Reaching for Fire

Abigail Mauney

To Tirayan, Moon, and everyone in room 1313 for keeping me sane throughout this crazy, wonderful journey.

CHAPTER ONE
Georges, 1667

Georges sat adjacent to the fireplace, a knife in one hand, and a chunk of firewood in the other. He was carving fingers into the edge of the log. They grasped for the cool sunlight that was pushing its way in through the crack beneath the door, attempting to escape their fiery fate.

Amelie pushed her way in through the door, with a cold wind combatting the warmth of the fire. It shut with a heavy thud, and she reclined into a chair on the opposite side of the table.

She pulled thick, wool gloves off of her hands. "I swear if it gets any colder out there, our sheep will freeze to death."

"They've got wool for a reason, Amelie. They're just the same as your hands in those wool gloves, toasty and warm." Georges continued carving.

As she set them down, she noticed what Georges was working on. Surrounding him on the table were piles of gears, pegs, and twine. Some wound together, and some that curled in upon themselves at the tug of a string. The hands were all he could make as of recently. Overall, he was a kind soul, rough around the edges from his work as a shepherd, but with eyes that could light up a room when he smiled.

"When will you stop with these projects, Georges? You know what Père Fournier thinks about all of this. You can only be healing for so long."

Georges looked at his left sleeve. The fabric caved in and folded right where his wrist should have begun. There was no hand. The carving in his lap continued to reach for the door, as if asking to be free.

She moved her chair closer to his. "It's been a year now. You should be well."

Georges took in a sharp breath before tossing the hand he was working on into the fire, watching the fingertips slowly become singed in the flames. "I'm just curious." He lifted what should have been his hand. "What if *this* didn't have to be anymore? I could build another."

"Oh you and your building!" She stood from the chair and began to pace. "When you took it up as a hobby, I expected you to build fences and cabinets but not… you know." She trailed off. "Can you not see that you've become obsessed with this?"

The fire had eaten its way down to the knuckles now.

"You just don't understand what it's like, Amelie! Each night, the pain I feel, burning, creeping down my arm and through my fingertips. Fingertips that I no longer have! Each night it feels like I'm losing it over and over again!"

The two of them stared at the gears scattered across the table, giving their tempers a moment to calm.

"Let me help you." she said, returning to her original softness. "Let Père Fournier help you! Pray! Anything to make you stop carving those- those *things!*"

"They're not things!" Georges set his knife onto the table with more force than he originally intended.

Amelie clearly didn't believe him. "Tell me then, what are they? Could you say in confidence that those are good, Godly things?"

Georges didn't respond. Amelie was about to comment on it, but he lifted his hand to stop her. Beyond the walls of their house, there was an audible rustling in the grass.

"Someone's outside." Georges whispered, thinking that if he stood as still and as quiet as possible, that he might be able to hear who.

Amelie listened for the sound, and panicked upon hearing them. "Put the carvings away."

Georges didn't appreciate the comment, but it was still a good idea. He swept his hand across the table, moving the gears off of the table and onto a cloth. Once they were all gathered, Elise tied it up for him and hid the bag behind a pot of herbs sitting on a shelf.

They were both startled when there was a stern knock on the door. The two shared a glance, acknowledging that they were ready to open the door. As Amelie made her way to greet the guest, Georges slipped the carving knife that was sitting on the table into his pocket.

Georges could make out the voice of the village priest from through the door after Amelie had opened it. "It is Père Fournier. We need to speak with Monsieur Lambert."

Before Amelie had time to question them, four men in red cloaks made their way into the one room house. The first thing Georges noticed was the mens' cloaks. They were a vibrant scarlet color, which was certainly unlike any of the garments that he'd seen in Edris. They were rich enough that they could look like the king's stuff, but what business would they have with a small village shepherd?

With all of them inside, it was quite cramped, but that didn't stop them from starting their scan of every inch of the house. He reached out defensively to stop them, but his hand was swatted away.

Fuming, he approached Amelie and leaned next to her. "What gives them the right to do that? What could they possibly be looking for?" He whispered, careful that they wouldn't hear him. Fighting them over his comment would only worsen the situation.

Amelie, however, didn't respond. She had a vacant expression as she watched them search the room, but Georges couldn't pinpoint whether it stemmed from her being worried about the searching or from something else. He could tell that she was thinking about something else as she watched, but there was no telling what that was.

Before he could ask Amelie what was on her mind, Père Fournier approached Georges with a slow stride. "Monsieur Lambert, how it saddens me to see you today." His hands were resting behind his back, and he had a pitying gaze.

"Saddens?" George questioned.

"Surely you must know." He stopped his pacing at a point in the room where the firelight was behind him, causing him to become a silhouette. The shadow was threatening, outlining the edges of his vestment and his disapproving stance. Even with his frail figure and fading hairline, it made Georges' blood turn to ice. "Did she really not tell you?"

She? Did he mean Amelie? There had to have been some sort of misunderstanding. "If this is about missing church in recent times, I can assure you I'm just figuring out how to properly use a Bible without causing havoc." He lifted his left arm, highlighting where the hand should be. "Missing hand,

and all that."

"Oh please, we both know that's not the reason."

He played with the objects lining the shelf he was standing next to, which just happened to be the same shelf that the carvings were hidden on. "It's actually a very different matter."

Georges was beginning to get nervous about how close he was getting to the gears, but if he let it show on his face, there would be even more problems. The entire situation felt like walking on eggshells.

Père Fournier continued his speech. "You see, they are from Rouen," He gestured to the men who had followed in behind him. "And I admit to having confided in them about your recent… hobbies."

His heart started racing, and the room started to spin. There was no way that he could have found out about them. The only person who knew he was even carving the hands was Amelie. He wondered how she was faring with all of this, but the question was quickly silenced by her taking his hand.

Thank you. He mouthed.

Amelie nodded.

"My hobbies?" Georges asked, trying to keep his voice steady. There was still a chance that it could be related to something else.

Père Fournier stepped forward, running his hand along the edge of the shelf. It was straying dangerously close to the bag of gears. "I've heard rumors."

The men, who had just been searching visually until this point, were beginning to move things around now. They were moving chairs and beginning to rummage through the objects on the shelf. Georges reached out again to stop them from prodding, but Amelie grabbed his wrist. Georges gave her a glare, but Amelie was still focused on Père Fournier.

"Rumors?" She asked.

"Yes. Recently, I was told about carvings that would come alive." Père Fournier knew just what to do to keep them both frozen in place. "Carvings that grasped at things of their own volition."

"That's ridiculous!" Georges stammered. "How could that be true?"

"They mentioned their worry over the state of your recovery. You must understand that I am only concerned for your wellbeing, Georges." The priest grinned. He was lying.

Georges let go of Amelie's hand and stumbled back. There was no way that it could have been her, right? Maybe someone had seen him carving through the door.

Amelie watched anxiously as he stumbled backwards. He kept going until he knocked into one of the shelves behind him, knocking a cup and some flowers onto the floor. He didn't notice her watching. He was still questioning who could have possibly done this to him.

"I found something!" one of the men in red piped up from across the room. A bag of Georges' failed carvings was in his hand.

Georges felt like all of the breath had escaped his chest. He needed to sit. Until this point, he'd always wondered how people fainted from stress, but those questions were thoroughly answered as the edges of his vision blurred. He made his way to sit in one of the chairs around the table.

Père Fournier looked across the room and nodded at the find. "Madame Lambert, I can understand how this may be unnerving to you, but I need you to step back."

She nodded, and solemnly took a step away.

"Are you not going to help?!" He looked to Amelie for

some sort of concern on her face, but the resolve was telling.

"We ask for cooperation through this effort, Monsieur Lambert." Père Fournier warned. "If you are truly innocent, the questions will answer themselves."

First was the sound of the gears spilling out onto the table, then the larger carvings that followed behind. Even Georges thought it was an unsettling sight to watch the disfigured and damaged wooden hands unfurling as they fell out onto the table, and Père Fournier was even harsher, there was no chance that he could explain himself after this. One of the men in red tugged at the strings that held a finger together, and jumped away as it curled in on itself.

Georges flinched. It definitely wasn't good.

Père Fournier looked at him with disgust in his eyes. Georges didn't even bother with trying to give reasoning. No matter what he said to rationalize his actions, he could tell that Père Fournier wouldn't believe it. Instead, he would ask for forgiveness. "I know it looks bad, but I swear I'm an innocent man."

"I think I've seen enough." Père Fournier sighed. "Men?"

The men in red quickly formed a circle around the chair he was sitting in, then pulled his arms behind his back. They did so with a painful amount of force, and each time he struggled to pull himself free, the men only tightened their grip on him. He looked into Amelie's eyes to search again for any sign that she would step in to help, but she had returned to her vacant expression.

"I didn't expect it to happen like this." Georges could hear her mutter.

He wondered what that meant as he continued to struggle.

"Ah," the priest chuckled. "Now you're showing your true colors."

"What?"

"Would an 'innocent man' be fighting so hard to escape the church?"

"An innocent man would fight to vindicate himself." Georges glared.

"An interesting thought, but I'm afraid that I would rather not risk the chance for you to enchant us with spells or trickery." Georges looked around the room. " It really is such a shame this will all be burned. It's a beautiful place, really."

"Burned?" Amelie broke from her stunned state.

"Well naturally," Père Fournier's eyes lingered on the table covered in gears and fingers. "That is what we do when we find a witch. This entire place is contaminated."

"You mean to say…" Amelie couldn't finish the sentence.

Père Fournier nodded. "Georges Lambert, has been accused, and found guilty of, witchcraft."

Georges had known that this is where the ordeal would lead for a while now, but the words being spoken aloud were even more sickening to hear. There was no escaping a sentence to witchcraft. Not in a small village such as this. Even with the King's Edict that lessened the punishment, the crown's reaches didn't extend this far into the countryside.

"I can understand the need to take Georges, but our house?!" Amelie begged.

"Amelie!" Georges shot, offended by the fact that she had asked for the house to be spared before he was..

"I'm sorry, but it has all been touched by Satan. Burning is the only thing that can purge his touch and purify the space," Père Fournier began to exit the house. "But I do understand your concern. I'm sure that someone else in the village would take you in if you asked kindly."

Georges was pulled out of the door, and the cold air felt like a slap to the face. He'd not had an opportunity to put anything warm on before he was dragged out, and he doubted that they would let him at this point, so instead he tried to focus on Amelie's voice.

"Please! Think of our sheep! What will we do with them, then?" he heard her say.

First the house, and now the sheep. Still, she hadn't mentioned him.

"They will be distributed among your neighbors for safekeeping." Père Fournier replied.

"And what of my livelihood?" Amelie's voice again. "Without a job or a permanent home, I'll have no way of sustaining myself!"

"You would have done better to make more plans for yourself after confessing your husband's crimes to me." Père Fournier said, becoming annoyed with her questions.

"You're right," Amelie relented, falling behind Père Fournier as they walked. "I will figure out something."

Georges froze, falling out of step with the men in red and disrupting their pace. He wished that he could have been surprised by the admittance, but that wasn't the case. It was the loss of all hope entirely that he'd been wrong that hurt him. "You let me burn so easily after eight years under the same roof? Amelie! "

Silence.

He tried to claw his way through the wall of guards that had formed around him as he was being brought to the church. He didn't care that it would get him into more trouble, in fact, he was probably already a dead man walking by this point.

What he needed was to see her listen to him at least one last
time.

Instead of Amelie, he saw Père Fournier who had
put his arm around her in a protective manner. He whispered
something into her ear that Georges couldn't hear, then she
nodded, remaining facing away from him.

"Amelie! Amelie, please!" He reached through the
quickly closing gap before being quickly shoved back into the
center of the formation.

"If you know what's best for you, you'll keep moving."
The man grunted.

"Does it really matter?"

The man chuckled. It was a deep, guttural laugh.
Parisian.

They traveled quickly through the field. Georges did
his best to take in the imagery one last time. In the summer,
the fields would have been flowering, and trees lining the
edge of the forest would have given shade to the houses that
shepherds had built. They didn't have much, but they were still
a community. Now, though, the grass was dead, doors shut, and
the bare trees of the forest offered only their jagged branches
on the horizon. Even the sheep blended into the frosty grass.

Soon enough, the grass turned to stones beneath
Georges' feet. They were entering town, which was getting
closer to the church. As they got into the more populated areas,
they slowed their pace as well. He was being made an example,
no doubt, becoming a warning of what could happen if you
disrespected the church.

As they walked, a man approached them. "What's
happening here?" He asked.

Georges recognized the voice as the town butcher. He
was an honest man, and Georges had sold many sheep to him

over the years. There was still a small sliver of hope that the townspeople might defend him in place of Amelie.

"He's been found guilty of witchcraft." Père Fournier said, almost sounding as if this were an everyday occurrence.

"Lord," He uttered, clearly pondering something. "What's going to happen to him?"

"He will be burned tomorrow morning."

"God. That's awful." There was a pause. "Do you think it contaminates the sheep?"

"Pardon?" Père Fournier stopped entirely to process the question.

"The witchcraft. Does it contaminate the sheep?"

Georges for a moment almost wished that his demise would come sooner. There was no way that the butcher had just asked such a question so nonchalantly. It seemed that somehow everyone valued sheep over his own life today.

"I'll give you a Livre if I can take the meat." The butcher added on, clarifying what he wanted out of the cursed sheep deal.

Père Fournier thought it over for a moment before he answered. "If you want, I suppose it couldn't hurt."

Georges was even more furious at the response than the question. If the sheep were going to go to anyone, they should go to the families that needed it, not to the already-wealthy butcher. There was no time to linger on the matter, though. With the scale of everything else that had happened already, this was hardly the most surprising thing he'd experienced thus far.

The rest of the walk went smoothly and quietly. The only interruptions they experienced were the occasional onlookers, but they didn't cause any damage other than to Georges' pride. Now, they had nearly completed the walk to the church.

It was a depressing building on the outside, made of cobblestone with a wooden annex added after its original construction. On the inside it was peaceful but lifeless. The cold light of winter made its way through the large, stained windows behind the altar, dousing the pews in multicolored light. Centered between the windows was a large stone crucifix. It had been there longer than he could remember, no doubt something from the town's founding. Its eyes seemed to watch them as they filed in through the main doors of the church. Here, it was filled with reverent silence, which allowed his mind at least a small ease.

"To think that tomorrow might be the first time that this church will be full on a Sunday in quite some time." Père Fournier looked out into the rows of empty pews smiling.

"What?"

"I suppose you've been home for quite a while, so you wouldn't know. Barely anyone comes anymore, a part of the changing times I suppose. However, I don't think anyone will want to miss a witch trial."

"Trial?" He questioned. Was there really any trial to be had if he was already convicted?

Père Fournier didn't answer the question as he continued to speak. "You must understand that it's a matter of consistency over anything. All witches must be tried fairly."

"Fairly." Georges muttered. That certainly wouldn't be the word he used to describe it.

They brought him down the hallway and into the annex of the church. This area contained a few small cobbled holding rooms, as well as the priest's living quarters. The hallway was dark save for the candlelight emanating from them. Georges was brought into one of the holding rooms, which were usually used only for the worst criminals in the village. He hadn't seen them used for years, but now he was becoming their first visitor for quite some time.

As they entered the room and his eyes adjusted, he realized that the holding room wasn't the most horrifying thing that he would encounter. In the center of the room, sat a rusting, iron cage complete with an absurdly large lock.

Before he could even process what it was meant for, the men tied his arms behind his back and tossed him into the cage. Since he couldn't break the fall, he fell face-first onto the floor. It hurt, but he needed to keep a straight face. He wasn't going to let the men get any sort of satisfaction from knowing the pain they caused him.

"The room alone wasn't enough for you?" Georges grumbled. "The cage too?"

Père Fournier leaned against the side of the cage. "Do you like it? It's German. These kind gentlemen brought it with them. Something about it supposedly blocks your communication with The Devil ."

Georges sat up against the wall of the cage. "Where did you find such a thing?" Just how long had this been planned for these priests to have direct access to witch cages imported from Germany?

Père Fournier again didn't answer the question directly. It seemed to be becoming a theme. "You must be controlling those… *things* of yours *somehow*, and I can't have them crawling in here and helping you escape, so no expenses can be spared."

Georges almost laughed at the absurdity of it all. "Of course you couldn't. "

"You seem to understand well enough." Père Fournier grinned. "Your wife will be here shortly, by the way. She wished for one last conversation with you."

Georges was taken aback, but was excited. If Amelie had wished to speak with him, there must have been something that he missed earlier. Now that they were talking in private, they could figure a way for him to be freed.

Shortly after Père Fournier left the room, the door creaked back open, and Amelie's head peeked in. "Père Fournier, I think you sent me to the wrong room."

"It's the right room, don't worry!" Georges was desperate to get her attention. He crawled to the edge of the cage that was closest to her, realizing how surprisingly difficult it was to do with his wrists tied.

"Oh Lord, what have they done to you?" She was shocked as soon as she'd adjusted to seeing the dark.

"It's awful, Amelie, but I'm glad that you're here now." Georges smiled. Seeing her face made everything from the last hours seem like a dream. "So what's our plan to get me out of here?"

"Get you out of here?" she asked. "What do you mean?"

Georges froze. "What do *you* mean?" he stared into her eyes desperately. "I thought that you were here to help me out of this. God, don't tell me that you actually told Père Fourier?"

Amelie avoided his eyes. "Georges, I'm not here to get you out of the cage." He could tell that she was choosing her words carefully. "You know I am always honest with you, Georges, but I couldn't just leave you in your current state." She paused. "But I didn't know that it would go this far!

"Amelie!" he cried. "Do you not understand that this will have me killed?!"

Tears formed in her eyes and she choked on her words. "Père Fournie said that he could save you. He said that it wasn't too late for you to see God's light."

Georges stared at her, unable to decide where to begin. "What reason could you have to do this?"

"You've not seen yourself! You spend all day crafting wooden hands, you spend all night screaming in your sleep. You look utterly miserable! How do you expect me to let this all just happen before me? Especially when… it doesn't matter now." Amelie turned away from him entirely.

"And you didn't think to talk to me first about it?" Georges spoke softly, hoping that she could be reasoned with.

"I just don't want you to be tempted by The Devil, Georges. I love you too much for that to happen to you." Georges could tell that she was crying. "I'm just here to say that I'll be okay. I found another man who promised to marry me. You don't have to worry about me."

"Another–" Georges fell back. "Amelie, are you listening to yourself?! I'm innocent! We can fix this!" he said desperately. "God, Amelie, I'm not even dead yet!"

"I thought you could be happy for me, at the very least."

He was wrong to have had hope in her. After everything that they had been through together, after their entire shared life, she was only coming back to say that she had found someone else to take care of her. "Fine! Leave me to die here then, but don't think that I'll come running back to greet you at Heaven's gates. You can leave that to your new husband."

"It's been a good six years." she said quietly. "I want you to know that."

"We both know it's been longer than that."

She started to say something, then stopped. "Goodbye, Georges."

Amelie waited for a goodbye in return, but he had decided not to give her that. After a few more moments, she left, shutting the door behind her. Georges was now truly in pure darkness, alone with the silence of the room and his racing thoughts. He'd woken up this morning with only the thought that it would be another regular day, but so far he had been accused of witchcraft, learned that all of his possessions were to be burned, learned that *he* was to be burned, and discovered that his wife had left him before he even died to be with another man. It was more than any person should handle. It was inhumane.

=There were no means of escape that he could think of, so for now the least he could do was to try and get comfortable. He sprawled out onto his stomach. The cage floor scratched against his face, but it was better than crushing his tied up wrists.

With nothing else left to do, he cried. He cried until the tears were streaming down the sides of his face and wetting his hair. His arms throbbed beneath his back. His heart was aching. Everything just *hurt*. The phantom pains started creeping back into the place where his hand would be. They started off slow, but quickly turned into searing, stabbing pain. Of course they would come back now, as if imminent death weren't already bad enough.

He tried pulling his right hand to grasp his left wrist, but was met with the rope that kept his arms together. The phantom pain still seared in his hand. He needed to feel his wrist at least. He needed to feel that the pain wasn't real, but just pulling at it wasn't going to help.

He took a deep breath and cleared his mind. The logical thinker in him was beginning to take over again. The knots were designed for people with hands, so his best option would be to pull upward rather than to the side.

Tugging upwards on the knot still wasn't easy, but with

enough time, it started to gain slack, which gave him hope. The more he pulled, the closer it came to becoming entirely undone. Once he believed that he had enough space, he wriggled himself free. Immediately, he fell back onto the floor of the cage holding his left wrist in his hand and waiting for the pain to subside.

He sat like that for a while. It felt like the pain subsiding had given him an entirely new perspective of the room. Now he noticed the cobwebs on the ceiling and vomit stains on the floor surrounding him. He was almost glad that he was resting on the floor of the cage rather than the room. He could see every groove in the wood of the door to the room. It couldn't have been locked. It almost taunted him with how easy it would be to escape. For a moment, he entertained the idea, pondering ways that he could possibly escape the church. It wouldn't honestly be hard. Instead, the difficulty came from getting out of his cage.

The thoughts started to feel more like solving a puzzle, and he had never left a puzzle unsolved. It would be a waste to start now when he needed it most. What point was there to letting himself waste away in the cage overnight? Determined now, he listed in his mind the things that he could use.

The knife.

He'd stuffed it into his pocket earlier that day before the events unfolded. No one had bothered to search his pockets before throwing him into the cage. Most likely, they'd assumed that he wouldn't be able to do much without the help of Satan or his left hand. Never before had he been so thankful for his condition.

He pulled the knife out of his pocket. The only thing that he could reach from inside the cage was its absurdly large lock. He'd managed to get things unlocked without keys before, so this would be no different. It couldn't be.

One way or another, there wasn't going to be a witch in this cage tomorrow.

CHAPTER TWO
Petime, 1684

Petime hobbled through the town center of Edris. With each step, her crutch struck the brick path beneath her. The villagers had always feared her, mainly because of her choice in crutch. It was a modification of old, rusted scythes that farmers had lost use for; with the grips sawed off and replaced in the positions more suitable for her arms. They were bound with tightly-wrapped twine, and were sealed with birch glue. The sound it made as it hit the stone road struck out like a sort of warning to the surrounding villagers. As if to say, "Stay away! Little Reaper is here!". Such a lovely nickname to be gifted.

Although it benefitted her travel in the end, she could never truly get over the twinge of guilt she felt as the paths formed before her. The first scythe-crutch had been made in an act of desperation, purely because there was nothing else around. As she grew into them though, she realized that she somewhat liked the aura they gave her. Despite the fear she received, it was one of the few things left in her life that made her feel powerful.

There were other things too, of course, like the way that she didn't smile in public, and the way that she didn't care to be polite. She figured that if other people were going to be rude to her, she'd have no obligation to be polite in return.

As she walked past, a mother pulled her child away from Petime. She needed to get vegetables for her family, so the logical reaction would be to ignore it. Still though, she didn't want to be seen as something that children should fear. The mother of that child was going just a little bit too far.

Think of the vegetables.

"Why is she wearing pants, Maman?" Petime heard the child ask.

"No matter the reason, it's indecent." the mother replied. "It would be best not to wonder about such things."

Petime's eyebrow twitched. She couldn't just leave it at that. "It's so I can walk with my crutch!" she put on her kindest face, which still turned out somewhat sour. She thought it was a good response, however, the mother didn't appear to agree with the sentiment.

"Don't speak to my child that way!" she pulled her child, who was now trying to escape her grasp, even closer.

Petime groaned. "I was just answering her question."

"Did you just groan?!"

"Maybe." Petime squeezed every ounce of enjoyment out of the mother's sour face as she could.

The radius between the crowd of the busy street and Petime had grown a bit, with more and more people coming to the edges to watch their interaction. The crowd, it seemed, thought the groan was equally distasteful.

Petime paused, then rephrased her statement. She needed to think of the vegetables! "I apologize. I just wanted to explain that I wear pants because skirts get caught in my crutch."

"Maman says that God took your leg on purpose!" the child said suddenly.

"She said *what-*" Petime slowly set down her empty basket and gripped her hands a little bit tighter. The vegetables could wait for just one little scuffle.

"Excuse me!" The interaction was interrupted by a cheery voice breaking through the circle. "My apologies for interrupting."

Everyone turned their gaze to see who it was. The long, light brown curls and radiant smile were a dead giveaway. Camille. Beautiful, perfect reputation, could do no wrong, perfectly pious church-going Camille. It seemed like everyone was at the edge of their seat to see how she would respond.

"Petime, I think that it would be unwise to continue speaking at this point." She smiled, telling Petime that it would be for her own good if she let her handle this. "As for you," she knelt down to be at eye level with the child, changing her tone to be warmer, "I urge you to remember that no one truly knows what God is thinking."

Petime realized how close she'd been to starting a fight, thankful that Camille had been there to help. The rest of the villagers seemed to be satisfied with that conclusion as well, and were slowly falling back into the regular foot traffic. It had truly been the perfect response, one that addressed both sides without getting involved herself whatsoever.

Camille checked to make sure that no one was watching them, then pointed in the direction of the farmers' houses. Petime understood the meaning by now, they were to meet up and speak there more discreetly. They'd been friends so long that communicating like this was almost second nature. Camille's reputation would be damaged if her friendship with

Petime was revealed to the public, so they had developed codes to communicate without making others suspicious. It hurt. It really hurt, but that was the price to pay for the only friendship she had.

They both made their way to the spot through different, roundabout paths. Petime arrived first with Camille following shortly after. The farmers were out in the fields, so hiding within their nest of houses was the perfect place to speak.

As she approached, she noticed Camille brushing down her skirt and readjusting her hair. She was the daughter of the butcher, making her one of the wealthier girls in the village; constant lessons on piano and etiquette filled her schedule, as well as being invited to gatherings and events.

Camille was one of Petime's first and only friends. Despite the facade that she presented to everyone else, she was a grudge-holding, witty person who loved to explore the forest and run through fields. Since Petime had no care for how people presented themself, she'd seen through the act immediately when they were children. Around that time, Petime had just recently lost her leg as well, and Camille was one of the only people who didn't treat her any differently. Quickly, they bonded over being the only two who truly understood what they were like beyond their appearances.

When Camille caught notice of Petime, she immediately let her guard down, slouching as she walked and letting her smile fade away. "Did I do alright? I felt awful talking to you like that." She searched for the words. "That woman was so *stupid*."

Petime laughed. The immediate change in tone never failed to amuse her. "Your mother would faint if she heard you say that."

"She would faint, and then have my head." Camille

corrected, momentarily lost in thought of what that might entail. "I'm so glad I found you though. I was looking for you!"

Camille walked towards the woods, and Petime followed along. She was most likely going to walk along the path that connected the shepherds' field to the village since it was relatively secluded. Its intended purpose was to connect the shepherds' fields and the marketplace more closely, but it also made for a perfect spot for the two of them to spend time together.

"So, why were you looking for me?" Petime asked, Camille should technically have been on her way to a piano lesson by now, so it must have been important whatever it was.

"It's my mother again." Camille sighed. "She's thinking about getting me another tutor."

"She can't be serious, can she?"

Camille nodded. She was staring at the ground as they walked, kicking stray stones to the side of the path.

"I think I have something that might brighten the mood." Petime grinned.

"Is this going to be like that other thing that you showed me?" Camille asked, raising an eyebrow in suspicion.

Petime layed sarcasm over her tone. "I don't know what you could possibly be talking about."

Camille couldn't hide her giggling now. "I was worried I'd get a scar for weeks! *Weeks,* Petime!"

"Just trust me." she veered off of the path and into the foliage.

Camille looked into the brush hesitantly, then followed Petime in. Petime was good at navigating through the foliage, and had grown accustomed to making sure her crutch avoided all of the stones and roots that came with the forest floor.

"Petime, how far is this off the path?" Camille asked, pushing brambles away from the edges of her skirt. "I don't know how much more of this my clothes can take."

"Not far! Don't worry." The trees were already thinning out, which meant they were about to reach their destination.

Sure enough, they reached it just moments later. Petime stepped away to reveal a clearing with large, rectangular stones eerily organized into a large circle. She guessed that they were remaining indications of a civilization before them now. If there were people here now, there had to be people there before her, even if all that was left of them was overgrown by moss and lichens. She'd been told that stuff like this would be witch's things, but she'd also been told that *she* was a witch's thing, so she didn't fully believe them when they said it.

"What is this?" Camille stepped hesitantly into the clearing, examining the stones that surrounded her.

"It can be anything we want! I don't think anyone else in the village knows about it!" Petime sat on one of the stones and set down her basket of vegetables. "It's the perfect place to meet together!"

Camille walked up to one of the stones, examining it for a second. "This doesn't feel right. These stones do have moss, but only moss. They're unnaturally clean."

"I'm sure there's nothing to worry about." Petime laid back entirely onto the stone, basking in the sunlight. "Come on, just relax for a minute. The sun is nice."

"And what if it's witchcraft? Or it's haunted?"

"Then it'd be haunted by the ghost of the Handless Witch I suppose." Petime said, still basking. "He's pretty common a story around here."

According to the stories, around seventeen years ago, there was a man accused of witchcraft who had escaped his condemnation through the works of Satan. She'd never believed it to be real, but it made for a good way to scare children.

Camille jumped. "Shh! If you say his name he can hear you! Maman said he can be summoned from the underworld itself." .

"He's clearly not real." Petime sat up. "They said the lock to the cage was on the floor the next morning. Satan wouldn't care to open the lock itself, he'd just leave it there."

"Fake or not, there are still valuable lessons to be learned from the story." Camille continued to look at the stones. "And if the witch were going to show up anywhere, it'd certainly be around here."

She knew that Camille was a lot more nervous about witchcraft than she was, but sometimes it still felt like her assumptions went too far. "I see Père Fournier has been making an influence on you with his sermons."

"My mother says that religion is of the utmost importance, and if we stray from His path, the Handless Witch is an example of what our fate will be." Camille proudly recited.

"You're beginning to gain an uncanny likeness to him. I think you need a break." Petime slumped back. "Everyone else has stopped attending masses. Why don't you?"

"I don't think…" she trailed off in the middle of her sentence, going entirely still. She was looking somewhere behind the treeline.

"Camille?"

"Petime. Run." she said it in a hauntingly deadpan tone.

She wasn't amused. "What do you mean run? I have no legs."

But Camille had already taken off into the woods. She

was entirely out of sight, leaving Petime on her own. She felt her heart rate start to rise from the anxiety. She couldn't have this happening, not right now.

"Camille?" Petime shouted. "Camille! Don't leave me here!"

There was no sign of Camille. Petime scrambled to grab her crutch and started walking as fast as she could to follow Camille. It was at moments like these where she cursed her inability to run.

"Camille?" she shouted hopelessly. "Camille!"

Petime looked behind her into the clearing to see what Camille had been so scared of, and that is when she saw it. There was the shadow of a man standing, watching her.

She bit her lip to keep from screaming, suddenly understanding why Camille had taken off so fast. Without her full focus on the ground it was a constant battle to keep upright now. She couldn't outrun whatever the thing was if it decided to chase her.

She walked as fast as she could until she saw the path up ahead of her. She'd convinced herself that the path was safe. If she made it there, then whatever was in the woods wouldn't follow. That was the only thing keeping her going.

"Petime! Is that you?" Camille must've heard her coming up towards the path.

"Yes." Petime shouted back breathlessly. She didn't know whether her voice carried far enough or not, but her main priority at the moment was to keep walking.

As soon as she made it onto the path, Petime collapsed to the ground in pure relief. She had Camille with her, so she was safe now. As long as someone else was with her she'd be okay.

Camille held onto her crutches and attempted to calm

her down. "Take deep breaths. It'll be okay. If it were going to chase us, it would have by now."

"Did you see it too?" Petime dared to ask.

Camille nodded, eyes flickering between Petime and the woods. "I think that we should tell Père Fournier." She said, starting again towards the main path. "We can turn right instead of left when we reach the path and–"

"No." Petime shook her head. "We can't."

"What?"

"Whatever's there has yet to bother us yet, and I don't want to see a town at war with rumors of a ghost." Petime was already mentally listing the things that could go wrong if they found out about what they had seen. "You know how they are about witches."

Camille furrowed her brows weighing her options.

Petime knew Camille's family, and also knew that she could only hope that Camille would see her reasoning. "You know what they'd think if Little Reaper was the one who warned them about it."

The village was so scared of witches, especially ones who were missing limbs, that when Petime had started using a scythe as her crutch, they believed it to be a bad omen. She spent her life being quiet and careful, but even then, there had still been too many close calls to her being deemed a witch herself.

"We can leave it be, then.," Camille finally decided. "But we have to swear not to tell a soul about this and to never return."

"I had no plans on doing either thankfully." Petime caught the last of her breath, then took her crutch back from Camille.

"Will you be okay to walk home on your own?"

Camille asked anxiously. "I don't want
to leave you alone but…"

"You have a lesson." Petime knew where this was going already.

"How did you know?"

"I've known you long enough to remember your schedule, so don't worry. I'll be alright as long as I stick to the path." She was definitely lying to some extent, but it was the least she could do to ease Camille's worries. "Weren't you planning on telling your father that you didn't want to play anymore?"

Camille looked up at the sky. "I was originally, but," Her eyes returned to Petime. "I'm not as strong as you are."

Petime stayed quiet for a moment before replying. She wasn't necessarily "strong", she just did what she had to. Before she spoke again, she lessened the seriousness in her voice. "I could tell him for you?"

Camille laughed. "I don't think he'd like that very much."

Petime chatted with Camille for a little while longer before they both actually decided to part ways. Once they were ready, they gave each other a hug and turned in opposite directions, Camille heading towards her lesson and Petime heading home towards her brother.

CHAPTER THREE
Camille

Camille took a deep breath as she left the scene. Her stomach turned at the thought of leaving Petime all by herself in the woods. She knew what kind of trauma that she carried along with her. However, her dress was already wrecked from the unexpected run through the woods. It was easy enough to take precautions when going at a walking pace, but some damage was bound to happen when fleeing a ghost.

She didn't know particularly what Petime had seen, but she knew that it wasn't as much as she had. The figure had a dark cloak, and carried a satchel over its back. She could feel that it didn't have good intentions, and her suspicions were only confirmed when she saw that right at its left wrist, it had a solid, wooden hand. Whatever it was had reacted to them talking about it just like her mother said it would, but it wasn't summoned by The Devil. When she made eye contact, it seemed to have genuine fear in its eyes. It seemed to be clinging onto its soul. It was *alive*.

Camille cleared the thoughts from her mind, figuring that it would be best if she returned to her home to freshen up before she went to her piano lesson. Her teacher was always harping on about the state of her outfit, noticing even the smallest mud stains at the bottom of her skirt. God knows what she'd think about the gashes that tore at it currently.

Sometimes she prayed that she would be allowed to wear commoners' robes. Her father worked as a butcher, which put her in a wealthier position than the rest of the village, but also made her feel isolated on occasion. She couldn't complain. It was a comfortable life compared to some of the others in the village, but sometimes those opportunities felt like they were the same things that held her captive.

By the time she reached her house, she was already well into the realm of late even if she weren't covered in bramble scratches and mud. Her mother's pursed face as she opened the door was perhaps even more terrifying than the ghost.

"Camille, what did I tell you about getting yourself messy?" She tutted, taking the bottom of Camille's shredded skirt in her hand. "How did you even manage to do this"

"I'm sorry Maman, I'll be better." Camille murmured. She'd promised it at least a hundred times by now, and broken the promise equally as many. She was waiting for the day that her mother would no longer take that excuse.

It wasn't this time though, and instead of saying anything against her, Camille's mother knelt down and started brushing away stray blades of grass that had attached themselves to her skirt. It was a futile effort, but Camille appreciated the concern nonetheless.

Her mother spoke as she cleaned. "Mon ange, how is it that each day you come home looking worse than the last? Yesterday it was berry stains, and today you look like you've been dragged through the woods by a wolf." Her voice was a note of pure disappointment. "It is a chore keeping up with your affinity to wrecking dresses."

She chuckled, unsure of how best to reply. "You know me, Maman."

Her mother sighed. "Well, be on with you then. I'd rather you be a punctual topiary than late and clean. I'm sure that Madame Chelault will lecture you enough anyway."

Before Camille could say anything more, she was getting pushed out the door. As soon as she was out, it shut behind her. It felt like she hadn't even been inside.

Her lessons took place in the church, which wasn't a far walk from the stores. Both were fairly close to the town center because of the village's function as a rest stop for those traveling between Rouen and Paris. Though, the church was receiving fewer and fewer patrons with each passing year due to the shifting views of religion in the larger cities of France.

When Camille arrived at the church, she cursed the doors for their telltale creak, perfect for letting people inside know exactly who was late and how late they were. Up near the front of the nave, Madame Chelault sat at the piano, her wrinkled face lit only by candlelight inside.

"You're late." she croaked.

Camille nodded. The woman sounded like she was on the edge of death, and always dressed as though she were going to a funeral. Whenever Camille asked about the outfit, she was scolded on how it was rude to comment on people's looks.

"You look like you've been dragged through the woods–"

"By a wolf. I know." *Rude to comment on people's looks, huh?* Camille reveled at how similar Madame Chelault sounded to her mother at times.

"It's rude to interrupt. Now, come. Play for me." The ancient woman slowly stood up from the bench to take an overseeing position of the piano.

Camille walked through the church to replace Madame Chelault on the bench. There was no way for her to practice at home, so each time she started playing, she could only pray that she sounded good enough. She took a deep breath in. This time was no different.

When she started playing, the notes sounded sweet, but soft. It wasn't the worst mistake she could make on the list of things she could mess up, but she knew Madame Chelault still wouldn't be pleased.

"Louder!"

Camille shrunk in on herself, but followed the command.

"You look like wheat collapsing in the breeze right now! Straighten your posture! Men like good posture." she continued to belt out commentary over Camille's playing.

The rest of the song continued in the same way. Madame Chelault wasn't satisfied, but she never was. As soon as the song was over, she gave even more critique that she "just didn't have the chance" to give while Camille was playing. And just like always, the critique turned into stories of the various reasons that men had rejected her over the years. She always cycled between the same three or four, but Camille thought the woman might be so senile that she didn't realize it.

Her mind wandered off as the old woman spoke, and she imagined herself in Paris instead, unbound from her parents' wishes and able to explore the city freely. Whenever travelers visited her father's store, they shared the most wondrous stories about it, so it had become somewhat of a dream that one day she would be able to see it with her own two eyes.

The rest of the lesson continued on in this format.

Playing, then talking, then more playing, and a bit more talking. It was the same every time. There was only so much commentary that one woman could give, and there was only so much that Camile could handle.

The time seemed like it was passing at least three times slower than usual. She practically ran out the door when Madame Chelault said that she couldn't bear to hear any more piano played by a "depressed stalk of collapsing wheat" that day. Even ending early, it felt like an eternity.

As she exited the building this time though, she was greeted by an unfamiliar sight. There was an unusually lavish-looking carriage resting in front of the church. There were a few villagers gathering luggage out of it and placing it in front of the door, but its main inhabitant was nowhere to be found.

Her gut twisted.Upon further inspection of the scene, she could see her mother and Père Fournier standing in front of the church speaking to each other. If they were speaking about something together, they were plotting, so she braced herself for what was to come next before she even considered the idea of approaching them. Once she was sufficiently prepared, she forced a polite smile and entered the conversation.

"Greetings Maman, Père Fournier." she said with her most ladylike smile. She hoped that she would earn back at least some degree of respect from her mother after daring to speak in public with the torn skirt.

"Oh, Camille! How wonderful it is to see you!" Père Fournier grinned back. She noticed that his teeth were yellowed and cracking. "I can tell the others that you are done with your lesson now."

"I apologize if I was any inconvenience."

"None at all. We were just waiting to bring in the luggage he had carried with him." He gestured to a pile of trunks that looked just as lavish as the carriage. "In fact, I was just speaking with your mother about an exciting opportunity."

Camille risked a questioning glance at her mother, who had a beaming smile on her face. She couldn't tell whether this made her more or less worried.

"You see, we will be having a long-term visitor to our village in the coming weeks, and I would love it if you would be able to show him around."

"He's from Rouen! And he's your age!" Her mother continued beaming. It was clear that she couldn't contain her excitement about the matter.

Instantly, Camille recognized what was happening. Her mother only ever acted that way when she had found her a potential suitor. She had been vying for years to get Camille married off, but every man she deemed worthy so far had been too apprehensive of marrying a girl from such a small village. However, whoever this was sounded like they were staying for a while, meaning that her family didn't have to go through all of the work of planning travels to meet him.

Her worries must have been showing, because Père Fournier gave her a pitying smile. "Don't be nervous dear. You'll be alright. It's not until tomorrow, so you can have time to think about what you'll say thoroughly."

Père Fournier disappeared back into the group of people moving the luggage, leaving her and her mother standing alone. She didn't know what exactly she had wanted to say in response, but she didn't want to say it here.

Camille began to walk back towards the house, and was followed closely by her mother, so she knew that she wouldn't be allowed to dodge the conversation entirely. As soon as they made it inside, her mother grabbed her hand, gesturing for her to come upstairs. If it was an upstairs conversation, she knew that it had to be serious.

"He's going to be a good husband for you." her mother said once they had made it entirely up the stairs.

She didn't reply. She had no opinion in the matter since she hadn't even met him.

"I saw him, and he's fairly handsome."

Camille shot a concerned glance at her mother. "Maman, if I were mistaken I'd believe that you were the one marrying him, not me."

"Camille! Watch your words." She huffed, but continued her speech. "I know that the idea of getting married can be scary, but I've gone through the same things that you have, so if you ever need to talk about it I'm here…" her mother said the last part in a more comforting tone at least. It was nice to know that she wasn't mad.

"Thank you Maman," She knew that what her mother said was genuine, but the fear still lingered on her mind. "But I think I'm going to sleep now."

She didn't bother greeting her father downstairs, choosing instead to go straight to her room. The worries were catching up to her as she fled her mother's words. She didn't want to marry anyone. Every other suitor she'd seen at least seemed unattainable in some way. She knew deep down that they would refuse her, but this one seemed like she actually had a chance.

If she were to get a husband now, she would never have freedom. For the rest of her life it would be like her piano lessons. Doing something for someone else even if she didn't like it, bending to their every desire. As soon as she reached her bed, she fell into the sheets and cried.

CHAPTER FOUR
Petime

Petime had finally reached her house. It was a small, wooden shack that rested along the back edge of the fields near the forest. Much like the other houses in this area of the village, it had one room covered by a thatched roof. The place wasn't much, but it was home for her. She somewhat liked the way that the sunlight peeked through the holes in the straw on sunny days, and the way that the door was always open to let in the fresh air during the summertime. They weren't fancy, but they were what she knew.

Outside, her brother was resting in the tall grass, bathing in sunlight instead of doing his chores. She approached as quietly as she could, careful not to disturb his rest. That was, until she got right up next to him.

"Bah!" she shouted as loud as she could, and directly into his ear.

Her brother jumped up from his restful state, initial terror morphing into pure disappointment. "What do you want Petime?"

"Why aren't you doing your chores? I thought you were

supposed to give the sheep water hours ago." She looked out onto the field. If she could tell what a dehydrated sheep looked like, she was sure that those sheep would fit the description.

Leon glanced at the empty water troughs. "I'll get around to it in a bit."

Petime gave a disapproving stare.

"Just a little bit longer?"

Even more disapproving.

"Pleeease?"

"No, the sheep need water." she said, trying to sound tough. She didn't want to be the one who ended up taking the blame if their parents got home early.

Leon groaned, then started to make his way into fully standing up. When he did, he eyed her empty hands. "Speaking of chores, weren't you sent out with a basket?" Leon asked, with a hint of mischief in his voice. He knew that he'd found something out.

Petime looked down at where the basket of vegetables *should* have been, and confirmed that it was, in fact, not there. The last place that she could remember having it was when she was sitting on the stones in the woods, which meant that it still had to be there where she'd left it. She also realized that she would have to retrieve it. Alone. Where she'd vowed never to return. With a ghost.

Petime scrambled to think of a lie. "I was picking berries in the clearing on my way home and must have left it in the berry patch. I should be back in no time if I return to go get it."

"So you're saying that there is more time for me to rest in the sun\?" Leon grinned. "It really would be a shame if Mere were to find out about your irresponsibility."

He wanted to bargain. She knew his games, and

unfortunately she wouldn't be able to win this time because she didn't have anything to combat him with. She sighed. "It does seem that way doesn't it."

"So, you get the basket and I don't tell our parents?" Leon grinned.

"Sounds like we have a deal." Petime grumbled. Leon was getting sneakier every day.

"Yay!" He did a little victory dance before dropping back into the grass to rest some more.

Once he had laid down, Petime made her way back onto the path. Although her brother was bothersome sometimes, she felt obligated to protect him from hardship. She understood better than anyone the horrors that the villagers were capable of if they didn't like someone, and Leon was already at a disadvantage thanks to her condition. She was lenient on him because she didn't want him to become another victim of her reputation.

As she got closer to the edge of the woods, Petime felt anxiety returning. It certainly wasn't the most nervous she'd felt that day, especially considering that she had seen a ghost, but she also wasn't excited.

The further she made it in though, the more unbearable it became. Sweat started dripping down her forehead. The silence became larger, and she jumped at the sound of every twig snapping and bird chirping. Anything that disrupted the silence of the woods immediately became a threat to her imagination. There were wolves lurking around every corner, and bears hiding behind every tree.

At the same time, she was becoming increasingly curious about the ghost that she'd seen. Camille looked like she'd known more than she was letting on when Petime replayed the memory in her mind, so there might have been something she was missing. Maybe she'd been right about the stones being witch's things. Maybe there was something else to it?

Petime lingered on the thoughts as she looked for the break in the foliage that led to the path. All she could hope as she looked was that she hadn't dropped the basket somewhere in the middle of the woods. Once she found the spot, she took a deep breath and moved the initial wall of bramble and leaves away, convincing herself that everything would be alright. The anxiety from earlier hadn't gone away, and now she was worried about the figure as well. She quelled the thoughts by convincing herself that there would be no way that the ghost was still there. He had to have moved on to taking care of some other ghostly matter by now.

Even after initially pulling the leaves away, she was startled. Sitting on a large, flat stone was the basket of vegetables that she had left behind at the stone circle. She immediately started searching through the events of the day to figure out how she might have left it there, but each time she did, the last place that she could remember leaving it was on the stones. There was no way that Camille had grabbed it, so this meant that it was the work of someone else. Moreso, it was just far enough off of the main trail that passersby wouldn't see it, but Petime could notice it as soon as she started going back to retrieve it.

She looked around for any other explanations, and when looking at the ground, she found one. It was hard to notice at first, but there was another set of footprints that originated from the direction of the woods. They couldn't have been hers or Camille's because they'd run out a different way. Someone had come from inside the woods, and the only someone that she knew of that lived there was the ghost.

She approached the basket with the smallest steps she could, reaching out to it with hands shaking. There was a large possibility that it could have been cursed, or worse. She wanted to leave it behind so badly, but she couldn't do that to the rest of her family. Leon wouldn't hesitate to hold up his end of the bargain, and they had trusted her with the job. It was one of the few things that they trusted her with, so she couldn't fail them.

She realized that he might be there watching that very moment as well, so she spoke into the woods just in case. "Monsieur … uh, ghost man? If you're still here watching, I'm an awful victim. I've only got one leg and I'm poor. So please take someone else. Thank you?" She felt stupid, but at least it would get her message across.

When she felt a burst of courage, she reached out and grabbed the basket, waiting for a moment in case anything terrible happened to her. After a few moments of nothing though, she realized that she was probably safe. Immediately, she searched inside of the basket just in case, and was greeted with something that definitely wasn't there before. There was a small piece of paper buried amongst the vegetables, and on it were four words. She couldn't understand what they said, but she knew that it certainly hadn't been there before.

Part of her wanted to leave the paper behind. This was definitely a trap. It was probably some sort of curse that condemned you to haunting as soon as you read it. However, another part of her wanted to take the paper with her. There was something about not understanding what it meant that bothered her.

She held it in her hand, debating for a while on what to do with it, until she came to the conclusion that she wouldn't part with it until she knew what it meant. She would say prayers over it tonight to dispel any unholy energy that it had, then give it to someone else to read. Thankfully, she already had a person that she was thinking of.

CHAPTER FIVE
Camille

Camille was awake and getting ready much earlier than she usually was. Her mother was bustling around her in the room, picking out which dress she thought was prettiest and braiding her hair. According to her, it was of the utmost importance that Camille looked her best for the potential suitor.

"Do you know what he's like?" Camille tried to sit down, but was urged to keep standing.

"He's from Parisian high society, and is supposedly a very kind young man. He's also close to the Lord, and is becoming an aide to Père Fournier."

"What reason would he have for that if he's coming from high society?" Camille gained a shred of hope. If he were training to become a priest, he wouldn't be allowed to have a wife in the future.

"I don't know the reason, but I know what you're thinking, and don't. He's a rare opportunity and we both know it." Her mother tied another ribbon into her braids. "His only downside is that he looks a little bit… miserable."

"Miserable?" She was already questioning the fact that

her mother had referred to him solely as an opportunity, but she only questioned even further when she realized that his only real description thus far was "miserable". Camille decided she would wait to make a judgment for herself before she listened to anything else her mother said.

"When do I leave for the tour?" Camille asked.

"We will meet them at the church this morning." Her mother was nearly done with dressing her. She was in the admiring phase of checking over her work. "Although, it would be wonderful if your outfit could survive the walk."

She wasn't ready for these kinds of pointed remarks so early in the morning. "I promise it is all on accident, Maman."

"I was a young girl once too, Camille." Her mother said wistfully, reliving some memory that Camille couldn't see. "I allow you leniency since you are not yet married, but you need to understand these little adventures will stop once you find a husband and settle down."

Camille froze. She'd been trying so hard to make these excuses believable this entire time just for her mother to have known the entire time that they were fake? "What if he wants to be a farmer? Then I could help plant seeds all day. What if he wants to be a shepherd?"

"No!" Camille's mother said in a tone louder than usual. "Sorry." She cleared her throat. "No. You will not be marrying a man of such low status with all of the work we've put into your development."

Camille slumped over. "It was only a joke, Maman. You know I wouldn't disobey your wishes."

"One that wasn't funny. Marriage is a serious matter. It is the difference between living a comfortable life or one of hardship. Always remember your value. You know too much to be the wife of a shepherd."

"What if he's rich, but he's an awful, miserable person?" She threw the word miserable into her description, hoping her mother would catch on.

She seemed to have, and gave a grumble of disapproval. "What you gain, not how you feel, is the most important factor in a marriage. Now, head to the church and give him a chance."

Camille nodded solemnly. On her way downstairs she found her father cutting meat behind their house. She would give so much just to be out there learning alongside her father. When she was a child, he'd taught her just a little bit before he realized that she liked it more than her classes. Once he deemed it a distraction, he stopped letting her learn.

"Camille, are you alright?" one of the villagers asked. "You're slouching!"

She panicked and straightened her back. Barely realizing that she was outside to begin with, she'd let her mind wander so much that she'd forgotten her posture. "I apologize for worrying you. I was just examining this flower."

The villager seemed to accept the excuse, and continued on their way, but Camille was left shaken. She needed to be perfect. No form of distraction would be useful to her in the long run.

As she got closer to the church, she saw that Père Fournier was standing outside the church alongside a man who was slightly shorter. Her initial thought was that she was late, which would make her mother proud. Her second thought was the worry that it was too late to make a good first impression now, but at least she could smile.

"Good morning Père Fournier! The weather is beautiful isn't it?" If she turned their attention towards something that was pleasant, they might think the same of her by association.

"It really is!" Père Fournier smiled. "Although, we have

no time to waste. I'm sure Juste is very excited to meet you."
He looked over to the other person who was standing beside
them, who Camille figured must be Juste.

He seemed to be lost in thought, whispering what
Camille guessed were prayers under his breath and staring at
the ground. If he had slept in the last three days, she couldn't
tell through the deep bags under his eyes. His hair was such a
deep brown it looked almost black. It wasn't cared for, or even
touched, in at least a week. Miserable was certainly a polite
way to describe him.

"Are you going to introduce yourself?" Père Fournier
asked.

Camille realized that she'd been spending just a little
bit too long questioning Juste's appearance. "Oh, yes! It is so
nice to meet you, Juste. My name is Camille."

He looked up briefly from his prayer and muttered,
"Juste Laurent."

Juste spoke almost as quietly as he whispered his
prayers, so it was really a guess whether or not she'd actually
heard him correctly. Laurent sounded familiar to Camille
though.

She racked her brain thinking of where she had seen it
before, and an image of the Laurents in the butcher shop came
to mind. Whenever she'd seen the Laurents come in to buy
meat though, they were dressed in lavish outfits and traveled
in luxury carriages. The carriage may have matched, but the
person in front of her was wearing regular peasant's clothing
and seemed eternally lost in thought. He couldn't be related to
them, could he?

"Well then, now that you two are introduced, I'll let
you go on ahead with the tour." Père Fournier pushed forward,
clearly getting bored with watching the two of them stare

wordlessly at each other.

"Oh! Of course. Shall we go?" Camille asked. She didn't want to be an inconvenience any more than she had to be.

Juste nodded.

Camille prayed that the reason he wasn't speaking wasn't related to her, then started to lead him through the town's marketplace, which was adjacent to the chapel, surrounding the main plaza. Here, some of the pathways still were lined with stones, but they slowly morphed into mud the further they walked.

As they were touring the place, Juste examined the areas that he passed through, but never said anything. He simply scanned the areas over visually, arms crossed and mouth whispering ever more prayers.

Camille was fed up with his overall lack of responsiveness. "May I ask a question?"

Juste nodded.

"What are you praying for? You seem so dedicated." She attempted to sound polite, but she could still sense a bit of edge in her voice.

"My parents." At least he was talking now.

"Oh, do you miss them?" Camille latched onto the opportunity to start a conversation with him. "What are they like?"

"They're dead."

Camille froze in place, an awkward smile still stuck on her face. "Oh! I am so sorry to hear that."

"Don't be. They were sinners. They deserved it." There was something robotic about his voice when he spoke. It felt almost like he was reciting something that he'd been told.

"Even if they were sinners, it's not wrong to miss them.

They were your parents after all." She tried her best to console him. "Their actions were their own choice, not yours."

For a second, her words appeared to have gotten through to Juste, but when Camille blinked, he was back to his usual, depressed, praying self. "They were sinners. God decided their fate, and I must understand that."

Camille thought about reaching out to him, but quickly retracted her arm. There had to be something that she could do to fix the situation. She was known for being able to cheer people up, so she figured that Juste would be no different. "Do you want to pray together?" she ventured.

Juste stared. "Why?"

The silence wore away at Camille, and she started rambling to explain herself. "I just saw you praying before and thought you might want to do it together…"

"*Blessed be the Lord God of Israel…*" Juste abruptly began reciting the prayer.

She didn't know what to do. The prayer was unfamiliar to her, so she wasn't able to follow along. Instead, she held her hands together and looked solemnly at the ground beneath her. Hopefully the sentiment would be enough.

"*because He hath visited and wrought the redemption of His people.*"

As the two of them were praying, Camille noticed footsteps approaching them. The footsteps of someone with a crutch.

"*As He spoke by the mouth of his holy prophets,*"

The footsteps were approaching rapidly, and Camille could only now hope that Juste would finish the prayer before she got close enough to start talking.

"Good morning, Camille! What are you doing?" Petime's voice cheerfully blurted out. "Oh. Did I interrupt something?"

Camille froze for a second, then turned towards Juste. He glared at Petime with eyes that could kill.

Camille immediately tried to reduce the damage, stepping in front of him to explain the matter. "Juste I'm so sorry, this is Petime. She is a wonderful person I promise, don't worry about–"

"She interrupted my prayer." Juste said in a growl-like tone.

Camille had never heard a person sound so angry before, and had run out of ideas on how to try and calm the situation. Juste had now started making his way around her to continue to stare at Petime, who just looked genuinely confused.

"Sorry, I didn't know what you were doing." Petime fidgeted uncomfortably as she spoke. "Do you want to finish the prayer? I'll wait…"

"You are that Little Reaper, hellbent on severing my connection with God. Père Fournier warned me about you. "

Petime stared at him. "I have no idea what you're talking about, but you seem like you need to calm down a little bit. Have you had breakfast yet?"

"I will not accept The Devil's invitation." Juste stalked closer to Petime.

"I am no Devil, but you certainly appear to have seen him recently." Petime's chuckle turned into a pointed laugh. "You look like you just crawled out of your coffin."

"Yet you're the one carrying a scythe." he scowled.

Camille watched in horror as the event unfolded in front of her. They were so caught up in insulting each other that she couldn't get their attention if she tried. Why was it that her voice always disappeared just when she needed to speak?

48

"Now, get away from me!" Juste shoved Petime, throwing her off her balance.

"You!" Petime writhed on the ground. She had stumbled a little way back before inevitably falling. Her crutch sat a few feet away from her on the ground.

"Me? What about me!?" Juste replied indignantly.

"You've just shoved someone using a crutch." Petime snatched her crutch off the ground and stood up to meet his face. "Don't you think that is deserving of a little judgment?"

Juste grumbled. "God wouldn't have crippled you if you didn't deserve it–"

Camille fought her anxiety to push between the two of them again. "May we take a moment to calm down please? I know you met in bad circumstances, but I think that there is still potential for a peaceful outcome here."

"An unfinished prayer is a sin, Camille." Juste fidgeted with his fingernails as he spoke, clearly uninterested in the idea of making up.

Petime raised an eyebrow. "Really? I didn't know that."

Juste didn't look up. "You know, it's bold of someone who is missing a leg to trust themself with a blade as a crutch. It seems counterintuitive don't you think?"

Petime lunged forward ready to fight. It was only Camille that stopped her.

"Juste!" Camille shot. Part of her had to admit that she was happy he was becoming more social, but she would have more happily accepted it in any form except hurling insults at Petime. "Could we please say this in a more welcoming tone?"

She glanced at Petime, who was probably already thinking of her next three responses to whatever he replied. Petime noticed that Camille was looking at her, and gave her a questioning glance. Camille used it as an opportunity to plead for her cooperation. Petime, thankfully, seemed to understand what she was asking.

"I apologize for my manners." Petime spoke in a much calmer, warm tone. "Sometimes my jokes can get out of hand."

"Now the witch knows her place." Juste smirked.

Camille watched Petime have a full, silent internal battle with herself. She could see every stage of Petime preventing herself internally from all-out warfare.

"*Anyways*, Camille! I have something to ask you about." She appeared to have picked the redirection approach. A good decision.

Juste seemed to have calmed down to at least a begrudging neutral for the time being, so she'd probably have time to answer Petime's question. "What do you need?"

"Can I ask you what this means?" Petime stepped forward with a wrinkled piece of parchment in her hands. She didn't know how or where she'd acquired the paper, but she read the words anyway.

Meet tomorrow. Same place.

"Do you understand what that means?" she asked, unsure of what to make of it. Why would someone need to meet Petime somewhere? And why would they share that fact through a note?

Petime thought about the translation for a moment before she responded. "I'll explain later, I don't trust *him*."

"Good!" He retorted.

Before they could exchange more unpleasantries, Petime took the paper and made her way back towards the shepherds' houses. It had been a decently high quality cardstock that it was written on, which only left Camille with more questions than answers.

"I wouldn't trust her if I were you." Juste muttered, probably noticing the questions in her gaze.

"Why not?" Hopefully she could gain at least a reason on why he was so quick to fight her.

"She's clearly a witch," He watched Petime as she disappeared over the horizon. "Or at least communicating with one. Think about it, a mysterious letter sent to someone who can't read, wears pants, clearly has the mark of sin upon her."

Camille was unsettled by how many details he'd noticed while he was seemingly filled with rage. "How did you know she can't read? The mark of sin?" Camille asked. "Where are you getting all of this?"

"She's a peasant, so it can be assumed she wouldn't know more than basic words. As for the mark of sin, God takes things for a reason, and her leg is only evidence to that fact."

"I guess you could make those assumptions." Camille spoke slowly, speaking as she still thought over the words.

"They're not assumptions, they're inferences." Juste said, proud of himself.

Not wanting to get into an argument with Juste, Camille left it at that. She didn't want to admit it, but part of what he was saying had some merit to it. Something wasn't adding up.

In her head, her piano teacher's voice lectured her on all of the mistakes she'd made throughout the conversation. If there were any chance of him being a marriage candidate to begin with, they were certainly ruined now "You know, I think I must get going." She stepped away from him. "I'm sorry to cut it short, but I think that all of that energy was a bit too much for today." It wasn't even noon yet, but what she said wasn't a lie. She really was tired.

"That's alright," Juste retreated back to his usual,

quiet self. One of the benefits of his lack of concern was its consistency. "Just remember, be careful around that girl."

She smiled and nodded, even though she didn't want to. "I'll keep note of that."

CHAPTER SIX
Juste

Juste thought about his morning as he returned to the church. Initially, he agreed to the tour because he wanted to make friends, but he wasn't sure of how he felt about Camille. She seemed nice enough, but it felt like she was holding back through their interactions with each other.

Nonetheless, he needed to complete the prayer to his parents. He couldn't leave himself with even a small mark of sin. He needed to live. He couldn't be like his parents.

Entering the church, he realized that this was the first time that he was truly able to see it since he had arrived. There were surprisingly many pews filling the nave of the church despite their emptiness. At the apse, there was a large stone crucifix which seemed to stare into his soul. There was something unusual about the building, but he couldn't quite figure out what just yet.

However, a church was a church, and the prayer was his first priority. He picked one of the many pews, and knelt down. As he started to whisper the words of the prayer, the crucifix became increasingly noticeable. Its eyes seemed to peer into his soul, knowing all of his deepest, darkest secrets. Unable to take it anymore, he looked up at the statue. When he stared into its blank eyes he was immediately thrown into the night of his parents' death.

It was raining. Heavy. It seemed like they couldn't get a word in without being interrupted by a crash of thunder. They had seen the rain coming and had made the decision to try and make it to the next town before it hit them, but they were thoroughly stuck at this point.

His mother was trying to say something, but he couldn't hear her. There was more thunder outside, and the carriage veered from its linear path, sending him and his parents slamming into each other along the seats.

The eyes of the crucifix continued to stare.

Even though he knew there should've been thunder there, the memory was silent. The carriage veered even farther off its path and skidded to a stop. He knew there was rain and thunder, but he could only feel the vibrations of the stormy air now. He saw his father's lips move, and his mother's response, but heard none of it. His father got out of the carriage.

He shifted in the pew to escape the crucifix's gaze.

His mother followed. As they made their way through the door, a wall of rain was let into the carriage. Both of them were gone for a little while, but Juste had no reason to be worried yet. He wasn't even curious until one of their servants entered the carriage.

"I need to tell you that we will be stopping here for the night." He mouthed in the silent voice of the memory. He was so unaware of the horror that was about to unfold.

The stare was burning now.

He looked towards the window.

Juste needed to leave the room. He couldn't stay

beneath the crucifix's gaze any longer.

The horse fell into the river.

He stood up. He needed to get out.

There was thunder. Then there was silence. The only sound that he remembered.

He screamed, curling over in the middle of the church. He stayed that way until he felt Père Fournier's hand on his shoulder. The world came flooding back to him at that moment as he realized what had been happening.

"Are you alright?" Père Fournier asked.

"Yes," Juste took a deep breath, attempting to appear like nothing had happened again. "I was just thinking."

Père Fournier didn't believe him though, and immediately pried further. "Was it about your parents again? I know your servant said that you had a… troubled relationship with the past."

Juste cursed his servants for being so open with his emotional state, but considering his circumstances, it was probably for the best. Here he would have the chance to recover. He was no longer trapped in the carriage that killed his parents. Père Fournier could help him work out his emotions.

"You're right. If I'm to be honest, I was thinking about the night my parents died." He paused. "Sometimes it happens against my will."

"Our Lord does everything for a reason, Juste. If they died, they were *meant* to die." Père Fournier took his hand off Juste's shoulder. "And you were *meant* to live."

"I might just have been lucky."

"God never makes mistakes, Juste."

"Then what makes us so different?!" Juste snapped. "What sets me apart from my parents who died that night?" He didn't know where the outburst had come from, but it was a question that had been on his mind for a long time. If there really was a reason for him to be alive right now, what was it? Was he saved purely on the fact that he was deemed a good person by God?

"You have a purpose, Juste." Père Fournier said. "And that's what sets you apart from them."

"If I do, it's hard to see. All that I've done since I've come to stay in this wretched town is walk around for a little while and get harassed by a legless witch girl." He was breathing heavily as he finished speaking, overcome by his emotion.

"Ah, Little Reaper. I suppose you met her on the tour?"

"She's dangerous. She wanted to hurt Camille." Juste said. "She came up to her babbling about something with a note. For all we know, it could have been a curse."

Père Fournier paused at the mention of a note. "I think it would interest you to know that Little Reaper's story digs deeper than that." Père Fournier was solemn. "Since they were children she has been tricking Camille with charms and spells into being her friend."

"What?!" Juste was caught off guard. Camille had seemed so normal, but was her kind intervention purely a way to protect Little Reaper? "The note wasn't normal. It was written on cardstock. I would think that there are more witches based on its contents."

"Elaborate, please." Père Fournier's tone suddenly became serious.

"She attacked us during prayer. And afterwards pulled out a note that described something about a meeting. It was very vague." Juste went over the details.

Père Fournier stroked his beard. "So whoever wrote it must be smart enough to read."

For a moment, neither of them spoke, and the silence of the church was deafening. Père Fournier was thinking very hard about something, looking at the ground with a furrowed brow. Juste realized his hands were still shaking. The conversation that had initially been started to comfort him was now focused on a different subject entirely.

The thought was interrupted by Père Fournier. "If I am not overstepping, I think I may have found your purpose, young Juste."

He tried to conceal his excitement of the potential of having a purpose. "And what is that?"

"How do you feel about killing a witch?"

CHAPTER SEVEN

Petime

Petime turned the letter over and over again in her hands, sitting on one of the stones in the stone circle. She'd made the decision to come back despite all of her better judgment. She couldn't even confide the full truth in Camille because of their pact. If she knew that Petime was here, she'd be livid. Here was uncomfortable, her mind perceived every sound as a threat, but still, something told her that she *needed* to do this.

Camille was growing apart from her whether she liked it or not, and Petime was still left with barely anything to claim for herself. Camille could go to high-society parties with her other friends, but she was left with nothing more than the life of a hermit shepherd.

The letter had been too vague for her to truly know if she was showing up at the right time. It had only said, "Meet tomorrow, same place." which in of itself didn't provide much information on the time. No matter what happened though, she was prepared to wait because she was going to meet this ghost one way or another.

It was a while before anything happened, but soon enough, there was a rustling sound in the trees that was progressively getting louder. It didn't sound like an animal. There were discernible, distinctly human footsteps emerging from the sound of the leaves. Terror shot through her bones. How would it be making footsteps if it were a ghost?

As she regretted every decision she'd ever made, Petime watched a dark-cloaked figure emerge from the edge of the treeline. As he stepped into the sunlight, she could see that it was an older man. As her eyes trailed down to his arms, she noticed one distinct feature. A wooden hand.

She wanted to scream at the sight of him. Petime had never expected the Handless Witch to be dead, but it was because she thought he wasn't real to begin with, but as it turned out, the stories were entirely true. She scrambled backwards on the stone she was sitting on, but it was to no avail. He was coming closer, slowly but surely.

The figure stopped abruptly, breaking its slow, haunting emergence from the woods. "Oh my, I probably should've taken the hood off. I apologize." He spoke in a surprisingly anxious tone.

Petime struggled to respond, still trying to comprehend what she'd just witnessed. A confused "What?" was all she managed to get out of her mouth.

Petime watched in horror as The Handless Witch pulled the cloak off of his head. His wooden fingers curled around the edge of the fabric just like those of a natural hand. If the stories of his escape were true, she had no reason to doubt the validity of his practice of witchcraft either.

Even through her terror though, she recognized his friendly aura. He had a warm grin, weathered by many years of hardship in life. She could only imagine what could have happened after his escape, especially if he was living in the woods like this. If he were a ghost, he'd certainly have her fooled.

"Are you wondering how I did that?" He predicted immediately. "It's a common question, don't worry."

Petime nodded cautiously.

The Handless Witch was surprisingly eager to elaborate, immediately getting lost in the explanation. "Inside of us are muscles that control different motions in our body. For the hand, those muscles are in the bottom half of your arm. When those muscles work, they change their shape, and my design uses that to my advantage."

Petime curled her fingers into a fist. He was right. She could feel a slight change in the way her arm felt. Examining the hand closer, she realized there were strings spanning all the way up to his forearm with a belt near his elbow. This was far beyond even the medical advancements in the city.

"Interesting, right?" he smiled.

She grabbed her crutch, ready to stand. This was something that she shouldn't get into. Even as a skeptic of witchcraft accusations, there was no way that he could have done all of this without some sort of outside help. Despite his friendly demeanor, something wasn't adding up.

"I'm leaving." she said, turning around.

"Wait!"

"I'm not waiting!" she continued walking back towards the path. "I'm not foolish enough to fall for your tricks!" She stumbled over a rock, and cursed herself silently for not paying attention to where she was going. All she could hope was that she made her point.

The Handless witch sighed. "If I'm going to be entirely honest, I've been watching you for a while."

Petime regathered her footing. "And that makes it better?!"

"I promise, I just want to ask you a few questions. I seldom meet other people who are… like me."

Petime understood what he meant. She'd never seen anyone who was missing a part of themself either. Even if he was a demon, the question seemed genuine enough. "Alright," She had decided to answer, but not to put herself in danger. "But on one condition."

"And what is that?"

"You need to explain *your* story to me truthfully first. I'm struggling to believe that you're human. You must understand that much at least." If he could say something that made enough sense to her, she'd continue speaking with him, but otherwise, he couldn't break his deal. According to what Camille had said, evil creatures loved deals.

"That is reasonable. Although, I will warn you that you might want to sit down again." he chuckled. "It's a long tale."

Petime set her crutches down and returned to her place on the stone. Hopefully it was worth it.

"The truth is that my name is Georges," he started, "And I *was* detained for witchcraft. However, they had left me with my carving knife, which I used to escape. After that I was able to make it onto the road to Paris to find shelter. The journey was… hard, but I made it eventually."

Petime thought about the possibility of unlocking a lock with a knife. It wasn't easy to do, but it wasn't unheard of.

"There I found a space where I was able to pursue my desire to create replacement limbs, which clearly turned out well enough." Georges took a moment to look at his hand. There was a sense of pride in his eyes. "Since then, I've returned to this village for reasons unrelated, staying out of sight. You of all people should certainly understand the desire to stay away from the village folk.”

"I do." Petime said. He wasn't wrong that they were far from accepting people. Petime took a moment to process all that Georges was telling her. She didn't believe that it was a lie, but she didn't sense that it was the whole truth either. "So what was this place?" she asked, curious of how he would respond.

When he told his story, he seemed suspiciously vague. For the first time, Petime saw him look somewhat nervous. She'd definitely caught onto something.

He appeared to be struggling internally over how to respond. "I wouldn't be able to tell you in good faith."

"In good faith? What do you mean by that?"

"I will not elaborate on that." Georges was attempting to change the subject as quickly as possible. "However, I held up my end of the bargain, so now it is your turn to speak."

Petime didn't trust the answer, but she also didn't want to leave just yet. As more things continued to leave loose ends, she found herself needing more answers. "Since you can't answer where you have come from, allow me one more question as a replacement." Petime bargained.

Georges nodded.

"How does your hand work?" She asked, hoping that it would answer more than one of her questions. If he could explain how it worked, it might help to prove his innocence as well.

"They're called gears." The Handless Witch explained, noticing Petime's curiosity. "They're pretty common in cities, but not so much so in these small villages. Rouen and Paris both commonly use them, although not like this."

"And the gears allow the hand to move?" Petime realized that he still wasn't answering her question.

"Not entirely, but they play a large part in it."

"What else works to keep it moving?" Petime looked at the hand again. "The strings?"

"Very impressive that you noticed that." He chuckled, "You are correct in pard, but I'm afraid that how it truly works is more than I can share in one conversation. You certainly are a curious one, though."

Petime could feel her embarrassment on her cheeks as she tried to maintain a threatening aura. She knew she was curious, but she didn't want to be called on it. At this point, it was less curiosity and more of a need to learn. If Georges could make something like that, there was a chance that she could as well. There was a chance to create something that would improve her life. She would be able to finally have something that was solely *hers*.

"Alright, you've convinced me that you are real," Petime took a deep breath. "But later, come back and teach me about that hand."

Georges stood for a moment in silence. His face was a cross between confused and nervous. He probably hadn't encountered a question like this before, especially if he'd spent the last years of his life living deep in the woods next to the village, so now he was figuring out how to react to her question.

"I suppose this calls for a test," he spoke slowly, as if not entirely finished thinking. "To see if you're really ready."

"Test?"

He pulled something out of his pocket, something that Petime quickly realized was a dagger, and hurled it at her. She scrambled back, pulling herself out of the way in time. The dagger flew past her and into a tree behind.

"What was that for!?" she shouted. "That's a twisted

joke, throwing knives at a person without a leg! I knew you were The Devil's worker!" she grabbed for her crutch, ready to leave.

"Wait! No! Come back!" Georges exclaimed, realizing the error of his ways.

"What could possibly make me want to do that?!" Petime had a stare that could kill. It took a certain level of confidence to be able to ask such a thing after nearly killing them.

"That was the test!" Georges was descending into an anxious spiral. "Although, now that I think about it, I suppose I could've asked a riddle, but I've never had to give a test before! It was just customary and…" He trailed off, looking to her for a response.

Petime continued looking at him with a worried face. She hadn't understood any of what he'd just said, so there was no way she could respond.

Georges, realizing this, took a moment to collect himself before speaking again. "I apologize. In short, to determine your readiness, I needed to give you a test. Although, I've never given one before, so I just did the first thing that came to mind… and that was a knife." By the end of the final sentence, he was speaking barely above a murmur.

"Ready for what?"

"Les Tunneliers." Georges said with more confidence. "We are a society of those interested in science. To join, you must first prove your willingness to learn, which you have just done, so congratulations!"

"And that willingness was proven by my ability to dodge a knife?" Petime questioned. "And what do you mean by science?" Her anger was getting overcome by more questions now. Things were quickly spiraling to a point beyond her comprehension.

"It was a mistake!" Georges shot, clearly regretting his actions.

Petime couldn't help but chuckle at his reaction.

"Anyway, when I speak of science, I mean the pursuit of learning. We do things like building wooden hands and creating machines that can light up rooms. Nearly all technological advancements were built by us before they escaped into society. As such, you must swear to never tell a soul of our existence."

"Why not?" Petime wondered about the other things that could have been their doing. It was hard to imagine something on such a scale when she'd spent her whole life in one small village.

"There are many who think that our work is witchcraft before they understand it. Many use it as a place of refuge. The church especially will jump at any chance they get to accuse people of witchcraft, and despite the edicts passed that make conviction difficult, they will get their way."

"Edicts?" Petime asked. She'd never heard of such things.

"The one I speak of was a law that redefined the way that witchcraft was classified. It changed the way that trials were held."

Petime could tell that Georges wasn't saying everything again, but this time she wasn't as concerned with it. She wasn't sure what had changed, but she felt like she could trust him now despite everything that had just happened. There would probably be a lot more that she needed to learn if she were to become part of this society.

"So, can I trust that you won't tell anyone else about this?" Georges asked again.

What she was agreeing to wasn't just lessons like Camille's. This was an opportunity to join a whole new league of people, a swear on her life, an opportunity to gain the independence that she wanted, but at what cost?

Petime weighed each option carefully. If she decided to do this, she couldn't tell anyone. Not Camille, not Leon, not anyone. However, she'd also regain her freedom. She could feel what it was like to stand on two legs again.

"I'll do it." she said. "I'll join you." No chance like this would ever come again.

Georges held out his wooden hand, and Petime shook it, signifying that the deal had been made.

"Until the next full moon, you won't be a full member, so resolve any loose ends in your life now, because it may be your last chance." Georges warned.

It was ominous, but she understood. Committing to this would require her to leave what she had behind. It hurt knowing that she'd leave the few things that she did love, but there was a feeling of excitement that was taking over. She was part of something. She had something to look forward to.

"When you want to find us, follow the trail of ferns." Georges grinned. "That's your first challenge."

"What?" Petime asked.

However, her question was to no one, because when she turned around, Georges was gone into the brush of the forest. She didn't know where to begin, but she would get there somehow. A small challenge wasn't going to stop her.

CHAPTER EIGHT

Petime, 1671

Petime and her father made their way down the path that connected the village to the fields. Her father walked, but Petime ran back and forth along the trail in front of her father, having too much energy to go at such a slow pace.

"Papa, can I please go back home to play with the sheep?" she said, slowing momentarily to a walk.

"Petime, you begged to come along with me." her father lectured. "You should have made a better decision for yourself if you knew that you'd be this energetic."

"But I didn't!" Petime latched onto his arm and started swinging back and forth. "Please?"

"No. It won't be that long."

"*Please?*"

"No."

"Please please please please?" Petime wasn't going to give up, and she knew that her father would give in sooner or later.

The incessant pleas continued on for a few more minutes until her father's spirit finally broke. "Fine," he gave in. "You can run home Just be careful, alright? You've never traveled the path alone before."

"Yay!" Petime cheered. She had already started running again by the time her father finished his warning. Being careful was common sense.

As she got further from her father, she started to feel the excitement of traveling alone. She'd never heard the woods so quiet before, and she'd never had so much control over how she traveled. If she wanted to look at a stone, she could, and no one would be there to stop her.

She didn't stop to look at the stones this time though. It was summer and the weather was nice. The splotchy sunlight through the trees running over her face combined with a slight breeze as she made her way down the path made for the perfect weather. On top of that, it had rained just a few days prior, so the earth was still soft beneath her feet. Perfect running weather.

As she neared the end of the path, Petime slowed to a walk. Even with all her energy, she had still managed to tire herself out. The only thing keeping her walking now was her want to see the sheep at home.

As she continued, she heard a sound coming from somewhere deeper into the woods. It sounded almost like someone crying. After a moment of listening, Petime was able to find out which direction it was coming from, but still not what it was. Her father had warned her to be careful, but if someone was in danger, that was more important. If she were able to find it, she'd be able to help. Her parents would be so proud.

Following the sound, she'd come to the conclusion that whatever was crying wasn't human. Her heart skipped a beat when she saw it. It was a sheep standing deep within the trees, bleating anxiously, and just further beyond the sheep was a wolf lurking in the trees.

Time froze for a moment as she weighed her options. She probably hadn't been noticed by the wolf yet and could easily escape, but she also couldn't just leave the sheep to the wolf. They had become like family to her, and she wouldn't leave family behind. "Hey wolf! Over here!" She stepped forward, immediately being overcome by fear.

Almost instantly, the wolf snapped its head towards her and started running. She was satisfied by her plan's success for only a brief moment. Then she realized how quickly it was running, and directly towards her.

She'd made a mistake, a huge mistake.

Petime turned around as quickly as possible, sprinting through the trees. The sheep was long gone by now, but would hopefully make its way back to the fields. Her goal now was the treeline. Wolves didn't leave the forest during the daytime, so as long as she made it there she was safe. Hopefully, she'd be able to outrun the wolf for at least that long.

"Help!" She knew that there was a slim chance of it working, but called out anyway.

Her eyes remained straight on the forest ahead of her. There was no reason to check behind her shoulder because the frantic crunching of leaves behind her told her exactly where the wolf was, and it was getting closer. Her legs were starting to sting, but the adrenaline allowed her to keep pushing forward. The path was within eyesight now. That was better than forest at least.

"Anyone! Please!" She called again, but to no avail.

She clambered onto the path, nearly falling over as the surface changed, but quickly readjusted and kept running. There was a brief moment of relief as the wolf encountered the same issue. Thankful for even the smallest bit of extra distance between them, she kept going.

Now her lungs were burning along with her legs. Scratch that, everything was burning. The last thing that her father had asked her to do was be careful, and she had thrown his request away. Now she was paying the price for it. She might never see her family again.

"Help! Wolf!" she shouted one last time, hoping that maybe she was close enough to the forest's edge for someone to hear. She couldn't lose hope now.

To her surprise, she heard voices in the distance. They gave her the renewed hope that she so desperately needed, allowing her to push the final way through to the edge of the woods. She could see the trees thinning, and the edge of the field slowly came into view. All she had to do was make it up the hill. The voices were getting nearer to her.

"I'm over here!" she shouted.

Tears of relief filled her eyes as she saw two farmers crest the top of the hill. They were holding their hoes in hand and waving them around. As soon as she saw them, her legs gave out, having gone well-beyond their capability. She fell face first into the ground in front of her, but she didn't hear the wolf's pace slow.

The farmers began yelling and hitting the tools against one another, which slowed it down, but not before it sunk its teeth into her leg. Starting from there, a searing pain shot through her entire body. After the initial pain had calmed itself, Petime could feel the ground moving beneath her. She must have been being dragged away by the wolf. She scrambled to latch onto one of the roots that was nearby, clinging on desperately.

The farmers continued to slam their tools together and

yell, which eventually caused the wolf to loosen its grip and slink away into the woods. Petime was thankful to be alive, but terrified of what her parents would say. Hopefully she'd saved the sheep at least.

"Are you alright?" one of the farmers asked.

"Of course she isn't! Look at her leg." the other retorted.

"Let's take her to the priest. He'll know what to do."

Petime was too tired to say anything, and allowed them to carry her to the church, at some point falling asleep. When she woke up, she would have believed the whole thing to be a dream if it weren't for the pain still stinging her leg when she woke up.

"Petime? Are you awake?" Her father asked.

She immediately started crying. "I'm so sorry Papa. I wasn't careful."

He leaned over to give her a hug, it was the sign she needed. A silent "It's okay as long as you're safe now."

They stayed like that for a while, until the village priest entered the room. "I heard crying. Is she awake now?" he asked with an odd lack of concern in his voice.

"She's awake Père Fournier." her mother said anxiously.

"I've been looking through my records, and I have some unfortunate news." He sighed, allowing for a dramatic pause. "The only way to be sure that she'll be safe is to entirely remove her leg."

Petime froze. "What?" she stammered.

He held an ancient-looking book of medicine in his hands, open to a page on amputation. "We don't have anyone experienced enough in medicine here to treat you, so the best solution would be to remove it entirely."

"Is there anything else you can do?" Petime's father left her side, and approached the priest. "What if it heals itself?"

Père Fournier shook his head. "It would be best to take care of it immediately."

Petime shifted her leg around beneath the blanket. It hurt, but she would prefer the pain to having no leg at all. Her father was no longer by her side and she was scared, faced with the prospect of losing it forever alone.

"I am obligated to share as well," Père Fournier continued on, still seemingly unaffected by the magnitude of this ordeal, "That she may not live through the amputation."

After the news, the room went silent, leaving Petime alone with her thoughts. Not only had she made a mistake, but there was a chance she would have to pay for it with her life.

She looked around her for anything that she could use to help her stand, and noticed an old scythe leaning against the back of the bed frame. As her parents continued to speak to Père Fournier, she grabbed it, using it as a crutch to stand up out of the bed.

When she stood up, hopping slowly to the center of the room to speak, Petime was proud of herself. However, she was the only one who thought so.

Her mother looked down at her, shocked. "Dear Lord, look at what she's holding! It's an omen of death!"

Petime stumbled backwards onto the floor, confused. Was it because she was holding the scythe? She looked at Père Fournier, who was also backing away slowly from her. Her father was doing the same.

Everyone in the room looked genuinely terrified, leaving Petime scared and confused. "What did I do? Please, tell me."

No one responded. They all just stood, staring.

However, a few moments later, Leon broke the silence. To the best of his toddler ability, he had waddled up next to her.

"Yay!" he beamed.

She smiled. He'd barely begun to speak yet, so she was glad that he'd spent one of his first words on her. It made her so proud that for a moment, she even forgot how the others in the room were staring at her.

The decision was made. She was going to live through the procedure. Despite not comprehending the reactions of the adults, she wanted to remember how Leon had reacted, and not waste his confidence in her. If it took using a scythe as a crutch for the rest of her life from this point on, then so be it. She would prove anyone else who doubted her wrong.

CHAPTER NINE
Georges, 1684

Georges stared at the trees that surrounded either side of the path as he pushed his way forwards, the forest was still just as thick as it had been when he'd started his journey. He'd been walking for days now with no sign of food or shelter anywhere, and by now he didn't even know what direction he was traveling in. All he knew of this path was that eventually it would lead to either Rouen or Paris, and either of which would be better than the village that had tried to kill him.

Somewhere out there his wife was getting married to another man, and somewhere out there Père Fournier was furious. His last words to anyone were silence. He hadn't even been able to fight back for himself as he left.

He caught himself dwelling on the past. There would be no more of that. This was the start of a new chapter.

His stomach growled. Despite being able to find water at the river that lined the path, food was scarce, and it was beginning to have its effects on him. He could see himself getting wearier by the day. It was a bout of bad luck that he'd not seen anyone on the path yet. If only he could find a traveler

to ride with, a village, or even an abandoned camp site. It
would be enough for him.

As if God had answered his prayer, the top of a church's
spire appeared over the top of the hill he was approaching.
The church would likely have food for him to eat and a place
for him to rest. Not all of them could have priests like Père
Fournier.

He started running towards the church, fueled by the
thought alone of being able to rest. His shoes, worn already,
slammed against the path. His legs burned, but he didn't mind.
This was the final push he needed. He didn't stop running until
he reached the door of the church, where he fell to his knees
and knocked on the door.

"Please," he knocked, "May I take refuge/"

There was a worryingly long silence, but after a few
moments the door creaked open to reveal a middle-aged priest.
He seemed warmer and friendlier than Père Fournier. He
smiled as he greeted Georges at the door.

The look quickly turned to worry at the sight of him
though. "Dear Lord, you look like you've been stranded for
days. Are you alright?"

"I've been chased by a corrupt church. Please, I beg
that you will let me stay and rest, even if only for a night"
Georges pleaded. He knew he looked like a beggar, but he
didn't care.

"Oh, you poor soul, of course you can stay. You need
to recover from all that you've been through. Come on inside."
The priest held open the door to Georges.

Georges nearly cried as he entered the church. He
couldn't stand, so he crawled up the steps and into the door.
His faith in the priest hadn't been misguided after all. He
came to rest on the floor of the church, waiting for the priest to

return.

The priest, who had disappeared off into some cellar, returned with a few loaves of bread in his arms. "Eat. You need it."

Georges took the loaf and started tearing away at it."How can I ever repay you?" He said between bites. "I will work, I can clean. I was a shepherd before I left, so I can tend to livestock too. Anything that I can do for you I will."

The priest only smiled. "All I want you to do now is rest. Take a good, long nap if you want. There are more than enough pews here for the travelers."

Afterwards, he left Georges alone to eat in peace. It was strange to be hearing total silence for the first time in a while. He'd grown accustomed to the sounds of nature as he'd been walking over the last few days. It only occurred to him just how far he'd traveled now.

Once he'd finished his food, he was filled with new energy, but exhaustion nonetheless, so he took the priest's offer to rest on the pews. Laying down, it felt like heaven to him. Even the hard wood of the pews felt like the softest bed in all of France. It was so comfortable that he didn't realize that it was shaped differently from the other pews. He didn't recognize that it sat just a little bit closer to the ground, just a little bit closer to where he'd entered the door. All he knew was that it was comfortable enough to fall asleep.

He woke up feeling strangely warm. It was the middle of the winter, so there shouldn't have been as much heat as there was. It was warm even for summer. It was beginning to get uncomfortably so.

He opened his eyes in a panic, realizing that something was wrong. Immediately, he was greeted with the image of the priest from before in front of him, holding a lit torch. The pew wasn't on fire yet, but it was about to be. Upon trying to escape, he realized that his arms were bound just like they had been back in his village.

"You were so gullible." The priest laughed, playing with the torch. "You were so desperate!"

"You," George rasped. "You betrayed me."

"No, witch. You betrayed the church. My dearest friend, Père Fournier, told me all about it." The priest paused, staring into the flame. "Now watch what God's glory can do."

Georges panicked, struggling at the knots that held him to the stake. The priest was getting ever closer with the flame, and he was running out of time to think. The desperate escapes were beginning to become familiar to him. Was this his life now? Nothing but a series of running and escaping ropes?

The thought grounded him again. This wasn't the first time that his wrists had been bound, and this probably wasn't the first time that they'd been bound without accounting for his lack of a left hand. He'd done this before, and he could do this again.

He waited, sweat forming at his brow as the priest drew closer and closer. If he moved too early, his plan wouldn't work, so he could only pray for now that his wrists were bound incorrectly.

Eventually, when the priest was moments away from setting the stake ablaze, Georges pulled on the knot that held his wrists, and he felt immediate relief as his arms became free. He'd been right, and startled the priest at the same time. That alone was enough for him to snatch the torch from the priest.

Thankfully, the priest's confidence had prevented him from binding anything more than Georges' hands. so it was easy enough for him to escape the pew. Before he did though, he threw the torch at the priest, sending him into a shrieking fit as it rolled across the ground towards him. It was ironic that he could have no trouble burning another, but was so scared of fire himself.

Georges snatched a few more loaves of bread and made his way out of the church. Only once he was a good distance away did he look back. From the top of the hill he saw that there was a fire beginning to spread inside the church, and that smoke was beginning to billow out of the windows. Part of him wanted to be sad, truly, but another part of him was beginning to believe that it was deserved.

CHAPTER TEN
Juste

Juste sat across from Père Fournier at his desk. It was the first time he'd ever been allowed to enter the church's office since he'd arrived at the village. He'd assumed initially that he wasn't allowed to enter for privacy reasons, but now he was beginning to have his doubts. It seemed normal at first glance, but the more that Juste looked around, the more unusual things he noticed.

The walls were piled high with miscellaneous church objects. There were shelves that he could see were stacked with spare candles and chalices, but an unnervingly large amount of locked drawers were also present. However the biggest thing he noticed were the letters. Surrounding him were stacks and stacks of letters all written in blood-red ink.

"Are you prying into my private life already?" Père Fournier muttered as he shuffled through a stack of papers.

"No, I—" Juste tried to think of something to say, but lost the words. "Sorry." It was embarrassing getting caught.

"You should be more careful when you're sneaking around. You look like a bumbling idiot staring like that."

He shrunk in on himself and nodded. This wasn't starting off well. The two of them were supposed to be discussing the matter of hunting the witch, but now all that he was doing was beginning to doubt his abilities.

"Are you done being disappointed in yourself?" The priest asked. "I found the papers you need to sign."

"Why do I need to sign papers?" Juste looked at the documents gathered in Père Fournier's hands. They were written in the same ink.

"Just a few terms of the agreement. Don't worry about it." Père Fournier slid the papers to Juste.

When Juste flipped through the pages, he realized that they were some sort of contract. There was no way that this much could have been written recently though, so they must have been made before he arrived, which immediately raised his suspicion. Before he could begin reading through it, he was stopped by Père Fournier.

"Don't bother reading through it. I am a busy man." he tapped on the desk impatiently.

"I figure it would be best to know what the terms are before I agree to them, don't you think?" Juste asked, equally impatient.

Père Fournier sighed. "In short, it just says that you will be loyal to me during the time that you are hunting the witch. In return, I'll provide the materials. Does that satisfy you?"

"I suppose." Juste wasn't entirely sure, but he signed his name on the line anyway. Père Fournier was a priest, so what ill intentions could he really be capable of?

Père Fournier was only satisfied once he saw the name written in. "Wonderful. Now, listen carefully to the plan that I am going to give you. If you follow it accordingly, you won't need to get that Camille girl involved in things more than is necessary."

Juste liked the idea of that. He didn't want to harm more people than necessary. "Alright, what do I need to do then?"

"I want you to marry her."

"Excuse me?" Juste was sure that he'd misheard the priest.

"I suppose you *are* blind." Père Fournier grumbled. "The girl's family is clearly interested in seeing you as a potential suitor for their daughter. If you accept their offer, you can both protect Camille while getting closer to the witch."

It made sense to him, but it was also a very large commitment for such a short amount of time. There was still hope that his family might show up to take him home, so coming home with a wife would be a terrible idea.

"Why do you believe that the best option is to get close to the witch?" Juste finally asked. "Do you not worry that she'll curse me as well?"

Père Fournier chuckled. "I suppose you'll learn in due time. But no, I'm not worried. Talking to someone can get you places, Juste. You would do best to learn that."

"I suppose that's why you have all of these letters?" He chanced another look around the room. The collection must have spanned over many years.

"From friends in higher places." he grinned.

"Paris?" Juste asked.

For once, Père Fournier was the one who seemed caught off guard. "How did you guess?"

"You still have an accent." Juste replied. He knew it well, being that it was the same one his family had.

"I see you have more to you than meets the eye." Père Fournier grinned. "You might do well at this with proper training."

Juste returned the smile. "I'm happy to learn while I stay."

"Well, if you are so excited to learn, then let this be your first lesson. Get close to those who you perceive as a threat. Let them show their deepest, darkest secrets to you first. This will allow you to wait until they are at their weakest to strike." Père Fournier seemed eerily excited at the idea of doing so.

Juste was getting increasingly unnerved by Père Fournier. He was getting both more cryptic and more concerning as he spoke. Would his parents be proud of what he was doing if they looked down upon him right now? Up? If God took them from the Earth, should he even want their pride? Was it bad that he still wanted it even if it wasn't something desirable?

His thoughts were threatening to spiral again, and he could feel it. With all of the new things he'd learned about the priest that night, it was probably best that he didn't return to him with more personal matters, including this one. He needed to get out, and fast.

"If that is all, then I will be leaving now." He said, managing to sound like his mind wasn't spiraling.

"If you have any more questions then go ahead." Père Fournier said, already becoming distracted. At least both of them were ready to be done with each other.

Juste stood up from his chair. "I don't."

"Good. Then you may be on your way." Père Fournier looked up from his work. "I expect daily reports on your progress as well."

"What are you? A tutor?" Juste retorted without thinking. His hands were already shaking, and right now he needed space more than he needed to question Père Fournier's methods.

Père Fournier glare was more than enough warning not to proceed any further.

Juste gladly took it and left the room. As soon as he had rounded the corner, he crouched over and started taking deep breaths. He only now realized how uncomfortably warm the air inside Père Fournier's office had been. As he calmed himself, he repeated the priest's lessons over and over in his mind.

Get close to those who you perceive as a threat.

Let them show their deepest, darkest secrets to you first.

Then you can wait until they are at their weakest to strike.

He needed to start his planning now if he were to ever make progress towards his goal, and the only thing he had so far was Père Fournier's offer, so it looked like he was going to have to take it.

CHAPTER ELEVEN
Petime

Petime laid in the grass next to her brother, enjoying the morning sunshine and pondering the events of the day previous. There was so much to think about, and so little time until the next full moon. Judging based on its current phase, she'd give it a few more days, a week maximum, until that point arrived.

"It's so nice when we're able to relax like this." Leon commented, still watching the clouds float across the sky. "I like when we don't have to worry about chores."

Petime scoffed. "Leon, you say this like you ever do your chores to begin with."

"Based upon yesterday, I was still better at mine than you were yours." He sat up. "What happened to the basket anyway? How were you able to just forget it in the middle of the woods?"

Petime didn't know how to respond, so she just shrugged.

Leon groaned. "You're such a menace."

"And proud of it." Petime noticed the sound of one

sheep approaching her from behind. When she turned around, she was face-to-face with a hungry ewe. She shrieked and fell backwards into the grass, which caused Leon to start cackling.

"You think this is funny don't you?!" Petime shouted from the grass. The ewe was standing over her now, as if threatening her for food.

"How could I not?" he said through his laughter.

"Her soulless stare that contains the hunger of a thousand starving mountain lions!" Petime fought. "Get up! We're starting on our chores.."

"What happened to relaxing?" Leon whined.

Petime gestured at the hungry ewe. It already looked like it was thinking about whether or not Petime's hand was food.

Leon sighed. "Fair enough."

They stood up from their places in the grass. Leon started preparing to herd the sheep into the grazing area for the day while Petime began her journey to the creek to gather water. Despite being able to travel well on other surfaces, something about the tall grass didn't agree with Petime. She often found herself tripping and stumbling through the fields ever since she started using a crutch to walk. Despite everything, there were still often days where she wished to have a leg again.

By the time she had reached the creek, she was deep in thought about Georges' wooden hand. He was able to grasp things and move his hand almost entirely normally. If she could build one as well, what would she regain the ability to do? Running, walking, even getting out of bed in the morning would be easier. Before she could do that though, she needed to be able to get to the tunnels to begin with. Without finding them, she wouldn't be able to learn at all.

The need to find the place started to take over her mind, so she returned home quickly. Once she was there she set the water bucket down next to the house and immediately started towards the woods. She hoped that Leon would at least appreciate the fact that she'd brought water home even if it wasn't fully distributed to the sheep. Walking through any more of the long grass today sounded like too much of a hassle.

All that she'd been given to find Georges again was the clue to follow the ferns. It was easy enough to guess that she'd need to make it back to the stone circle, but the rest of it confused her. There was always the chance that it was meant to be that way on purpose as a test, but if it was, she wasn't going to let that stop her.

Arriving at the stone circle, part of her expected something to be different, maybe for there to be some sort of hint to follow or a secret door that had opened up, but there was nothing that she noticed right away. For all she knew, it still seemed to be a perfectly normal forest clearing save for the stones.

She thought back to what Georges had said. "Follow the trail of ferns" wasn't exactly that helpful considering that there were several types of ferns that grew naturally in the area. There was a fern around every bend if she looked hard enough.

Petime began to do just that, examining every fern that she came across. If she looked close enough at all of them, she would be able to find *something* that was different about at least one of them. Her quick scan eventually led her to a fern whose leaves were oddly curled in on itself compared to the others. Upon first glance, one would just assume it to be somewhat wilted, but with a closer look, it seemed to be perfectly fine. It had rounded leaves, and spores on the underside of the tops of the fronds, unlike any native fern she'd seen. A few feet away, there was another fern that looked almost the same, and even further away there was a third. She'd found it. This had to be it.

Petime's suspicion was only confirmed the longer that the trail continued. It went so long that she began to get worried even. There was still a clear trail of ferns, but she'd yet to find anything. Looking around, she realized how deep she had strayed into the forest. Maybe she had gone too far.

Suddenly, the forest started to seem much larger than it had before, threatening to bring back memories she'd rather not revisit. She thought she was imagining footsteps as well, until she noticed a cloaked figure emerge. However, this one didn't look like Georges, he was much younger, probably closer to her and Camille's age. Petime nearly toppled over from the unexpectedness of it.

The cloaked figure noticed her. "Sorry, did I scare you?" He quickly pulled down his hood to reveal a worried face.

"Oh! Um, are you allowed to do that?" This was the second time it had happened, but it never failed to surprise her. She didn't know the rules of the society, but she figured that if they had such mysterious cloaks they'd be more secretive of their identity.

"Oh Lord, you're right!" The person panicked, quickly pulling his hood back on. "I don't know if you're allowed to know who I am yet."

"Yet?" Petime raised an eyebrow.

"Well, Georges said you should find us first, and you're pretty far away…" The figure trailed off. "Although you are still on the trail."

"So this *was* the trail!" Petime took the victory where she could find it.

"Yes, but again, you're far past the tunnel. I suppose

you are Petime?"

"I am!" Petime beamed, proud that she was recognizable. "Would you be able to lead me back to your, uh, wherever you live?"

"I don't see why not." The figure had the same sort of anxious tone that Georges had.

Petime wondered if they were related in any way as the two of them started on their journey back to the tunnel. He probably didn't understand the magnitude of the favor that he'd just done her, but he could live without knowing that fact for the time being.

"So, have you ever seen the tunnels?" He asked as he walked.

Petime shook her head, confused by the question. Was that not what she had just been out here looking for?

"You'll like it there I think. They've trapped lightning in bottles, and it can kill you if you even so much as touch it." He seemed like he was off in thought. "My name is Adrian, by the way."

She was intrigued by the description, she wanted to see what they'd invented that could possibly trap lightning. "Nice to meet you Adrian. I'm excited to see this place."

Adrian didn't respond, and instead continued to look out into the forest, which created an awkward tension for Petime.

"So where are we going?" She asked, attempting to break it.

He pointed off into the trees. "That way." It wasn't a very useful response, but at least it wasn't more silence.

"So, uh, how does one get into these tunnels?" She asked, realizing what might be a fatal flaw in this plan.

Adrian tilted his head at her, confused. "You… open the

door? Then you go down the ladder?"

"We might have a small issue…"

"What do you mean?" Adrian asked, only getting more confused.

"I'm missing a leg…" There was no way that she would be able to get down the ladder with crutches.

He looked down, then jumped back as if this was the first time he was noticing this about her. "Georges didn't tell me that!"

Petime stared at him, confused for a moment. Had he really not noticed that she was missing a leg for this entire span of time? Despite the strangeness, something about it was oddly refreshing to her. Spending her entire life in the village, it had been one of her most defining features for as long as she could remember.

Adrian misinterpreted the reason she was staring. "Don't worry, not many of them use actual ladders any more! A lot of the ones in Paris have doors as well. A lot have code words to enter though. They're a pain to remember"

He said it all as if it were the most normal thing in the world, but to Petime it felt unreal. Code words and secret tunnels were all things out of her wildest imagination, but with every new detail she learned, she only got more excited.

"How do you know how to find them without a map?" Petime asked, mind beginning to race with more questions.

Adrian shrugged. "After long enough, you start to remember the locations."

"That's interesting. How often do you travel?" If the tunnels spanned all the way out to Paris, they had to go there often.

"The members of this tunnel don't travel often. This space is more of a resting site for others who are traveling.

It's safer than being out in the open. People tend to give information while they visit though." Adrian explained.

This was bigger than she had initially imagined it to be. She'd always wanted to see the city in her lifetime. "How many tunnels are there?"

Adrian was silent again, but this time he didn't look out into the forest. His face went inexplicably blank.

Petime backtracked as quickly as possible. "I'm sorry if I touched on something sensitive."

"Don't worry about it." Adrian mumbled.

Petime gave Adrian some space after that, not wanting to provoke him further. She knew what it was like to have someone bring back sour memories, and she had her own things to think about as well. All of this still seemed so big compared to her life in the village. Was she really ready for such a big jump?

After a bit more walking they approached a small clearing in the trees. Seeing it definitely made Petime feel better about missing it the first time that she had passed by, because it was barely noticeable amongst the brush. Adrian, who had been leading the way, stepped aside to reveal a large, wooden door in the ground. It looked almost like it would lead to a well, but when he lifted it up, it revealed a ladder descending into the unknown.

Adrian started climbing, and then gestured for Petime to follow. "I promise it's safe. Mostly."

Petime instead stood awkwardly at the edge of the hole, wondering how she would be able to get down. Never in her life had she used a ladder, partially because she'd never had a use to, but mostly because she didn't know whether or not it would be possible to do so. She sat down in the grass, then inched as close as she could to the edge.

"Could someone catch my crutch?" She hoped the answer would be a yes.

"You mean the murderous-looking scythe thing?" Adrian's voice yelled back up.

Petime was surprised that he'd paid that much attention without commenting on it."Yes! That one!"

"Got it!" A pair of hands entered Petime's field of view from the top of the door.

Petime took in a deep breath, then dropped her crutch down the hole. There was no going back now, because quite literally she would be unable to walk home if she didn't make it down there to retrieve it. Somehow, this only filled her with more determination. She'd never climbed a ladder before, but today was going to be the day.

She gripped the ladder with both hands, then dropped her leg onto a bar below them. She was one step of the way down, which was progress. After taking a moment to figure out what to do next, she lowered her hands, then jumped down again, repeating the process until she reached the bottom. It was painfully slow at first, but each consecutive jump got the slightest bit faster. She was learning things already!

Adrian was waiting at the bottom of the ladder, crutch in his hand and ready to pass it off. Petime dropped off of the ladder much less gracefully than she had climbed, simply falling onto the ground and accepting her fate. Adrian stared at her for a moment, then set the crutch down beside her, which she didn't mind. Her arms were burning from clinging onto the bars for so long, and didn't have the strength to hold on any longer, but she had really done it!

Once she started to examine her surroundings, she realized how elaborate they were. The tunnel was surprisingly large, with tall, arched ceilings. As she looked downwards, she realized the brick walls formed numerous pillars throughout the room and were surrounded by shelves that held various artifacts and books. It was a collection larger than any she had ever seen.

The place was surprisingly bright as well. Secured onto the walls there were rows of oil lamps that served as the main light source, but also lanterns Adrian had mentioned which buzzed with lightning.

A man who she immediately recognized as Georges came out of an archway along the side of the main room that she assumed led into another, smaller tunnel. Petime noticed that there were a few others as well, wondering where they could lead to.

"Petime! You're here!" Georges said with excitement. "I didn't know if my clue was too vague or not."

Petime sat fully up, only then seeing the rest of what filled the room. Somehow, the contraptions that filled the room made the lamps of lightning look like children's toys. What stood out to her most, though, was a map on the wall that had dozens of tiny red pins stuck into it, and dozens more tiny black ones. "I found my way, don't worry!" She said proudly. "It was a test of my intelligence, wasn't it?"

"Uh..."

Before Georges could say anything, a woman around the same age as Georges emerged from the same room, chuckling. "It definitely wasn't. He's just bad at coming up with clues."

"Elise, don't embarrass me in front of the newcomer!" Georges said quietly.

She smiled. "You do that enough for yourself. Don't worry."

Geroges cleared his throat. "Anyway, I will give

you your official welcome now, Petime. Welcome to Les Tunneliers! You will be fully initiated on the night of the next full moon, as is tradition. Until then, you have time to see if you enjoy being here. Though, please note that if you join, you will have loyalty to us above all else. This is to protect the community for generations to come."

Petime had never seen Georges look so serious, but she nodded. The idea of allegiance wasn't an issue for her since she'd sworn no loyalties previously. As long as she would still be able to visit her family and Camille, she'd be okay with anything.

The other woman approached Petime and held out her hand. "My name is Elise, Georges' wife." She paused. "Surprisingly, I was also accused of witchcraft, but in a different village. We run this tunnel together, just the three of us, so it's become somewhat of a close-knit family. Although, I'm sure that you will fit in equally as much in due time."

Petime couldn't help but believe in Elise with her warm smile. "What's the next step?" She only wanted to ask the one question, but it only opened the floodgates for her to ask more in rapid succession. "When do I start learning? What do I learn? Do I have to live here now too?"

"Whenever you want, whatever you're interested in, and that highly depends on how sneaky you can be." Elise answered just as fast.

Petime's mind returned to earlier that morning. "Can I start with learning how Georges made his hand?"

Elise looked at Georges for confirmation.

"That's alright with me." Georges shrugged.

"Can I ask one last question?" Petime was already overflowing with excitement, but she still wanted to know one last thing.

"Of course!" Elise smiled.

Petime glanced at the ladder leading down into the room, then turned back to Elise. "Does all the learning that we do need to be science?"

"In what way?" Elise considered the question. "Do you mean social experiments? We have plenty of people who do those!"

Petime took a moment to attempt to process what Elise had just said, then decided to ignore her concerns. "I want to do physical training." Petime ventured. "Sometimes I feel like my leg puts me at a disadvantage, and I want to make up for that lack of strength elsewhere."

"Actually, I think that's a job that I can help you with!" Elise skittered over to a bookshelf and grabbed a few journals. "When I first met Georges, I was researching some of René Descartes' work, specifically having to do with phantom pain in limbs. While I was at it, I ended up learning a lot of techniques that could help you build strength." Elise's eyes lit up as she thought more about what this joint work could teach the both of them. "Oh, this will be so exciting!"

Petime liked the fact that someone was excited to work with her, and was even more excited that there was the potential for her to feel some degree of normalcy in her life again. The thought of running barefoot in the fields resurfaced in her mind.

The following conversation involved a lot more about the logistics of her intermediate period between being part of the society and being part of the village. They determined that the terms would be that she could visit freely so long as she went undetected, she wouldn't share any information about the tunnels, and she would plan her visits in advance. Altogether, they were pretty reasonable terms.

94

When everything was said and done, it was time to climb the ladder again. Climbing upwards was an entirely new challenge. Getting a crutch out of the tunnel would be much harder than getting it into the tunnel as well.

It didn't prove to be as much of an issue as she thought it would be though, and after a few failed attempts, she settled into a rhythm where she hooked the blade of the scythe between the bars of the ladder as she climbed.

Just like before, the steps started off slow, but quicker as they progressed. There was a sense of triumph as she climbed out of the door at the top and into the grass. She had done it all by herself, without anyone else's help. It was the start of something big, she could feel it.

CHAPTER TWELVE
Juste

Juste walked with Père Fournier in the direction of Camille's house. It was early enough that the birds were just beginning their morning songs, which also meant that the streets were strangely empty. He wanted to make the proposal as discreet as possible so that the witch wouldn't find out about his plans. He also wanted to make it at least somewhat of a special moment to share between him and Camille. He was marrying her after all.

Juste thought about his life just a few months earlier. He was staying in mansions, spending every night comfortable and warm in bed. People complimented him for how kindhearted he was and how beautiful he looked. Now he was here, in Edris, France, a place that no one had heard of, dressed like a peasant and planning to kill a witch. He had no parents, nothing left of his travel supplies, and slowly dwindling hope for his family to retrieve him. Just what had happened over the last few weeks?

"So, Juste, are you ready to be a married man?" Père Fournier poked.

"If it's for the witch hunt, yes." Juste sighed, somewhat annoyed that Père Fournier was interrupting the quiet.

"That won't change the fact that you're married." Père Fournier wasn't wrong, but it wasn't a comforting thought.

"Maybe I'll call off the wedding once I catch the witch." Juste suggested. "I don't know, and I don't particularly care. Once this place is free of the witch, my work is done."

"Your work *here* is done," Père Fournier shifted into a quieter, more threatening tone. "But the work of a witch hunter is never truly complete."

"Doesn't my contract say otherwise?" Juste countered. "Technically, my work *is* done after I complete that.

"And you think that the Lord will be satisfied with that answer?" Père Fournier asked.

Juste didn't respond. He didn't want to.

Père Fournier sighed. "I think it's about time that I tell you a secret, Juste. There are tunnels beneath France. Tunnels that hold communities filled with unspeakable horrors."

Juste, although intrigued, didn't understand why this mattered. "What horrors?"

"Witchcraft. Things that move on their own. Lightning captured in lanterns." Père Fournier easily listed off each addition to the list. "Witch hunters fought them until two years ago when things fell into disarray."

So that was what he was going for. "This all sounds like fiction to me." Juste said, trying to appear like he wasn't curious to know more. "If this was true, then how have I heard nothing of these witch hunters?"

"To fight a secret, the counterattack needs to remain equally as secretive. The trick is to lure them into a sense of safety, Juste."

He remembered as much from the lesson, but he hadn't

expected it to apply on a scale this large. "Why would you share this secret with me then?"

"That is a conversation for another time." Père Fournier grinned.

Before any more could be said on the topic, Père Fournier was knocking at the door to Camille's house. Juste prayed that the two of them wouldn't be waking Camille's family from their sleep. He needed them to be in as good a mood as possible if this was going to go well.

While they waited at the door, Juste couldn't help but think that some of Père Fournier's words were meant to apply to his plan with Camille as well. It was a veiled warning to keep their plans secret.

Camille's father was the one who answered the door. "I apologize but–" he cut himself off once he realized who was at the door. "Oh, my, I'm sorry! What can I do for you two gentlemen?"

"I believe Juste has a question for you." Père Fournier smiled and rested a hand on Juste's shoulder.

Juste was caught off guard, not expecting Père Fournier to leave the duty of asking the question to him. It made sense though. If it were the priest asking for the marriage, it would be seen as strange. "I was uh, wondering if I would be able to ask for your daughter's hand in marriage?"

Camille's father stared at him. His initial face of disbelief slowly morphed into a large smile. "I'll be right back."

He wasn't in the house long, and quickly returned to welcome them inside. The place was very quaint compared to what he was used to, but had noticeably better furniture and decorations than what he had seen elsewhere in the village. From speaking to Camille, he could also guess that she'd had some form of proper etiquette training as well. She must have been one of the wealthier people in the village.

Her father was quick to iron out the details. The marriage would be in exactly four weeks, giving the family just enough time to prepare while also being as hasty as possible. After that, they began to discuss matters of dowry and announcing the engagement to the public. Throughout all of this, though, he noticed that Camille and her mother were nowhere to be seen.

Juste took one final look around to make sure he wasn't missing anything. "Sorry to interrupt the conversation, but may I ask where Camille is?"

"Oh, uh," her father chuckled. "She is upstairs right now talking with her mother about the matter."

It was reassuring to know that at least she was going along with it. "I hope she is as excited as I am, then!"

There was a slamming sound upstairs, and he saw Camille storm down the stairs, tears in her eyes. "I don't want this!"

Maybe she wasn't. "If Camille doesn't want to be married I—" He was cut off by Père Fournier.

"Women are very emotional creatures, Juste." he said. "I'm sure she'll come around to the idea in due time."

"That's what I was trying to tell her." Camille's mother said, trailing down the stairs behind Camille.

Juste glared at him. If Camille was truly against the marriage to this extent, he didn't want to go through with it. He could find another plan. However, Juste recognized Père Fournier's way of telling him to take a step back. This wasn't Juste's plan anymore, it was his. This marriage was for a greater purpose, so the feelings of Camille would have to take a step back for the benefit of killing the witch. That wasn't any reason that he couldn't at least try to come to an agreement, though.

Juste looked out the door Camille had run through, still open and swinging. She probably hadn't made it too far. "Père Fournier, if I may, would I be able to speak with Camille myself? Maybe talking to her will show her how good an opportunity this is."

"Of course, son." Père Fournier said kindly. *Son.* The word lingered in his thoughts.

Juste whipped around to attempt and follow her, but before he was able to leave, he felt a tight grip on his forearm.

"Just don't do anything foolish. Alright?" Père Fournier whispered just quiet enough that only the two of them could hear.

Juste was terrified, but he nodded. Thankfully that was enough confirmation for Père Fournier, because he loosened his grip afterward.

When he made it outside, she was nowhere to be found, so Juste put himself in her shoes. If he'd just found out that he was being married to a man that he didn't like, he would probably want to go somewhere where he could be alone. Following that logic, he walked along the outskirts of town to search for her.

It wasn't long before he found her. She sat next to the edge of the river, hunched over herself. She definitely wasn't happy.

He approached slowly. "Is it okay if I sit down?"

She looked up at him, revealing a face that was puffy from crying. "No."

Unprepared for the answer, he stood there for a moment, then sat down anyway. "Well, I," he didn't know how to phrase it. "I think that we can make terms."

"Sorry?" she sniffled.

"You don't want to be married to me, right?"

"I mean," She hesitated, caught off guard by the question. "Well, if I'm to be honest, then no, but I really have no choice in the matter." The crying in her voice was clearing up as she explained herself.

"The truth is, the decision wasn't entirely mine either." Juste admitted. "If there is something I can do to make this a smoother process for both of us, then I will do it."

Camille smiled, which sent relief through Juste. "There is actually one thing!"

"What are your terms, then?" he asked.

"I want to be allowed to roam free," she said. "I want to be able to go wherever I want, when I want to."

"Ah," Juste hesitated. He'd expected something more emotional from her, such as no hugs or no being seen together in public. Spending time outside of the house was a different issue altogether. It would pose issues to how the housework was going to be done. He was sure that witch was the cause of such irrational demands. "Are you sure about that?"

"I'm sure." she said.

Juste sighed. "I'm sorry, I can't allow that." At the end of the day, he still needed her to be a wife after all.

"You're just like the rest of them aren't you?" Camille looked out over the river, hunching back over. "I guess I couldn't have expected to receive such generosity."

"If you want to negotiate later, I'm still willing. However, your safety is important to me, and there are dangerous people out there. God does everything for a reason, and I'm already in debt. I can't risk him taking you from me as payment."

"Steal me from you? In debt?" Camille grumbled. "Are

you listening to yourself?"

"It doesn't matter." He muttered.

Camille continued to stare out over the river. "If you need to, you can talk to me."

"About what?" This was the first time in a while that someone had truly offered to speak to him about his well being. He knew that it was her politeness, but part of him still wanted to entertain it.

Camille further curled in on herself. "I don't know, but you seem troubled. I don't want to marry a troubled man."

So that was it. She wasn't being nice out of kindness, but rather to save herself from being married to a man who was too emotional. It made sense, but it stung.

"I see." He muttered as he stood up to return home. Altogether, it had been an unsuccessful venture.

"Wait," Camille said, unfurling from her position. "I misspoke. I didn't mean it like that."

Juste turned to look at her.

"I just meant that I would rather you be happy if we're going to spend nearly all of our time together, so you can talk to me if something is bothering you."

"I think I understand now." he said with an edge to his tone. He wanted her to still hate him, and he wanted to ignore the warm feeling in his chest that he had at her offer. This was all for the sake of the witch.

CHAPTER THIRTEEN

Camille

As Juste walked away, Camille returned to staring out at the river, running her fingers through her hair. She probably looked like a mess. She'd forgotten all of her manners. If anyone saw her now, she'd be done for. She'd had an opportunity to bargain for herself with Juste and she'd wasted it. Now she was going to be trapped forever as the wife of a man who loved God more than he did her. If only he would spend half the minutes he spent praying speaking to people, he might not be half bad.

"Camille?" Petime's voice called out. "What are you doing here?"

Camille didn't know why she was out near the river at this hour, especially being alone, but it was none of her business to ask. Despite her better judgment, she put a smile on her face. It would be easier for now to pretend that everything was alright.

"Petime! Good afternoon!"

Petime waved back, and immediately descended into rambling. "I have such exciting news for you. Although, I can't really tell you about it, but I'm sure that you'll be excited to know that it's there!"

Camille tuned out her voice. She had secretly hoped that Petime would notice that something wasn't okay. She hoped that Petime would notice that she was being quieter than usual. Anything.

"Anyways, I'll fill you in on the rest later, alright?" Petime smiled. "I need to do some chores."

"Oh, may I come with you?" Camille had no idea what had followed that statement, but if she was going to be filled in later it didn't matter. She needed a distraction. "I can help out if you want."

Petime looked towards the forest. "Uh, I suppose so, but only for a little while, okay?"

Camille hesitated. Normally Petime would be overjoyed to have so much time to spend with her. Maybe she had missed something important.

Petime stood up, and Camille followed suit. It probably was just her worrying about things that didn't exist. With a deep breath, she began to feel the worry ease from her chest. She was going to make the most of it.

"So, this thing that you wanted to tell me about?" Camille prompted Petime to tell her more.

Petime didn't respond. She was turned in the opposite direction as she asked, looking off somewhere into the woods.

"Petime?" Camille tapped her shoulder. "Are you okay?"

Petime whipped her head around, startled by the tap. "Oh! Yeah," She took a breath to regain her composure. "I'm fine, just a little bit distracted."

"I can see that." Camille muttered. Camille knew that Petime hadn't been paying attention, but she let it slide.

"Speaking of which, I have something to share." She stopped, realizing that Petime was staring into the woods again. "Petime!" Something wasn't right.

Petime turned around, realizing that she'd been caught again. "Sorry."

"Are you okay?" Camille asked. Her own problems could wait.

"I'm just a little bit distracted with everything that's been happening." Petime admitted.

Camille stopped walking. "Alright, you're going to tell me what "everything" is. Even if it's a secret, you're clearly worried about something."

"I promise I will, but I should really get going now. I'm late to start my chores, and I need to have them done fast today. How about we finish this conversation later?"

"But I offered to help–" Before Petime could hear Camille's reply though, she was walking hastily away in the direction they had just come from. If she had really needed to be doing her chores, why was she backtracking? The only thing in that direction was the stone circle.

Juste's warning about her getting into the witches' things came to mind. She didn't want to believe it, but some of his predictions were becoming accurate. Somehow, that made her even more nervous to be married to him.

The more she thought about everything, the more trapped she felt. She was being cornered into a life that she wouldn't be able to escape from. Petime was distant, and Juste was getting closer. Maybe it was a sign. It didn't matter how she felt in the end. No matter where life would bring her, she was only needed to make everyone else happy.

CHAPTER FOURTEEN
Petime

Petime scurried away from Camille as quickly as possible, knowing that she would notice that it was in the direction that they had just come from. She knew that she should've said that they couldn't walk, but Camille had looked like she needed it. The attempt wasn't good enough though, and she knew that. She wanted to get to the tunnel as quickly as possible to do her work. The ideas on her brain were taking up too much space for her to really pay attention to anything. She would apologize to Camille later, but that wasn't something to worry about now.

Now that she knew what the ferns looked like, it became exponentially easier to spot them, which made her journey to the tunnel exponentially faster than it had been last time. If anything, the journey had become almost calming to her.

When she reached the clearing, Elise was standing there waiting for her along with some setups that hadn't been there last time. There were various pieces of equipment that she couldn't even guess the function of. Some had large stones attached to ropes, and there were others that looked like a horizontal ladder, there was even a wooden bar that connected two of the trees.

"How long have you been standing there?" Petime asked, confused. They'd agreed upon a time to meet, but that time had only been specified as "mid day".

"Oh, not long, we have ways of detecting when someone gets close to the tunnel." Elise beamed. Petime could tell by her reaction that it must have been her who'd created those detection methods.

"So you're saying that the first time, when I walked too far…"

She looked away from Petime playfully. "I won't say anything confirming nor denying that we saw you."

Petime sighed. "I look forward to learning how that works one day. Also, were these things here the last time I came?" Petime asked, glancing at one of the things that Elise had set up.

"These are what I've been working on that should help you build muscle in your upper body! My thought is that if you are missing potential strength in your legs, that building strength in the upper body will be the best first step." Elise explained. "After that is when we will start working to increase the strength in your remaining leg."

It was a really interesting idea, but it couldn't have been easy to assemble everything. "How did you assemble all of these things so quickly?"

"The truth is that I had the ideas sketched out a while ago while working with Georges." Elise admitted.

Georges had gone through the same type of training with Elise? It made sense when she thought about it, and it also made her feel comforted in a way. She wasn't the first one to do this, and Georges had seemed successful enough.

Elise looked through her journal, which appeared to have an entire new page dedicated entirely to her. "Speaking of which, before you move to a replacement limb, I want you to talk with Georges about updating your crutch instead. As it is right now, I don't know how it would be able to handle intense movement. A replacement will provide for a short-term solution while you work on your leg."

Petime was offended by the remark towards her craftsmanship. "I think that my crutch is perfectly fine!"

Petime had worked on the skill of making crutches even when she didn't need a new one. There were always farmers who were getting rid of old scythes, so it wasn't hard to find materials for new projects. The glue was probably the hardest part to come by out of any, but Petime was able to make it from the birch trees that she found near the village. The scythe she had now was her most complicated, but also the best-built. It included a small extension to the handle to be more comfortable for her height. The only visible issue was that the blade of the scythe itself, worn from many years of use, wasn't sharp at all, and was beginning to rust around the edges. Even that was only an aesthetic issue though.

Elise kicked her foot at the joint where the extension began, and Petime watched in horror as the crutch almost broke.

"If you could abstain from breaking my crutch any further, I do need it to walk!" Petime shot, then took a deep breath. "But I do see your point."

"Don't worry, we have everything we need here to repair it thoroughly, but it does appear like it will need some updates." Elise examined the place where the crutch had bent. "After we build your upper body strength, the new crutch will be a key to your balance as you work your other leg."

"So where do we start?" Petime asked, desperately trying to move on from the breakability of her creation.

In hindsight, that was a question she'd regret asking. The two of them spent a significant chunk of time afterwards having Petime hang from a tree repeatedly, and seeing how long she could pull her weight. This was followed by lifting increasingly heavy objects and throwing things to see how far they would go.

Even after the exercise was done, the painstaking journey down the ladder and into the tunnel was even worse. She'd dropped her crutch down to Adrian like before, but even so, she was still tired. As she climbed, it seemed like it would be an eternity before she reached Georges' work desk.

When she reached the bottom of the ladder, she painstakingly picked up her crutch and dragged herself to the desk. Sitting on it were hundreds of differently-sized gears, all with different types of teeth, stray pieces of leather, wooden bars, and even some metal rods sitting on the desk. As she looked at them, she thought about how much work had probably gone into making each of the components.

"So, Petime. Elise told me that you need a new crutch that can handle more movement?" Georges asked, approaching the desk behind her.

"Yes." Petime grumbled.

"And you're partial to scythes, I assume?" He asked.

"If it is possible, I just feel more comfortable with them." Petime admitted. She'd never really thought about it before, but they almost felt like they were a part of her.

"I knew that I was right for saving it then!" Georges disappeared behind one of the archways, then quickly returned with a new, taller scythe. "They're called war scythes. When farmers were stuck close to wars, they realized that the regular angle of the blades wasn't effective against enemies, so they readjusted them to be parallel to the rod of the scythe. This one here had an abnormally long pole, which I figured I could use for another machine, but I think it's found a better cause. I'll leave it to you to find a design that works."

Petime took it from his hands, in love with it already. It was the prettiest scythe she had ever seen. There was no rust, and the wooden handle was smooth and varnished. She realized that she would need to add the grips back on, but that would be an easy task for her. There was so much potential within the scythe.

Once they had finished discussing their ideas, they drew plans. Georges taught her step-by-step all of the things that she needed to think about as she drew schematics. After a few failed attempts, Petime was ready to draw them on her own. She sat next to Adrian, who was engrossed in his own project. He seemed focused on his work, staring into the schematics of something about four times as complicated as her own, which made it all the more surprising when he started speaking to her.

"What is it like living in the village?" Adrian asked, still looking down at the page.

Petime was caught off guard by the question. "What do you mean?"

"Just, is it nice living out there?"

"I suppose it is. It's nice spending time with the sheep and being around other people. Even if they aren't the nicest sometimes." Petime stared at her own design.

"What are sheep like?" Adrian asked.

Petime stared at him until he looked up as well. "Have you never seen a sheep?"

"I've heard Georges mention them, but he never

described what they are." Adrian said. "I was born in the tunnels, so I haven't seen much of the outside world.

Realizing that fact explained a lot about his demeanor. He was very accepting as a person, but had little grasp on the social aspect of life. Petime tried to think of a way that she could even begin to describe the concept of a sheep to a person. They were fluffy, and hungry, but she couldn't describe how they bleated when they were anxious, or how they reacted when scratched behind the ears.

Petime came to a conclusion. Sneakery. "How would you feel about seeing one?"

Adrian returned to his work. "Georges and Elise would never allow me to do anything like that."

"Then you should go without telling them!" Petime smiled. She had become used to the idea of sneaking around from all of her years with Camille.

"I don't want to break the rules though." Adrian looked at Petime, then back to the schematics quickly, trying to distract himself.

Petime was determined to get him to visit now. "If you want to collect the most accurate details though, don't you think it would be better to see one with your own eyes?"

Adrian't will was breaking. "I suppose you make a good point, but I'd still be breaking the rules."

"But you'd be breaking the rules *for science*."

Adrian stared at the schematics for a little while longer, not immediately replying, but Petime knew that it was only a matter of time before he would give in to her suggestion.

"I'll do it."

There it was. "Great. Then meet me tomorrow night near the edge of the woods. Just after sunset."

Adrian nodded quickly, then got back to his work, as

if focusing harder would hide the fact that he'd just agreed to break the rules. Neither of the two spoke on the matter again.

CHAPTER FIFTEEN
Camille

Camille walked the rest of the way home in disappointed silence. She knew that it was just one bad day. One bad day wouldn't matter in the face of many, and if she was caught frowning too much her mother would be displeased. However, one bad day was a lot more threatening when it determined the course of the rest of her life.

She needed to speak to her mother again about the marriage again. Deep down, her mother was a girl just like Camille. She must understand Camille's feelings to some extent. This was Camille's chance to have at least *something* turn out positively about the day.

When she walked into the door, her mother was already there, and pulled her into a hug. Camille returned the gesture, happy to be with her family again.

Camille didn't hesitate to start speaking. "Maman, he's dreadful! He speaks so much about sin and witch hunting! It's all horribly unsettling."

"Let's get you upstairs before your father hears any more of this." Her mother said comfortingly.

When Camille spoke to her mother, she always had the serious conversations upstairs out of earshot of her father. It was a firm belief in their house that all emotional matters should be kept between the women of the house.

Her mother started speaking once they were up the stairs. She'd brought them into her bedroom. "I think that marrying a witch hunter would be a good idea. It would keep you safe. Especially with how much you spend time with that legless girl." Her mother put her hand on Camille's shoulder. "If you marry Juste, you'll be safe from any curse she could put on you. And even if you hate him, he'd be off hunting witches most of the time anyway."

"Witch hunter?" Camille asked. She'd known that he disliked Petime, but he certainly hadn't mentioned being a witch hunter.

"Père Fournier said he has found a profession in witch hunting recently." Her mother said, clearly confused that it hadn't been common knowledge.

If what her mother was saying was true, she had a good point. With him off witch hunting, he'd be spending most of his days out of town where he couldn't dictate what she did which meant that she would have a significant amount of time to herself. Still, would living a life of solitude be what she wanted?

"I'd rather marry for love." She came to her conclusion. It wasn't worth the benefits she'd have if she couldn't love anyone.

"And where will you find that in a place like this? Travelers seldom wish to meet a village girl, let alone marry her." There was understanding in her mother's eyes, but she wasn't going to back down. "This is an opportunity for you to gain status. He is related to a noble family."

"But he's awful!"

"He's the best thing you'll get!"

The two of them stared at each other. Unsure of what to say next.

Camille wondered under what circumstances that her mother and father had gotten married. They didn't share much about their story, but she knew that her mother was his second wife. It wasn't common for people to remarry, so what had been their reasoning?

"What if I can find a man better than Juste?" Camille said, an idea forming in her mind. If Juste was the best option she had currently, it wouldn't be hard to find someone better. "I'll make every effort to search for a man that I would prefer before the wedding. If I do, could you promise to call it off?"

"Do you truly think you can find someone better than Juste?" her mother asked.

"Yes."

She raised an eyebrow. "Do you truly think you can find someone better than a man who is wealthy, close to the church, and willing to marry a girl from a small village?"

"Yes?" Camille repeated, but with less enthusiasm. Maybe this would be harder than she thought.

"You have until one week before the wedding date." her mother said calmly. "Nothing more."

Camille hugged her mother, thankful that she'd allowed her to do this. "Maman you are the best mother the world could ask for!"

"Of course I am," she chuckled. "Just know that the man has to be *better* than Juste by my standards. It won't be easy."

"Of course, I'll keep that in mind." All of the terms of the deal were fair, but Camille couldn't argue that they weren't difficult. She would need to stay within the realm of the village as well. It would look suspicious if she traveled so soon before the wedding. "May I ask one more thing?"

"Go ahead." Her mother sighed. "While I'm in a good mood."

"Since I am to be married anyway, may I stop taking piano lessons?" Camille prayed that she would say yes.

"I figured you would have asked that question sooner, honestly." her mother stood up from the bed. "I'll allow it on the condition that you can keep yourself tidy until the wedding. If I have to clean your dress so much as one more time, I'm telling Madame Chelault that you'll be back."

"Alright! Done!" Camille grinned and ran out of the room.

She immediately set off in search of Petime, hoping that since she had finished her chores she wouldn't be as distracted. As she walked, she was careful to keep every ruffle of her skirt clean. Even through the tall grass of the field, she was sure to walk delicately to avoid stains.

The walk was longer than she expected though because Petime was nowhere to be found, which was unusual for this time of day. The sun was getting close to setting, so there was no way that she would still be doing her chores by this point, right?

A voice from behind her interrupted her concern. "Petime?"

Juste.

"Good afternoon Juste." She didn't bother turning around. "Why are you here?"

"I could ask you the same question." He paused. "Are you going to see the witch girl?"

She bit her tongue to restrain herself from spewing

a slew of insults. "You know that it isn't polite to say that, right?"

"But it's the truth. You know that she is bound to have cursed you by now!" Juste grabbed her hand, making Camille flinch. "She's dangerous Camille."

"And how can I prove to you that she isn't?" Camille whipped around, meeting his eyes.

Juste stared at her for a moment. There was a look on his face that she couldn't quite identify. Though, he quickly recovered and cleared his throat. "How about you pray with me?"

"Pray?"

"If you are cleansed by God's light, it may weaken her hold on you." Juste explained, letting go of her hand. "Then you'll be able to see through your cloud of delusion."

"I'm not delusional." Camille huffed.

Juste didn't seem surprised by her answer. "Those under the influence of witchcraft cannot see their own delusion. Especially women."

His last words had tested her, but she remained smiling. Any thought of visiting Petime was cleared from her mind. All that she could think about now was that she was going to pray tomorrow, and she was going to prove him wrong.

"Shall we pray tomorrow then?" Camille knew it was an offer he couldn't decline.

"Tomorrow sounds wonderful." Juste smiled.

CHAPTER SIXTEEN

Juste

Juste headed back towards the church, satisfied with himself. He had convinced Camille to pray with him as well as distracted her from visiting the witch girl. From what he had seen, instead of going towards the fields she had headed back home. Although he felt some remorse for calling her delusional, it was the hard truth that she needed to hear.

As he walked back, the memory of her defiant face haunted him. He didn't know why. Maybe it was the fact that she'd looked at him with such resolve. He was intimidated, nothing more. That was definitely it. He'd seen many beautiful women, but none so quick to defend themself.

He wanted to keep lingering on it, but he was getting close to returning to the church, which meant that he needed to report something to Père Fournier. The engagement was set as of this morning, but they both knew that. Other than convincing Camille to pray with him tomorrow, there was nothing more that he could add to his progress.

Thankfully he was blessed with more time to think, because when he entered the church, Père Fournier was nowhere to be found. Juste took a seat in one of the pews, knowing he'd turn up eventually. He enjoyed the quiet that the space provided him. Somehow, the sounds both from outdoors and indoors seemed to fall quiet in the large room. He recited prayers until they were the only thing that filled his mind. The eyes of the crucifix would not beat him this time. He was worth God's light. He was worth living.

He knelt for a long time praying like that, hoping that answers would come to him. As he prayed, he watched the sun's light slowly fade through the stained glass and descend into night. The only lights inside the church were a few lone candles.It occurred to him then that the priest had never returned.

He stood up, heading down the hallway to look for him, thinking that he might have just missed his entrance. "Père Fournier?" he called. No response.

Juste walked into the back of the hallway, checking the office. Père Fournier was nowhere to be found. Although, the large stacks of papers were still sitting atop his desk. It wasn't right to snoop, but it might give him a clue as to where Père Fournier was hiding.

He walked up to the desk to check the content of the letters. Nearly all of them seemed like personal letters, written back and forth in neat cursive. Instinctively, Juste's eyes wandered towards the names signed at the bottom. It was hard to imagine the idea of Père Fournier having friends.

However, when he glanced at the papers, there were no names associated with them. No visible ones, at least. In the space where the names should have rested was only empty space. All that connected them was a single wax seal. It was intricate, similar to the seal of the king, but not quite the same. It depicted a flame that crept up its center, with flowers and herbs surrounding it, all burning in the wax flames.

"Do you need something?" Père Fournier's voice came from behind him.

Juste looked away from the letters as fast as possible, being careful to avoid looking like he was snooping, but the look on Père Fournier's face told him that he had been caught.

"I was just looking at this seal, Père Fournier." There was an element of truth to what he had said. He was simply not sharing the full reasoning.

"Ah, it's a pretty one isn't it." He paced towards Juste. "There's not many places you'll see this seal now. They stopped production of them two years ago, actually." He picked up one of the letters and stared at it wistfully. "Were you looking for me? I heard you call my name."

Juste couldn't understand how Père Fournier had been close enough to hear his name. He hadn't been in the hallway or any of the rooms along it, and there weren't any available places to hide that he knew of.

That he knew of.

"I reasoned that you'd probably want to hear my progress for today." Juste said timidly. Any focus he'd had from before was dissolving away from the stress of being caught. If anything, Père Fournier's apparent calmness towards it all was the worst part.

"I'll let you have tonight without a report." Père Fournier set down the letter, then tossed a log into the fireplace.

"Thank you." He left the room as quickly as he could without seeming like he was in a rush, and as soon as he was in the hallway he felt his breath returning to his chest. Losing it was beginning to become a trend when he was around Père Fournier.

He crossed the hall and entered the room where he

was staying for the time being. It was small, but it had ample furniture and a window on the side, so it would do. Inside was a bed, a rug, and a large wooden chest to store his belongings in. It wasn't as much as he'd had at home, but he didn't mind since that was all he needed.

Laying down in his bed to sleep, he found that he couldn't. There was too much on his mind to be able to be tired in any capacity. First was the confusion surrounding the fact that Père Fournier had come out from seemingly nowhere. Then it kept circling back to his conversation with Père Fournier, Camille's defiant face, and the seal placed on every single one of the letters. All of it was spiraling far beyond what he could rationalize. Père Fournier had mentioned secrets, and Juste was beginning to believe that he might be part of one of them.

He groaned, then stood up out of the bed. He headed to Père Fournier's office and to Juste's surprise, he was still awake, lounging in a chair and staring into the fireplace. In his hands were a quill and journal, but it seemed like he had stopped writing long beforehand.

"Have you come back to search my room more?" Père Fournier grumbled, not looking away from the fire. "It's getting tiring."

"I was actually coming to speak to you." Juste chanced a few steps further into the room. "I wasn't able to sleep."

"Is it about your parents again?"

Juste's heart stung at the mention of them. "No, it isn't. I just wanted to ask you something."

The priest finally turned around to look at him. "And what is that?"

There were so many things for Juste to choose from, whether it be Camille or the secrets or anything else, but there was one thing weighing on his mind more than the others.

"What makes a person evil?" he asked.

"What's got your mind on that?" Père Fournier seemed even more annoyed than before.

"I just want to know whether or not I'm a good person. Truly."

"Come sit down." Père Fournier gestured towards another chair adjacent to the fireplace.

Juste obliged, and sat down in the chair. He made himself comfortable, knowing that whatever they spoke about, it was probably going to be a long conversation.

"What makes you a good person is whether or not you follow God's will." Père Fournier explained. "If you do whatever you can at all times to follow the path that he has intended for you, then you are a good person."

"And what if you feel as though you have lost that path?" Juste asked.

"Then you allow others to guide you. Everyone can lose their way when searching for God's light. All of it depends on what you do to return to it." It was the most priestly thing that Père Fournier had said so far.

"And what happens if even then I still stray?"

"Why are you asking all of these questions all of a sudden?" Père Fournier looked at him with suspicion in his eyes. "Are you planning on going back on our plan to kill the witch?"

"No of course not," Juste scrambled. "I just wanted to know whether or not I was doing the right thing."

"The right thing for you Juste is to allow yourself to be given orders. God is watching you especially closely. To be a good person, you must allow yourself to become my puppet. Do you understand?"

Puppet. Juste didn't like the description, but he also valued his life, so the decision was a clear one. He nodded his head.

"Wonderful." Père Fournier said. "Now, do you think you can sleep?"

"I have one other question, actually."

Père Fournier sighed. "You lied when you said it was only one. That is three prayers tomorrow morning for you."

"Alright." Juste didn't agree, but accepted the punishment regardless.

"Now what is your question?"

"The seals on those letters…" Juste started, beginning a train of speaking that went on much longer than he wanted it to. "You said that the seals went out of production two years ago, which is the same time that the witch hunters fell into disarray." Juste met Père Fournier's eyes. "Is there something that you aren't telling me here?"

Père Fournier sighed. "I really should be more careful around you."

"So that means that there is?"

He shut his journal, preparing to put out the fire. "Nothing that you need to be concerned with tonight. If you couldn't sleep before, you certainly wouldn't be able to sleep if I were to explain all of that."

Juste accepted the answer reluctantly, knowing that there was nothing more he would get out of Père Fournier tonight. He got out of the chair, ready to leave the room as well when the priest stopped him.

"Just remember, Juste." he said, staring into the dying flames. "You need to be a puppet."

CHAPTER SEVENTEEN
Petime

Petime woke up the next morning feeling like death. Her arms were hurting, her leg was hurting, everything was just *hurting*. She knew that it was all of the work that she had done yesterday beginning to pay off, but it was a heavy toll when she needed to be out of bed first thing in the morning to help her brother with chores.

Once the two of them were outside, they immediately got to work. This morning, they were awake before their parents, meaning that they could speak more freely as they tended to the sheep, and today was no exception. As soon as they made it outside and the door was shut, Leon was speaking. "Petime, you look like you were visited by an actual reaper in your sleep. Are you alright?"

"I'm fine. I just wandered the forest for a little too long." she explained.

"I don't know what's been happening to you, but it can't affect your productivity. First it was the basket of vegetables, and now you're walking around looking more like the undead than usual."

"More than usual?" She shot him a disapproving stare. "I said what I said."

She grumbled something unintelligible, then grabbed some of the buckets for the sheep's water. It was going to be a painstaking journey to the stream today, so she might as well start it sooner than later.

"Don't die while you're out there!" Leon shouted as she trudged through the grass.

"I hope you get trampled by a sheep!" she shouted back in an equally mocking tone.

"That's not very nice to say to your brother is it now?" another voice added from beside her.

Petime was so startled that she jumped, crutch catching on the grass. With an ungraceful tumble, the buckets rolled just far enough away from her that she was going to have to crawl to pick them up. It was horrifyingly embarrassing.

"What do you need, Juste?" Petime asked, daggers in her voice.

He lifted his hands. "Calm down, calm down. I'm here for a peaceful reason this time."

"And what could you of all people possibly have in the business of peace?" Petime laughed at the absurdity of the idea.

"I want to make a truce."

Petime stood back up and grabbed the buckets cackling, but when she looked into his eyes, they were dead serious. He really wanted to create a truce with her.

"What caused the sudden change of heart?" She wasn't unwilling to accept the personal growth, she just found it highly unlikely.

"I'm going to marry Camille."

Petime dropped the buckets that she had just finished collecting. "What?!"

Juste puffed out his chest, proud of the fact that he'd managed to surprise her. "Well, if I'm being honest. Neither of us really wanted to, but we had no choice in the matter."

"Oh." Petime returned to a deadpan tone. "So you're unbearable *and* an idiot. You're a man with everything and you still get roped into an arranged marriage?"

"Of course you don't understand." Juste scoffed. "It's something that a peasant girl like you wouldn't understand."

Petime, between her fury towards Juste, realized that that must've been the reason that Camille was so insistent on speaking with her yesterday. She'd been in a moment of need and Petime had entirely ignored it. She'd really messed up this time.

Juste prevented her from dwelling any further on the matter. "Anyways. How do you feel about that truce?"

Petime's gut reaction was that she didn't like it, but if it was going to help Camille, she would agree to it. She would do anything that it took to help Camille out in her marriage, especially if it was to someone as miserable as Juste. If Petime was certain about anything, it was Camille's disapproval of the matching. "If it's for Camille, I'll do it."

"Good!" Juste helped Petime gather her buckets. "What are your conditions?"

"How about you stop calling me a witch?"

"That's doable," Juste shrugged. "On the condition that you never speak to Camille again."

Of course there was a catch. When she was speaking to Juste there always had to be a catch of some sort. She was a fool if she'd thought any differently. "I won't agree on those terms."

"Why not? It's for Camille's own good!" Juste pressed.

"What about Camille losing me is any good for her?"

Petime replied, equally as adamant.

Juste took one of her buckets and handed it to her angrily. "You're a *witch*. You certainly must know what harm you are doing to her!"

Petime slapped it away, refusing the offer of help. "Would you stop with the witchcraft accusations? I urge you to think about it, to really think about it, and ask yourself what motivations I would have to curse my only real friend in this town."

"I don't think I will, actually!" Juste shouted.

"This isn't going to happen. In fact, I'm going to go speak with Camille *right now*." Petime walked away, leaving the buckets in the grass where they'd fallen. She would be able to finish gathering water later.

She hopped through the field as quickly as she could, leaving Juste standing behind her. Thankfully, he at least had the decency to stand still, allowing her proper time to make her dramatic exit. She didn't know if her temper could handle any more of the man.

She was furious at Juste for implying that she was casting spells on Camille, but she was also furious at herself for allowing the tunnels to come in the way of speaking to her friend. Hopefully she would be able to reconcile things before it was too late.

CHAPTER EIGHTEEN
Juste

Juste watched the witch hobble away on her crutch as if she could conceivably gain any sort of distance on him. It really was pathetic, but it left him with an opportunity. While he was sure that she was away, he could examine her house for clues. If there was anything that she was hiding, it was likely that it was stored somewhere close to where she lived, and hard evidence would be good to have for his daily report.

After staring at her disapprovingly for a satisfactory amount of time, he approached what he believed to be her house, and looked around the surrounding field. Her brother was nearby tending to the sheep, but he didn't seem to notice Juste's presence. Figuring that he was well hidden, he used the opportunity to sneak into the inside of the house.

When he entered, he nearly froze from shock. Along the far wall of the house, two people who he instantly recognized as the witch's parents were sleeping in a bed. He cursed himself for opening the door so loudly, and quickly pulled it shut to avoid letting light in. All he could do now was hope that her parents didn't wake up, and if they did, that the darkness would mask his cover.

Once his eyes adjusted, he took in the contents of the house. The whole place seemed dank and musty. It was like everything was moments away from disintegrating. He wholeheartedly believed that if he were to lean against the side of the table in the center of the room, it would break in two. There were two other "beds" in the house, although they were closer to collections of rags on the ground. He assumed that one was for the witch and the other was for her brother. Thankfully, though, the witch's bed was easy enough to identify because there was a bundle of crutches sitting adjacent to it.

They were all different sizes, ranging from child-sized to nearly large enough for the witch to use now. There was also one that was snapped in half entirely. He didn't want to imagine what had happened to that one. It felt almost like a portal into her childhood, which was tempting to linger on, but not what he was looking for. He needed to find anything that would be incriminating, and a crutch wouldn't be nearly enough to prove her guilt.

He started rummaging as quietly as possible through the bed, becoming increasingly aware of how bad it would look if he were caught. All he could do was pray that he found something quickly.

The prayers were answered shortly, though. While he was searching, he started to hear the telltale crinkling of paper crumpling, which immediately caught his attention. Peasants didn't usually have access to paper. It was quick enough to locate through sound, and soon he was holding it in his hands. He instantly recognized it as poorly-drawn designs for some sort of crutch unlike any of her previous ones. There were no numbers or measurements yet, so either the idea was fresh or the witch had no writing comprehension skills, but he was sure that it was hers no matter the case.

Before he could debate on what to do with the drawings, he noticed that the sound of snoring had come to a stop, and there was rustling coming from the other side of the room. He could take the paper with him, but then the witch would know what he had been up to.

Making his impulse decision, he hid the paper in the blankets once more and snuck towards the door. To Juste's horror, there was clear movement coming from the other side of the room now. They were about to get out of bed.

He cursed himself under his breath as he struggled to push open the door silently. It was caught on some sort of stone from outside. He aimed to get it open as narrowly as possible as to not disturb the darkness of the room, but it seemed like it was going to have to come fully open for him to escape at all.

"Leon, close that door. It's too bright out." A man's voice mumbled.

Juste nearly fainted when he heard the voice speaking to him. In a panic, he slipped through the door, shutting it as fast as possible behind him, immediately running behind the house in case the parents came looking for him. Once he was behind, he pressed his back against the wall and slid down in relief. Leon was her brother's name. Interesting.

The schematics were the more pressing matter though. This meant that she was learning from somewhere, or *someone,* which in turn meant there were more witches, and they were working together.

"Leon?" The same man's voice called out. "Leon!"

"Yes Papa?" a younger voice called back. It was much more distant than his father's.

"I swear he was just inside." the father's voice said

again. "Unless it was someone else."

Juste heard footsteps approaching the back of the house causing him to spew another bout of curses. This would be a delicate process.

As the footsteps of Petime's father rounded one side of the house, Juste made his way along to the other. The circling continued for a few rounds of the house, until her father finally deemed it safe enough to disappear back into the fields to go speak with the real Leon. The entire time, Juste could hear his heart pounding in his chest. That was too close for comfort.

As soon as he was certain that Petime's father wouldn't see him, he started sprinting back towards the church. A good portion of the journey was spent convincing his hands to stop shaking from the nerves of being stalked round and round a house. If Père Fournier were to see him, he would probably laugh, or worse.

By the time he had actually made it to the church, he was calm for the most part thankfully. When he called out for Père Fournier, he was sitting peacefully at his desk. Part of him was expecting the priest to pop out from behind a wall again like last time, but it was quite a relief that he didn't.

"I have news to bring you." Juste said, hoping that he wasn't interrupting anything too important.

Père Fournier didn't look up from his work. "And what is that?"

"I have evidence to prove that the girl is really a witch!" Juste beamed.

Père Fournier continued scritching letters onto the document. "Come back when you have something better for me then."

"What?" Juste stammered. Wasn't evidence what he was looking for?

"It doesn't matter whether the girl is a witch or not. It only matters whether she is dead or alive."

"I'm sorry?" Juste stepped backward. "Please explain this to me further."

"It doesn't matter whether the girl is a witch or not. We are trying to eradicate the *idea* of her." Père Fournier droned. "Years ago, we let a witch missing a hand escape, and it has damaged the reputation of the church. What do you think the villagers think of a legless girl running free? They have the potential to gain sympathy."

"You mean to tell me that it was never for the people's wellbeing?" Juste felt sick to his stomach. Père Fournier hadn't helped him because he believed the witch was a genuine danger, he'd just cared about the reputation of the church.

"I think that it's time you hear the full story, Juste." Père Fournier said solemnly. "You're getting close to putting the pieces together."

"Alright…" The explanation had better be a good one, or Juste didn't know what he was going to do.

Père Fournier stood, beginning his signature, slow pacing. "In Paris, the witch trials had a golden era. A time where witches were properly convicted, where the population lived in peace, and where God's light held the ultimate power. However, as time progressed, less and less of those witches were convicted. In fact, some of the trials even ended in their escape. The King couldn't live with that sort of danger roaming free throughout the city. So in response to this darkness, he created Les Saints Chevaliers."

"The Holy Knights?"

"Yes. They were a group that lived to… *take care* of those who escaped their condemnations after the trials took place. We were restoring order to the city from behind the curtain."

Juste's stomach continued to churn. "When you say you took care of them. That means that you--"

"Killed them, yes."

"How does that reflect God's wishes?" Juste asked desperately. "How were you okay with doing that?"

"It *saves* them, Juste." Père Fournier emphasized. "It stops them before they stray too far from His light."

"Then how does killing people like Petime have any effect?" Juste asked, unsure of how to take this. On one hand, they were saving people, but how they went about it seemed like unnecessary violence.

Père Fournier sighed. "Think of how many doubts she spawns regarding the validity of the church, Juste. Her sacrifice would bring dozens of people back to the church at least. If not hundreds." The priest spoke with a terrifying note of greed in his voice. "Think of your parents. Her death would have been able to save them too. The witches are the messiahs of the greater populus. God does everything for a reason, and creates everyone with a purpose. He simply creates them with the purpose to die."

Juste hadn't realized it, but Père Fournier had paced to the other side of the room with his speech, and was admiring his portrait that hung from the wall. After a dramatic pause, he pulled on the corner of it, causing it to swing open like a door. Juste watched as it pulled away to reveal a collection of daggers built into a notch in the wall. Part of him was amazed, but a larger part was worried for his safety as Père Fournier approached holding a knife.

Juste took a step backwards, but found he was backed into a corner. "What… is that for?"

Père Fournier continued forward silently, and Juste

held his breath. He lifted the knife up as he got within stabbing distance, but instead of thrusting it forward, pressed it into Juste's hands, and curled his fingers around it.

"I'm asking you to do the right thing, Juste. Kill the girl. Save them all. You can be part of Les Saints Chevaliers. You can do His bidding."

Juste let go of his breath, thankful that he was going to live through the experience. He looked into Père Fournier's eyes and saw nothing but sincerity behind them. God did everything for a reason, and Juste had lived for this, whether he liked it or not.

"I will."

CHAPTER NINETEEN

Georges, 1682

Georges walked through the tunnel holding Elise's hand. In the hand that was free there was an oil lamp that illuminated the rest of the dark tunnel before them. Water dripped in through the ceiling, and the entire thing was made of bricks, just like their own.

Elise pressed her own free hand to the brick wall. "They don't understand underground masonry." she sighed. "It looks awful."

Georges took his own look at the masonry. She wasn't wrong. "They're priests, not architects. Besides, that might serve as an advantage to us."

"I hope it collapses."

Georges held back a snicker. "That would be ideal, wouldn't it?"

"Hold on." Elise pressed a finger to George's mouth. He sincerely hoped that it wasn't one of the same fingers that had just touched the disgusting brick wall next to them. "Do you hear that?"

Georges listened, and then realized what she was

talking about. Somewhere in the distance there was yelling. Not an argument though. It was motivational yelling, like someone was speaking to a crowd. The type of yelling that someone used to deliver news that was important. The point of their mission was to gather as much information on Les Saints Chevaliers as possible, so that sound would lead them to exactly where they needed to go.

"I hear it." Georges said, shifting into a hushed tone and blowing out the light of the oil lamp. It was dark, but it would hide their presence better. If there was a gathering, there would surely be some form of security.

"Good idea." Elise squeezed his hand, then broke away.

The two of them waited for a moment for their eyes to adjust to the light, then followed the sound. As they got closer to its source, they made sure to stay pressed against the walls of the tunnels to stay hidden.

The further they walked, Georges noticed that the tunnels were getting larger. Based upon the entrance they had managed to find, he couldn't even comprehend how they'd hidden such a large network. By the time they neared the voice itself, it sounded like it was being projected into a large hall. Where exactly were they?

"Stop." Elise whispered. They were almost next to the voice now.

After a few moments of listening, Georges realized what was happening. "It's a sermon."

The man preaching the sermon had a booming voice that carried throughout the hall. Georges could only imagine the size of the crowd that he was preaching to. The whole thing was unsettling to imagine to say the least. Especially being only the two of them deep into enemy territory.

"Let's see if we can get a little bit closer." Elise said,

motioning down to the end of the hall. They were approaching a corner, and if Georges had to guess based upon the sound of the voice, he'd say that it led into the room itself.

He nodded, and as they crept closer, he started hearing the words of the sermon clearer. They had transformed into something else entirely.

"Let each and every one of them burn for what they have done! They live like worms beneath the ground, becoming the very underbelly of this city! We need to be rid of those pests once and for all! For years, we have silently cared for this beautiful city, and now it is time to do the ultimate good. Even if The King has declared us broken, our spirit will remain strong!"

There was a roar of cheers that erupted throughout the chamber. The walls and ceiling vibrated with its power, so much so that pebbles started to fall from it. Georges glanced at it, hoping that it could survive the blow.

"They're talking about us." Georges murmured.

"They're going to get rid of all of us." Elise replied.

"I don't think any of us understood their true numbers until now, and if they're organizing…"

Elise took Georges' hand again. "The King doesn't know what he has done, truly. In his effort to save us, he has condemned us all."

Their conversation was interrupted as the roar of the crowd died down, and the leader began to speak once again. "Go, brothers! Unleash the light upon this world! Let the purifying flames creep burn them out!"

They were about to move. Hundreds of people with a freshly renewed thirst for witch hunting were about to be filing out of the room they were standing directly next to.

"We need to go." Georges said frantically.

Elise nodded. They had no time to waste. If they were
going to bring the news back to their tunnel, they needed
to survive the trip back. Georges lit the oil lamp yet again,
unconcerned about stealth now. Their main priority was escape.

The two started running, but in their original effort
to find the sound, they had strayed deep into the tunnels of
the priests. They had a vague idea of which way could be
considered out, but at the speed they were running, it was
a guessing game as to where they'd end up. Georges swore
that he heard footsteps behind them as well, but there was no
looking back. If he did, he had convinced himself that there
would be a worse fate than death lurking behind it.

In a stroke of luck, he saw a light emanating from one
of the paths, a natural light. "Elise!" He pulled her towards it.

They made it out, escaping through a door into a small
alley between two buildings. There was a crowd outside, so it
was easy enough to blend into. It seemed perfect, almost too
perfect, but as long as they were out, he would accept that it
was fate.

Once they had mingled into the crowd, they stared at
each other silently, unsure of how to react to what they'd just
heard, and Elise pulled him into a hug. He didn't look back. He
didn't hear the laughter that rang out behind them.

CHAPTER TWENTY

Camille, 1684

Camille woke the next morning and began her usual chores. She hoped that during the coming months, she would get things a little easier due to the deal between her and her mother, but she couldn't escape things entirely. Petime probably wouldn't be awake at this hour anyway.

The more she thought about it, the more she realized that the strange things had been happening ever since she'd seen the ghost at the stone circle. After that day, she'd barely seen Petime, and when she had, she'd always been distant. Maybe it was a coincidence, but it all seemed like it was too much to ignore.

She finished hanging the last piece of laundry on the line, then sat down. She needed to talk about it all to someone, even if that someone wasn't her friend. She needed someone who would still give her honest advice no matter what, and there was only one person she could think of who fit that description. She went inside to talk to her mother, and found her sewing upstairs. "Maman, may I speak to you for a minute? I finished the laundry."

"Of course Camille. Come in." She said, not looking up from her sewing.

Camille fidgeted with her hands. "What do you do if you feel like someone is… hiding something from you?"

Her mother pricked her finger as soon as Camille had said the words. Camille could tell that she had made a mistake already. She stepped forward to help looking for a bandage, but her mother held up her hand.

"Don't. If someone is hiding something from you, figure out what it is, and if it is something bad, tell Père Fournier. Immediately." Her mother said in a flat tone unlike anything she'd heard before.

Camille saw her mother's hands trembling, unable to tell if it was from the pain or something else. "I don't think it is something that bad. Don't worry Maman."

"That's how I lost him, Camille!" Her mother immediately covered her mouth. She'd said too much.

Both stood frozen in place and unable to break eye contact. Camille guessed that she was speaking about her last husband, but there was no way to be sure. Not many women in the village remarried, and Camille could tell that her mother felt shame for doing so. She never had shared the story of what happened. All she knew was that he died. Now, she was sitting on the bed, threatening tears.

"Maman, it's okay. I won't ask about it." Camille hugged her mother. "If you don't want to say anything else, I understand."

Her mother wrapped her arms around her stomach, staring into a memory that Camille couldn't see. "Camille, my last husband got caught doing bad things. I just don't want that happening to you too." She wrapped her arms tighter. "It hurts. It hurts so much."

"It won't, I promise." Camille pulled away from the hug. She knew that her mother preferred her emotional moments to be private, so she took the box of bandages off the shelf, and silently placed it on the bed next to her before leaving the room.

She returned downstairs to clear her mind. The thought of her mother plagued her focus. Her trembling hands and distant stare threatened Camille to heed her warning. They whispered the idea that Petime might be more dangerous than Camille thought she was.

She found herself behind the shop holding the knives that her father used to carve the meat. She'd learned how to toss them when she was fairly young purely as a side effect of her proximity. Now, she tossed them at the wooden boards behind their house to release stress.

She shot a knife at the board, and it hit its mark. However, along with the normal *thunk* of it hitting the wood, there was also a "Hey!" from behind it.

"Petime?" She was surprised, but it wasn't an unwelcome visit. "How did you get here?"

"Well I saw you walk around back, and I was going to surprise you, but then you looked angry so I hesitated—and there were knives." Petime continued to ramble for a few more seconds before she realized that she was speaking for too long.

"Anyways, I wanted to apologize."

"For what?" Camille asked.

"For not listening to you yesterday. I found out about the marriage." Petime dug shapes into the dirt with her crutch as she spoke, appearing like she wanted to shrink into nothingness. "I'm sorry."

A wave of relief flooded over Camille, and she accepted the apology. It had just been one bad day afterall, and Petime was returning back to her usual self now. "It's alright. Speaking of, were you okay?"

"I was distracted." Petime admitted like it was any sort of surprise. "I've just had a new way to pass my time recently."

"And what is that?" Camille prayed that she would give an answer that didn't involve witchcraft.

"I've been… exercising!" Petime said happily. "Speaking of which, I have a large favor to ask of you."

"What is it?" Camille was hesitant, she could tell that Petime wasn't telling the full truth as she spoke, and now she was asking for a favor?

"Can you meet me in the fields?" Petime said in a hushed tone. "Tonight?"

"What would we be doing in the fields?" All she wanted was a normal answer, and now she was being asked to sneak out to the fields in the middle of the night. This wasn't witchcraft. It couldn't be.

"I can't exactly tell you, but you've given a tour of the town before, right?"

She stared at Petime, even more confused by the followup question. At least witchcraft *probably* wouldn't involve giving a tour of the town. "Yes?"

"I know it sounds strange but–" Petime was cut off.

"Everything you say sounds strange, Little Reaper." Juste emerged from behind one of the boards. Why was it that everyone had decided to find her in her yard today? Could she not just throw knives in peace?

Camille grimaced. "Hello, Juste."

However, he didn't return the greeting. He was already enthralled by scowling at Petime, who was returning the gesture.

"I thought I told you to stay away from her." Juste

threatened.

"We made no contract." Petime scoffed. "It was all empty threats."

"God makes no empty threat, *witch*." he hissed.

Camille, in a burst of temper, threw a knife towards the board behind Juste, just narrowly missing him.

"Dear God!" he jumped back.

Petime snickered.

"I just wanted to come out here and throw knives, and you two immediately start attacking each other the moment you make eye contact!" she shouted, taking a moment to gather her breath afterwards. "Can you both just calm down?"

Petime thankfully nodded, even though she looked like she would still jump back into the fight the moment she was given the chance. Juste took a step back as well, but still scowled.

"She has a bad influence on you." Juste muttered, not breaking eye contact with Petime.

"Juste…" Camille warned.

He took a deep breath, then turned towards Camille. "Ignoring Little Reaper over there," Juste said, clearly still hiding jabs at her within his speech, "I think that now would be a good time for us to pray together."

"How romantic," Petime interjected. "Do you invite the Lord on all of your dates?"

Camille turned away from the both of them, struggling to maintain her composure. If her mother emerged to see what all of the commotion was about she'd already be done for, but if *she* was the one who was caught yelling, it'd be exponentially worse. She'd already given up on making both of them happy, so she was going to have to pick one or the other.

"Petime." Camille whipped around with a renewed

sense of conviction in her voice. "I will be there, but please, I beg of you, leave."

Petime nodded, slinking off down the street.

"Juste." Camille faced him. "Let's go pray."

"I'm glad that you're choosing the right path." he smiled.

Camille rolled her eyes. "I'm choosing the path that doesn't end in you two murdering each other."

"You still defend her. You must be truly hexed." Juste looked at her pitifully. "You go as far to throw knives now. I pray that God will clear your vision."

Camille decided not to share the fact that she had been throwing knives since her childhood. It was a battle that she didn't want to start at the moment. All that she needed to do was pray for just long enough to appease him. If it got out that she'd refused his offer, the town would have reason to question their relationship.

Neither of them spoke as they walked towards the church. Juste looked like his mind was still on Petime based upon the occasional scowl that crept over it. Although, Camille never could be too sure when it came to him.

As they entered the church, Père Fournier was lingering near the door, looking like he was ready to speak to them, but when he realized that Camille was trailing behind Juste, he slithered away into the depths of the back hallway. She wondered what it could have been that she wasn't allowed to hear about. What compelled the members of the church in this village to act like this?

Juste picked seats for the two of them right in the center of the frontmost pews. Camille had never sat so close to the altar before, and it was strangely unsettling. That along with the fact that the church looked very different than when she attended masses. Without being livened up by the people who filled it, the place seemed almost like a crypt.

"Let us pray for Camille's return to the light." Juste said to no one in particular.

Camille knelt down, looking into the eyes of the Crucifix. They gazed back at her, almost in a pitying way, reassuring her that her pain was seen. Upon seeing His stare, she tucked her face into her hands, praying instead for a way to escape.

CHAPTER TWENTY-ONE

Juste

Juste hid his smile as he prayed for Camille. When he was able to sneak glances at her, she seemed deep in prayer, which meant that he was successful in convincing her to stray from the witch. He would be able to save her without the need for violence. If only he could convince the whole world to pray, it would be so much easier.

The two of them stayed like that for a while, praying. It was only them and the crucifix in the empty nave of the church, creating a direct connection with God.

"Alright." Camille leaned back onto the pew. "I think that I have been sufficiently enlightened."

"Really?" Juste's heart leaped. "Are you going to stop speaking with her?"

Camille leaned further back into the seat. "No."

"What?" Juste was confused. Were the witch's enchantments really so strong that even prayer couldn't cleanse her?

"You've barely given her the chance to speak for herself, and yet you make a judgment on her character so easily. You preach so often about the Lord's doing everything for a reason that you have become blind to the things that aren't of his doing."

"She's a *witch*, Camille."

Camille stood up from the pew. "And how do you know that?"

"I have proof!" Juste immediately regretted the decision. No one else was supposed to know about the details of his work, at least not yet.

Camille sighed. "I don't know what this proof is, but I urge you to speak to her about it yourself. You can tell that she doesn't have much concern for societal standards, but she always has her reasons."

Juste bit his tongue. "I don't think you understand." If he could only share the drawings, he could explain, but that would require him to admit to sneaking around as well, and that would only make things worse at this point.

"I think that I understand perfectly." Camille looked at him with a certain shadow in her eyes. It was the stare of someone who was beginning to lose hope, and it dug into Juste like a dagger. "I wish you a good day."

She exited the pew, leaving Juste standing alone. He didn't bother to watch her leave, instead listening only to the heavy creak of the door as it opened, then slammed shut. Camille's expression was burned into his memory. Hopelessness, he knew that feeling well.

He looked at the Crucifix for help, almost expecting it to whisper some sort of answer to him, but it just continued to stare. He knew that The Crucifix was capable of pity, but only for Camille. To him it only spit fire, searing flames of judgment for his sins.

He wasn't going to wait for it to burn him again. Juste left the church as well, finding himself walking towards the woods. He didn't know exactly where he was going. All he knew was that he was going to hunt for the witch.

He'd heard of the path that the shepherds used, and wanted to examine it for himself. It was easy enough to find, but the atmosphere was different than he'd imagined. Once he was fully onto the path, the woods blocked everything else about the world out, leaving him with only his thoughts. It was a welcome peace coming from the bustle of the village center. He could focus on the birds chirping in the trees, and the clouds forming overhead. As he continued further, he approached a clearing full of short, leafy bushes. The path looked like it was well traveled to the clearing, which piqued Juste's interest. Something important had to be over there.

He strayed from the main trail, realizing only then what the bushes contained. Strawberries.

It was ironic seeing so many of them now. His mother had always spoken of how much she loved wild strawberries, but he'd never tried one himself. Juste had helped her grow a garden of them at their home, spending a large portion of his free days running around and watering the bushes, and still the ones here thrived tenfold even without human intervention. He'd had plenty of those, but she'd always said that the wild ones tasted better.

She was a good person. She had to be. Juste had never seen her do one thing wrong, but still God decided to take her.

"What is your reason?" He whispered to the air.

There was a gust of wind. They were becoming increasingly frequent, and now a significant layer of clouds was forming above him in the sky. He continued to stare at the strawberries, though, thinking of all the time that he'd spent with his mother. Maybe Camille had a point. If he'd learned about her whole story, maybe he could have saved her. If he learned about Petime, would he be able to save her too?

He slowly walked towards the berry bushes. He wanted to take one, but it felt wrong doing it without his mother next to him. They'd do it together. That's what she always said. The first time that he tried a wild strawberry, they'd eat them together.

That wasn't an option now, though.

"Maman, please forgive me."

He took a berry from one of the bushes, and as soon as it broke away from the vine, a flash of lightning filled the sky. Juste dropped the berry immediately, hands shaking. A slow roll of thunder followed after.

His heart was racing and his hands were trembling. "I'm sorry. I'm sorry! Please don't do this." He didn't know who he was speaking to, but if something was listening, he hoped it accepted his plea. He didn't deserve to die. Not like this.

He was wrong. They couldn't be saved. None of them could be saved. Père Fournier was right in his resolve, and Juste never should have doubted him. He had sinned by even thinking about the possibilities, and now God was punishing him for it.

This was his life now.

CHAPTER TWENTY-TWO

Camille

Camille waited in her bed until she was sure that her parents were asleep. Escaping in the night was easy enough, but only if she was careful. Usually, the only time that she'd do it was in early summer when she watched the glow worms with Petime. This time was different though. There was a note of mystery to it; meeting at a new location, and for some reason, using her skills of giving tours. Her stomach tied itself in knots wondering just what Petime was up to. She could only hope that she hadn't wrongly defended her this morning to Juste.

Once she heard distant snoring from the other room, Camille made her way down the stairs, careful to avoid every creaking board. The stairs were the hardest part of the journey, but she passed them with ease. The rest of the way to the field was nothing comparatively, and she snuck out the door, traversed the village streets, and reached the fields just as easily.

As soon as she reached them, she could instantly locate Petime. She was lurking near the edge of the treeline on the outskirts of the field, staring somewhere into the forest. She didn't know what was out there, but her worries were only increased. Nothing good could come from a forest in the night time.

Camille, disregarding her better judgment, walked the rest of the way to the treeline to meet up with Petime. "I was worried that I wouldn't find you at first!" Her excitement still showed through all of her anxiety.

Petime, startled, nearly collapsed to the ground upon hearing her voice. Once she realized it was only her though, she took a deep breath and recollected herself. Remaining silent, she put her finger to her mouth and pointed at the sheep.

Camille looked out over the field of sleeping sheep. No matter how cute they were, they would probably be a nightmare to deal with if they were to wake up. "Sorry." Camille whispered.

"Don't worry." Petime whispered back. "Now, are you ready to go meet him?"

"Him?" Did this mean someone else from the village was involved in all of this too? Her mind started shuffling through an entirely new set of concerns. There were increasingly few rational explanations to Petime's behavior remaining.

Petime continued to look back and forth between Camille and the forest as she spoke. "There is someone that I need to introduce you to. He may act a little bit strange, but I promise that he is a good person at heart."

Camille felt an odd twinge of jealousy hearing Petime talk about him. She'd always told Camille that she was her only friend, but it seemed like that was changing now, and without her knowledge at that. How long had the two of them known each other? She'd come here for resolution to her concerns, but they were barely speaking at all.

Without time to dwell any further, Camille saw a light beginning to appear in the distance brighter than any glow worms could possibly be. She stepped back immediately. "Is that coming from the woods? Petime. What aren't you telling me here?"

Petime returned her questions with nothing more than an excited grin, causing Camille to assume the worst. Something had happened that day in the stone circle, and Petime was almost certainly interacting with The Handless Witch. There was no one else that would be coming *from* the woods and producing such an unearthly light. There was a brief, brief moment where she almost wished Juste was there with her.

When he emerged, he was wearing a cloak. Camille stood her ground despite wanting to run away because she knew that running would only make matters worse, but she was going to need to speak to Petime about this later.

The cloaked man quickly pulled the hood down as soon as he saw Petime, revealing a much younger figure than she had expected. He had platinum blonde hair and bright, blue eyes, both of which were uncommon traits for the village. She'd definitely remember if she'd met him before. However, he did have both of his hands, so it wasn't as bad as she'd initially thought. It wasn't enough to quell her fears entirely, but it was enough to convince her to give him a chance. Something about him seemed to draw her in despite her better judgment.

"Camille, I want to introduce you to Adrian." Petime finally decided to speak. "He's my friend from the woods!"

Adrian stared at Camille for a second, then whipped around towards Petime. "You didn't tell me that there'd be more people here! You're not supposed to tell anyone about us!"

"Who is us?!" Camille couldn't help but catch his phrasing. There were more than just one of him?

"She's fine, don't worry." Petime assured him. "Plus, she's way better at giving tours."

"Petime, she's already questioning me! I just wanted to see a sheep for God's sake." Adrian collapsed in on himself with clear regret in his eyes. It was a strangely relatable feeling to Camille.

"You do realize that I can hear all of this unfold, right?" Camille couldn't help but smile at the absurdity of the situation.

Adrian collapsed more.

Petime circled around him anxiously, making sure that he was okay. "I figured that if you were going to sneak out, you should make the most of it. Just give it a chance?"

Camille watched the back and forth continue, unsure what to make of it. Based on the way that they spoke to each other, it was clear that she was missing some context. She wanted to ask, but was too nervous to interject.

Adrian eventually caught onto this, and broke up his and Petime's conversation by shooting his hand out towards Camille. She didn't know how to return the gesture, and just stared at him, still trying to comprehend what was happening.

Adrian's serious face melted into an anxious smile. "That is a normal greeting, isn't it?" Adrian paused, then looked at Petime for confirmation. "Isn't it?"

Petime nodded. "Don't worry Adrian, I think that Camille's just not used to getting many handshakes."

Petime was right. She wasn't used to getting many handshakes at all, but the feeling was oddly refreshing. Seldom were women even given the opportunity to, so it made her feel important. She reached out and grabbed Adrian's hand, giving the best handshake that she could.

"That was weak." Adrian looked at her hand, seemingly examining if it was okay.

"Oh, sorry!" Camille was a flurry of anxiety. She didn't want her first impression on him to be a bad one. "Do you care if I try again?"

"Sure." Adrian said.

Camille shook his hand a few more times until he'd concluded that it had gained enough strength to pass his test.

"You two are so perfect for each other." Petime said cheerfully.

"What do you mean by that?" Camille could feel the blush on her cheeks, and was never more thankful for the cover of darkness.

"You'd be really good friends!" Petime turned around, starting the walk into the village. "Anyway, we've got a job to do. Camille, do your thing!"

Camille realized only now how utterly distracted she'd been by Adrian. She'd never questioned the light, she'd never questioned why he was emerging from the woods, and she'd even been willing enough to give him a handshake. He was dangerous.

Camille noticed that Adrian was still looking at her and appearing conflicted. Multiple times as they climbed the hill towards the village, she watched him start to say something, then cut himself off, then start to say something again.

"You don't need to be worried to speak to me." Camille said, tired of wondering what he was thinking about.

"Oh!" Adrian appeared surprised that she'd been paying attention to him at all. "I just live further down the path. I've never been into town. That's why I've never seen a sheep." He grew quieter and quieter with every following sentence.

Camille recognized the lie instantly, but she also recognized the sincerity behind his words. He wasn't lying because he had ulterior motives, he was lying because he didn't want her to be scared. At least, that was what she wanted to believe.

She started to lead them back around towards the village, but as soon as Adrian saw a sheep, they were forced to pause.

He stopped dead in his tracks, staring into the fields. "*Is that a sheep?*"

Petime shushed him, since they were close enough to wake them again, but nodded in affirmation.

"They're so *soft*!" Adrian looked almost like he was going to break out into a squeal.

He truly hadn't seen a sheep before. The ewe sitting in the field was no more wooly than usual, and Camille wouldn't even describe it as particularly adorable either. Yet here Adrian was, in pure awe at its presence.

"Can you explain to me how you've never managed to see a sheep before?" Camille asked in a whisper, being careful to wait until he'd had his moment.

"No." Adrian replied quickly, returning to his regular tone.

Camille realized that she was going to have to accept a lot of bizarre answers when she spoke with Adrian, which only became more clear as the evening progressed. However, compared to all of the other things she had had to come to terms with lately, this one was alright. Even though she knew

she *should* have been getting a sense of danger from him,
she knew deep down that he wasn't dangerous. There wasn't
witchcraft involved, only secrets, and secrets were okay for
now. She smiled at the absurdity of it.

Adrian's marvel towards ordinary objects became a
sort of trend throughout the night, and the group would need to
pause at each statue, building, or nighttime creature, but they
reached a nice rhythm as they moved from place to place as
well. Camille made sure that she shared small facts about each
of the places that they stopped, noticing the way that it made
Adrian smile. The time flew by, and soon enough, the tour had
ended and they were back in the field. Petime was leading the
way, leaving her and Adrian trailing next to each other in the
back. It was all too short for her.

"What is your favorite place in the village?" Adrian
asked Camille as they inched around the sheep. He was still
glancing at them on occasion.

"Hmm." Camille thought about her own favorite
memories of the town. "If I had to choose only one, I'd say the
banks of the river. When I'm there, I don't feel the need to keep
up appearances for anyone else. " She dropped her voice down
to a whisper. "Don't tell Petime, but I have a spot that is still a
secret from her."

"Your secret is safe with me." Adrian returned the
whisper.

Camille continued on with the description, smiling
at her memories as she did. "At night, the most magnificent
glow worms fill the sky. Usually I go out and watch them with
Petime, but sometimes I go alone."

"Would it be alright if I saw them?" Adrian asked. "Of
course, we don't have to!" He stumbled over the second half of
the sentence.

"Sorry?" Camille blinked.

"It's just that I saw no glow worms tonight, and they sound very nice to see." He paused. "And you're very nice to listen to."

Camille stared at him again, at a loss of words for what to say. It was a compliment, but it wasn't masked in the slightest.

Adrian's nerves only worsened when he saw Camille's reaction. "Sorry. Did I do something odd? I don't speak with others much."

"Oh, no! I'm just… Thank you!" Camille was stumbling over her words now as well. "Thank you."

"Why would you thank me? It's the truth."

Camille didn't make eye contact with him. She didn't want to stumble over any more of her words while processing what he'd said. His lack of hesitation was going to be the death of her composure.

Once she was ready, she returned to the conversation. "I don't think we can see the glow worms tonight though. It's much too late.

Adrian nodded. "I figured as much. Can we see them tomorrow then? Or the night after?"

Camille went over the logistics of sneaking out again mentally. "I mean, I suppose we could. Let me go tell Petime." She began walking slightly quicker to catch up with her.

"Wait!" Adrian stopped her. "Didn't you say that the place was private? We can go just the two of us."

Camille froze in place, questioning whether she'd heard him right. "Alone?" She gulped.

"I don't want you to bring more people than you are comfortable with."

Camille immediately let out a sigh of relief. Of course it

was just him misunderstanding the implications of what he had just said, nothing more. "I am alright with the idea of sharing my space if it makes you two happy."

Adrian looked at her for a few moments, then shook his head. "Let's go somewhere else then."

Camille was taken aback by the sudden change in direction. "Why?"

"You're prioritizing our wants over yours. From what it sounds like, this place is important to you because it allows you to be yourself, so it would be wrong of me to intrude upon that safe space." Adrian explained.

Adrian wasn't wrong, and Camille hadn't even realized it until he'd pointed it out. Throughout the last couple days especially, she'd barely made any decisions for herself. She didn't know that she needed to hear Adrian's words tonight, but they made her feel oddly comforted.

"Thank you for saying that." Camille made sure to look him in the eyes as she said it.

Adrian looked away. "There is no need for that."

"I have an idea of where our second place might be, though!"

"May I know where it is?"

"It's a secret!" Camille grinned.

"How will I know where to meet you then?" Adrian asked with a strange sincerity.

"Same place, tomorrow night." Camille glanced ahead of her. "Don't tell Petime either. I'm going to make a decision for myself this time."

Adrian nodded, and after that the rest of the walk was quiet. Camille wasn't certain of what had made her so bold, but it wasn't an unwelcome feeling. Petime had made a good choice in making Adrian her friend. If anything, he was certainly better than The Handless Witch.

"What are you two talking about back there?" Petime looked back at them, unaware of what had just unfolded. "Hopefully it's nothing too interesting."

"Nothing interesting! Don't worry." Adrian replied. As he did he smiled at Camille.

Camille returned the grin, and they continued walking. She didn't know what she was getting herself into exactly, but she was slowly coming to terms with the fact that it was happening, and that she was going to be okay with it.

CHAPTER TWENTY-THREE
Juste

Juste woke up to the unpleasant sound of church bells ringing directly above him. Their sounds, meant to be heard throughout the whole village, were more than enough to wake someone directly beneath them. He knew that they meant a town meeting was to be called, but he didn't know why Père Fournier would ring them today of all days. He figured that if he was going to, he would've at least told him about it first.

No matter what he thought, though, he was going to have to go outside to see what it was all about, so he got out of bed and got ready as quickly as possible. He flung himself out of bed and got changed keeping his hands over his ears as much as humanly possible. The sound being better outside was one of the only things that motivated him.

His plans to get outside as quickly as possible were interrupted when he ran into Père Fournier in the hallway.

"Why are you ringing the bells?" Juste asked, the bells were still unbearably loud. "And without warning?"

"I have a wonderful opportunity to share with you and the town, Juste!" It was one of the few times he'd seen genuinely excited over the last few days. "It has to do with your induction into Les Saints Chevaliers."

Juste raised an eyebrow. "I thought that they were a secret?"

"Of course, the event is masked beneath another." Père Fournier explained.

It gave Juste no real idea of what the surprise was or what it was going to entail, but he was sure that it was intended to be that way. Juste was just relieved that it wasn't a true emergency taking place.

Père Fournier led the two of them outside where they stood to wait on the porch of the church for the people in the village to gather. Those who were already there were murmuring amongst themselves, curious to hear the news. Only once he was sure that everyone had arrived, the priest hushed the crowd, signaling that it was time to make his big announcement.

"Hello everyone!" His voice carried over the people more than Juste thought possible for a man of his age. "I am here to announce that we will be having some very special visitors in the coming weeks."

There were more whispers throughout the crowd. This *was* a common travel route, so it wouldn't be unheard of for a well-known member of society to stop here on occasion, but with knowledge of the ulterior motive, Juste gained a new level of concern.

"There are going to be four high-ranking members of the church, and friends of mine, coming to the village in two weeks' time. I would greatly appreciate it if you tidied your homes and prepared gifts for those days. I strive to make them feel as welcome as possible here in Edris."

High ranking church members, most likely from Les Saints Chevaliers. Juste's stomach twisted at the thought of how they might test him when they arrived.

"Since the spare space in the chapel has been taken by the newest member of our community, Juste Laurent." Père Fournier took a moment to gesture towards him. "I will ask one of you to host them for the village."

People began raising their hands to volunteer themselves, slowly getting noisier. The visit would be an opportunity to elevate their status through their connection to the church. Juste knew better though. There was more than enough space for more guests in the church. Père Fournier had probably known for a while now who he was going to pick.

Juste's suspicions were confirmed as Père Fournier continued. "While I appreciate the enthusiasm, there is no need to volunteer yourselves. I have already made the decision on who I trust to take care of my friends."

The crowd went silent, eagerly waiting for who it was.

The priest slowly lifted his finger, dragging everyone's eyes along with it. It came to rest directly over the witch and her brother, who were standing near the back of the crowd. "I trust that your family would be more than happy to take care of our esteemed guests?"

He'd seen her arrive earlier, but was previously trying his best to ignore her. Now she was unmissable, standing shocked and separated from the rest of the crowd. They stepped away from her and her brother, forming a sort of circle around them.

Juste was equally as nervous. If the other members of Les Saints Chevaliers were getting involved in his work, it wasn't a good sign. If Père Fournier was bad on his own, he couldn't imagine how the others would try to test him.

Père Fournier leaned closer to Juste, dropping down to a whisper. "Seems you have a time limit, don't you Juste?"

He was giving a deadline. Juste needed to have the witch caught before the deadline in order to miss whatever repercussions they had in store for him. He had to admit that it definitely gave him motivation.

"Scary isn't it? I love seeing the look on people's faces as they realize they have something to be worried about." Père Fournier's grin turned all the more unsettling. "Head into the chapel. We will continue our discussion there."

Juste almost felt pity for the witch. On the way inside, he caught sight of her surrounded by half the village, no doubt being bombarded with proposals and offers. The whole ordeal was going to be detrimental to both of them. For Juste, because of the deadline, and for the witch, because of the stress. With the added responsibilities of preparing for the guests, she would be harder to get alone. Just what had Père Fournier been thinking when he planned this?

He took in a deep breath and cleared the thoughts from his mind. Père Fournier had a reason for everything he did, and Juste needed to trust in that. He just needed to wait in the chapel until he had further instructions.

Waiting in Père Fournier's office, he prayed a rosary. With each prayer, he tried to focus more on his goal. He was realizing that becoming a witch hunter was more of a mental battle than a physical one. There was something about the witches that made one want to feel pity for them, and to see them as fellow humans rather than dangerous beings.

He never got the chance to complete it though, because Père Fournier wasn't too far behind. He'd only stayed back for a little while to calm the crowd.

Père Fournier walked in with a smile even larger than before. "Did you see that? She looked so utterly hopeless! That means we're close."

While Juste didn't like the witch, he understood somewhat what she must be feeling. From his time living as nobility, the events took a mental toll as well as a physical one, unexpected ones especially.

"You seem less than eager to be going through with this plan." Père Fournier noticed. "It was only intended as a motivation, I assure you."

Juste knew that he was lying, and was beginning to grow tired of it. "I think it will be detrimental to her capture, if I'm being honest."

"Detrimental?" Père Fournier sat down at the chair to his desk. "Please explain. This will be amusing."

Juste knew that he wasn't going to be taken seriously, but that didn't matter. It was better said than not. "You give me inadequate time to lure her into a false sense of safety. Based upon your own words, is that not the best course of action? How should I be expected to achieve this so quickly?"

"In some cases, yes." the priest acknowledged. "But this is a simple witch. Her death is required to right a wrong, not to prevent any sort of danger."

"So you say that she isn't a threat?" Juste questioned, restraining himself. Even if she wasn't dangerous now, there was nothing stopping her from becoming so.

"No," The priest shrugged. "I'm simply saying that her threat has not yet manifested. Pity is a dangerous thing, Juste."

"Do you expect pity to crumble your church in the span of two weeks?"

"Remember that you are still inexperienced." The priest warned with a new edge to his tone.

Juste struggled to maintain his composure. "I thought that I was a part of your little society. When will you start treating me like one?"

Père Fournier paused for a moment, then started laughing. "You think that you're meant to be doing real work here?"

Juste slammed his fist onto the desk. "Am I not?! Am I not hunting a witch? Am I not your puppet? What do you say that I am doing right now?"

Père Fournier remained unaffected by the outburst, and if anything seemed amused. "You're just as much a figurehead as she is, Juste. I needed someone who was young, who would cooperate."

"What?" Juste croaked, then shook his head. "No, no. I'm leaving." Juste fled from the room. If he stayed any longer, he would only say more things that he'd regret.

He wasn't serving a true purpose. It didn't matter what plan it was, or for what reason. All that mattered was that he was being *used.* Père Fournier had lied. He'd said that Juste had a reason to live, but that reason was nothing more than to be a sacrifice. What was the difference between him and the witches he was supposed to hunt?

CHAPTER TWENTY-FOUR
Petime

Petime watched as Juste slipped back into the church, closely followed by Père Fournier. No one noticed because they were too busy surrounding her and Leon. Even when the priest had come over to enlighten them on what the visit would entail, he'd said nothing of substance. It was all minor reassurances at best. Now, they were alone surrounded by the crowd. Leon tightened his grip on her hand as it got closer.

"I don't think that we were the right choice." Leon whispered.

"Maybe not the logical choice, but it was certainly the right one." Petime said, eyes still on the crowd.

"Why would they choose you?" someone grumbled. "Now they'll remember us as the town with the legless girl."

"Give her a chance," another laughed. "It'll be funny."

Another jutted in. "Can you send in a good word about our shop?"

It was all too much.

"Stop!" Petime shouted louder than she'd intended to. The crowd went silent at the sound of her voice. They'd heard her frustrated before, but they'd never heard her this angry.

"Please, please let Petime have some room to breathe!" Père Fournier had emerged again from the church seemingly as quickly as he'd disappeared the first time. "I need to speak with Petime and her brother." He urged the two of them to follow him through the crowd of people, and they were led into the church.

Once the doors behind them were closed, Petime unleashed her fury. "What is the meaning of this?! Aren't there a hundred better people for your respected guests to stay with?" Petime didn't care about reverence in the church or disrespecting the priest. This one deserved it.

Leon nudged her arm in a silent plea to calm down, so she bit her tongue for just long enough to wait for an initial explanation from Père Fournier. The least she could give him was time for an explanation.

"Calm down, calm down," Père Fournier spoke in a babying tone, as if they were around half their age. "I did this all for a reason."

Petime leaned back onto her crutch. "And what could that reason possibly be?"

"I wanted to show our guests that even the *poorest*, most *simple-minded* people in our village are still above regular peasant standards!" Père Fournier beamed. Petime couldn't tell whether his good mood came from his enjoyment of their reactions or from the plan itself.

Petime dug her nails into the palm of her hand. "Disregarding your pointed remarks, what are the requirements of 'above standard'?"

Père Fournier started stalking in the direction of his

office. "I'll leave that to you to figure out."

"You're not doing that." Petime prepared to bounce off her crutch and lunge at him. "You will at least explain to us what we are meant to do."

He turned around and waggled his finger. "Ah ah. I wouldn't try that if I were you. If you fight me now, the consequences will return tenfold later. Have a good day!" With that, he disappeared into the back hallway, smiling and unscathed.

Petime got ready to lunge at him for real this time, but Leon shook his head. "I don't think you should risk it just yet." He said, a knowing look in his eyes telling her he knew exactly what she had been thinking about doing.

"He's just so–" Petime couldn't even begin to think of a word that described him.

"Priests are supposed to be good people," Leon was trying his hardest to comfort her. "But I don't think that Père Fournier fits that description."

Petime muttered, staring down the hallway. "Leon, start heading home. I have one last thing to do."

"Petime."

"I won't get violent. Don't worry. I just don't want him to be able to use you against me."

Leon sighed, but walked away, leaving Petime standing alone in the church. Once she was sure that he wouldn't come back, she approached the hallway.

"Père Fournier, we're not done talking!" she called out. However, when she looked down the hall in front of her, it was entirely empty, and the priest was nowhere to be seen.

She wandered further down the hall, looking into each room to see if Père Fournier was hiding somewhere, but they were all empty. She got increasingly nervous as she made her way down, until there was only one room left. Upon checking it, it was also empty. Forget the Handless Witch. If there was a true ghost in the village, it was Père Fournier.

"Père Fournier?" she asked again, but quieter this time, knowing she wouldn't get a response.

An overwhelming sense of dread washed over her, like she was somewhere that she was never meant to be. She needed to get out of there as quickly as possible. She walked as quickly as possible out of the building. Her heart skipped a beat every time that her crutch slammed into the stone floor of the church, letting out a resounding sound that she was almost entirely sure was going to summon some sort of demon. There was no way that he could have just *disappeared.*

She slammed the door shut once she was out, then leaned against the wall to catch her breath. Her family was probably worried already, and if she came home like this they'd be even more so. She knew the route was a bit longer, but she could have the chance to calm down if she walked through the forest.

Père Fournier disappearing had left an even more terrifying taste in her mouth about the visitors that her family was going to be hosting. His disappearance was suspicious itself, and now he was inviting people to the village she barely knew, all at the same time that she had just joined the tunnels. There had to be some overarching reason that she wasn't seeing. Mulling over her thoughts as she walked helped, but didn't solve the problem entirely.

She stopped suddenly around halfway through the path. The sound of crying was just barely audible from just ahead of her. It sounded almost like a little girl. Quickly, Petime realized that it was coming from the strawberry patch.

Petime took a deep breath, and walked forward towards

the sound. Last time she'd followed the sound of crying in the woods, it hadn't turned out well, but she was older now, wiser. She could easily keep walking and ignore it, but there was the same pull that she'd felt as a child. She needed to help.

She found herself searching through the berry patch, looking for whoever was crying. "Are you alright?" Petime called out. "I'm here to help if you need it."

"Go away." a surprisingly masculine voice called out. A voice that definitely belonged to Juste.

Petime froze, startled by the voice associated with the crying. Once she truly processed who it belonged to, she was stifling her laughter. It would be so *easy* to let him keep suffering. She could just walk away. Still, Petime found herself a few moments later, greeted by a Juste who was sitting beneath a shrub and covered in leaves.

"Are you alright?" she asked again. "I, uh, heard a little girl crying. It seems to just be you, though."

She waited for a witty comeback, but there was a surprising silence coming from him. No matter how much she hated him, this was just unnatural.

Petime sat down beneath the bush next to him, dodging Juste's half-hearted attempts to swat her away. "Okay, you're going to talk about this."

"No, I'm not." Juste grumbled.

"Yes, you are." Petime searched her brain for the thing she thought would annoy him into speaking the quickest. "Until you're better I will only say nice things to you. How does that sound?"

"Awful."

Petime lathered on the fake complimentary tone thick. "You know, you look absolutely wonderful today! Sitting there, beneath this bush!" All she could hope was that Juste was just as uncomfortable with this as she was. "With the sun reflecting off of your *radiant* hair–"

"Okay, you can stop!" he groaned. "I'll talk about it."

Petime sighed in relief. "Thank goodness. Also, your hair looks like a mud-covered rat resting atop your head, you should really do something about that."

Juste grumbled something unintelligible as he emerged from the shrub.

Petime stood up as well, brushing the leaves off of her pants. It was a relief to see him as his usual, grumbley self again. "I suppose that you could say that we're both acting like witches now, hanging around in the woods and all that."

Juste stopped dead in his tracks. "What did you just say?"

"I mean, you could call it very witch-like behavior." Petime explained awkwardly. This would be the last time she ever tried to joke with him.

"Do you really think that I'm a witch?"

"No, no." Her only goal now was to escape the situation. Comforting him in the first place was already bad enough. "Don't worry, I was just joking!"

Juste continued to stare at the ground, not replying for a solid chunk of time. Petime didn't know whether she was able to walk away or not.

"Listen, let's make a deal." He murmured.

Was he really going to try this again? "If this is a deal like last time, I'm not accepting it."

Juste turned to meet her eyes. "I think you have reason to accept the terms of this one."

Petime looked away. She didn't know why she was unable to stand her ground, but something about his tone felt different. "Why is that?"

"I need you to disappear from this town. Forever."

Of course. She was a fool for thinking it could be anything other than that. "You know, I'm tired of you thinking that you can simply decide to keep me away from places."

Juste grabbed her arm. "This is for your own good, Petime!"

She immediately pried herself away from his grasp. "How is this any good for me?"

"Because if you leave, I don't have to be the one to hurt you!"

His words hung in the air. Petime's heart sank to her stomach. "Does he… want to kill me?" Petime choked. Suddenly, it made sense why the priest was inviting his friends to the village.

Juste nodded. "I don't want your blood on my hands."

"So you'd rather have me disappear?" Petime scoffed.

"Yes."

"I don't accept your offer then." Petime began walking away. He was choosing the coward's way out. "If you think that running away will solve everything, then you're weak, Juste. Come back when you're ready to fight." She stopped. "I'm sure that once he's done with me he'll be just as awful to you."

"I don't know who you're talking about."

"We both know that's not true." She continued her walk. If he was the one assigned to hunt her down, she trusted that she would have some time at least, and there were more important things to do at the house anyway.

"You know," Juste shouted. "I won't be this nice anymore! I'm going to have to hurt you, and you'll have to die knowing that you chose this for yourself!"

Petime's stomach turned again. She thought about

172

fleeing the tunnels for a moment, but that would make her the same as Juste, someone who ran away from the things that threatened them. She needed to go home and find every way to stand her ground that she possibly could. If not for her, then for her family. Her brother would not be a victim of her own circumstance. When she was in the tunnels, she needed to gain every advantage possible. She couldn't rest until she'd won. This was the beginning of a battle that she wouldn't accept losing.

CHAPTER TWENTY-FIVE
Camille

Camille pushed her way through the brush of the field, heart beating fast from the adrenaline. She was excited to go on another late night adventure. This summer was threatening to be her last with any semblance of freedom, and she wasn't going to waste it. Getting nearer to the edge of the woods, she noticed the same type of unnatural glow approaching the treeline as she had seen the night before. She had no doubt that it was Adrian, and she was proven even more correct as she saw a cloaked figure come clearly into the moonlight.

She took a deep breath to calm herself down, not wanting to seem like she was too excited for this. It would be breaking every law of etiquette that she had ever learned. For some reason, seeming polite mattered more to her now than it had before.

"Camille! Just in time!" Adrian smiled as they neared speaking distance with each other.

Camille trudged the rest of the way through the grass,

being sure to keep her skirt lifted enough to avoid grass stains. "Good evening. I hope the trip through the woods wasn't any trouble to you?"

"None at all." He turned out the lamp, flooding them with darkness. "So where have you decided to take me tonight?"

"You'll see!" Camille spoke cheerfully.

The beginning portion of the walk was surprisingly similar to the night before, just without Petime there along the way. Adrian stared again at the sheep again as they walked around the field, leaving Camille to wonder what could peak his interest so much about them. Even though he hadn't seen them before, he surely couldn't be *that* interested in looking at them.

Adrian seemed to take notice of her curiosity. "I know a shepherd. It's just interesting to see that he took care of so many sheep."

Camille took a moment before she responded, looking out at the sheep herself. Adrian knew a shepherd? His story seemed to get increasingly tangled each time they spoke to each other.

"Not one family takes care of all of the sheep here." Camille explained. "The flock just gathers together at night to avoid danger from the wolves."

"Ah, do they come around often?" Adrian asked. "With it being close to the forest I'd assume it's a decent threat."

"Unfortunately, yes." Camille watched one of the sleep shift around in its sleep. "Especially during the winter months."

"I can take care of that." Adrian's eyes turned towards the woods, clearly plotting something.

"How do you intend on doing that all by yourself?" Camille asked. "The shepherds have been trying for years to come up with methods that would keep them away."

"Oh!" He laughed awkwardly. "I was just reading a book on… Swiss shepherding methods?"

Camille shook her head, just taking it in stride. She could ask questions later. At least now he wasn't even attempting to mask the lies, which could be considered progress in his trust towards her?

"You're concerned about something." Adrian interrupted her internal monologue.

Camille stopped walking for a moment. "How did you know that?"

"It's written all over your face." Adrian said, "You get a very specific look to you when you're concerned about something."

"Oh!" Camille didn't know how she felt about him paying such close attention to her. "I guess I was just thinking that you were bad at lying."

"Oh, you knew that it wasn't true?" Adrian appeared to be taking a mental note.

"Where would one get a book on Swiss shepherding methods?" Camille asked rhetorically.

"I suppose a library? Although, it would probably only be available in the city." Adrian pondered the question, leaving Camille staring.

Adrian maintained eye contact with her for a few more moments. Both of them had come to a full stop along the path. "Oh, I wasn't meant to answer that, was I?"

There were a few more moments of staring, then they both laughed.

"Do you really have to lie?" Camille asked, although she already knew the answer.

"Unfortunately." Adrian said in a sigh.

Camille's mind trailed back to the events of the night previous. Petime had seemed to know something that she hadn't about Adrian. "Does Petime know the truth of your past?"

"Yes." Adrian looked at the ground.

She knew that it hurt him that he couldn't tell her too, it was written all over his face, but she didn't want to admit that it hurt her too. She tried to be happy with everything, knowing that it was one of the most important qualities of a lady to never be displeased with what they had, but sometimes it was hard.

She realized how long they had been walking, and that they were nearly to the spot. "Oh, look! Here we are!" She smiled, hoping that it would distract Adrian from the previous topic.

They were approaching a wooden arch bridge that crossed over the wider part of the river that ran next to their village. Camille ran forward and sat down on the edge of it letting her feet hang off of the side, and looking down into the water. It was the perfect distraction for her as well.

"Come, sit down!" She patted the ground next to her. "Listen to the water!"

Adrian joined her, careful not to disturb the sound. With both of them quiet, the sound of the water was audible beneath their feet, creating a relaxing scene.

"So this is your second favorite place in the village?" Adrian asked after a moment of listening.

"I'd have to say so. It's a shame that the glow worms don't come out as much near the path." Camille leaned back onto the bridge. "There are plenty of fish though."

"It's alright, you're better than glow worms." Adrian leaned back as well.

Camille was glad that she hadn't let him down, and she almost believed that she would get away with distracting Adrian too.

"Do you want to know more about me than Petime does?" Adrian asked, looking up at the sky.

Camille choked back every thought threatening to spill out of her mouth. "No."

"You're lying."

"So are you."

"Is that alright for now?"

"For now, yes." Camille sat back up, looking at the fish swimming in circles in the water. "Speaking of Petime, I must admit that I'm worried about her."

"Why is that?"

"The priest of the village has invited some high-ranking members of the church to visit our town, and for some unknown reason he thinks that they should stay with Petime's family." Camille waited for a response from Adrian, but there was none. When she looked over to see what the reason was, she found that he'd turned ghostly pale. "Adrian, are you alright?"

Adrian's face was ghostly pale, and she could see the sweat beading on his forehead. "I need you to not let her out of your sight until they have left the village. Do you understand?"

"I don't get it. Is it really that important?" Camille was beginning to worry about the whole thing.

"Yes. I'll gather help from my sources, but those people from the church aren't good. Their intention is almost certainly to hurt her." Adrian said, voice going faster.

Camille's stomach started to tie itself into knots. If Adrian was worried, it definitely wasn't good. He seemed to know a lot more than he was letting on already. "What is the worst that a few priests can do to Petime? You've seen her. She'd fight them without hesitation."

"This is different." Adrian muttered, staring somewhere past her.

Camille wanted to help, but she couldn't if he didn't share what he was thinking. "If you're comfortable, could you tell me what this is about?"

"They took my parents, Camille." Adrian whispered.

"What?" Camille wasn't sure that she'd heard him right, and if she had, she didn't understand what he'd meant. Was it priests that had taken his family?

Adrian looked down into the water to collect himself. "Something… similar happened to me when I was a child."

"I have all night if you want to talk about it." Camille chanced.

"Would you?" Adrian looked at her straight in the eyes, allowing Camille to see the desperation that was behind them.

"Of course."

CHAPTER TWENTY-SIX
Georges, 1682

"I don't think you understand. There were hundreds of them." Elise explained desperately. They were standing in front of the leaders of the tunnel, trying to explain what they had seen during their mission.

"That's impossible." The man pushed them aside. "To date, the largest group we've seen was around fifty, and even that was a once in a lifetime occurrence."

"Have you ever considered that it's because the tunnels don't have a unified record system?" Georges barred him from walking any further. "How do we know for sure what the other tunnels have seen? You'd think that for a place so bent on science, we'd have a better way to access each other's knowledge."

"Georges. Stay focused." Elise whispered to him before speaking back up to the man. "What we're trying to say is that we need to be prepared to work as a team in the event that something *does* happen."

"What could possibly–"

A thunderous sound shook throughout the tunnel, cutting off whatever else he had to say. It was an explosion. They faced each other, silently agreeing that this conversation would be put on halt for the time being, and ran towards the sound.

It turned out that a lot of other people had the same idea, and were all channeling towards the sound. Suddenly, another explosion broke loose almost immediately next to them. A cloud of dust was thrust over the crowd, causing Georges to lose the feeling of Elise's hand in his.

"Georges? Georges!" Georges could only faintly hear Elise's voice over the fray. It was most certainly an attack now. People were gathering anything that they could use as weapons, some even making scrambled attempts to organize.

"I'm right here!" Georges called back. He couldn't see Elise, but he knew that she would be able to find him.

Someone's sword swung into the side of his wooden hand with a loud clunk. George's face whipped backwards to see who the culprit was, but he only saw the outline of someone disappearing into the dust. Georges was left staring at the gash in the wood. It was chaos.

A few moments later, he was drenched in water coming from above him. Through the settling dust above them, Georges was able to see a hole in the ceiling, and buckets of water being dumped upon the group. Holy Water.

Thankfully, the water was harmless for the most part, so Georges was alright with letting Les Saints Chevaliers believe that it hurt them. The truly concerning part of what he was beginning to see were small fires breaking out all across the tunnel, burning into valuable work and resources, as well as filling the room with smoke. It reminded him of all the times he'd been threatened to be burned. It seemed like he would never truly be safe from the fire that chased him.

Elise pushed her way through the panicked crowd, meeting Georges. "I found you!"

"I knew you would." Georges grabbed her hand, but didn't linger long with it. "I need your help."

Georges had an idea. It had a high chance of failure, but it might be the only thing that would get them out alive. He planned to use their own weakness against them.

"What do you need?" Elise asked, prepared for the request.

"I'm going to need a bundle of the most terrifying-looking projects we have going on." Georges looked around at the fires. "Or, whatever's left of them."

Elise nodded, and Georges could only hope that it meant she understood what he was going to do, because there was no time to explain. "Do they need to be working?"

"No, just scary looking. Now, quickly! I have some work to do on my end as well." Georges glanced behind his back. It was time to do the same thing that had gotten him captured so many years ago.

Elise disappeared back into the mess of battle. Somewhere along the line of their conversation, members of Les Saints Chevaliers were filing into the room and getting involved in the fight as well. Georges had to believe that he would be okay.

While he waited for Elise, he slowly climbed to the top of the tallest tables that he could find, pushing a few men to the side. He hoped that they were on the opposing side of the battle.

"Members of Les Saints Chevaliers! Listen to what I am about to say to you!" Georges shouted at the top of his lungs. It was enough to grab the attention of those who were closest to him, but not the entire room. "Listen to what The Devil has to say!" He added. The word "Devil" seemed successful in gathering the attention of those who'd missed the first call.

Georges spotted Elise in the corner of the room still grabbing the last of the materials. He'd need to stall for time. "I am here to end this battle, once and for all!" He shot his wooden hand into the air and wriggled its fingers. The gash was clear to see.

A wave of shocked murmurs made their way throughout the crowd upon seeing the hand. They had started to form a circle around him, fully invested now with what he had to say. "I, The Handless Witch, spoke with The Devil , and knew of your arrival!"

Elise was now poised near the edge of the crowd, waiting for his signal. It was all lining up perfectly.

"I have crafted a device that will allow me to curse all of you!" Georges twisted his arms into another, even more dramatic position. "Any who invaded this place for Les Saints Chevaliers will be doomed to an eternal life of suffering and sadness! You will bear no crops, you will bear no children, and you will only live in misery for the rest of your days!" He gave one final twist of his arm, like he was pulling something from the air, and Elise threw what she could towards him. They clattered onto the floor in front of him perfectly, sending the members of the crowd closest to the front jumping backwards.

It remained quiet for a moment, until someone started fighting the heap of machinery. It hurt his heart to see them be attacked, but machines could be rebuilt, and lives couldn't.

"Run!" He shouted, hoping that the others from the tunnel would take the opportunity to escape while they had it.

Georges climbed down from the table himself, and started making his way towards the door alongside Elise. As they pushed through the crowd, he saw some people still fighting, but there were a good amount running as well. He wanted to save them, and tell them that it was time to run, but he couldn't.

The area surrounding the exit to the tunnel was entirely empty. The priests must not have wanted anyone knowing that the battle was taking place, which was a sickening thought, but useful for the sake of their secrecy in this case.

After him, only a few more people followed. Together, they added up to maybe a quarter of the full population, which still left a significant number of people missing.

A boy no older than fifteen pushed his way into the center of the group sobbing. "You have to save them! We need to go back! They took my parents!" He fell onto his knees, tugging at the bottom of Georges' shirt.

Georges spoke as tenderly as possible, ignoring the stares of those around him. He knew that they wanted to say that it was hopeless, but he wouldn't accept that answer. "Who are your parents? We can look for them when the battle has concluded."

"When you were talking! They tied my parents' hands and dragged them away!" He broke into sobbing again. He hadn't answered the question, but his response was still concerning in its own right. "They said something about burning them at the stake."

Georges' heart dropped. If what he'd said was true, there was little hope that they would be able to find his parents now. Especially if they weren't still in the tunnel.

He took the boy's hand nonetheless. "I'll look for them."

The boy nodded, and Georges turned to the rest of the group. There was a lot left to discuss.

CHAPTER TWENTY-SEVEN
Adrian, 1684

As Adrian walked back into the woods, he started thinking over the events of the night. He'd told her everything. He'd shared the story of his entire childhood with Camille against all of his better judgment. She still didn't know the full truth, but she had heard the story of how his parents had died, and now Les Saints Chevaliers were coming for them again as soon as he was beginning to feel whole again. He wouldn't allow them to take more than they already had.

What concerned him most was Camille's comments on Père Fournier. Later into the night, she had mentioned him and the way that he acted. He had definitely heard Georges mention the name before as well, and it wasn't in a positive tone.

His mind continued to race until he arrived back at the tunnel, he tried to enter as quickly and as quietly as possible, but with each step he took, the ladder let out a large creak. He flinched with each one, knowing how light a sleeper that Elise was. Adrian had never had a problem with the ladder until now, but then again, he'd never snuck out until now either.

By the time he reached the bottom, he was met with Elise standing behind him, arms crossed. "And what are you doing out this late at night?"

He'd most certainly been caught. "Uh." Adrian searched his brain for an excuse. "I was going to the bathroom."

"Outside?" Elise questioned. "Even with the chamber pot?"

"Sometimes you just want to go outside!" Adrian retorted, still trying to play it off.

"For multiple hours?"

Adrian realized that she had definitely seen him leaving, and this was definitely a test. He hated when she did that. "You could've at least told me that you knew I was lying."

"I wanted to test your integrity." She grumbled in a tone that told him that they would be having a longer conversation in the morning. "No matter that now though, what were you out there doing?"

Adrian thought about the best possible way to phrase it. If he told them about Camille now, he would surely be prevented from seeing her again, and that was the last thing that he wanted. He would be alright if he lied for just a little bit longer.

"I was going for a walk." At least it was partially the truth?

"Assuming that you know better than to lie to me now, I'll accept that answer. Were you meeting up with Petime?" Elise guessed.

Adrian figured that her thinking that he was meeting up with Petime was better than her knowing he'd been meeting with Camille, so he nodded. "However, she said something concerning to me." Adrian paused. "She mentioned Père Fournier."

"That old menace is still alive?! I thought he died years ago!" She shouted without thinking, then covered her mouth with her hands. "If that woke up Georges, we're dead." Her voice was muffled, but Adrian could still understand every word perfectly.

"You are very right." Adrian whispered in return. So much for quietly sneaking in.

He knew that this conversation would've happened one way or another, but he would have much preferred if it didn't happen in the middle of the night. The only blessing so far was that his mention of Père Fournier had distracted Elise from spitting out a punishment for the time being.

The two of them heard rustling from where Georges usually slept. They turned to look at each other. They were dead.

Elise sighed. "Before he wakes up, tell me what happened so that I can do the talking. If he hears it coming from me, he might take it better."

"Père Fournier has invited some high-ranking church officials to stay at Petime's house, and she is going to be evaluated on their stay before they leave." Adrian explained as quickly and quietly as possible.

There was a long sigh from Elise as she realized just how bad the situation was. "That sounds like a cover up…"

"Les Saints Chevaliers." They both said together.

"Dear Lord, this isn't something that you should be dealing with right now." She pressed her fingers to her forehead. "Do you know why they're hunting her down?"

"I don't think that it's about us," Adrian explained. "I think that it has something to do with her leg if my

188

interpretations were correct."

Elise started pacing. "They're connecting her to Georges. Lord, this'll be a conversation to have."

Georges emerged from his bedroom holding a candle, and wearing a look of pure, tired rage on his face. "What are you two doing up at this hour? Yelling, no less!"

Elise walked up to him as gently as she could, and rubbed his arm. "We were just discussing something. If you want to hear about it tomorrow we can–"

Georges cut her off. "No no, if you are up shouting about it, I want to know what about."

Elise took a deep breath. "Père Fournier."

"God! Of course it is. For him to have finally died would be too good for me. What is it this time?" He groaned.

"He's sending members of Les Saints Chevaliers to stay with Petime, but there is no reason to believe that they are onto our base right now." She added on the second part quickly.

"Is Petime involved with the church?" Georges worried.

"Not that I believe?" Elise questioned, looking at Adrian for a response.

Adrian shrugged. "That would be my assumption as well." He just wanted to go to sleep.

Georges spent an excruciatingly long moment thinking before he spoke. "I'll allow her one chance to explain herself, but if she is involved with the church in any way, she is prevented from returning here, or to any of the other tunnels, ever again."

Adrian's heart felt like it was trying to escape its chest. "I think that might be a little harsh." If Petime wasn't allowed to return, she wouldn't even know the reason why. His tower of lies was threatening to crumble more and more as the longer they spoke.

Elise prevented him from spiraling any further with an attempt to help. "I agree. We should give Petime the benefit of the doubt here. Adrian explained that the reason for them staying with her is simply because she's missing a leg, so it most likely doesn't relate to her connection with the church."

"Oh, so my reasoning is faulty?" Georges snapped.

Maybe it wasn't helping.

Adrian was glad that Elise was on his side at least. If they worked together, they might be able to calm Georges down. They both knew that he had a particular sensitivity to matters relating to the church because of his past, but that didn't mean that there wasn't a possibility for him to back down.

Georges looked at their faces, his own expression twisting into one of desperation. "You two don't understand the danger that she's in! You don't understand the danger of the church!" Georges grabbed Adrian's hand. "That "visit"? It's a death sentence!"

"What?" Adrian managed to stammer, still startled from Georges' outburst.

Georges didn't hesitate to continue the explanation. "Church after church invited me to stay, and do you know what happened to me every time? They tried to turn me into a pile of ashes! They'll no doubt do the same to her. It's what they do to all of us."

The guilt continued building in Adrian's chest. "Please, don't jump to conclusions—"

"No. This isn't a matter of conclusions, it is repeated evidence. I'm not going to be bothered with any more priests! I'm tired of the church, and I'm tired of the fires they set." Georges sighed. "We'll pack her things, and she can find somewhere else to stay."

190

"Georges, she's barely been here a week!" Elise interjected. "We can't just leave her!"

"She's leaving tomorrow. That's final."

Elise reached out for him, but it was too late. Georges was already storming back towards his bedroom, making it clear that he wasn't going to discuss the matter any further.

"I'm sorry Adrian." Elise said softly.

Adrian walked away as well, not bothering to respond. He was too.

CHAPTER TWENTY-EIGHT
Petime

Petime found herself grinning uncontrollably as she strolled along the trail of ferns. Usually, she'd be bothered by the long walk through the unforgiving terrain, but she was ready for it this time. Her family had fallen into a frenzy of work preparing for the visitors, making this her first true break in a long time.

Upon arrival, she lifted the lid to the tunnels and made her way easily down the ladder. From visiting the tunnels in her free time, she'd gotten better at navigating its bars. She was excited to share her progress, but when she reached the bottom, she noticed that everyone was staring at her.

"Is everything alright?" She asked. It was somewhat unsettling.

Georges was the first one to speak. "Why didn't you tell us about the matters relating to the church?"

She shrunk back against the ladder. Georges had a look in his eyes, like his anger went deeper than he was letting on.

Never had she seen him look so cold. "How do you know about that? It happened yesterday, and I haven't seen any of you all since it happened."

"There is no need to lie." Elise stepped forward now as well. "Adrian told me everything."

"I'm not lying!" She looked desperately at Adrian, hoping for some sort of explanation, but he avoided her eyes in favor of staring at the floor.

"Don't look to him for answers." Elise lectured. "He was honest about what you had said about the priest coming to visit."

Petime didn't understand how the news had even reached them. The only person who she'd even spoken about it with was Juste. "I told you before only learned about this yesterday!"

"You went out walking with him last night, Petime. That can be forgiven, but your lying can't be." Georges spoke again, sounding even more disappointed in her.

"Adrian, please! Tell them that I'm not lying!" Petime had to cling onto any hope that she had left, especially if she were to survive the coming days.

Adrian continued to look at the ground.

"He's a *priest,* Petime. Nothing good can come of interacting with him." Georges pulled her attention back. "His actions could put our whole operation into significant danger."

"I wouldn't let that happen." Petime argued. "Are you so quick to lose trust in me?"

"I said the same thing once. Everyone did, and now the tunnels are *dying* Petime." Georges looked toward the pin-covered map on the wall. "The red ones are those of us that are left."

There were only a few clusters of the red pins left in the

outer regions of Paris and Rouen. The rest were a deathly blak.

"I'm sure that we can work together–" Petime was cut short.

"No. If the church is involved, I am making no exception. You will not be allowed to return here."

Petime shook her head. "No, this isn't right." Her shock was beginning to transform into anger. "This is the time where I would need your aide most, and yet you leave me to the wolves."

Georges waited patiently for her to finish speaking before he continued. "We do have one last gift for you. This pains me as much as it pains you, but I will prioritize the needs of my family, and that requires that you leave."

Georges left the room, giving her a moment to think. Both Elise and Adrian were silent as well, watching her every move as she stood next to the ladder. It stung to be thought of as an outsider again. Even here, in the most accepting space she had found, she was unable to stay. Not once had she been someone's first priority.

Georges returned holding a large crate.

"Might I ask what it is?" Petime questioned. At least they were excluding her along with presents.

"It's all the supplies you should need for your new crutch, and some training exercises from Elise. I figured it's the least that we could do." Georges set it down beside her. At least he seemed to have calmed down now. "I was excited to work with you, but we can't have the church coming anywhere near our operations."

The calm cleared her mind as well. Even though she disagreed with his actions, she could understand their origins. She understood the need to protect family from harm. She understood the need to protect those around you from experiencing the same hardships, and would do the same thing if her own family were threatened. What she didn't understand was why this was happening.

"Thank you." Petime murmured. The least she could do was attempt to stay strong in front of them. "For everything."

Petime looked at the crate, already feeling the tears stinging her eyes. At least this would be enough for her to sustain herself for the time being. She would be able to figure out something else later. She felt tears stinging in her eyes, but no matter how much she wanted to, she wouldn't let herself cry in front of them. She wouldn't be able to sleep at night if she let herself do that. Even when Elise hugged her, and Georges joined in, she didn't cry. Even when Adrian stayed away, she didn't cry. She still had a chance to learn on her own, and one day she would return as someone worthy of being in their tunnel.

"May I ask one more thing?" She continued looking at the crate.

"What is it?" Georges asked.

The sadness subsided, leaving only an awkward atmosphere. "Can someone help me carry that back to the village…?"

"I'll do it!" Adrian jumped up from his floor-staring.

"I suppose that that can be arranged." Geroges trailed off into his own thoughts, almost like he was regretting his decision of letting her have the materials.

She figured they should head out before Georges had any reason to question his decision further. "I'll make sure that they stay well hidden."

The work to get the box out of the tunnels was surprisingly quick with Adrian's help. He'd got it up the ladder, and was beginning to tie it around his back as preparation for the journey.

Once she was sure that no one else was within earshot, Petime glared at Adrian. "What did you *do?*"

He slumped over, clearly expecting the topic to come up sooner or later. "I didn't mean for any of it to turn out like that. I'm truly sorry."

"I can't even begin to comprehend what that means." She looked away, again, unable to face him. "How did you even find out about what had happened?"

Once he had secured the box, he started walking. "I would rather not say."

"And I would rather not be kicked out of the tunnels, Adrian!" Petime shouted, causing a flock of birds in a nearby tree to flutter away. She hadn't meant to be that loud, but she didn't want to apologize either.

He sighed. "I visited Camille again last night."

"Camille?!"

Adrian spoke wistfully when mentioning her. "She's so incredibly nice and sweet. I just wanted to see her again."

Petime could barely believe what she was hearing. "She's engaged to be married, so don't get too comfortable with her."

Adrian frowned, making Petime just the slightest bit happier.

"I'd appreciate it if you two didn't talk about me on your escapades as well." She grumbled.

Adrian waited a while before speaking again after that, but when he did, it was filled with worry. "Speaking of that, there was another reason that I asked to walk with you."

"What else could you possibly have to admit?" Petime said.

"The visit might have more to it than just the priest's

doing." Adrian warned.

Petime had no clue what he was hinting at. "Explain?"

"Georges believes that the priest in the villages has connections to a group known as Les Saints Chevaliers. They are witch hunters who gather in a manner similar to ourselves, and they are hellbent on destroying all of us."

So that was why Georges was so scared Petime thought. This was something larger than just him, and that meant it was all the more dangerous. First Juste had warned her, and now Adrian was as well.

Adrian continued his description. "Their group was formed a while after ours was. No one knows the exact date, but we can guess that it was sometime around 1645, following the coronation of King Louis XIV. Convicted witches were winning their trials, so he formed the group as a way to tie loose ends."

Tie loose ends was the nicer way to put it. They were formed to kill them.

Petime was beginning to connect the dots, and a sinking feeling formed inside of her. As long as this group existed, witches were still being killed, and if the Les Saints Chevaliers had destroyed all of the tunnels in Paris already, there was no telling what they'd be able to do to the tunnels in the smaller surrounding towns.

Juste had come from Paris according to Camille, and he had immediately been spouting nonsense about sins and witches. He was immediately taken in by Père Fournier, and the two of them seemed rather close. Part of her didn't want to believe it, but there was too much that connected him to Les Saints Chevaliers for it not to be at least a possibility.

Petime didn't speak to Adrian for the rest of the walk onwards. Even if it was her last chance to speak with him, she knew that both of them were too lost in thought for it to really be about anything too meaningful. She needed to speak with Juste and Camille more than anything, Camille to find out what had happened, and Juste to prove her suspicions wrong because Adrian didn't appear to want to help explain anything more. It was time for her to do the rest of this on her own.

The thoughts were enough to carry her through the rest of the walk until the both of them were approaching the stone circle, and Petime realized that this goodbye might be her last one to the tunnels for a long time. "I guess this is it then." She murmured, still unsure of her feelings about everything that had happened today.

Adrian shrugged. "I believe we'll meet again, in some way or another."

She tried to not let herself be annoyed by how lightly he seemed to be taking it. "Do you think I'll be allowed back?"

"Probably not."

"You'd better pray that he does, or else I'll never forgive you." Petime forced out something resembling a laugh, but she wasn't exactly joking either. The events of the day had left her with some major doubts about his character.

Adrian didn't respond to the comment, and proceeded with untying the ropes around the crate. Once he was satisfied with his work, he returned back into the foliage leaving Petime alone. Transporting the crate had been such a long process that now the sun was threatening to set. It was better than nothing at least, and for the time being it was her entire foreseeable future as well.

She sat down on one of the rocks, knowing that it would be time to return home soon. Her family was probably wondering where she had disappeared to since they had become more concerned with her whereabouts after the recent events. Despite everything though, she felt like she had earned a break. When she returned home this time, she would be able to focus entirely on her family, which was important with the events coming up, but it also meant returning back to her normal life and saying goodbye to the one thing that made her special.

Maybe a simple life was her destiny afterall. Maybe it was too much to hope for something more than that.

CHAPTER TWENTY-NINE
Camille

Despite being tired as ever, Camille woke up early the next morning. Adrian had left with instructions to keep a close eye on Petime, so she would try her best to follow them as much as she could, even if that meant waking up before the sun to go and check on her. No matter the time, the walk to her house was still refreshing, and if anything it was even more so now due to the village's early morning emptiness.

After arriving at her destination, she sat on the top of the hill that overlooked the shepherds' fields for a while to watch Petime do her work. It took a moment to find her initially, but once Camille could pinpoint her, it was an easy thing to watch. For missing a leg, she worked very diligently, which was a side that Camille had never really seen of Petime beforehand.

"I see that I'm not the only one enjoying the hills this fine morning." Juste's voice chimed from behind her.

Camille slumped over. Out of every person in the

village that it could have been, she preferred his presence the least.

"Why are you here?" She asked, hoping that whatever it was that he needed would be brief.

Juste sat down in the grass next to her. "Well, I was walking by, and I just so happened to see my fiance sitting on the hillside, so I thought that I'd join you."

Camille didn't trust the answer, but it was better he was here than with Petime. She probably needed a break after the stress she'd been under over the last few days.

She decided to be direct. If they were going to be married, there was no point in playing dumb with him for his affection. "We both know that this place is out of your way Juste. Why were you really here?"

Juste shrugged. "I think we both know the answer to that, and it's hobbling around down there."

Camille was seething from the way that he'd described Petime. "You would do best not to speak about others in such a manner."

"I think you're the only one who would defend her."

"That is the problem, not the solution." Camille held her ground against Juste. At least he was here bothering her rather than down there bothering Petime.

"Camille, you're so kind to everyone you meet," Juste smiled. "And that's dangerous, but I'm here to protect you now."

Camille couldn't help but compare him to Adrian, who had allowed her to express emotions other than gratitude. She wanted that feeling back, not this.

Petime, as they were speaking, had been moving to start work on another chore, one that had her facing directly towards the both of them sitting on the hill. Once Camille realized it, she scurried behind a bush to stay out of sight, and Juste followed closely behind.

He grinned at the sight of her crouched alongside him. "I see now that neither of us wanted to be seen, did we?"

"You don't know my reasons." Camille scowled.

She took it as a chance to return home for her morning chores, leaving Juste behind the bush as she escaped the scene. She had been able to watch Petime for a while at least, and Juste didn't seem like he would be anything more than a nuisance for the time being.

When she arrived home, she worked with her mother to cook breakfast in the kitchen like they usually did in the morning, but she was tired and distracted. With everything that been happening recently, her mind wanted to be anywhere other than the kitchen. She only returned fully to reality after dropping an egg onto the table, cringing as its insides started to spill out onto the wooden table.

"Camille, what a mess you're making today!" Her mother snipped. "Are you sick? Do you need to rest?"

"No, Maman, just thinking." She started to clean the egg yolk from the table. "I'm sorry."

Her mother, unsatisfied with Camille's pace, took the rag from her hand and started wiping the yolk away herself. "What could you be thinking about that is making you act like this?"

Camille reached out again to help, but was gently swatted away by her mother.

"You just rest for a moment and talk to me about your dilemma. I'll take care of this." She spoke only out of her concern for Camille.

Camille appreciated the gesture, allowing herself to take a seat while her mother worked. "I've just been wondering what will happen with the marriage, that's all." She wanted to say more, but it would be against her better judgment to tell her mother about Adrian just yet.

"Have you found yourself another suitor?" Her mother asked, getting back to cooking.

Camille was shocked about how quickly her mother had caught on. "I think I might have, but I don't know if he'll be up to your standards." She needed to be careful of how she phrased things.

Her mother looked around the kitchen. It was only the two of them. "No one seems to be around, so you can tell me. I won't share." Her mother had a slight grin as she spoke, which made Camille believe that she was genuinely interested in listening.

"Well, he looks very nice." Camille figured that talking about it could only help her work out her thoughts.

"Continue." Her mother nodded along.

"Well, he also acts very kindly," she added, "And he doesn't make me feel uncomfortable like Juste does."

"That is all good, but how wealthy is he?" Her mother asked. Camille figured that she wouldn't waste any time getting to the important questions.

The problem was Camille didn't have an answer to most of them. Every time that Adrian had shared his backstory, he filled it with a different story. She was lucky if they shared even a slight commonality to gather insight from.

Her mother raised an eyebrow at the silence, noticing Camille's hesitation. "At least you can say that it's marrying for love."

Camille was startled by the remark, unsure of whether her relationship truly counted as love yet. If the previous standard were Juste, she'd rather marry a sheep.

"Your reaction is telling, Camille." Her mother chuckled. "Do you know his profession?"

"He is a farmer… I think?" Camille didn't know how to respond to this question either.

Her mother sighed. "I want to give you my blessing, truly, but do you expect that I'll let you marry a maybe-farmer over the son of a noble family? You must realize that no matter what you feel for each other, I can't approve based upon that alone."

"Please Maman, just give me a chance to learn more about him." Camille begged.

"I'll let you have that chance as long as you stop sneaking out in the middle of the night to do it." Her mother said it so calmly that Camille almost didn't believe what she'd heard.

Her mother tutted. "Do you think that I don't know when you sneak out? I'm your mother, Camille."

She couldn't admit the truth, so she was going to defend the lie until the very end. "I don't know what you're talking about Maman. I would do nothing of the sort."

"Camille, don't do this."

She had to. Otherwise it'd eat away at her pride. "You must have heard an animal outside."

"Camille. I want to help you in any way that I can, but lying to me isn't the way to earn my trust." Her mother lectured. "For that, you'll be staying in this house until further notice"

"Maman!" Camille stood up from the chair.

"It would be unwise of you to continue testing me, Camille." Her mother was clearly warning her not to go any further on the subject.

Once the defiance wore off, Camille realized the gravity

of what she'd just done to herself. She'd committed to being trapped at home unable to speak to Adrian, unable to watch over Petime, and becoming a perfect target for Juste.

"I can take care of breakfast. Go to your room if you're going to cry." Her mother knew her well enough by this point to have predicted her reaction to the punishment.

Camille gladly took the opportunity, and rushed out of the kitchen to her room. She'd ruined everything. She was supposed to meet Adrian again, and now didn't even have a way to tell Adrian where she was. There was truly nothing she could do.

Once she had made it to her bed, she fell into its comfort. She enjoyed the quiet for a while, until she heard voices from outside her window. They were muffled due to the thick cloth that covered it to keep the heat out, but she knew that she recognized them. This was her chance to talk to someone.

She rushed out of her bed and pulled the curtains apart, revealing Juste and Petime both poised like they were ready to fight.

CHAPTER THIRTY
Georges, 1682

Georges looked out onto the streets of Paris from his hiding space. In the end, the group had decided to split off into smaller groups for easier hiding. Elise, Adrian, and he were one of them, and had found a relatively hidden spot beneath one of the bridges of Paris. It was strange seeing people wander the streets now, unaware of all that had happened the night previous. Les Saints Chevaliers had made quick work of repairing the damage.

Georges had promised Adrian that he would go out and look for his parents today as well, but there wasn't any real way to find them. Even if they'd left a trail of evidence, they'd likely been taken to a place that was riddled with priests, making it near impossible for Georges to infiltrate. He was also left with equally scarring memories of the day previous. There was a lingering doubt in his mind of whether or not he'd even be able to return to the tunnel itself.

"Georges." Elise approached him, speaking in a tone just below a whisper.

"Elise?" He asked. "Is everything alright?"

"He's asking if you've found his parents yet. What should I tell him?"

"From what I've seen, there has been no sign of them yet, but I also haven't searched everywhere."

"So it's a no?" Elise questioned.

Georges sighed, knowing that he'd never be satisfied until he'd truly looked for them everywhere. "No. There is still one more place that I can look for them." Georges grabbed her hand.

Elise shook her head. "You can't be thinking—"

"Their tunnel. Yes." Georges was equally apprehensive about the idea, but he knew that it was important that he went. "Think about it, Elise. If they were captured, where else would they be taken?"

She grumbled something unintelligible, unable to deny his logic. "Just don't do anything stupid, okay?"

"Of course I won't." Georges smiled.

Afterwards, he started towards the old entrance into their tunnels that they'd found. It was a dangerous endeavor to pull off alone, but it would also be easier to sneak in unnoticed being only one person. He'd made it into the bases of Les Saints Chevaliers before, so what was to stop him now?

Georges wandered the streets of the city until he found an entrance into the tunnels of Les Saints Chevaliers. They weren't hard to find if someone knew what they were looking for. Almost always, it was a large, wooden door with large flames carved into its facade. They also had distinct iron locks similar to the one that had been on his cage back at the village.

The locks' similarity left him with a clear advantage when it came to picking them. It was a skill that Georges had practiced a lot since the incident.

Using a skeleton key, he breezed through the wards

lining the lock. Georges celebrated his small victory as the handle twisted open easily and the door swung open. This one revealed a much more sinister-looking tunnel than the one before, but that wasn't enough to scare him yet. He peered inside to see what he was dealing with, and realized that right near the entrance, there was a long staircase that led down into a walkway. This one went deep, but it might be an advantage if he was looking for Adrian's parents.

As he explored the tunnel, he realized that although the first walkway was small, it fed into increasingly large tunnels. The further he made it, the older they looked. He noticed there were pieces of mortar between the bricks of the arched ceiling crumbling away to the floor even without the help of a roaring crowd. He noticed evidence of a secret door along one of the tunnels as well. Despite being intrigued, he needed to keep moving. He could only wonder how the priests had got their hands on the technology. For how much they disliked the pursuit of science, they always seemed to have its latest advancements in their grasp.

He came to a sharp turn in the tunnel, which was the moment he started smelling smoke. His heart started pounding in his chest. The combination of smoke and tunnel was a newfound hatred of his. He pressed his back against the wall praying that no one was around the corner. If someone were to find him, there'd be no place to hide.

He looked around the bend in the tunnel, and thankfully it was empty, so he proceeded further. After that turn, he could see the beginnings of a large room at the end of the hall. No, large would be an understatement. It was enough to hold a crowd at least three times as large as the one he and Elise had seen, and as he approached it, the smell of fire became much worse, and strangely metallic.

As he got closer to the edge, a muffled voice became audible from around the wall. The same voice from before. "Gentlemen!" It called out. From here he could recognize it as an older man. "Today, we celebrate the successful raid of three more tunnels of Les Tunneliers, Les Sorcières Sanglantes!"

A cheer erupted from the others in the room. *The Bloody Witches.* It was concerning to say the least. Under the guise of the noise, Georges chanced a look around the final corner in the wall. The room was circular with a tall dome room and large enough to comfortably fit the crowd. He'd heard rumors about Les Saints Chevaliers having something like this, but he'd never believed them. Now though, presented with the undeniable evidence, he was left with no other choice.

What rested in the center was what concerned him the most, though. There was a group of large crosses, all reaching up from the floor to near the top of the ceilings, flames creeping from the bottom upwards. They were about to host a witch burning.

His gaze turned to two priests who were dragging in a woman. She screamed and kicked against her captors despite all odds being against her. Her hair had been cut so short that Georges almost didn't recognize her. It was Adrian's mother.

He turned away before he could witness what happened next, knowing that if he went in there now, what he had seen would never escape that room. Majorly outnumbered and underprepared, it was an impossible fight. He had failed.

He ignored every sound behind him and left the tunnel. The gathering in the tunnel made it a lot easier to escape thankfully, so he was able to walk this time. As he did, he said a prayer for each person he had been able to see when he'd looked in.

The hard part wasn't escaping the tunnels, but escaping

the haunting images that they'd left him with. Once he was back through the door and into the streets, he scribbled down the details of what he had seen, knowing that it would be important for later but also hoping that it would help it to escape from his mind. Even after drawing it though, the imagery still stuck firm in his mind.

Returning back from his search, Adrian ran up to him, waiting eagerly for his parents to be trailing behind Georges. Georges could only watch him slump over when he realized that they weren't there.

"Did you find anything?" Adrian asked despite already knowing the answer.

"I'm sorry. I didn't find anything." Georges avoided Adrian's gaze.

"Elise said that this was your last effort…" He connected the dots, and tears formed in his eyes.

Adrian ran away, leaving Georges alone with Elise, who had trailed behind Adrian at Georges' return. As Adrian ran past her, she reached out, but Georges shook his head.

"Leave him." Georges leaned against the brick wall beneath the bridge.

Elise brought him into a hug, and they stayed like that for a while. Her brows furrowed. "You smell like smoke."

"If I'm being honest," Georges looked around to make sure that Adrian was still out of earshot. "I did find something."

"What do you mean by that? You're worrying me."

Georges took a breath, preparing himself to explain. "I found the room where they were burning them. There were too many to take on alone."

"Oh," Elise hugged him tighter, both in mourning and empathy. "I'm so sorry."

"I was deeper into the tunnels than I think we've ever

made it." Georges murmured. "When I looked inside that room, I could only think of one thing. The Sanctum."

"What? That's just a myth! It was confirmed years ago that all of the leads were dead ends." She stepped away from him. "It was a plot to keep us distracted, nothing more."

"I saw evidence of secret doors Elise. What if we had simply missed them? In that dark, I don't think I would have seen them if they weren't already open for the burning. You don't know what I saw in there."

"Do you want to talk about it?" Elise asked in an attempt to change the subject to something more positive. "I'm here to listen."

"Honestly, I don't know. There was… a lot." Georges admitted. It was one thing to see such a scene, but it was another to see your friends being dragged into it. He still carried the guilt of not helping. Part of him almost wished that he'd sacrificed himself to fight.

Elise only had pity in her eyes. She was worried for him, but she didn't know how to express it. "I'll be here when you're ready." She said it quietly.

Georges nodded.

"What do we do now, then?" Elise asked.

"I have no idea." Georges muttered. "Based on what I heard down there, three of us have been attacked, so there is no telling who is available to help us."

Elise froze. "I just heard the news today while you were out. Dear Lord, what is happening down there."

"That leaves us with seven tunnels left in Paris. What should be the epicenter of our operation is dying." Georges turned to face the wall, slamming his fist against it. "The priests are out here throwing festivals and burning our friends, and we're crumbling."

"Don't think like that!" Elise shot back.

"I'm only telling the truth!" Georges was angry, tired, and grieving. A change in mentality was out of the question, at least for the moment.

"Can the truth wait until morning then? There might be more news by then." Elise suggested.

"More news of another tunnel burned?" Georges faced Elise again. "And what of Adrian? His parents are– He needs a family right now."

"One step at a time."

"Yes, but how much of that do we have left?"

CHAPTER THIRTY-ONE
Petime, 1684

Petime had been on her way to speak to Camille when showed up to be in her way. She'd already had more important things on her mind, such as everything that had unfolded with Adrian, and this was the last thing that she needed. Now, she was arguing again, burdened with his antics and drowned-rat hair.

"If there were ever a day that I would wish for peace, it would be this one. Please spare me one day of peace." she pleaded. All that she needed to do was talk to Camille, and then she'd be able to leave.

"I'm sorry, witch, but I can't allow that to happen." Juste shot back, ready to take a challenge. "I told you the terms of my offer."

"I know, I know. You need to prove yourself to the big important priest to overcome your crippling sense of worthlessness." She attempted to push past him. "Now, let me keep walking. We can fight later."

"Oh, you asked for it." Juste fell back into a defensive stance.

So this is what her days were going to be like now. Yesterday, she'd been told that she'd never be allowed to visit the tunnels again, and today, Juste was finally gaining confidence. Next thing she knew, she would be coming home to find out that the sheep had learned how to fly.

Juste swung at her, and she hit him with the stick end of her scythe crutch, momentarily resting on her one good leg. She continued walking past him, enjoying the fact that Elise's training had worked.

"God! That hurt!" Juste groaned, grabbing his stomach.

"I barely hit you! Now, go running back to your little society and don't bother me again." Petime realized the errors of her action only after it was too late. Technically, she wasn't supposed to know about any of that yet.

Juste looked at her, a cross between terrified and intrigued. "How do you know about that?"

So he *was* part of the society. Petime admittedly wasn't surprised, but a small, strange part of her was disappointed by the news. If he wasn't part of it, there was still at least a chance for his redemption, but he'd made his choice clear now.

Juste was becoming increasingly anxious at her lack of response. "Who was the one who told you?"

She smirked, figuring that speaking with Camille could probably wait just a little bit longer. It was too good an opportunity to mess with Juste to pass up. "Do you really think it's not terribly easy to pick up on the fact that you're hiding something? It was only a matter of time before I found out." Petime crafted the response that she thought would scare him most.

She was rewarded briefly by Juste's fearful stare, but

when she blinked, it was gone, and he looked angrier than ever.

"You won't let the secret get out." he growled.

"I never planned on it, unless you plan on killing me anyway, in which case I might tell a few people." Petime shrugged, knowing it would make him mad.

"God, to think that I ever suggested peace between us."

"Finally, we can agree on something!" Petime smiled.

"Stop!" Camille's muffled voice shouted from the window above them.

Both Petime and Juste turned up to see the curtain of Camille's window be pulled away. She ran into her room for a moment, then returned to the window, poking her head out of the wall.

"Stop it both of you!" She shouted breathlessly.

"She intends on harming you Camille!" Juste shouted back up. "I'm just protecting you!"

"What?!" Petime said to Juste in a regular tone, turning her attention away from Camille. "Quit spouting nonsense."

"She doesn't have to know I'm lying." Juste whispered, clearly proud of his response.

"I hate you."

Both turned back to face Camille, who was still leaning out the window. Once she realized that their attention was back on her, she started speaking again.

"I'm sure that she doesn't actually intend on hurting me Juste. What did you want to speak about?" Camille asked towards Petime.

"Can you come down and meet me?" Petime asked, beginning to get tired of all of the shouting.

"Unfortunately I must stay inside for the time being." Camille sighed. "And don't ask about what I did to get here." She added the second part abruptly to the end.

Camille knew Petime well enough to know that those were exactly the questions going through her head. The last time her mother had gone as far as keeping her inside the house, she had ruined a brand new pair of dress shoes, so on the scale of mistakes she could have made, it had to be bad.

"Well I can't speak about anything until *this one* leaves." Petime complained. "So we might be here for a while"

"In that case, I will stay by your side to protect you Camille!" Juste puffed out his chest.

Petime's blood boiled. Beside the fact that he was clearly showing off to impress her, there was going to be no way that she was able to speak with Camille now. She looked around the area to assess her options. Juste was making himself comfortable in the grass, so it was clear that he wasn't lying when he'd made his claims about waiting as long as it took for her to leave. There were certain battles that just weren't worth the energy they took to fight, and this was one of them.

"Camille. I won't tell you about it now," Petime called up, trying to create an explanation that would clue Camille in while also leaving Juste confused. "But I can tell you that it has to do with a certain man who loves watching sheep."

"But I hate sheep…" Juste muttered.

A moment of realization washed over Camille's face as she realized who Petime was talking about. "You know?!"

"I know." Petime nodded. "You have some explaining to do!"

"I certainly do." Camille replied.

The look on Juste's face as they ignored him was priceless.

"I'll see you, then!" Petime waved up at Camille. "And hopefully I *won't* see *you*." She glared at Juste.

Even though she was stressed in many areas of her life,

Camille's presence was one of the few constants, which made her one of Petime's closest allies. Despite wanting explanations and a place to release her anger, she couldn't be mad when the two of them were working together.

CHAPTER THIRTY-TWO
Juste

Juste watched the witch galavant off into the bushes. He had no idea what she and Camille had been talking about, but what was more concerning was how much knowledge the witch had acquired. She knew about Les Saints Chevaliers, and Juste knew that the secret was too well-guarded for her to have found out from him or Père Fournier, which could only mean that she had contact with someone another witch.

If he were able to uncover an entire clan of witches, wouldn't it be better in the end even if it took a little while longer? If he weren't able to make the deadline because of that, would it still be enough for the other priests to be satisfied? Père Fournier already thought him nothing more than a figurehead, so maybe this would be his chance to prove that he was different.

Camille had retreated back into her window, so it was getting increasingly awkward to be standing outside. Figuring it was time to return home, he started back towards the church, but noticed an unnatural shape mixed amongst the rocks. When he examined it closer, he found that it was a screw, and a relatively new looking one like that.

Juste fidgeted with the screw in his hand. He had no doubt that it was dropped by the witch, but still didn't understand why she would have it on her person. Her crutch was bound with twine, and none of her shepherd's tasks would require one.

His mind immediately returned to his previous thoughts. An outside source. Père Fournier had mentioned earlier that there were communities living beneath the streets of Paris, so what was stopping them from existing here as well? It would make sense for Petime to have found one of them, it was just a matter of finding out which one, and in Père Fournier's office there had to be at least something within his stacks of letters that would help him figure out the answer.

He left Camille's house, thinking about how he would begin his search. He would first look through anything that had the seal on it, figuring that the best place to find information on a secret society would be in the workings of another secret society, but the plan heavily depended on Père Fournier's absence. If he had made anything clear over the time he had spent with Juste, it was how heavily he guarded his secrets.

His prayers were answered when he found the church almost entirely empty. He made his way back, careful to disrupt as little as possible. His first strategy was to search through the piles that looked newest and smallest first, and as he opened the letters from those piles, he found that many of the most recent letters were finalizing the details of the visit. The dates trailed back months, which made Juste realize that the priest had been planning this for longer than he'd initially thought. It was unsettling that Père Fournier had been planning even before he'd arrived in the village. It wasn't what he was looking for right now though.

He realized that many of the letters followed the same format, talking about plans and actions rather than giving any sort of information, which made Juste believe that instead of letters, it might be wiser to look for a log or journal of some sort. What was strange was that as he looked around the room, there were no books anywhere. It felt like the more he searched, the less he found.

He looked over the spot where Père Fournier had opened the secret door previously, noticing the hinges against the edge of the picture frame. They blended with the wall well at a glance, but when Juste was this close, they glaringly stood out. Even moreso, it was the only painting in the room. The rest of the walls remained empty, serving only as the backs to shelves.

The futile searching began to get the best of his temper, signaling that it was time for a break. He returned the stacks of letters to their original places and paced down the hallway, still looking along the walls. He realized that there was only one other notable, framed painting hanging in the church, and that was the portrait of Père Fournier hanging in the hallway.

Juste examined it on a whim. It certainly did seem like it could be hiding something, but he would have thought the same of the painting in the office as well. The only thing in front of it was a small table, so it could be moved easily enough.

He pushed the table aside, careful not to disturb any of the decorations sitting on top of it, and started feeling around the edges of the painting looking for hinges. At first he found nothing, but just before he was going to stop searching, he felt the telltale bump of hinges. He jumped a bit coming across

it, but the fear was quickly overtaken by curiosity. When he
tugged on its edge, the painting swung open to reveal a small,
dark tunnel. When he peered into it, it was clear that it led
to *somewhere*, but Juste had no idea where that was. He had
expected something like a bookshelf at most, so certainly not
this.

Conveniently, there was a candle holder at the entrance
of the tunnel. The candle inside looked relatively new, telling
him that this place was still used as well. He wasted no time
in lighting the candle, and starting slowly down the tunnel. Its
floor of the tunnel was covered in dust, and the entire place
cold, which was a strange contrast to the summer air outside.
After a small distance, the tunnel opened up into a larger
room, and the candlelight revealed a cluttered collection of
bookshelves and witch hunting paraphernalia.

Upon first glance, it all looked normal, but as he
examined it closer, he realized that he couldn't be more wrong.
The first thing he saw was a jar of jewelry sitting on the desk.
Women's jewelry. As he noticed more, he realized that amongst
the clutter were various devices intended to kill witches.
Numerous knives, stakes, and bows lined one of the walls,
more than one small village could ever need in a lifetime, and
bottles of poisons lined another. He tried to ignore the idea of
Petime being the victim of one of them forcing its way into his
mind. It made him feel sick. He didn't have time to examine it
all too thoroughly anyway because he needed to find as much
as possible before Père Fournier's return.

He scanned the bookshelves, hoping for something
that might be useful. If anything, he knew he was on the right
track at least, because the things filling the shelves down here
seemed more informational. There were shelves of books on
the history of Les Saints Chevaliers, and a few on different

types of weapons, but nothing on the other societies beneath Paris.

One book did catch his eye, however. It had a leather cover, and seemed more-worn than the rest of the other books. It was also significantly less dusty than the rest, meaning that it had been moved at least somewhat recently. He pulled it from the shelf, and was about to open it, when he realized that there were furious footsteps coming down the hallway.

"Put that down." Père Fournier's voice growled.

Juste almost dropped the book, but decided to stand his ground. He'd tried being apologetic before, and it had failed, so now it was time to try confidence, no matter how false.

"And what if I don't?"

Père Fournier fully stepped into the candlelight. "Don't test me when you're in a room full of weapons."

"A young man against an old priest? I think I'd have an advantage." Juste smirked, knowing that it would damage the priest's pride. It was a dangerous game to be playing, but he was committed now.

"I must say that you're developing quite the personality." Père Fournier stalked closer, making Juste increasingly anxious. "At least it is better than your previous timidness.Now hand over the book."

Juste noticed that the usual edge in Père Fournier's tone had a hint of worry to it now. There was no doubt in his mind that the book contained at least something useful.

"Why can't I read this one?" Juste kept the book in hand pulling it away as Père Fournier grabbed at it.

"I don't need to answer your questions." Père Fournier continued reaching for the book. It was almost entertaining to watch.

Juste had never seen him so unnerved about anything

before, so he had to admit that it was an interesting sight. However, he valued his life as well, so he handed it over. "Do you have any suggestions on what I should read then?"

Père Fournier took the book, then straightened himself out. "What do you need to know?"

"Information on the other societies that you'd mentioned."

"Why in God's name would you need that?"

"I don't need to answer your questions." Juste stood still after he said it, waiting to see whether the boldness would pay off or not.

Père Fournier grabbed a book from the shelf, and handed it to Juste. "This one should have the treasonous society's history if I'm not mistaken. If it is unsatisfactory you may choose any other books you seek from *this* shelf." He gestured towards the opposite side of the room. "I suppose it was around time that you learned about this place anyway."

Juste took the book wordlessly, then left Père Fournier alone in the secret room. Despite having the answers that he'd initially been looking for, the forbidden book lingered in his mind for much longer. It looked like it was a journal of some sort, from what he'd seen. and if they were all books from Père Fournier's private collection, Juste could only assume that it was his. Just why was it so important that it remain unread?

After reaching his room, he slumped into bed and tried to clear his mind from thoughts of the leather journal, and started reading the book he'd been given. The book was what he'd been looking for, but it seemed wrong. It depicted a society of mindless servants to The Devil that supposedly lived beneath the streets of Paris and Rouen along with Les Saints Chevaliers. The people in the descriptions didn't even seem human, and Juste knew that even witches had human qualities

too. If Little Reaper had proven anything, it was that. Witches
were nothing more than sinners; humans that were once holy,
led down the wrong path. They were to be pitied. They were
creatures that needed a humane end.

He thought about all of the things that the witch had
said to him in the berry patch. She had tried to help him
with his struggles despite not being on good terms with him.
Moments like those were what made The Devil 's tricks so
powerful, and this book didn't account for any of it. Moments
like those were what made people like Camille so vulnerable to
their tricks.

From what judgments he *could* make from the book
though, he believed this was definitely the group that Petime
had allied with. The schematics, the screw, all of it pointed
towards the fact that she was making something for The Devil.
Juste closed the book and set it down on the bed. It was late
enough now that Père Fournier should have been asleep, and he
needed something new to read.

He returned quietly to the bookshelf in the hidden
room, this time deciding not to use the candle. It was a lot
darker, but less risky in the event that Père Fournier woke up.
The tunnel in the dark seemed strangely sinister, and it took
constant focus to avoid stepping on anything along the journey.

To his surprise, the leather journal was still sitting on
the bookshelf where Père Fournier had left it when he got
there. Juste was worried that he might've decided to hide it out
of distrust towards Juste, but it seemed like he hadn't thought
that he would be bold enough to try anything.

Juste reached out for the book, then stopped himself,
wondering if it would be a sin to take it. He'd been asked not
to, but he was also taking it to further the mission of Les Saints
Chevaliers, Père Fournier had told him that they carried out

God's will. If it was for that reason, God would surely turn a blind eye just this once, right?

He took the journal. It felt a lot heavier in his hands than he would've imagined, and buzzed with an energy that it didn't seem to have earlier. He didn't have permission to see this, and he knew it.

As he opened it, he was greeted by pages filled with handwritten writing. All of it was organized into tidy paragraphs that left almost no margins. It was hard to read in the dark, but he could make out common words like "tunnels", "church", and "doorway". Among the words, there was also a name that showed up repeatedly. "Guilliaume Gramont" showed up multiple times in almost every page that was written. Juste didn't recognize it, but he knew that it was definitely important.

He flipped through the book one final time before returning to his room, wondering if Père Fournier would really know that it was missing if he were to take it. It was filled through its final page, meaning that there would be no purpose to return to it anytime soon if it were a journal. This book seemed like it had the first hand accounts of secret societies that he needed. Things that would go more in depth on what it was really like to hunt a witch. Things that would show what he needed to do to uncover what the witch and her friends were hiding.

He squinted, seeing what he could make of the situation in the dark when another book caught his eye. It was very similar in size and color to the journal. The only difference was that it wasn't bound with leather. Acting in a moment of what he thought was pure genius, he took the other book and pushed it into the hole that the journal left. It wasn't perfect, but it wasn't noticeable at a glance either. God would keep his head turned as long as he didn't get greedy.

Juste wasted no time in leaving before he could regret his decisions. Upon returning to his room, he hid the book carefully in a trunk of his belongings, then laid in bed to sleep. As he rested, thoughts of the journal's potential contents filled his mind. There was so much more to learn, and it was all at his fingertips.

CHAPTER THIRTY-THREE

Camille

Camille paced around her room for what must have been the hundredth time. She had made a promise to Adrian to see him again, but the solution she'd come up with was a little bit outrageous. On her bed rested a rope made of clothes and fabric. It was strong enough to hold her weight, but that wasn't the hard part. She needed to climb down the face of her house, and if she fell, she was doomed.

She made another lap around her room. Even if she was scared, she still needed to see Adrian. A promise was a promise after all, and if her parents were to find out, the worst that they could do was confine her to her room for even longer. The confinement was already going to last until her marriage, so it couldn't get any worse than it was for her already.

The choice wasn't even a choice.

She took a deep breath, then dropped the rope through her window. She looked at the rope, dangling along the side of the house. She needed to climb that.

This was the make or break moment of the entire situation. With her eyes closed, she gripped onto the rope and swung around and out the window. In a moment of pure relief, she landed safely against the side of the stone brick home. While it wasn't the most comfortable feeling in the world, it was still a much better alternative than falling to the ground.

Climbing slowly down, her arms burned from holding her body weight. It occurred to her that this would, unfortunately, be the easy part. For every rope that she climbed down from, she would also need to climb back up. She couldn't focus on that now though because she needed to make it back to Adrian.

She was already late, so her usual walking pace through the village was a sort of half-run more than anything. A shuffle. It was a solid shuffle. All that was on her mind was being able to speak to Adrian, even if it was only one more time.

As she reached the edge of the woods, she saw the telltale light emanating from Adrian's lamp, and breathed a sigh of relief. He hadn't left without her.

"Adrian!" She ran up to him, stumbling through the tall grass.

"Camille, good evening!" Adrian smiled.

"Before we speak for too long, there is something I need to talk to you about." Camille could feel her voice shaking. She could already imagine her parents running through the field after her. Even if it was a false worry, there was still no time to waste.

"Me too." Adrian admitted.

"You go first." It was an unexpected answer, so she was caught off guard.

"We need to stop talking about Petime." Adrian explained, continuing the trend of unexpectedness. "I need for her life in the village to be separate from mine."

"That's alright." Camille replied. It would be easy enough, especially since speaking at all would be in question soon.

Adrian started walking along the field. "Now, your turn."

Camille had lost her sense of readiness after Adrian's contribution. "I, uh," She stammered. She had trained for years not to get caught on her words, and still when it mattered most, it had no effect.

"Take as long as you need to be comfortable." Adrian comforted her.

Camille nodded, taking a few moments to process what she was going to say. Voicing it out loud made it real. They hadn't even known each other for that long, so for all she knew, the news might mean that this was the last time that they ever saw each other.

"I'm technically not supposed to be here tonight." Camille felt like she was off to a good start. "I have been confined to my house. I'm sorry." She became quieter and quieter as she spoke. Now she wasn't doing as well.

She noticed Adrian's facial expression change into one which was part shock and part sadness, and a wave of guilt washed over her. This was all her fault. If only she had been more responsible, none of this would've happened.

"That's alright, we can get Petime to–" Adrian paused. "Never mind."

"What do you mean?" Camille questioned. "Petime can still speak to us freely! That's a great idea!"

"Not anymore, actually." Adrian looked out over the field of sheep. "There was a reason behind my asking for us not to speak about her anymore."

"Why? Is everything alright?" Camille mourned the loss of a potential way to communicate, but Adrian's feelings were more important in the end.

Adrian sighed. "She got into trouble with my family because of something that I said. Now we're not allowed to speak anymore."

"I'm sure it's alright." Camille paused. "Also, you have a family?" She hadn't even considered the possibility of that until now.

"It's… hard to explain." Adrian stared at the ground, fidgeting with his feet and drawing shapes into the mud with his shoe.

"Then tell me the truth. If there were ever a time to tell me the truth, it would be now, right?" she ventured.

"It's a danger to you!" Adrian was clearly struggling against his answer. "I can't risk putting you in harm's way."

"Then why isn't it a danger to Petime?" Camille stepped forward, not realizing how close she was to Adrian. "What did she do differently?"

"She chose the danger for herself." Adrian replied quieter, accepting the shrinking distance between them.

"I would choose to be in danger too if it meant I could be in danger alongside you." Camille grabbed Adrian's hand. "Lord, I climbed out a window just on the off-chance that I wouldn't be too late to meet you!"

Adrian stared at her. "You did all of that for me?"

"Of course I did."

"Why?"

"I don't know." Camille murmured, realizing that the question took more thought than she was able to put into it so suddenly. She'd unconsciously been asking herself the same question for a long time.

"Neither do I, Camille." Adrian took Camille's other hand. "But I want to find out."

"Then tell me the truth." Camille pulled away, wishing that she didn't have to.

"I–" Adrian started, then stopped again, then started again.

Camille hid her smile. "Take as much time as you need to be comfortable."

"Stop stealing my words!" Adrian joked.

"Focus then!" Camille reminded him. She'd been too caught in the moment to remember her time limit before, but it was creeping back into her thoughts. She wasn't prepared for what came next.

Adrian took a deep breath, then said everything. He spoke about the tunnels. He spoke about Georges and Elise. He spoke about his past, his true past, and he even spoke about the future that he wanted. Camille took it all in as well as she could, knowing that she'd have the time to process it all later, but it was still a lot for anyone to handle.

It put a lot of things in context for her. She had been right about Petime being distracted, and it made more sense why Juste had been following her every move so closely. There was a battle that Petime was going through that Camille had been almost entirely absent from. It made sense why Petime hadn't shared anything about it, but that didn't stop it from hurting. She was defending her life from evil priests and threats to her livelihood, and she hadn't even come to anyone else about it.

The entire explanation had also taken a lot longer than Camille thought it would, pushing the boundaries of how comfortable she was with staying out late, but it was worth it. No one had come looking for her yet, but that wasn't a luxury she could afford to rely on for much longer. She wished she could stop and slow down, but she needed to keep moving.

"Adrian—" Camille started.

"You need to go, I know." He sighed.

Camille nodded. "As much as I would love to stay and talk for longer, I don't know when or where my parents will come looking for me. Now that I know about… everything, I need to make sure that I can be there for Petime when you can't."

"I still feel so guilty about all of it." Adrian said, voice filled with pain.

"Petime is one of my best friends, and also one of the kindest people you'll ever meet. While she may be mad now, she'll forgive you in time. Don't worry."

Adrian accepted the comfort. "I can only hope so."

"Thank you for telling me the truth. I won't forget how much courage that took."

"Thank you for giving me reason to overcome my fears." Adrian smiled.

Camille fully turned away, unable to look at Adrian any longer. If she looked at his smile any longer, she'd want to stay longer than she already had, and she'd already spent too much of her time.

"Wait, Camille?" Adrain grabbed her wrist before she could walk away.

"Yes?" Camille replied, gritting her teeth, but still looking forward. She knew what was behind her.

"I will find a way to send you messages, no matter what it takes."

"And I look forward to them, then." Camille broke away, tears forming in her eyes. She didn't want to stay confined to her house. She didn't want to be married. She didn't want her friends and her life to be thrown into such turmoil. All she'd wanted was to enjoy her final days before married life.

Camille sprinted home, not caring about the sweat or the stains or how she looked. The running was helping to clear her mind as well as getting her home faster. It was going to be an awful morning on her muscles, but she didn't care.

When she got home, she was greeted with the unfriendly reminder of the fact that she needed to climb back up the makeshift rope. It hung out her window still, swaying in the nighttime breeze. She approached it carefully, then grabbed onto the rope, preparing to start climbing.

"Don't even try." Her mother's voice came from behind her.

"Maman!" Camille was too frozen with fear to do anything anyway. There was no way of predicting what was going to come next.

"Go to sleep. We are talking about this tomorrow." Her mother muttered, still carrying her threatening tone. "I don't know who I raised, but she is a better daughter than this."

Camille bit back tears and nodded. Her mother wasn't wrong.

CHAPTER THIRTY-FOUR
Petime

Petime rested on one of the stone circle's large, mossy stones organizing the contents of the box that Georges had given her. With the recent events, working on her new crutch had become her only remaining chance to fight back. There was no telling what would happen once the visitors arrived, so she'd at least need *something* that she could use as a weapon against them.

It was clear that the box's contents had been thrown together haphazardly, but Petime still appreciated the sentiment. Among the materials for her new crutches, Elise had left some copies of writings by Ambroise Pare as well. They detailed the process of creating smooth looking, comfortable replacement limbs. She'd also included some of Georges' plans for his own hand that he'd built.

She spent a large portion of the day working on the construction of her new crutches, paying careful attention to each and every detail. There was no room for error with such limited supplies. Her crutches' new design was similar, but still had some differences. Mainly, they allowed for a wider range of motion. The two forearm-height crutches would allow for more balance when doing more intense movement as well as make her regular motions easier to carry out.

The process went relatively quickly since it followed the usual process of making a new crutch with the exception of a few modifications. She didn't know whether it was natural talent or something else, but by the late afternoon, she had nearly finished what had been predicted to take multiple days. All that was left was to attach leather padding in some places along the crutch. She'd saved it for last due to her limited supply of animal glue from the tunnels. It was different from the birch glue that she usually made for her previous crutches, being a lot stronger and more reliable. Georges and Elise had left the last of their already limited supply in the box for her, so she couldn't let it go to waste.

With a careful hand though, even applying the glue turned out to be simpler than she'd anticipated. The animal glue easily bonded with both the wood and the leather that were used for the crutch, so there wasn't much issue with the placement at all.

Once everything was applied, she held the finished products out in front of her, admiring her work with a renewed sense of self-confidence. The assembly had gone as perfectly as it could have. After she had sufficiently appreciated her hard work, Petime laid them to dry on one of the adjacent stones, taking in the scenery of the area around her. The calm summer day seemed unaffected by all the stresses of her daily life. This was her escape, and she would find a way to prove herself worthy of it again.

She stood up using her old crutch, and started to walk

again. The feeling of the farmer's scythe in her hand was old and familiar, but she was ready to try out something new, something that allowed her more freedom.

The only thing left in her plan for the day was to visit Camille. Having had time to calm herself after the initial shock of being kicked out of the tunnels, Petime now wanted answers more than anything. For the past few days especially, there had been so much happening that they'd barely been able to see each other, and every time that they *did* have the time, Juste had been there to ruin it in some way or other.

It made more sense to her now knowing that he was part of Les Saints Chevaliers, but Petime couldn't tell whether that made her more or less forgiving of his actions. His desire to protect Camille had been one of the only remaining admirable things about him, but knowing that the desire stemmed from the wishes of the church tainted that fact. For a while, she would even go as far as to say that he would be capable of redemption, but the thought was pushed far into the back of her mind.

She continued through the woods and into the town, only to meet Juste himself. Speak of the Devil. There was a good attempt at veering from her previous path as quickly as possible to go down a different side street, but Juste caught onto her presence as quickly as she had onto his. Petime shot a quick string of curses under her breath as he stopped what he was doing to approach her.

"Look who it is! I'm so happy to see you!" Juste scoffed with pure, sarcastic positivity.

"I'm not." Petime did her best to keep shuffling down the alternate route, but Juste continued to follow her.

"Might I ask where you're headed down that dusty backroad?" Juste asked. "You wouldn't possibly be trying to avoid me, would you?"

Petime wished she could walk faster, but with her crutch, she had no hope of outwalking Juste. "You have been living here for what, a week? Why do you know the backroads so well? Are your priest friends not keeping you busy enough?"

Juste scowled. "I have plenty to do, thank you. And if I were you, I wouldn't forget that one of those things is killing you."

"You don't seem to be doing well with that." Petime rolled her eyes, giving up on the potential to escape him.

"Might I ask where you really want to go, then?" Juste changed the subject. "I surely hope that it isn't to spend time with Camille."

It seemed like she had been right in her assessment that he was purposefully barring her from seeing Camille, and it only made her more furious. "I will be speaking to her one way or another, and *you* won't be involved."

"What, so you can possess her?" Juste fell back into a defensive position.

"Do you really want to fight me?"

"Yes." Juste nodded. "If it means protecting Camille."

Petime leaned back on her crutch. "I only want to speak with her, not possess her! You're certainly thick-skulled if you still believe that I'm hellbent on possessing her."

Juste seemed to take personal offense to the statement. "I'm doing you a favor! I'm stopping you before The Devil can steal what little bit of your soul you have left!"

"I'd like to point out that your 'favor' results in my untimely death." Petime grumbled, readying herself for whatever he was about to do next.

"Any God-fearing citizen would know that life is only a test to see how loyal we are." Juste hissed. "Only sinners fear death."

Petime, fed up with arguing, slammed her crutch into the ground to gain stability, then grabbed the collar of Juste's shirt, pulling him close to her. "You would do well to fear it too, then."

She pushed him away, sending him tumbling into the dirt. She hadn't expected him to be so easy to fling around, so the whole ordeal had been much more dramatic than she originally intended. What she had just done would only serve to enrage him, and that was possibly the least productive outcome of this conversation.

Juste stood himself up from the dirt. "This isn't you. Can't you see that Satan is possessing you?" There was a surprisingly genuine tone to his voice.

Petime almost faltered, but caught herself. "You don't get to dictate who I am, Juste."

He stood up slowly, not breaking eye contact with her. "I do, actually. I have seen your moments of kindness. In those moments you seem like a real, genuine person." He circled around her, reminding Petime eerily of Père Fournier. "But now, your words are filled with poison. You are no longer the girl you once were Petime. Let's see how The Devil fights back."

He snatched the crutch out of Petime's hand, and broke it over his knee. As she fell to the ground, she heard its sickening crack. The splintering wood seemed to splinter her soul as well, as if she was losing a part of herself. She knew it was bait, but she was left with no choice but to fight now.

"I forgive you for your sins, little witch. It is a shame that you had to fall this way." Juste said pityingly.

Petime scanned the area for whatever she could find, and spotted one of the pieces of her crutch on the ground next to Juste. It had been his mistake to leave them there for her taking. She snatched the piece with the blade from beneath his feet, causing a twinge of grief upon looking at it. She remembered the years she'd spent with the crutch that now tapered off into a sharp, splintery end. She'd never had to use the blade before, but this crutch wouldn't lose its life for nothing.

"What do you intend to do with that? I'm not some piece of wheat—" He was cut off by Petime slashing the scythe's blade into the bottom of his leg.

She made sure to only graze it enough to cause a surface wound, something that would hurt, but wouldn't be dangerous to him. As tempting as it was to make him truly understand what life was like without a functioning leg, no one deserved that fate. All she needed right now was time to get away.

"Christ!" Juste cursed, grabbing his leg and stumbling over from the pain.

"You'll probably want to address that!" Petime noted. "Clothes can make excellent bandages if you're willing to spare some."

"I don't need your advice!" He spat through gritted teeth. "Was slashing me not enough for you?!"

"It's alright if you want to lose your leg too. I was just giving my thoughts." She took the broken halves of her crutch in her hands, and began crawling away as fast as possible. It was a mortifying experience, but there was no other choice.

Behind her, Juste staggered to his feet. Blood was beginning to show through the tear in his pants where she'd hit him. He looked first at her, then his leg. After a moment, he shook his head and started towards the river. "You'll pay for this, witch!" He shouted as he walked away.

"Alright!" Petime shouted back. She needed to appear like everything was alright. If she could feign confidence, Juste wouldn't know how terrified she truly was from the whole encounter.

She ripped a strand off the bottom of her shirt, and used it to tie the two pieces of her crutch together. Under her weight it barely supported itself, but barely functioning was still functioning. She still needed to talk to Camille, and this might be the only time she would be able to for a while to come. Juste was getting more dangerous, and now that the first blow of the fight had been dealt, there was nothing stopping Juste from dealing the next one.

CHAPTER THIRTY-FIVE
Camille

Camille spent her morning worried sick. After her encounter with her mother last night, she knew that she would be furious, but as the day had progressed, the two of them had barely spoken at all. Her mother had passed by multiple times, seeming almost as if nothing from the night prior had happened at all. Camille could only dread the moment that she decided to address it, and as time went on, the feeling only got worse. So much so that it was almost a relief when her mother stormed into the room with that serious "We're going to have a talk" face. Whatever was coming was going to be bad, but it couldn't be as bad as the waiting that had preceded it.

"It's nice to see you, Maman." Camille said quietly, attempting to be void of any strong emotion. If she could gauge her mother's mood before she started speaking, it would be better for both of them.

"I know what you're trying to do, and I want none of it." Her mother sat on the bed. She was certainly furious, and fed up with Camille's attempts at strategy. "I came here to talk about last night and you are going to sit down and listen to me speak." She let out a large sigh. "What could possibly be worth sneaking out *again* after I explicitly told you not to?"

Camille remained silent.

"Don't think that I don't know about your little night time adventures off into the fields Camille. Once or twice in the summer is fine, but multiple nights in a row is simply unacceptable!" Her eyes were daggers into Camille's soul. "Do you know what people would think if you were sneaking around after dark? An *engaged* woman doing Lord knows what?"

"I suppose I–" She was cut off again.

"Don't bother, because I won't hear it. I don't want a harlot daughter! I have given you *every* opportunity that I can to enjoy your days and search for another suitor in *regular daylight hours,* and this is how you repay that favor?" Her mother's face was red from emotion. "You will not be leaving this house again unless you want your windows barred and your door locked. I don't even know what to do with you Camille."

Locks? Bars on the windows? She would become a prisoner in her own household. The guilt was consuming her. She had failed so badly that her mother believed that it was the only option left for her. "You can trust that I will do whatever you say to the best of my ability from this point on, and will do my best to practice my skills as a future wife during the time between now and my marriage." Camille took a deep breath to calm her nerves. "I understand that you must've been worried sick about me, and I can only hope that that begins to make up for it."

"Feigning repentance won't work either." Her mother

said flatly. "Say that again when your words aren't baseless."

"I was only trying to make you happy." Camille said, tears stinging her eyes. "I understand now how much I've hurt you, and I want to make it up to you in any way I can, whether I'm happy about it or not."

Her mother's gaze softened, and she pulled Camille into a hug. "At least now you're being honest with me. I appreciate that. Let's work through this together alright? All I want for you is a good future."

"I know."

"Just be careful to stay away from the witches." Her mother's face turned sour, and she pushed herself away from their hug. "I've heard rumors from the priest that they are running rampant in the town, and that the legless girl is the cause of all of it."

"Petime?"

"Don't say her name! It may curse you!" She looked around, as if making sure that uttering the name hadn't summoned anything.

Camille fought the rage that was welling up inside of her. Her mother had never been happy that she was friends with Petime, but this was going too far. "Just because you think she's a witch doesn't mean that you can believe baseless rumors."

"That girl is a blemish on this village. She's just a reminder of the old Handless Witch. It's God's way of mocking us for letting him free." Her mother spoke in a hauntingly calm voice. Camille could hear the priest's words coming through her voice.

"May I ask why you are so utterly obsessed with the idea of witchcraft sometimes?" Camille asked.

"Because it is dangerous!" Her mother snapped.

"Did you know the Handless Witch personally?" Camille questioned, raising her own voice in return. "How do you know what his true intentions were? Even then, how is Petime related to him?"

"He was my husband, Camille!" Her mother shouted.

A wave of deafening silence fell over the room. Suddenly, things were starting to make sense. When her mother had said that her ex-husband had gotten in trouble with the church, she had meant that he was convicted of witchcraft. She had lost her husband to its effects, and she didn't want to lose anyone else.

"I'm sorry that that happened." Camille didn't know what to say. Her first instinct was to give her mother a hug, but she knew that she probably wouldn't want one at the moment.

Her mother sighed. "I couldn't keep it to myself forever. I just want you to know that I am doing everything that I am doing out of *love*." There was a weakness in her eyes that Camille hadn't thought possible.

"Maman, I know that. Always. Don't worry." The emotional whiplash was confusing, but it felt like this was the first time they'd truly made progress in a while.

Her mother continued to reveal her past. "I didn't want to leave him. I said that I had to. I pretended like I didn't care because I knew that your life was more important." Tears were forming in her eyes.

"My… life?" Camille stammered, just beginning to realize the implications of what that meant.

"I was expecting, and I knew that your father was going through a rough time in his life. I knew what the village was beginning to think of him, and I couldn't take that risk."

"So that means…" Camille was too dumbfounded to finish the sentence.

"You're his child, Camille. You look just like him." Her mother started crying.

Time seemed to stand still. She was the child of a witch. She was the child of the same witch that Adrian was working under. Unknowingly, by being kept here, she had given up on so much more than she had thought. She didn't notice the tears forming in her own eyes.

"I understand why you want to spend your days out with your friends, but do you understand why I can't let that happen?" Her mother whispered. "Why I can't let you get hurt? I've done *everything* for you, Camille. Just do this one thing for me."

Camille decided not to tell her mother about Georges. She seemed at peace now, if that was any small grace. She really had sacrificed everything for Camille's wellbeing, and the only way that Camille could return her favor was through this.

"I'll do it, Maman. Don't worry." Camille murmured.

CHAPTER THIRTY-SIX

Petime

Petime continued painfully slowly on her broken crutch until she reached Camille's house. She could feel now that the cloth tying it together wasn't going to hold for very much longer. The only thing that kept her walking was knowing that this was likely her last chance to speak with Camille. She could see it getting closer in the distance, but her pace was so painfully slow that it wasn't really a motivator.

Only after she reached the house itself was her leg allowed a sigh of relief. "Camille?" Petime shouted, waiting for her to appear from behind the curtain.

"Petime?" She popped out almost right on cue. Her face was red from crying recently.

"Are you alright up there?" Petime tried to appear less concerned than she really was.

"It's been alright I suppose." She was lying, but if she didn't want to talk about it just yet that was okay with Petime.

"Oh Lord, what happened to your crutch?!"

"Your fiance." Petime grumbled.

"Juste did that to you? He's worse than I'd imagined." Camille leaned forward against the window sill. "I haven't even seen him in the last few days. I hope he's alright."

"I hope that he falls into the river." Petime complained. "They've got him wrapped up in a plan to kill me. The idiot is so far deep into their lies that he can't see he's being used."

"They probably used his parents…" Camille trailed off, worried.

"Speaking of that, since I've taken care of him for the time being, we need to get out everything we need to say *now*." Petime refocused herself. She had a mission when she came here. "Juste has been getting more serious about keeping us separate."

Camille nodded. "I think there is a lot that we need to talk about."

"I want to apologize." Both of them said at once.

Petime felt oddly relieved as she heard that. It gave her a sense that even though what had happened wasn't ideal, it wasn't on purpose.

"I should've told you about Adrian." Camille said.

"I should've told you about The Tunnels." Petime replied.

"I never meant for you to get kicked out because of me Petime." Camille sighed. "I was just so caught up in the fact that Adrian wanted me to be a part of his team that I was quick to spill secrets. I didn't even think that they might hurt you."

"To be fair, you didn't know at the time that Adrian was part of a secret society with a horrible fear of the church." Petime chuckled.

"I don't understand. Even though some of its members

are corrupt, most of them are still good, right?" Camille wondered. "The church as a whole is still good, right?"

Petime didn't know how to answer the question. Her experience had been so limited that she wanted to say that it was all bad, but she knew that making those assumptions would be acting the same as those who called her a witch.

"I don't know." Petime settled on that answer. "It's hard to forgive someone who tries to kill you."

"I can imagine."

There was a silence between the two of them.

"What do you want to do about Juste?" Petime asked.

"I need to get married to him." Camille sighed. "I have no choice."

"What?!" Petime shot back. "Even after everything he's done?" The words stung.

"I need to do it for my mother's sake. It was stupid that I thought I could be with Adrian. It was just a wish in the end." Camille looked up at the sky. The sun was beginning to set.

"And when will you stop acting for your family? Your family is the one keeping you trapped here, and they are the ones that are sending you away to be married to him. You have done everything they've asked since you were a child. What else do you owe them?" Petime didn't hold anything back. She thought that Camille had at least learned something from spending time with Adrian, but now she was giving that up too. It was essentially worthless that Petime had been kicked out at all now.

"I owe my family everything! My mother sacrificed her love, her home, *everything* just for me. She sent her husband to die just so that I could live, so in turn I owe my life to her." Even from the yard below, Petime could see the tears forming in Camille's eyes as she said this.

"Your mother did what?" Petime stammered.

"My father is the Handless Witch." Camille admitted. "And my mother was the one who told the church."

Time seemed to freeze as Petime heard the news. Everything she'd heard from Georges' perspective gained a second perspective. Camille's mother had done all of it to protect her child. A child that Georges didn't even know he'd had, and Camille was following down the same path. If Camille had to make a choice between Petime or her family, would she do the same thing that Georges had?

"I– I don't know what to say." Petime said, voice shaking. "You think that all of this is okay? Do you not see that you're doing nothing more than continuing the pattern?"

"Even if I am, it's what I need to do!" Camille shot back. "Not everyone has choices like you do. Do you know what I would give just for a sliver of the freedom you have? You can go outside, you can spend hours a day with no one knowing where you are without consequence!"

"It's because no one cares if I'm gone, Camille."

Camille reached out her hand like she was going to say something more, then retracted it. "I really want to run away, Petime. Trust me."

"Do you? If you knew that it would hurt your family if you left, would you still make the choice to live for yourself?" Petime asked, standing up from the ground. She groaned as she pushed herself off of the ground and onto her broken crutch.

"We both know my answer." Camille replied coldly.

"And that is why I can't trust you." Petime sighed. "I really hoped that we could reconcile, but it seems that we're just too different."

CHAPTER THIRTY-SEVEN
Juste

Juste struggled to stay on his feet as he made it to the river. The pain searing in his leg was more than he'd ever experienced before, and it was beginning to make him feel sick. The only good thing was that the bleeding in his leg had slowed. Although, every time the wound even gently brushed something, that stopped being true. This was a punishment, a reminder from God that he couldn't hesitate. If he had only acted on his instincts earlier, the witch wouldn't have had a chance to injure him like this.

Even trying to ignore the wound, the walk to the river felt like it lasted an eternity, with each step taking more effort than the last. It was embarrassing to feel like this. He felt weak and exposed. For a brief moment, he almost felt pity for Little Reaper, knowing that this was how she lived her life every day, but a sharp reminder was given to him each time that his leg flooded with pain that this was intentional. She was dangerous.

After the walking had concluded, he collapsed at the

edge of the river. Crawling the rest of the way to its edge. Before he could return to the church the wound would need cleaning, especially if he was going to approach Père Fournier. Sitting on the bank of the river, he took a moment to look into his reflection in the water. He looked awful.

Not wanting to linger on the moment, he started the cleaning process. The cold river water washing over it made him dizzier than ever, but he fought through the pain, knowing that it was for his own good. After a while, the cold water running over it started to feel soothing, like it was putting out the fire of pain in his leg. Thankfully, when the blood was wiped away, he found that the cut wasn't as deep as he'd originally thought. It would heal up just fine even though it hurt like The Devil.

He sat like that for a while, letting the water wash over him, not wanting to imagine what Père Fournier's reaction to all of this would be. If he showed any sign of weakness from his injury, there would certainly be a punishment waiting for him eventually. He didn't want to return to the church, but he had no choice. Standing up was probably the hardest part of the process, and any of the comfort that he'd had beforehand was dissolving away. Ahead of him was another equally grueling walk to return to the church.

When he arrived, Père Fournier was already waiting for him with a disapproving look.

"Are you going to help me?" Juste asked, voice still raspy from the pain.

"No, I'm just here to make sure that you don't bleed onto my floor. We can't have blood stains inside of a church, you know." Père Fournier tutted.

Juste didn't have the willpower to hide his anger. "I've already cleaned the wound!"

Père Fournier crossed his arms. "I don't understand why you think you suddenly have the right to speak back to me, Juste."

"I apologize." Juste glared at him. There were so many more things that he wanted to say.

"You seem mad." Père Fournier noted. "Was it the witch who injured you?"

"I am bleeding, I am tired, Lord, I have walked across the entire village on an injured leg! Of course I am mad!" Juste shouted.

He pushed his way past Père Fournier and walked down the hallway, not caring whether or not he got blood stains on the carpet. Behind him was the sound of footsteps beginning to follow him, then stopping, but he didn't care. Tears stung his eyes as he walked on. Père Fournier hadn't said anything wrong, but he had certainly touched a nerve. Juste knew that he was weak, weak enough to be beaten by a witch. A witch who, at this point, had shown more consideration for his emotions than the priest ever would. It was ridiculous. Satan was truly trying his hardest to compel him to the dark side. He always came for souls at their weakest.

When he reached his room, he slammed the door shut, then sat down on the bed. Looking around for something to distract him, he remembered the journal that he had stolen the night previous. It was still resting in the chest right where he had left it, waiting to be read. The last person he wanted to see right now was the priest, but reading was better than nothing.

He reluctantly picked up the book and started flipping through the pages, quickly realizing that this book must have been one of the first journals the priest ever started. The voice in this book was a lot more timid than the Père Fournier Juste knew today. This voice wrote about his worries and anxieties and seemed like a genuine person.

The moment that Juste started to notice a chance was when Père Fournier joined Les Saints Chevaliers. He'd done it because one of his priest friends had invited him to a meeting, and he was curious about their cause. It seemed like Père Fournier had the luxury of choice when it came to his joining the society.

The next section of the journal detailed his first missions. While some things were similar between their experiences, Juste realized that there was something that clearly set them apart. Juste was worried about killing the witch, but Père Fournier seemed to have no issue with it at all. As he read, he was increasingly unsettled by the language in the pages. The shy, timid Père Fournier he'd met in the beginning was slowly transforming into someone who looked forward to the next mission, the next burning witch.

Juste's stomach churned reading the later chapters, but he didn't know whether it was because of his leg's pain or the unsettling transformation he was witnessing unfold in the journal. Père Fournier was losing all of his empathy, and Juste didn't want to become like that. Reading the journal almost felt like watching someone lose their humanity. Although he acted for the good of the church, Juste still considered Père Fournier one of the coldest people he'd ever met, and he was beginning to believe that it was all due to Les Saints Chevaliers.

There needed to be change. A society led for the sake of God shouldn't do that to people. Even if it was one of the holiest institutions, it wasn't immune to becoming corrupt. Maybe he was the first to notice Satan's hands taking hold of it since he was new, or maybe he was the first one to care, but this was his chance to make a difference in something. This was the purpose that God had for him.

Père Fournier had said himself that it needed a new leader, and Juste was the perfect candidate. He would play along with Père Fournier's plan for the time being, just until he gained enough status. Then he would begin climbing the ranks. Slowly but surely, he was going to become the change that they needed to see. He was going to show Père Fournier and whoever else tried to stop him that he had the ability to become the best member of Les Saints Chevaliers that they had ever seen to date. That was his plan, and his work towards it started today.

CHAPTER THIRTY-EIGHT
Petime

Petime was woken up by a sound that shot terror through her heart. The church bells were ringing again. When she looked to Leon for confirmation that he heard them too, his eyes were wide open, and filled with the same racing thoughts. Although they had a suspicion that the visitors would arrive early, no one in the family had been prepared for them to arrive this soon.

With all that had happened last night, she was feeling more hopeless than ever. She'd already lost Adrian, Georges, and Elise, and now she had as good as lost Camille. Even with their help, the battle would be tough, so what would she be able to do against a team of fully trained witch hunters alone? Her new crutches were still in the stone circle drying, so she didn't even have those to use to her advantage.

The old ones still laid next to her, cracked and tied together, waiting to fall apart. Hopefully there would be an opportunity to get her new ones before the old ones turned to dust. Even if they had a bad reaction to seeing an entirely new style of crutch, at least they wouldn't be falling apart. If they had reacted like they did to Georges' hand, it might be a bad idea to let them see the new ones, but there was no other choice.

Leon sat up from his bed. "They're here, Petime."

"And so early at that." Petime worried. Leon was seeing the full effects of what the church could do to her family because of her. It wasn't fair.

"Were we expecting anything different?"

"You're right." Leon's response had broken her heart even more. "I suppose we should get ready now then."

They woke up the rest of the family, and prepared as much as they could while they got ready. They wore their nicest clothes, tidied as much of the main room as possible, and filled a cup with some wildflowers from outside. Thankfully, they had already asked for a neighbor's help with the sheep when the time came for the visitors to arrive, so that was taken care of. It was requested that their entire family would have to go to greet the visitors, leaving no time to do much more, so all that they could do was hope that they had done enough.

"Is everyone ready to leave?" Petime's mother called out after a while.

The family all responded with various versions of agreement, and gathered at the front of the house. Despite being dressed their best, they looked otherwise unkempt due to the surprise nature of the visit.

Petime prayed that they wouldn't ask about Juste's leg. Her outburst yesterday might have put them in a much worse position than they would be in otherwise. The guilt was eating her alive.

The family walked out together, trying to look as much

like a comprehensive unit as possible. None of them interacted too much with each other on a daily basis, so it felt strange to be doing something all together. The last time that Petime could remember feeling anything similar was around the time she had lost her leg.

As they walked, Leon whispered to Petime. "We'll be okay, right?"

"Don't worry." Petime responded, keeping the second half of the sentence to herself. *Because they're only out for me.*

"Petime's right," Their mother joined in on the conversation. "They will be able to tell that we've been working hard for this."

Petime was reminded that they still believed that this was all due to random chance. She'd never been able to gather the courage to tell them the real reason that this had all happened. It was cowardly, but she felt like if she didn't tell them, she still had the potential to survive all of this unscathed. The danger wouldn't be real if she didn't speak it into existence.

Making their way to the village center, the other villagers looked at them with a strange mix of jealousy and relief. They wanted to host the visitors, but they were simultaneously glad that the burden wasn't on them. Petime wished she could tell them how lucky they really were.

Petime scanned the crowd for Camille, but didn't see her anywhere. Part of her was hoping that she'd at least have been able to leave the house to greet the visitors, but it seemed like her family didn't even want to risk that much. She pushed the thought out of her mind. She needed to focus on the matter at hand for right now.

The next faces she searched the crowd for were Juste

and Père Fournier. However they were equally as missing as Camille. Petime was more unnerved by their absence, because theoretically they should have been the ones doing the greeting and the announcing.

The worry kept her mind busy for the rest of the walk until they arrived in the town center. They were greeted by a carriage parked near the church. The ornate decorations that covered the outside and the lavish interior gave away that it was clearly from Paris. Petime would also guess that they were members of the church based on the religious undertones of the decor. When she was able to get a glance through the window of the carriage, it appeared to be empty, which might explain the absence of Père Fournier and Juste.

For what felt like an eternity, they waited, chattering amongst themselves about the reasons why it could possibly be taking so long for the priest and his friends to emerge. The crowd was chattering and buzzing with energy in the beginning of the wait, but it stretched so long that they started to lose energy after a while.

Eventually, the crowd fell completely silent. Only then did the doors of the church creak slowly open. Père Fournier stepped into an area close to the center, followed by five men. People gasped as they saw their outfits, which had colors brighter than most in Edris had ever seen. They wore deep scarlet robes, embroidered with gold details that shimmered in the sunlight.

Père Fournier was the first to start speaking, and his voice carried over the large crowd. "Good morning, and thank you for responding to the call of the church bells! I am here to announce that our visitors from Paris have arrived early!"

Everyone was clapping politely, but Petime knew that they were all wondering about the early arrival as well. Petime and her family weren't the only ones who weren't prepared for visitors to be walking around the village all day. The shop owners had surely been preparing their own plans to appease the rich guests.

"I urge you to do your very best to provide for these men if they step into your shops, or homes." He looked at Petime and her family. "I understand that they arrived early, so do not worry if it isn't the best you can provide." He paused. "Although, I'm sure that the hosts of our guests have been preparing for long enough now that it shouldn't be an issue to them."

Petime glared at Père Fournier. He had still managed to find a way to put them at a disadvantage despite everything. The reason was so well-crafted that she had to give him some respect for the phrasing, but it annoyed her to no end nonetheless.

"That's not fair." Leon grumbled, voicing her opinion exactly.

"Now, may our wonderful hosts come forward to show our guests where they will be staying?" Père Fournier smiled, looking at them. Of course he'd already seen them in the crowd, but he was doing this all for show.

The crowd obliged, and parted ways for Petime and her family to make their way towards the priests. She wouldn't be able to escape now. This was real, and this was dangerous. Once they reached Père Fournier and the others, the men all began exchanging greetings with each other. Despite it being a man's exchange, she still saw them sneak glances at her as well. It's like they weren't even trying to hide the fact that they were there for her. Usually she would want to send a nasty glare right back at them, but right now she was more cautious.

Père Fournier watched the whole thing unfold, intrigued

by how the two groups were interacting with each other. It only made Petime feel disgusted.

Once he was done observing them, he turned back towards the crowd. "Well, it looks like the greeting has gone well! For everyone else, I wish you a good day, and you are free to leave if you choose!" He turned to his friends, and switched to a much quieter voice. "Now, do you think that it is a good time now to see where you are staying?"

They looked amongst themselves, and nodded.

"That would be nice." one of them said.

Père Fournier smiled, then looked to Petime's mother. "I hope you understand, but there isn't much space left in the church with Juste occupying it. Would you be able to store their luggage at your house as well?"

Petime was livid. She knew that he was lying because even with Juste in the church, the place was still practically empty. There was more than enough space to fit all of their luggage, three times over, really. She knew that her mother felt the same, because there was a strange tension in the air between the two groups.

"Oh— of course." Petime's mother said eventually, most likely in an attempt to keep the peace. It was the smartest move she probably could have made.

Père Fournier gestured for his friends to pick up their luggage as well. "Wonderful."

They began the trip back to the house. Petime had positioned herself as far away from the men as possible, but they still had their eyes firmly locked onto her as they walked. She didn't quite know how to react to it, but she tried to stay calm and continue smiling.

"So, where is Juste?" Petime asked. She'd realized along the way that he had been missing from the group.

She hoped that she hadn't prevented him from being able to walk. If he couldn't, it was definitely going to be used against her later. It was only meant to be a scratch, but her rage had blinded her in the moment.

"Oh, I'm sure that you know the reason why Juste isn't here Petime." Père Fournier shot a glare at her that sent chills down her spine. They definitely knew.

Leon looked back at her, giving a questioning glance. Petime shrugged, hoping that he wouldn't question it any further.

"I don't quite know what you are talking about, but I certainly hope that he is okay." Petime replied. It was a struggle to stay calm, but she needed to play the part.

"You look sick dear," Père Fournier frowned. "Are you okay? I wouldn't want these wonderful gentlemen catching the plague."

She hated being called dear, but it was nothing she could comment on for the time being. "I assure you that I am plague-free, Père Fournier. I was just *so* worried because we haven't even formally introduced ourselves to our guests!" She turned to the men in scarlet robes, making sure she sounded as polite as possible. "May I ask your names?"

The men looked amongst themselves until the one in the front of the pack decided to speak. "We are knights of the king, in a sense. Our true names are only known to us and to God as long as we wear these robes."

Knights. What a clever way to refer to themselves without saying that they were part of Les Saints Chevaliers. If anything, it was smart. However, it also confirmed her suspicion that they were coming for her.

The group continued making their way back to the fields. After that exchange, there wasn't much conversation between them. It was an awkward, tense silence. Petime silently cursed the priest's unbelievably sluggish pace as they walked. There was no reason for him to be walking slower than someone missing a leg and walking on a broken crutch.

As they neared the house, Père Fournier began giving instructions to everyone. He guided people on where to take the luggage, and told the family what things needed to be prepared. The visitors waited silently behind him, overseeing the entire thing. Petime realized that through all of his instructions, not once had he mentioned her name.

As if on cue, he whipped around towards Petime. "And you, young lady, I have some questions for you."

"Questions?" She smiled, but it was only a mask for her anxiety. Whatever they were, they couldn't be good.

Père Fournier didn't reply, but instead pulled her around to the side of the house where no one could hear them speak. Once they were there, he took a moment to examine her. "I see that your crutch is… broken." He chuckled. "Are you really that careless?"

"I would urge you to stay out of my affairs." Petime warned.

"I think you will welcome this intrusion." Père Fournier started pacing back and forth. Pacing was never good.

Petime raised an eyebrow. "What do you mean by that?"

"I am giving you a warning to get your affairs in order."

"What?!" Petime snapped back. The sickness in her stomach came rushing back to her.

"You're a smart girl." He continued his circling. "I'm sure that you know by now that this isn't just a visit."

"Are you saying that–" Petime stammered.

"Unfortunately, yes, such is the fate of convicted

witches." He was acting sad, but an act was all that it was. "Although, I suppose I could make an exception." Père Fournier chuckled. "If you were to dedicate your life to God, he may smile upon you."

"No." Petime hissed. "Not after all that you've done."

"I figured as much." Père Fournier sighed.

"Why are you warning me about this anyway?" Petime asked. "What if I escape?"

"Oh, you won't be." He laughed. "I just felt like being kind today. Don't waste it."

"Then why me?!" She snapped. "What have I done to deserve this?"

"I'm getting there, calm down." It felt almost like he was speaking down to a young child. "Although you're a nice girl, the *idea* of you is dangerous. You're spreading around the thought that witches can recover their image, and that is where the danger lies."

"*But I'm not a witch.*".

"Oh, that isn't for you to decide. Haven't you caught on by now?" The priest stepped in front of her, locking eyes with her. "The moment you lost that leg of yours, you became a witch. Someone a long time ago decided that for you."

"That is quite possibly the stupidest thing I've ever heard." Petime grumbled. Comparing her to Georges was quite a stretch, even by his terms.

"For someone who isn't a witch, you certainly seem well-spoken." Père Fournier said, almost questioning her.

She couldn't tell if he was being serious or not. "Are you surprised that I can fight back?"

"No, I'm just wondering where you could have learned such things, whether it came from The Devil… or other sources." He held out the last part of the sentence, emphasizing it to her.

She didn't want to think about the possibility that he would know about the tunnel beneath the village, so she continued to act like she didn't know what he could be hinting at. "At this point, I don't care about Heaven any more. It can't be real. You're proof enough of that. At least The Devil cares for all of his subjects." If there was a chance that she could change the subject, it might prove useful to her.

"That is something that you and I can agree on, at least." He chuckled. "It's a shame. You really would have fit in with the knights if you'd chosen to work with us."

"What does that mean?" Did he really not believe in God either?

"You know what I mean." Père Fournier started walking away. "The offer still stands too, I suppose, but I know you won't accept, so instead I'd recommend to start saying your last goodbyes." He disappeared around the corner, leaving Petime alone.

The reality of what was happening was setting in. All of her worst fears had come true. The priest was going to find a way to convict her, and she couldn't do anything about it. Soon enough, she was going to face the same fate as Georges, except this time the priest was prepared. The world was spinning around her as she made her way back to the front of the house. She couldn't think about it anymore. She needed to be distracted even if only for a moment so that she could get her head back to where it needed to be.

Peeking inside the door to her house, she watched her family struggling to keep everything perfect for the visitors. They had all taken to sitting in various places of the house where they really shouldn't have been. A few of the men were sitting on the kitchen table, and a few more were sitting on people's beds despite there being ample chairs for them to be seated in.

Her family seemed to be making due without her. If she were to cooperate with Père Fournier's advice, they would continue to do so, and maybe even gain some status among the villagers. It was the logical decision. Her family would be much better off without her presence. If she could make one sacrifice for the sake of her family, this would be the time to do it. Camille had merit to what she had said before.

What she needed to do was disappear, and fast. If she could do that at least, there was a chance that they wouldn't come after her. From what she had gathered, the group seemed more interested in the idea of her being gone rather than her being dead.

While thinking, she came into eye contact with Leon, who was working on one of the chores inside. It wouldn't be right to leave without telling anyone her plans, so she gestured for him to come outside. He shot back an indignant look, pointing to his task, but Petime shook her head. It was urgent. Leon sighed, then made his way out of the door.

"Whatever this is, it had better be worth the lecture we will get from our parents." He grumbled as he exited.

"I need to leave." Petime admitted. "Now."

"What?" Leon stuttered. "Why?" He looked more confused than anything.

"I will— be gone for a while." Petime searched for the right words to say. She couldn't just leave without at least one person in her family knowing the truth. "It's for the good of all of us."

"What do you mean? Are you not going to come back? Petime, this isn't time for one of your whims." Leon shook his head, trying to process everything that was happening.

"You saw how Père Fournier and the others were looking at me, right?" She didn't have the time to lie. "I may have done something that got me in trouble with them, and I need to leave."

"So they won't take it out on us?" Leon was catching on surprisingly fast. It made her sad.

Petime nodded.

"You'll be alright though, right? Wherever you're going, you'll be safe?" Leon asked.

Petime stayed silent. She couldn't guarantee anything, especially not knowing where she was going to go.

"You will be safe, right?" Leon repeated.

"I can't say that." Petime admitted. "But I will try."

"Then promise to come back." Leon said. "Swear by it."

"I can't–"

"Swear by it!" Leon grabbed her hand. It was clear that he had no intention of letting go until she swore. He was more worried than she'd thought.

"I swear." Hopefully, it wouldn't end up being a lie. She couldn't leave him knowing she wouldn't keep her promise.

"Good," Leon was struggling to speak. Petime realized that he was holding back tears. "Now go."

He wanted to say more, but was restraining himself. Petime knew Leon well enough to know that. She wanted to stay too, but if she was going to make it to her crutches in time, she'd need to leave now.

Petime nodded, turning away from Leon. She couldn't look back. No matter what she did, she would need those to survive what was coming ahead. The walk there would give her the time to think about her plans and gain some distance from the priest. It was the only option now, because it was becoming

266

increasingly clear to her that even if she had wanted to stay, there was no place for her in the village anymore. Georges had realized the same thing so many years ago, and now it was her turn.

CHAPTER THIRTY-NINE
Juste

Juste paced throughout the church. Père Fournier's guests had come much earlier than he'd intended, and while he was still injured no less. Père Fournier was surely going to bring it up in conversation, and he'd be doomed. He'd just barely found his direction in this place, and now everything was going wrong. He needed to have everything taken care of as soon as possible, or at least have a plan to do so, by the time they got back.

Juste realized that he wasn't going to do anything productive until he got his mind in the right place, so he headed towards the secret room. Once he arrived in front of the painting, he avoided eye contact with it as his shaking hands slid the table in front of the painting aside. A few of the decorations toppled from on top of the table, but it was of no matter to him. He pulled back the painting, lit the torch, and made his way through the tunnel.

While he was down here, he wouldn't be able to tell

when all of them returned, which could be seen as both a blessing and a curse. While being in the secret room improved his ability to focus, it also kept him from knowing when the visitors would return. He scanned the room the same way that he had before, looking for anything that might be useful. If there was one thing that the priest lacked skill in, it was organization.

As he searched, it was becoming increasingly clear how pointless the endeavor was. Without a specific object in mind, there was no benefit to searching through everything. Each set of items would lead him down a slightly different path of ideas, only causing more internal conflict, so he shifted his attention to the bookshelves instead. *Something* in there had to be able to help him.

Searching through the shelves was a lot easier, because while still dusty and cluttered, the information within each book was still organized in some way. About halfway through the top shelf, he came across another journal. It looked newer than the other one, but only slightly so. He pulled it from the shelf despite being sure that it was one of the ones he wasn't allowed to read from. Desperate times called for desperate measures.

He didn't know why he chose it exactly, but it just felt *right*. Flipping through the pages, Juste glimpsed the word "weapon" on one of the pages. There wasn't much time left, so he just prayed that whatever this was would be useful. The page began with Père Fournier listing off how disappointed he was in the society, and how he thought that its punishments were too light. He mentioned the king as being "too lenient" and the punishments being "unfit for the witches' crimes". Then it delved into weaponry.

Juste gaped at it for a moment, not knowing whether

to be horrified or impressed. From top to bottom, the page was filled with sketches. Sketches of the incomplete ideas Père Fournier had for torture devices. Ones made specifically for witches. After the initial shock wore off, Juste slammed the journal shut. He was in a cold sweat, panting like he'd just woken up from a nightmare.It turned out that the books were just as bad of an idea as the searching.

Juste cleared his mind, attempting to come up with his own plan. If he could at least get the witch to the church, that would probably be enough for the time being. All that was left was figuring out how to get her there.

There wasn't much time to dwell on the idea. From upstairs, Juste could hear the sound of the doors to the church opening followed by the sound of mens' voices. They were back, and they were going to be meeting him formally now. He needed to make a good impression.

Haphazardly tossing the newer journal back onto the bookshelf, he left the secret room as quickly as possible. When he emerged from the painting, he noticed the priest and his guests standing just outside of the hallway. They were gathered as a group murmuring about something or other, but whatever it was sounded serious.

Père Fournier was the first to take notice of him leaving the secret room, and thankfully didn't mention it to the others. "Juste, I would like you to meet some of the other members of Les Saints Chevaliers. I'm sure that their visit means a great deal to you."

Juste couldn't look Père Fournier in the eyes after seeing the inside of the journal, so he smiled politely while focusing on the others. The thoughts of the contraptions filled his mind just long enough to realize that he was supposed to be responding.

Père Fournier caught onto the misstep quicker than he did. "Not in much of a speaking mood? I suppose that's understandable considering your defeat yesterday." He certainly wasted no time in bringing that up.

"Uh–" Juste started, at a loss for what to say. So much for a good first impression.

"I see that he's leaving the entrance into the back room a mess as well." One of the visitors glanced at the area next to the table. In his rush to get into the room, he'd forgotten to tidy up the table again after resetting the secret entrance. None of this looked good for him.

"I must ask, what is this about a defeat?" Another member asked. Juste was done for.

"Unfortunately Juste suffered an injury in a scuffle with the witch yesterday. It honestly was a mistake on his part, and I'm sure that he is ready for any chance he can take to get his revenge." Père Fournier turned towards him. "Aren't you Juste?" With the way that he phrased it, it was clear that it wasn't a question.

"You can't win every battle." Juste suggested, realizing how wrong he was in thinking that saying that would make him sound nonchalant. He wasn't helping his case.

"He needs some confidence on him. He speaks like a lamb." The first visitor remarked.

"He'll get there eventually, he still clings onto his sympathy at the moment." Père Fournier tutted.

"A trait you can't have in a profession like this, unfortunately." Another of the new men replied.

"Do you think that he's ready for the ceremony tonight?" A third man asked.

"He'll have to be, one way or another." Père Fournier shrugged. "In the end, it has been decided to be his life or hers."

"What do you mean by that?" Juste shot back a little bit too quickly. This hadn't been part of the plan before.

"I think that it's time that we should tell you just what exactly you're going to be doing tonight." Père Fournier smiled.

Time felt like it froze at that moment. Juste didn't want to admit that he was terrified of what was going to come next. He knew that he was hunting a witch, so there weren't many ways that it could get worse.

"You're going to be burning a witch." Père Fournier smiled.

"Burning?" Juste stammered. That was it. That was definitely bad.

"The same one you've been chasing around." Père Fournier explained. "You might want to start working on that though, because if there is no witch to burn, we'll have to get a replacement." He dropped his voice down to just above a whisper. "Her life or yours, Juste."

Juste felt the men's eyes on him from all angles, and his stomach twisted in knots. The pressure made him want to do nothing more than abandon everything altogether. He had done everything that he could for God's work, and there was still the potential for him to suffer because of it.

"Understood." He managed to say. Even if he wanted to disobey, it was a sin. There was no choice in his response.

"Why don't we all eat lunch now?" Père Fournier grinned. "I think that it's going to be a long night for some of us." He lingered on the last part, keeping eye contact with Juste. It was certainly a hint if he'd ever seen one. He had work to do rather than be eating.

The men all started filing into the hall that led to the

secret room, but as one of them passed by, he heard the name Gramont escape from his mouth. It immediately caught his attention. It was the same name he'd seen appearing in the journal.

This might be his chance to get an idea of who he was. He strained to hear the rest of the conversation as they descended downstairs.

"Gramont… coming tonight… leader." He heard from one voice.

"Agreed… important." The other replied.

Their voices were too muffled to hear much of anything beyond that, but what he'd heard was enough. Gramont was some sort of leader, he was coming tonight, and it was going to be important. This added even more pressure on him to catch the witch, and it was already approaching mid day, so he'd have to move quickly.

He gathered a bag together and left the church for the witch's house. If she hadn't tried to escape already, she would almost certainly be at her house. Keeping the visitors couldn't be an easy task for his family, so she'd have to be helping with the chores. While he walked, he began uttering prayers to himself. It helped to clear all the questions pouring over his mind.

He knew that his situation wasn't ideal, but if it would help him reach his goal, it was for the greater good. This is what God wanted from him. Even though it wasn't for the reason he'd thought, the priest wasn't lying when he said that Juste had a purpose in Les Saints Chevaliers. All he needed was to stay focused on that.

After a tedious trek through the village, he arrived at the witch's house. Immediately he could tell that she wasn't there. He also noticed that her family was all speaking nervously in the front yard. Something was awry. He approached them, and they all straightened themselves out immediately, turning to face him like soldiers in a line. He was unsettled at first, but it made Juste feel strangely powerful.

"If you're here to ask about our daughter, I promise I know nothing." The witch's mother said, voice wavering.

"Do you mean the wi–," He just barely caught himself. "Petime?"

"Yes, she left a while ago and hasn't returned. I'm so sorry." Her mother was visibly shaking. Juste's heart filled with guilt seeing her face. She was worried about her daughter, no matter whether she was a sinner or not.

The witch had finally decided to flee. After everything she had said about standing her ground, now was the time that she decided to break. It seemed like the two of them were both pushing their boundaries today. Juste bit back frustration, hoping only that she couldn't have gone too far. It meant that they were both becoming desperate.

"Maman, I told you that it'll be alright." her child consoled her. It threw Juste out of his thoughts and back into the conversation. He must have been Petime's brother. Leon?

"Shh, shh." His mother leaned down, trying to keep him from speaking up.

"I told you she promised to come back!" Leon pushed back.

"Leon!"

Juste looked at him for a moment. What he had just said was certainly something he wasn't supposed to share, but he wasn't going to waste the opportunity. "You." He pointed to the child. "Come with me."

The witch's mother gasped, leaving her father to step in front of the two defensively. It really was a heartwarming

274

family scene to see. He wanted to step away, but he had to do this for the sake of his own life.

Juste pushed past the witch's father and grabbed Leon's hand, leading him some distance away from his parents. It was just enough that they'd be out of earshot, but still within sight.

"What's your name?" Juste asked once they had reached a stopping point.

Leon crossed his arms. "Why did you choose me?"

"I see that you have just as much fight in you as your sister." Juste sighed, caught off guard by the overwhelmingly familiar lack of hesitation.

Leon leaned back onto one leg, reminding him again of the witch leaning onto her crutch. "So you'll also be able to guess that I won't tell you then." It was unnerving seeing them act so similar.

"What would make you tell me then?" Juste asked. Everyone could give their answers if they were offered the right reward. Leon couldn't be any different.

"You're just going to hurt my sister…" Leon paused. "Did the church send you as well?"

Juste was caught off guard by the response. He'd been able to rely on the church for the better part of his childhood, but was this what people were seeing from it now? The image of the traps drawn into the journal crept back into his mind. If Les Saints Chevaliers kept acting like they did, how many more people would they drive away from God?

Leon leaned closer to Juste, examining his facial expression. "You look like you don't entirely believe their views either. Am I right?"

"Watch what you say!" Juste took a step forward defensively, but it wasn't worth arguing about. It was clear that if he spent any more time here, it would just be wasted. "You can return to your family." He sighed, pressing his fingers into his eyebrows. The longer he lingered here, the less time he could spend searching for the witch.

He lingered where he was standing for a while, watching the child run back into the arms of his parents. Once Leon reached them, he got pulled into a tight hug. A type of hug that he'd never been able to give his own parents upon their return. They never returned like Leon did.

He shook the thought from his mind. It was nothing more than The Devil's tricks trying to distract him. *She promised to come back.* That was all that he had to work off of, and even that wasn't much of a clue. He felt sick to his stomach, but he needed to keep pressing onward. He was fighting for his life now. The only thing that he had left to do was to keep searching, hoping that she hadn't made it far.

If he thought like the witch, he might be able to think of where she might be. There was nothing better as of now to try, anyways. Although it wasn't easy to put himself in her shoes, he did know that there was one thing that all of her actions had in common. The forest. There had to be something in there that he didn't know about. If she was going to hide anywhere, it would be there.

CHAPTER FORTY

Petime

Petime fell face first into the grass once she had made
it to the stone circle, allowing herself to catch her breath after
so much frantic walking. She could only pray that she'd made
it there fast enough. She'd played a balancing game with her
broken crutch the entire way there, and that wasn't even to
mention the amount of times she'd come dangerously close
to tripping over roots and branches on her way there. There
was nothing more that she could do now though, just catch her
breath and hope. Petime cursed her crutches for making her so
slow, but also praised them for staying together. It had been her
last time using them, so it didn't matter what condition they
had ended the journey in, only that they had survived.

It was a blessing in disguise really. She'd been waiting
for any chance she could get to try her new crutches, and now
she'd been given the perfect opportunity. She could finally
see if they would do all that she hoped they would. Her new
crutches were sitting in the sun in the same place she'd left
them to dry. They beckoned Petime from her tiredness to give
them a test.

Sitting up slowly, she approached them. She didn't bother to stand all the way up, especially since that would require using the old crutches again, but she eagerly switched out her old ones for the new ones while sitting on the ground next to them. Immediately she recognized how much more comfortable they were. Georges had been right about adding the leather padding. They curved almost perfectly around her forearms so that they had some freedom to move, but wouldn't slip out. Standing up took a little while, but she got there eventually. Once she was up, she could begin the real tests. She took a few steps with the crutches, readjusting to the new type of walking. The strangest part though was how small they felt. Since they only reached up to her hips, they felt more like an extension of her legs than a hindrance. It was one step closer to something like Georges had.

She silently thanked Elise for the training that she'd received. Without it, her arms definitely would have been sore, but they adjusted to this movement quite nicely. The new crutches took a lot more upper body strength than her old ones ever did, but it was worth it. When she walked it was easier, and she could turn much sharper. They were well built. Once Petime grew accustomed to walking in the new way, it was time to try what she'd really been waiting to do. Running.

She practiced for a while, bouncing back and forth from one crutch to another at increasing speeds. Strangely, it didn't feel unnatural to her like the walking had at first. Once she found her way into a rhythm, it was almost like the muscle memory started coming back to her. Once Petime was ready, she stopped, prepared herself, then took off. Already she was going much faster than her previous crutches would allow, but she wanted to push these ones to their limits. And for a second she did.

For a second, she was back to her childhood, running barefoot through the grass with the wind in her hair. She felt that same, fleeting sense of freedom that she had when she was still young. It had been so long since she moved this fast.

However, it was only a second. Quickly, she tumbled into the dirt again. This time as she fell, she embraced it. Rolling onto her back and laughing after she landed. She could run. She could *run*. She sat up, cleaning off her face and clothes. It hurt, but she knew that running was possible now. At that moment, it seemed like she could do anything. She stared into the sky, smiling. She didn't need to tell anyone about this yet. This was hers. Although she'd wanted to show off the crutches before, now she wanted to keep that feeling to herself just a little bit longer. She could keep the running a secret until she really needed to use it.

The moment of happiness was short-lived, though. Gathering the crutches had only been a survival measure. She still had a multitude of religious figures and a severely-traumatized witch hunter chasing after her. Deep down, she knew that even though she'd won yesterday, Juste would stop at nothing to catch her. He was undoubtedly fighting for his life just as much as she was.

She shuffled through her options of what to do. There was really only one safe place left that she had to go, and they didn't want her back. Beyond that, the only other option was to set out on her own, and even though Georges had done it, it had only been just barely. She couldn't risk it.

The longer she thought about it, the more that Petime realized that there really wasn't an option. She'd have to test her luck with Georges and Elise again and hope that they would let her back. They would have to see how much she'd grown, the fact that she'd made her own crutches so successfully, and the fact that she really was left with no other choice. They all knew how she felt. They would have to help.

She heard voices in the distance, which sent a shock of pure terror through her. She didn't stop to think who it was, or where it was coming from. She just needed to go. She wasn't far off the path, so it was likely farmers, but there was still no telling where Les Saints Chevaliers were now or how close they were to getting to her. She'd spent too long already learning how to use her new crutches, so she couldn't waste any more time.

She stood up and started walking, realizing how much difference there was in her ability to travel. Things felt more natural now, and she could walk at different speeds if she wanted to. They were all such small things, but they added together. They were the small sliver of hope that she needed to keep pressing onward through the journey.

CHAPTER FORTY-ONE
Adrian

Adrian nearly fell out of his seat when he started hearing the warning bells to their alarm system going off. He never liked the sound of them. It was an elaborate set of tripwires throughout the forest that were tripped when someone got too close to the tunnels. This worked in tandem with a set of mirrors that allowed them to see the area surrounding the door. Occasionally there were false alarms, but this felt like too much of a coincidence, especially with recent events.

He stood up and headed over to examine the area surrounding the door through the mirrors, and was greeted with a distorted image of Petime. Not expecting the sight, he stumbled backwards from the looking glass. Georges was going to be furious.

"What was it?" Georges asked. "Another squirrel climbing the pipe?" He laughed.

"It was one time!" Adrian retorted. A while ago, a squirrel had managed to get stuck in the pipe that held the mirrors, causing a similar reaction. Thankfully, it was a good enough distraction from seeing Petime that his facial expression didn't give anything away.

Adrian just about believed that the issue would end there when the sound of loud banging on the lid to the tunnel's entrance filled the main room. A few seconds later it was joined by the sound of muffled shouting.

"What did you see?" Georges huffed, then gestured for him to move aside.

Adrian trailed quickly on Georges' tail. "I'm sorry Georges. I was hoping she wasn't here to see us."

"So it's Petime?"

"Yes, but–" Adrian was cut off.

"We'll leave the door closed then. Who knows what else she's brought along with her." He said flatly.

Adrian chanced another look through the mirrors, seeing Petime outside desperately knocking on the lid of the tunnel. She knew she could open it, but still she decided to wait for their permission. "Shouldn't we at least hear what she has to say?" Figuring that he'd been at fault for her getting kicked out to begin with, Adrian wanted to help her in any way he could at least.

"She's not getting in here." Georges made it clear that it was the final verdict. There was nothing that Adrian could do to change his mind.

"What's all of the noise about?" Elise emerged from around the corner, running into Georges as he was trying to leave.

"Petime is trying to get back in." Georges grumbled.

"Elise, don't you think we should at least listen to what she has to say?" Adrian prayed that Elise's influence might be enough to sway Georges' opinion. Even if *he* couldn't do anything else, she might be able to.

"We're safer when we're in here and she's out there."
Georges didn't let up on the cold, serious tone. "We can't break
the seal."

Elise decided to take a look outside for herself, moving
Adrian to the side as she looked through the glass. When she
pulled away, she had a worried look on her face. "Georges,
dear. For as much as you want to keep us safe, I think we're
worse off leaving her to keep making so much noise up there. I
agree with Adrian. We should at least listen to what she has to
say."

Georges sighed, turning away from both of them for
a moment to make his decision. Elise had really done it. Her
powers to convince Georges were truly a force to be reckoned
with.

Once he had decided, Georges turned around to face
them again. "We can't let her in here."

"What?!" Adrian was sure that Elise would have
convinced him.

"If I'm being honest, I worry more for myself than
I worry for her. I've been watching Petime's progress since
she's left, and she's been doing so well for herself." Georges
admitted. "She's finished the crutches despite everything that's
been happening, and I have no doubt that she would have
been capable of so much more. It makes me feel guilty for not
defending her."

"I think that is the reason that we *should* let her in."
Elise grabbed his hand. "It'll help you figure out how you feel
about everything, won't it?"

Adrian was shocked at the fact that Georges had
been keeping an eye on Petime this entire time, but it was a
reassuring thought that he hadn't left her entirely on her own.

Even after he'd promised to never come back to this village again, he still ended up staying just at its outskirts. Georges didn't want to admit it, but he still held it close to his heart, and Petime was part of that.

Georges' vision lingered on Elise's hand for a moment, then he sighed. "Alright."

As soon as Adrian heard the words, he rushed over to the ladder, quickly climbing up to open the door. At the top, Petime was just about ready to start another round of banging on the door when he emerged. When she saw him, her panicked expression melted away into one of relief. It eased some of the guilt still lingering with him knowing that he'd been able to help.

"Am I allowed in?" Petime asked as she sat back into the grass.

"Yes." As soon as he said it, Adrian started climbing back down the ladder to make room for Petime. On the way, he just narrowly missed her crutches as she tossed them down. Thankfully, the new ones posed a significantly smaller threat to him.

"Sorry!" Petime called down. "I did that a bit too early!"

Adrian smiled. He had missed her.

Petime bounded down the ladder surprisingly fast, slamming the door shut as soon as she was able to. She didn't usually act like that, which made Adrian a bit nervous. If someone *was* tailing her, Georges would never forgive him and Elise. At least she was safe here now. Hopefully.

Georges approached her, Elise trailing behind. "I know you must have come here for a good reason, so what is it?"

"They're here. Les Saints Chevaliers." Petime said breathlessly and in broken sentences. Now that she had a chance to rest, her fatigue must have been catching up to her.

"Did you… run here?" Elise asked.

Petime nodded. "Most of the way."

"Elise, ask her about her training later." Georges reminded her.

"Right, right. Now's not the time." She sighed.

"Do you have any idea what their plans are?" Georges asked.

"They intend to kill me."

Silence fell over the room. No one knew how to respond. If anyone knew Les Saints Chevaliers, it was them, and once witches were marked for death, it was rare that they escaped.

"I beat Juste in a fight yesterday." Petime explained further, still taking a small amount of pride when she described her victory. "I don't think the group is happy about it."

From everything Adrian had heard about Juste, he was happy that the fight had ended in Petime's favor, but he couldn't deny that it was incredibly stupid to anger him at such a time. Members of Les Saints Chevaliers held grudges, so if she wasn't caught soon, every member of that society would know her face.

Petime noticed the silence among them. "Tell me. I've already been told today that I should say my final goodbyes, so it can't get worse than that."

Georges was the first one to speak. "How did you beat him?" He asked. It wasn't what they had all been thinking, but it was certainly a welcome distraction.

"Sliced his leg with my crutch." She hesitated. "Is that bad?"

Georges inhaled sharply hearing her response. That meant that it was bad. "We can find a way to work around this.

Although… how opposed are you to fleeing the country?"

"That's a joke, right?" Petime smiled nervously. "Right?"

"You're the one who angered Les Saints Chevaliers." He shrugged.

"Now Georges–" Elise interjected.

Petime pulled the conversation back on track. "I swear that I didn't want to come here like this, but I had no other choice. If I don't do something, my family will be in danger too." She looked at her new crutches still resting on the ground next to her. "I knew that if anyone would understand the need to protect their family from these people, it would be you."

Georges looked at her with understanding in his eyes. It seemed like her words had touched him deeper than she thought. Based upon his reaction, even if Georges didn't have the words to express how he felt, he was going to do everything he could to help. Les Saints Chevaliers took lives from people, and no one here was an exception. They made sure that you felt pain. They made sure that you knew you were betraying God.

Petime, seemingly equally deep in thought, looked up from her crutches. "I'm going back to fight them." She said it with renewed determination. "I thought that the best option would be to run, but the only way to truly stop them is to fight back, isn't it? They won't let me go until their need for blood is met." She stood up, falling into a comfortable, determined stance. It was almost unrecognizable compared to when he had first met her.

Adrian realized that there was merit to what she was saying. Les Saints Chevaliers were never going to stop trying to eradicate Les Tunneliers. "I'll go with you."

Adrian stepped forward. He was doing this for his parents, he was doing it for those he'd lost when they attacked his tunnel, and he was doing it for those who had yet to discover the benefits that the society had to offer.

"Adrian!" Elise retaliated.

"I'm not risking more lives than necessary today. Do you really think you are ready for battle?" Georges seemed equally as worried as Elise.

"I'd say that right now, it's more of a passive-aggressive meal time." Petime commented. It earned her a glare from both Georges and Elise. Now wasn't the time. "But it is dangerous nonetheless. I agree." She added quickly, making sure to stay in their favor.

Adrian shook his head. "I don't think I am ready. No one ever is, but I need to do this for myself." He turned towards Georges and Elise. "I've lost everything to Les Saints Chevaliers, and I'm not going to risk losing you or Petime along with it. She'd benefit from having someone at her side who knows how Les Saints Chevaliers function."

Petime looked at him. There was a sense of hope in her eyes that Adrian had never seen before. He wanted to make more people feel like that. He was scared, but he couldn't keep waiting in safety while everyone around him fought. He needed to be a part of the battle to protect the things he loved. Hopefully, Georges and Elise would see that too.

"You will do no such thing." Elise began, furious. "We can't just run into battle blindly and hope that it will work out for us!"

"Elise." Georges began, his voice calm and decided. "We should let him go."

"Into danger?" She said, exasperated.

Adrian was just as surprised. He'd never have expected for Georges to be the one arguing for him to leave, but it only made him feel like it was more special. Georges wouldn't have said what he said without good reason.

Georges rested his hand on Adrian's back, giving a reassuring smile. "He's growing up. We can't keep him safe forever. If he wants to make this choice for himself, he should be able to do so, no matter how much we disagree."

"I just… He's like a child to us, Georges. A child we never had the chance to have." Elise looked at the two of them, tears forming in her eyes.

"And part of being a parent is letting them grow up."

Adrian was trying not to cry himself. He'd never even realized how much of a true family they'd become until now. Usually Georges was the last to trust younger members of the society with important tasks, so he was being serious now.

Before Adrian could dwell on it for too long, Georges signaled for him and Petime to follow. He was leaving the main room and heading into one of the rooms connected to the side of the main tunnel. Adrian realized that it was one of the rooms hidden behind a secret door. He'd never been allowed to see what was behind it.

Adrian chuckled when he saw Petime's reaction to the door. She hadn't been here long enough yet to know where all the secrets were, and she'd probably never seen a true secret door to begin with until now.

Petime inched closer to Adrian. "Do you know what's in there?" She whispered.

Her question was answered when Georges pulled open the door and rummaged through a crate of *something*. Neither Adrian nor Petime could tell what it was until Georges turned back around holding two daggers, smiling proudly. and Weapons. That place was filled with weapons.

"I have one for each of you." He beamed. "Make sure to keep them hidden. Les Saints Chevaliers also carry daggers, but they won't expect you to be doing the same. Their weaknesses always stem from their assumptions." When he spoke, there was a faint note of pain. He was speaking from experience.

Georges turned towards Petime. "They will think that *you* are weak more than anything, Petime. They think that because you are missing a leg, you aren't as capable, and until they know otherwise, I urge you to let them believe it."

Petime nodded firmly.

He turned to Adrian afterward. "Adrian, you've been preparing for something like this to happen your entire life. You've *seen* something like this happen before. Trust your instinct. You know what the right decision is, even if you don't think you do."

Adrian nodded as well, trying to stay as serious as Petime had.

Next was the message directed at both of them. "And know that I'll be here to support you no matter what. You can fall back onto the tunnels if you need to retreat. Elise and I will be prepared to help you in any way that we can."

Petime and Adrian shared a look. They were both ready to do this. An alliance had been formed.

"With that, I wish you good luck." Georges handed both of them their daggers as well as a few other small tools to keep handy.

Petime started towards the door immediately, leaving Adrian alone with Georges and Elise for a moment longer. He looked at the both of them, then pulled them into a hug. Out of all the things he'd realized about himself in the span of the conversation, by far the most important was how much they meant to him.

"I'm going to fight for you guys." Adrian's voice was

muffled by Georges' shirt.

"And us for you." Georges said in return. "Now, go make us proud."

Adrian finally broke away from the hug, then joined Petime.

"That was oddly heartwarming." She said as Adrian rounded the corner again. "It reminds me of my family. Speaking of which, can you grab my crutches?"

"How is that even remotely related to what you were just saying?"

Petime shrugged. "No idea."

"You're really going to make me carry them again?" He sighed.

"Always." she laughed.

"So, I guess that you have an idea of where we should be going first?" He said, picking up the crutches. They were cumbersome to carry up the ladder, but he didn't mind.

Petime followed quickly behind him. "I think that we need one more person before we really start making plans."

Adrian couldn't see her face, but he could hear the smirk in Petime's voice. She was talking about Camille. Even at the mention of her name, his heart started beating faster. Fighting alongside her was something he'd never even imagined.

"Are you alright?" Petime asked. "You seem strangely quiet up there."

Adrian panicked. "Oh, uh, yeah!"

Petime only laughed in response. Adrian didn't know what that meant, but he decided not to linger on it too long, at least not yet. As soon as the two made it out of the tunnel, Petime took the crutches from Adrian, preparing for another long walk. There was energy in the air around them. Even though it felt dangerous, it finally felt like he was coming close to something *complete*.

CHAPTER FORTY-TWO
Petime

The two of them descended into the thick of the forest silently. The outside sounds couldn't even begin to break the tense atmosphere that had formed as they walked. After they had left the tunnel, they were both on high-alert. There could be members of Les Saints Chevaliers around any corner, and they wouldn't even know it until they were in battle. Although Petime had escaped them for the time being, there was no doubt that they weren't too far behind.

Their destination approached quickly enough. With no distractions, the trip back to the village was much faster than usual, and they were beginning to see the outlines of houses through the trees. Instead of traveling through the village though, Petime made sure that they stayed towards the edge of the treeline.

"Would it not be faster to sneak through town?" Adrian asked.

"With a group of rabid priests out for my head?" Petime

continued walking.

"... You make a fair point."

"I will get you close to Camille's house, but you need to be the one to get her." Petime continued trudging along the treeline. They were nearly to the point where they would split off. "I would come with you, but I don't know who's out there."

Adrian nodded. "Unfortunately, you're pretty easy to identify."

"It's only funny when I do it." Petime grumbled.

"Noted."

"Also, are you okay?" Petime noticed that Adrian had been smiling nearly the entire time they were walking. It was threatening to return even now after the conversation between them had started up again.

"I'm just… happy to see her. That's all." Adrian grinned even wider.

So that was what it was about. Camille. "So, you have feelings for her then?"

"Well no," Adrian stammered, caught off guard. "Yes? Maybe? Wait, who are you even talking about?"

Petime sighed. "We both know who it is, Adrian, but I'll allow you to avoid the question for a little bit longer. What you are looking for when getting Camille is a butcher shop. If you follow the road ahead, you'll come across it just before the corner." She pointed to a street deeper into the populated area of the village.

Adrian welcomed the change of topic, and listened intently to the instructions he was given. "I'll do my best to find her."

"Good." Petime leaned against the back of a tree hidden by shadow. This was where they were going to split. "Also, don't get distracted, alright?"

"What do you mean by that?" Adrian had started walking towards the butcher shop already, but whipped back around to glare at her.

She shrugged. "I'm just saying that it seems like you have some things left to discuss with her, but now's not the time to do that."

"Do you have that little faith in me?" Adrian joked.

"Yes." Petime hid her chuckle and got comfortable in her spot against the tree. From here she could just barely see the edge of Camille's house.

"I'll be back." Adrian turned away again, walking off down the street.

He had an unexpected level of composure to him as he proceeded onward. Whenever he was in the tunnels, she'd only seen the less serious side of him, but here it was becoming apparent that he had a knack for sneaking around. It would definitely come in useful later.

When he approached the shop, he slowed to a stop, glancing at the sign. After a moment examining it, he walked in. Petime breathed a sigh of relief knowing that he had found the right place. All that was left was the wait for him to reemerge.

If she knew Camille's family at all, they would surely be out trying to capitalize on the opportunity presented by the rich guests to the town. The only thing left in question was whether or not Camille was still inside of her house.

After a few minutes, she saw Adrian exit through the doors of the shop. Thankfully, Camille followed behind him, which allowed Petime to release a large amount of tension she'd been holding. The two began walking down the street again, and thankfully made it back without much hassle.

As soon as Camille caught sight of Petime, she ran up and hugged her. Petime welcomed the hug, realizing that she still had a lot of apologies to make.

"I'm sorry." Her voice was muffled against Camille's shoulder. "I didn't even consider your perspective. I was stressed, but it was no excuse." Through everything that had happened today, Petime understood more than ever the value of sacrifice for the sake of family. Even if she didn't agree with how Camille acted, she still understood it now.

"Lord, I'm sorry too." Camille replied. "You were getting chased around by Juste. That alone would be enough to make anyone go mad."

The both of them laughed, and a wave of relief washed over Petime. Their friendship had survived yet another of the many tests thrown upon it, one of the many tests that they had worked together to overcome.

"I hate to break up the reunion, but Juste is also out for Petime's blood right now." Adrian awkwardly chimed in. "The entire group is, honestly."

Petime stepped back and refocused. He wasn't wrong. The rest of their conversation could be had later. All that mattered now was that the three of them were working together.

"Oh! I forgot to show you!" Camille beamed. "Look what I brought!" She reached into the pockets of her skirt and revealed a collection of butcher's knives. "My father's going to be furious!" Her cheerful tone did not match the implications of what she was saying at all.

Camille took one of the knives and flung it at a tree. It hit the trunk with a threatening thud, and the blade ended up at least an inch into the bark of the tree. Both Petime and Adrian jumped back upon seeing it. Petime knew that Camille could throw knives, but she'd never seen it in action.

"Is that normal?!" Adrian's face was a mix of shock and admiration.

"I usually just do it to relieve stress." Camille smiled, embarrassed. "Maybe I was a little more stressed in life than I thought I was."

"A little?" Petime raised an eyebrow. Although, the skill would definitely be useful to have in their arsenal. "Either way, we need to make a plan now."

After some discussion, they decided that they should move further into the woods. It wasn't worth risking being seen in the village, so the stone circle would be the safest place for them to freely discuss their next move.

As they walked, Adrian briefed Camille on everything he knew that she had missed while stuck inside. While he recounted the events, she only got more and more horrified. It would have been an entertaining sight to see if it weren't such an awful situation otherwise. The volume of information was so high as well that by the time that Camille was fully filled in, they were nearly back to the stone circle.

Petime didn't say it out loud, but she was becoming more anxious as the day progressed. It was nearly noon and she'd not seen any sign of Juste. She knew for a fact that Père Fournier would have sent him out looking for her at least, so that could only mean that he was close to finding them but now. He was incompetent sometimes, but not *that* incompetent. They didn't have any more time to spare.

As Camille processed everything that she'd been filled in on, the three of them arrived at the stone circle. Each took a place among the stones, getting ready for a long discussion.

"I think that it is best if we try and keep moving, otherwise Juste may find us." Petime was the first to start talking. They didn't have any time to waste. "We've spent too much time traveling. We need to face him head-on eventually."

"I'd agree with that, *Witch*." Juste's voice spat from behind her.

Petime nearly dropped her crutches as she scrambled up from where she was sitting. An overwhelming panic was starting to wash over her. Juste's voice had a different tone to it this time, something more sinister than their previous interactions. Adrian and Camille bolted into a standing position as well.

Petime's palms were sweaty against the grips of her crutches. "Show yourself, coward." When she looked for his voice, Juste was nowhere to be found.

Juste obliged, and slowly emerged from the foliage in front of them. He looked like a mess, covered in mud and scratches from brambles. The only thing she could imagine would get him in that condition was searching the open woods, which was terrifying. He was truly desperate.

"Did you think I wouldn't find you?" Juste grinned.

"What are your intentions?" Camille shot back.

Petime was surprised by the sudden burst of confidence from Camille, but it wasn't unwelcome. When Petime looked at her, it was clear that she had caught onto some aspect of Juste's behavior that she and Adrian were missing.

"Calm down little girl. I'm just here to make a deal." Juste raised his hands.

Camille's look could kill a man. "Little girl? Weren't I the one that you were weeks away from marrying? We are the same age!"

"You certainly have more of an edge to you when you're away from your parents." Juste noted. "I tried to save you. I really did, but now you have chosen your side."

"I– You–" Camille stammered. She quickly lost her confidence at the mention of her parents.

Adrian took a step forward in an attempt to take Juste's attention. "What do you want anyway? You said you were here to make a deal."

Juste smiled. "Finally, someone who is getting to the point. If you hand over the witch, I'll be happy to release you all unscathed. Although, that isn't your decision to make, is it?" He turned towards Petime. "What do you say? You've been oddly quiet now that I'm serious. I'll give you one last chance."

Petime froze, struck by Juste's confidence. He wasn't wrong. Before, she'd treated his threats as nothing more than banter, but now he was being serious. All of the attention was on her, and what she said next determined how she would be seen by him. She needed to be equally as dangerous.

"I've said that I won't accept your terms how many times now? Do you really need me to say it again?" She returned Juste's grin through a veil of anxiety. "Juste, what would your parents think about all of this?"

Juste was taken aback by the comment, which made Petime realize that she'd made the right move. He had one major weak point, and that was the mention of his parents. It was wrong to abuse that, but she needed to use anything she had to fight him.

After a moment, he staggered back, paralyzed by some memory. He grabbed his head and started shaking it. "Out! Out! Stay out of my head, witch!"

"I'm just asking a question. Is something bothering you?" Petime stepped closer to him.

"What are you doing?" Camille asked frantically. "That will only make him lash out!"

"It's the only chance we've got." Petime replied calmly

as she continued closer.

Adrian stood across the field, and Petime noticed him reaching for the dagger tied around his leg. He didn't think that this was going to work.

"Do the priests ask you the same thing?" Petime tried to keep her voice clear, but she faltered. She was too close to him for comfort.

This gave Juste the chance to snap back to reality. "The priests were the ones who saved me!" He grabbed Petime's arm so tight that his nails were digging into her skin. "When my parents died, the priests were the ones to come get me. When no one else came for me, they agreed to let me stay. When I felt more alone than ever, they gave me a purpose. This *purpose* is the only thing I have now, and I will defend it with my life. Now, *listen!*" Juste flung Petime away from him, sending her skidding through the grass.

The tumble was all too ungraceful. She felt her crutches land somewhere to the side of her, and she felt herself being scraped by the small stones that were scattered across the ground. All she could do once she came to a stop was make sure nothing was broken, make sure her crutches were still in one piece, and start crawling towards them.

Adrian pulled out the dagger now. He didn't move, but he was ready to attack at any moment. This was the start of the true battle.

Camille reached forward, holding out her hand in a futile attempt to stop Juste. "Are you sure this is a good idea? We can talk about—"

"I said stay out of my head!" Juste shot forward towards Camille, holding something that was a cross between a sword and a knife.

Adrian bolted forward as well, blocking the attack.

"What happened to not wanting to hurt us?" Adrian spoke through gritted teeth, his blade still pressed against Juste's.

Petime grabbed hold of her crutches and skittered back into a standing position behind them.

"You're right." Juste turned suddenly to look at her. "What's your decision? Surrender now, and your friends live. It's your choice."

Petime remained frozen for a moment. She almost debated accepting his offer until Camille looked back at her, giving her silent permission that it was okay to fight back. It was all that she needed to gain the confidence to reach for her own weapon. "You know, I almost pitied you Juste." She spoke quietly.

She broke into a run towards Juste, catching everyone thoroughly off guard.

"Since when could you do that?!" He stumbled away from Adrian. "You're missing a leg!"

Petime snorted, thoroughly enjoying his reaction. In her efforts, she's also managed to get a scrape at his forearm, sending him even further backwards.

Right. She could win.

Adrian took the opportunity to run behind Juste and restrain his arms, but he slipped away from him as he tried.

"Three on one doesn't seem very fair." Juste grumbled.

"You count me as a full person now? How sweet." Petime took the moment to catch her breath.

"May I ask what happened today? You seem stressed." Camille asked.

Everyone turned to look at her. She'd been quiet for a while now, so it was jarring hearing her voice. Petime realized what she was trying to do now though. She had always been good at breaking up conflicts with her words. Although, usually it was between children who got into scuffles on the streets.

"Stressed? Of course I'm stressed!" Juste stood up slowly, laughing maniacally. Somehow, the distraction was successful. "I'm being followed around by a gaggle of priests who will murder me if I don't capture her by tonight, when just yesterday I was slashed in the leg by her rusty old crutch-scythe thing! I lost to a woman in pants. *A woman in pants, Camille.*"

The priests were threatening to murder him. Petime realized what he was being driven by now. He feared losing his own life just as much as he feared losing her own. One of them was going to die.

"If they are threatening you, then why follow their orders?" Camille asked desperately. "It's not too late to fight back alongside us!"

Juste wasn't listening anymore. He was preparing to run towards Petime again.

She realized this, and called to Adrian, who was still behind Juste. "Adrian, grab him!"

She was too late. As soon as she uttered the words, Juste whipped around and shoved Adrian into one of the stones. Upon impact slumped to the ground, unconscious from the blow. Camille screamed and rushed to his side, tears in her eyes.

Petime saw Juste turn towards the two of them, but she wasn't going to let that happen. She tried running again, but she had lost the element of surprise.

"That won't work twice!" Juste managed to grit out, meeting her dagger with his.

The interaction only started a series of frantic attacks. Her dagger clashed with his blow after blow. As they fought, it became obvious that Juste would be able to overpower her eventually. It was a game of when Petime's strength was going to run out now. All that Juste had to do was last until then. She didn't intend on giving up, but it was becoming harder and harder to fight back with each hit.

The sound of Camille's crying was the only thing that let Petime know that they were still safe – or at least as safe as someone who just got shoved into a rock could be. Even while trying to draw him away from the two of them, she was lagging behind. Her mind forcefully strayed to what might happen if she fell to Juste, and a blade got uncomfortably close to her face. She was thinking like she'd already lost, and that would be a detriment to her. She could feel herself getting tired, but Juste only seemed like he was gaining more energy.

Petime tried to block out the negative thoughts, focusing on the positive instead. She'd improved so much over all this time. She finally had something that was *hers,* and she needed to defend it. Camille and Adrian both had other things to fight for, but this was all that Petime had. She might have found the only place in all of France that would accept a legless woman as an equal, and maybe that alone was enough.

She managed to sneak a glance at Camille and Adrian. Whatever had happened, it certainly wasn't good. He'd yet to regain consciousness after the hit. Camille was still crying. She couldn't just keep watching. She had to make a decision now.

"I'll accept your offer!" Petime shouted suddenly, causing a stop in the fighting.

Juste seemed unimpressed. "You're lying."

Petime shook her head. "If it means they'll be safe, I'll turn myself over." Camille and Adrian still had a life ahead of them. This was the right thing to do.

"Petime no!" Camille said, fighting her tears. "I can't

lose both of you!"

Petime bit back her own tears at Camille's voice, refusing to make eye contact with her. She needed to appear strong. "Camille, you've spent your whole life sacrificing things for me. It's time that I did the same." She knew that Camille would hear her voice wavering, and she would see right through the fragile disguise over Petime's emotions, but Petime still put it up anyway.

"Petime, you've spent your whole life fighting, and *now* is when you decide to take a page from my book?" Camille half laughed, half cried.

"He likes you too, you know." She smiled, gaining the courage to look at her. "Now go get him help. I'm sure you know where to go. Follow the ferns."

"I hate to break up this conversation, but I do have a deadline." Juste interjected, earning himself a glare from both Petime and Camille.

"God, you're unbearable." Petime snapped.

"And you're going to die! What's your point?"

He wasn't wrong.

Petime sighed. "Allow me one last thing then. I want to give my friend a hug."

Juste looked at the sky to see the position of the sun, clearly anxious about the time. "Alright, but make it fast."

Camille stood up as Petime approached her, and both were choking back their tears. Camille pulled Petime into a hug, and neither said anything. For a moment, the only thing around them was the weight of their silence, speaking more than words ever could.

After the moment was over Petime took her daggers and handed it to Camille.

"It's better than whatever you had in your kitchen." she

smiled.

"You don't have to give this to me…" Camille said, shocked by the gesture.

Petime pulled away from the hug, finally collecting herself. "I'd rather them in your hands than the priest's." Petime shivered at the thought of Père Fournier with a weapon.

"If you want it to be like that, then I won't fight it." Camille was still smiling, but tears were streaming down her face now.

"One last thing," Petime could barely say the words. "Tell Leon that he will still see me again… later."

"But he–"

"I know." Petime sighed.

Juste stepped closer to the two of them, grumbling at how long they were taking. "Alright, you've had your moment. Now, come with me."

Petime took one last look at Camille, who was getting in position to carry Adrian over her shoulder. She knew that Camille would make it. She was strong. They were both strong.

When she turned to look back at Juste, she saw him rifling through his bag frantically. "Are you looking for something?" She was hesitant to point it out, but he looked like he was struggling.

"…Something to bind your wrists with." Juste admitted sheepishly.

"Dear Lord, how did you make it this far in life?" It would be *so* easy to run away right now.

After a moment more rifling through his bag, Juste came up with a ball of twine. "This will work!"

So easy.

Petime sat down on one of the stones, eating her pride and waiting for Juste to figure out how twine worked.

"How does it feel to lose?" Juste asked, finally getting a hold of the twine's end.

"How does it feel to only win because the other side surrendered?" Petime asked in reply.

"You know, that is one thing that I can admire about you." Juste wrapped it tight around her wrists and pulled it tight. "You know when to give up."

She squirmed. "Careful! That hurts!" The twine burned as it dug into her wrists. She knew that the cry was futile, but it was still worth a shot.

"That won't be the worst that happens to you tonight, witch. Now, stand up." Juste stared at her for another moment, realizing that his plan had a fatal flaw.

"Please tell me that you've at least accounted for the fact *I'm missing a leg.*" Petime groaned, leaning over onto the rocks from pure disbelief. Every ounce of threatening energy he'd had earlier had dissolved into nothing.

He stared at Petime some more, as if it would solve the problem. "Give me a break! I've never done anything like this before. I was just told to bring you back to the church by dark."

"If you unbind my hands I can use my crutches?" Petime suggested.

"Not happening."

"I guess we'll both be dying then."

"Oh for God's sake, I'll just carry you." He grumbled.

Juste stepped forward, and picked her up. It was embarrassingly easy for him to do so. Instinctively, she kicked her leg in retaliation at first, knowing the effort was futile. At the very least, she needed to have her crutches alongside her. She hadn't put in all that work for nothing.

"Wait!" She searched her brain frantically for any excuse she could find to keep the crutches, still wriggling hopelessly towards them in Juste's arms. "At least grab my crutches! I'm sure that Père Fournier would love to have them as a trophy."

"And why should I give you a means of escape?" Juste questioned, not fully buying into the excuse.

"How do you think I'll manage that with my hands bound?" She asked, being sure to use the most grating tone possible. She enjoyed causing him emotional distress.

"Fine!" He snatched the crutches and set them on top of her. Petime didn't know whether or not it stemmed from the fact that she'd made a successful argument or from him being fed up with her, but she was satisfied nonetheless. "You will never stop being a bother, will you?"

"Nope!" She laughed.

After it subsided, however, the walk through the woods was mostly quiet. The only sounds were Juste's scattered mumbles. From what she could hear, he was whispering something about being better. Did he think that if he repeated it enough, it would come true?

Once she could tune out his muttering, she reached a state that had at least some semblance of peace. The downfall was that it also gave her more time to think. Her mind became plagued with endless questions. What if she had continued fighting, what if she had tried to run? She thought of Leon, and her broken promise to return home safely.

Before she realized what was happening, tears started streaming down her face. She had failed him as a sister. When she looked up at Juste, he was avoiding her gaze in some silent form of respect. He had granted her that much at least.

CHAPTER FORTY-THREE
Camille

Thanks to the events of the day, Camille had enough adrenaline in her system to be able to sling Adrian over her shoulder fairly quickly. She was practically dragging him along, but it wasn't impossible. Although, he was still unconscious, and worryingly limp against her body as she carried him. She had never learned how to tell if someone was alive or not, so she simply prayed for the best.

As she walked towards the tunnel, she didn't look back at Petime. Whether it be because she wouldn't or she couldn't, she didn't know. Everyone else had made a physical effort in the fight, and she'd done barely anything at all. Petime had even sacrificed herself, and Camille had just let it all happen. If she weren't there crying and had fought instead, how would the outcome have changed?

She followed the trail of ferns Petime had mentioned to the best of her ability. Although she'd never been told what they looked like, there were certainly ones that were distinct from the others. Following them was somewhat therapeutic really, and it helped her to keep a level head. The secret to remaining calm was to break everything down into smaller tasks until there were none left to do, and right now those small tasks were finding the ferns, following them one by one until she reached her destination.

After a few dozen ferns though, the journey started to get tiring. Adrian was getting heavier and heavier, and she was struggling to stay standing as she dragged him along. Her feet hurt, her back hurt, and her skirt was covered in mud and brambles. If her mother saw her, she didn't know what would happen. The only thing keeping her trudging onwards was the fact that she owed this to Petime. Her sacrifice couldn't be for nothing.

This continued on until Camille stumbled upon what she was sure had to be the place she was looking for. There was a large clearing in the middle of the woods, and directly in its center was a wooden door that led somewhere underground. *This had to be it.* She couldn't imagine any other reason that there would be such a thing in the middle of the woods.

Her suspicions were confirmed – and her heart nearly stopped – when the door flung itself open. As the door slammed into the ground with a loud thud, two people scrambled out of a tunnel and into the clearing. They must have been Georges and Elise.

"What happened to him?" The man asked.

Camille didn't have any reason not to trust them as of yet, so she answered honestly. "He was thrown against a rock, though I couldn't tell you his condition even if I wanted to."

"Don't worry, I'll take him from here." The man lifted Adrian off of Camille's shoulder, and swung him onto his own.

The weight lifted was a huge relief, and it allowed

Camille to return to her regular standing stance. When she saw Adrian being carried away, she didn't want to point it out, but he looked considerably worse than he had in the clearing.

"You poor thing, you must be exhausted." The woman approached her. "Do you think you can make it inside?"

All that Camille managed to get out was a halfhearted nod.

The ladder down into the tunnel didn't turn out to be as bad as she thought it would be, albeit somewhat hard to navigate with a skirt. Its wooden bars were comfortable and sturdy, well worn from regular use.

"Is there anything that you need dear?" Elise asked once Camille had made it all the way down.

"A nap would be nice." Camille joked, taking in her surroundings. She could tell they were impressive, but an overwhelming tiredness was starting to overtake her.

"We can arrange for that." The woman smiled.

Camille didn't remember much of what happened after that, so waking up some unknown amount of time later sent her into a panic.

The woman walked into the room upon hearing her stir. "You haven't been asleep long, don't worry. We've only just stabilized Adrian's condition."

Relief flooded over her. Stable and Adrian being together in the same sentence was something that she deeply needed, but it still didn't tell her exactly how long it had been. Petime was still somewhere out there.

Camille sat up in the bed, shaking off the last of her grogginess. "That's a relief."

"You're back to speaking again!" The woman did a small, happy jump. Camille liked her.

"You must be Elise then?" Camille smiled.

"How do you know about that?" Elise asked. "Actually, how do you know about this place to begin with?"

Camille looked at her. "Has Adrian not told you about me?"

"No, but I suppose it would make sense." Elise looked away, deep in thought. "He *has* seemed happier than usual recently."

Camille's face was suddenly very warm at the thought of that, and her mind returned to Petime's words. *He likes you too.* She definitely had a few things to say to him when he woke up.

"What do you mean by that, Elise?" The man stepped beside her.

Elise chuckled. "Oh, Georges. You really are blind."

Georges turned to face Camille, and bestowed upon her a judgment unlike anything else she had felt before. He was peering directly into her soul.

Elise reached out and grabbed his arm reassuringly. "If she dragged him all the way here, I think she's trustworthy, Georges."

"I don't like it, but I'll allow it." Georges sighed. "For now, what happened?"

His entire manner changed once he had stopped judging her. As Camille started filling them in on the story, she could tell that he was genuinely curious to hear all the details that she had to offer. It was a stark contrast to her conversations in the village, which usually ended with her feeling more like an object to be admired than anything else. It was understandable how Petime had fallen in love with its environment so quickly.

Once everything had been explained, Camille looked at them for what to do next. She really had no idea.

"I think that we need to stay here and let things pass."

Elise determined. "Petime made her decision."

A surge of guilt rang through Camille.

Georges shook his head. "Did she really have a choice, Elise?"

"What do you mean?"

"You know Les Saints Chevaliers. They rarely give a true *choice*. " Georges elaborated. "She likely knew of some consequence that we didn't. Besides, from the sound of things she is going to be kept in the same type of trap that I was. I can't just let that happen to her Elise. This is my chance to make it up to Adrian. Do you think he really wants to lose someone else?"

Adrian's parents. Camille knew a little bit on how they had died, but she didn't know that Georges was involved in it as well. Based on how he was speaking, Adrian might not know the fact either.

"I know that this is a very emotional topic for you, but if you think logically, it's better if we were all to stay here." Elise argued.

"To hell with whether or not it's emotional, I can't let history repeat itself. She's trapped in a cage and we should help her!" Georges snapped.

"And let someone else die in her place?" Elise was trying to sound angry, but her voice broke upon saying it.

Georges approached her, taking her hand in his own. "If you look around this place, what do you see?" He asked quietly.

"It's our life, our home." Elise said.

"And when was the last time that this place saw a new face? When was the last time that we can say we added someone new to our family?" Georges squeezed her hand. "Petime is the only new person we've seen join the society in ages when new members are something we desperately need. She is part of our family now. She is part of the future, and I know that if we work together as a team, we can protect her."

"I understand your sentiment, but we can't just run in blindly." Elise let go of his hand. "Like I said before, someone will only get themself killed."

"Then let us spend less time debating and more time planning!" Georges replied. "We have a whole tunnel full of weaponry for God's sake!"

Elise didn't reply.

"Our time is coming to an end Elise. We need to make way for the new generation, and none of our efforts will matter if they aren't *alive.*" Georges smiled. "Think about how I met you. Don't you want them to experience that too?'

"We did enjoy our travels." Elise chuckled.

Georges smiled. "So let's make sure that they do too."

"I do suppose that helping them would be the right thing to do." Elise resigned. "Alright."

The two of them continued their discussion, transitioning into planning things that Camille couldn't even begin to comprehend. She didn't bother trying to listen though, because she heard the telltale voice of Adrian grumbling from the other room. He'd clearly woken up to some extent. She stood up as quickly as possible and rushed over to him, ignoring the calls from Georges and Elise to be careful.

She rushed out of the room, and saw him lying on the ground against a wall. "Adrian?"

"Camille? Where am I?" He examined his surroundings. "Is this the tunnel?"

She nodded, then took a seat beside him. "We made it here thanks to Petime."

"If we're here then that means..." He trailed off,

realizing the implications.

"She's alive." Camille said, hoping that she was still correct with that fact. "For now, at least."

"Then we need to go find her!" Adrian said, shuffling to sit upright.

Camille held him down as best as she could. "You need to stay resting!"

"She's right." Georges said from behind the two of them, causing a mutual, startled jump.

Adrian frowned. "But Georges–"

Elise trailed behind Georges. "The three of us will be alright. You need to stay and recover."

Adrian looked like he was going to say something, then nodded, laying back onto his makeshift bed. "Do you at least have a plan?" He asked.

Camille turned towards Georges and Elise, curious to know the answer as well.

Georges stepped forward. "It's time that they felt the heat of their own flames."

CHAPTER FORTY-FOUR
Juste

As he brought Petime towards the church, the thoughts of Père Fournier's journal only became increasingly intrusive. Juste was better than that. He had to be better than that, right? He took no joy in doing this. He was only doing it because he had to. This death wouldn't be in vain, he would make sure of it.

Somewhere along the way, he had found a wagon for the witch. It creaked with every turn of the wheel and was caked in mud, but it did the job well enough. He hadn't asked whether or not he was able to use it, but if God were going to look down on him for stealing, Juste would have seen the punishment already. He would pay them back later anyways.

He took a glance at the witch, who had gone oddly silent. She was slumped over in nearly the same position she'd been in when dropped into the wagon. It was strange seeing her having lost her defiance. It meant that he'd actually done it. He'd actually captured the witch that he'd been hunting since the day that he arrived in the village. Still though, it didn't feel right.

"Are you, uh, doing alright in there?" He asked, careful not to make eye contact.

Silence.

It was deserved, honestly. He had sacrificed almost every relationship he had to capture the witch, and that included what little bit of kindness she had ever shown him. He didn't know why it hurt so much, but it left him feeling a strange void in his chest. If he could at least make amends with her before her death, it might ease his pain.

He kept trying. "I can get you something to eat after we arrive at the church. I'm sure one loaf of bread wouldn't make a difference." Kindness was what had sparked him into speaking at the berry patch, so maybe it would work here as well.

"This is the most embarrassing day of my life." She grumbled.

"What?"

She sat up against the edge of the wagon. "I've been captured by an idiot, and I'm stuck in a wagon meant for sheep excrement with my hands tied behind my back! If you were in this scenario, how exactly would you describe this day?"

He looked at the wagon. Sure enough, he was incorrect in his assumption that what was caked onto it was mud. "I agree that it would be embarrassing for you. Although, it's not bad for me!"

"Oh look, I'm Juste!" The witch had dropped her voice by at least an octave and was sounding as gruff as she possibly could. "I crawled out of my grave this morning and spent my energy capturing a legless girl with barely any experience in battle! I'm so proud of myself because it was so *hard to do.*"

The last three words were filled with extra malice, and were paired with a glare that could kill.

"Ah, you're returning to your usual self!" Juste smiled, knowing that now he could dig into her deeper. "I met your family, by the way."

Petime's face fell into an expression of sheer panic. "What do you mean by that?"

Juste pulled along the wagon happily. She had the same weakness that he did. "Oh, did you think that I didn't know about your family? I actually spoke with your brother today–"

"You leave him alone!" She thrashed against the walls of the wagon, trying to escape. "You said you wouldn't hurt anyone else!"

"I said that I would leave Camille and Adrian alone, that's it."

There was no response to that, but seeing the look on her face told him that he'd gone too far. Petime was back to her previous state.

"I'm sorry." Juste chanced.

"No you're not."

The village was nearly empty as the sun set. He thought of all of the families eating dinner, and wondered whether the priests were eating with the witch's family yet. Maybe she was thinking about the same. He had to admit that it would be painful to leave without a goodbye, but if it had happened that way, it was how God intended it to be. He'd never been so kind to Juste.

His mind wandered to Camille and Adrian, thinking about where they could have run off to in the woods. He'd never seen exactly where they were off to, but it looked like it was deeper into the woods. Where witch's things happened. Hopefully when the witch was killed, The Devil's grips on them would loosen as well, because the last thing that he wanted to do was to hunt another one of the group down.

He felt an overwhelming relief wash over him as they approached the church. His journey had come to an end, and he'd done it. The witch was in his grasp and his mission was complete. When he knocked on the door, there was no response, which probably meant that the others had left to eat dinner at the witch's house.

Juste's stomach growled as he stood. He could use dinner as well, but figured that it would be rude to join the meal late, and dangerous to leave the witch alone. There was no way that he would risk the chance of Père Fournier taking the credit for his work. It wouldn't be a hard job to watch her anyway. At some point during the last few minutes, she'd fallen asleep entirely, so all he would need to do was to make sure she stayed in the wagon. It would be more humane to leave her asleep than awake and stressed.

It was a challenge, but he managed to make his way inside of the church. The door creaked shut behind them, leaving the two alone in the large hall of the church. The place was brighter than usual, with lit prayer candles lining the entryway. People rarely came to pray on a regular day, but it seemed that the presence of the high-ranking church members was inspiring people to become closer to God. Now, he was faced with the judgment of the crucifix in the front of the room. Even warmed by the light of so many prayers, his stern, judging gaze pierced through the glow.

"I'm doing this for you." He whispered.

It made Juste realize just how much he had changed over the last weeks. If someone from his past life were to see him now, they'd barely recognize him. He wore the same peasant-brown clothes as the others in the village did, was covered in dust and injuries and grime, and was sitting in a small chapel, watching over a captured witch. This was what God had planned for him. This was what He wanted.

Taking a deep breath, he made his way towards the back of his church. He pulled the wagon gently along behind him, realizing that inside, its rancid smell became much more potent. Hopefully Père Fournier wouldn't say anything about it.

Upon reaching the room where she would be staying, all that he saw initially was darkness. It was only when his eyes adjusted to it that the cage came into view. It was the same one they had used to contain the Handless Witch so many years ago, or so Père Fournier had told him. It was strange to imagine him trapped behind it. It was cold, and somewhat damp, and he knew it would disrupt the witch's sleep, but it was what he needed to do in order to stay safe.

He pulled the wagon the rest of the way into the dark room, and tossed the witch's crutches onto the ground. They dropped with a clatter much louder than he had anticipated, which set the witch into motion.

She stirred slowly. "Was I asleep?" It was spoken in an unnaturally peaceful voice, like she hadn't remembered where she was yet.

"Yes." He said as he opened the door to the cage. Its key was made of large, rusting iron that scraped against his hands.

"Of course you would let me spend my final moments asleep." She turned and faced the ceiling of the room. "I guess it was peaceful at least. I had a dream that there was a fire. Any ideas as to what that means?"

"Studying the meaning of dreams is the stuff of witches." He replied uneasily. It seemed like somewhere in the process of being taken away by him, she'd lost all of her fear.

Maybe it was a coping mechanism, or maybe it was her giving up, but it was unsettling to watch.

When she saw the cage, her eyes widened just a little bit. She was nervous.

"Don't ask me when the others will be here." Juste said, inferring her next question. "If you want, I can keep you company until then."

Petime shrugged, shifting back into her unbothered state. "If you want."

Juste said nothing more, and instead moved on to lifting her out of the wagon and into the cage. He had to shake off the unnerving feeling that he was getting from doing so. Something felt like it was about to go wrong.

As he was preparing to shut the cage's door, the sound of the main doors opening nearly gave him a heart attack. His instinct turned out to be correct. In a panic, he slammed the door to the cage shut, earning a disgruntled look from the witch.

"Juste?" Père Fournier called out. "Are you here?"

"I am!" He replied, peeking his head out the door into the hallway. The light seemed nearly blinding after being so long in the dark. "And I think you'll like what I've brought home!"

Once he popped his head back into the room, he listened to the group of footsteps get increasingly closer before eventually reaching the room. The look on Père Fournier's told Juste everything that he needed to know.

"I see that you managed to do it." He spoke with a tone that sounded almost like it had a note of disappointment.

Juste had an unreasonable desire to test Père Fournier's patience. "Did you not have faith in my abilities?"

"Did you train him to have such an attitude?" One of

the members standing behind Père Fournier peeked over his shoulder.

"That was entirely his own doing." Père Fournier uttered through gritted teeth.

"So, what happens now? Does she get a trial?" Juste enjoyed the displeasure he had caused. It was powerful knowing that they couldn't belittle him when he'd completed his mission. However, he knew an embarrassingly small amount about how the process would go.

The group laughed, including the witch, which Juste's face to flush bright red. He could understand the priests, but his captive too?

"A trial!" One of Les Saints Chevaliers chuckled, wiping a tear away from his eye. "I must say I think that's the funniest thing that I've heard all night!" He paused to catch his breath. "And that is saying something, because I saw that peasant girl's family trying to entertain."

Juste peeked back through the door into the darkness, seeing the witch. He knew that the comment would affect her, so he tried to give a small reassurance, but she didn't see. She had taken on a horrified expression, and grabbed into the sides of her skirt, as if compressing them into nothing would ease her pain.

"I think that you should leave her family alone. They weren't part of this." Juste commented. "We hunt witches, not their families."

The amusement faded from the man's face, and he slipped into a much more ominous tone. "Be careful, if you speak too much like that, God will start to look down on you too. You are not immune."

"He speaks the truth." Père Fournier chimed in. "Be wary of how you act around here."

Juste bit his tongue, knowing when he needed to stop. He wanted to say more, but he didn't have *that* much power yet.

"Speaking of which, I'm going to speak with the witch in private." Père Fournier said.

Before Juste could protest, he was being pushed out of the room.

CHAPTER FORTY-FIVE
Petime

Petime sat with her back to the iron cage, hands still bound, but now being surrounded with a ring of salt as well as a ring of holy water. Once everyone else had left the room, Père Fournier immediately accessed some secret stash of holy water and salt that he'd had hidden in the walls. It was a precaution, no doubt, but a pointless one.

Petime sighed and leaned back against the bars of the cage, waiting for the next thing to come. She'd been in there for a while now, and as much as she didn't want to admit it, was resigned to the idea that she wouldn't be escaping any time soon. The thought that Camille and Adrian at least were safe in the tunnels was her only solace. She glanced at her crutches, which were sitting in the corner of the room surrounded by their own circles of salt and holy water. It would have been laughable had she had the energy.

Despite the irony though, a part of her also ached to be with them again. Being without her crutches for too long had started to make her increasingly anxious. She had worked so hard to make them, and the idea that they would be left to waste made her furious. If she could, she would have reached for them through the bars of the cage, but Père Fournier warned her that if she disrupted the salt circle in any way that her fingers would burn off, so it was best not to break that illusion of a barrier quite yet.

She wished that Georges had been willing to teach her lockpicking before she was kicked out of the society. She'd asked him to show it to her a few times, but he'd never actually explained to her how it worked. All she knew is that it involved sticking a small piece of metal into the lock. As she continued to look out, she noticed the sound of soft laughter coming from Père Fournier.

"What are you looking at?" Petime tried to appear unbothered by his presence.

"I'm just enjoying seeing you finally put in your place." He walked closer so he was able to look down at her. "Didn't I tell you that I would win?"

His laugh made her feel sick to her stomach. "And yet you're still here with me."

"Just for one more little chat, nothing more." The priest dusted the remaining salt off of his hands. "I promise that after that, I won't bother you again."

Petime realized that he was enjoying seeing her reactions to his words, so she made sure to keep a straight face moving forward. "You don't know, I might escape yet." If there was anything that would give her the motivation to, it would be getting away from *him*.

"Oh, are you expecting help from your friends?" Père Fournier crouched down to be at eye-level with her. "The friends that ran off into the woods like cowards? Juste told me that one of them was injured pretty badly, so they won't be coming back if they know what's good for them."

Even though Petime could tell that he was just trying to get a rise out of her, it took a surprising amount of strength to keep a level head. Juste probably hadn't hesitated to share the story of their battle, which meant that the priest knew all about her embarrassing capture. Thankfully, she was able to bite her tongue for the time being. She would save her mean words for Juste later.

"You're finally getting better at my little game." He stood back up, returning to his pacing. "For that, I'll give you a little reward."

Whatever the "reward" was, Petime didn't want it. It brought up a sense of disgust in her so deep that she couldn't help but move to the far side of the cage, getting as far as possible from Père Fournier. "What is your business with Juste anyway?" Petime faced towards the wall. "You two seem strangely coordinated."

"Still so concerned about the business of others, witch. Even though it no longer matters, you still act as though you care." He paused to inspect her. "You really are interesting. Both you and that little boy."

"Care to explain?" It was strange to hear Père Fournier refer to Juste as a little boy. Even though he acted childish, he still was more than that, but if she were to disagree Père Fournier would stop talking. She'd managed to keep him going for this long, and this was her opportunity to get more information. If not for the benefit of telling the others, for the benefit of knowing the reason behind her death. "There would be no consequence to telling a dead girl your secrets, and I know how much you love to talk."

"I don't deny it." He grinned. "I suppose that I can

share just a few of my plans."

Petime returned the smile, playing along. At minimum, for all the time that he spoke, it was still time that she was alive. She leaned against the bars of the cage, knowing that if she was able to get him started on a tangent, it would be a while before he stopped.

"My plan is quite genius, really. It goes far beyond just you and Juste. Ever since Les Saints Chevaliers stopped working under the king two years ago, members have slowly been leaving our ranks. There is a lack of interest from the younger generations, but Juste however has presented me with an opportunity."

"He's definitely gullible enough to fall for anything." Pettime muttered.

"You're bold to say such a thing, but you aren't incorrect. I needed someone who could serve as a figurehead, or more accurately, a puppet."

If she wasn't sick to her stomach before all of this, she certainly was now. The idea of using someone as a puppet, even Juste, was wrong.

"Alongside him, I will bring in a new generation to Les Saints Chevaliers. A generation that is loyal to me, and will follow my orders above all else." He continued. "And if you're wondering what the first of those orders might be, it will be to get rid of your damned tunnels."

Petime tried to hold her composure, but she was sure that Père Fournier could see her reaction.

"They're already dwindling, but Les Saints Chevaliers will only stop once they are eradicated entirely. Only once every witch is dead, will our job be done. Me and a close friend of mine have been working to make sure that that happens." Père Fournier smiled.

Part of her wondered why she was still trying to buy time at this point. She knew that Camille and Adrian weren't coming back, but something told her to keep holding out, even if just for a moment longer. Now though, she knew she needed to find the others and tell them this information. She had been prepared to die, but if her life was at stake anyways, what was to say that she would go down without a fight?

"Who is your accomplice?" She asked. Hopefully this would get him onto another tangent.

"So wonderful that you would ask. He is the leader of Les Saints Chevaliers!" Père Fournier said as if she would recognize him. "Of course, he didn't start out that way, but someone had to fill in for the king after he left us. He is a longtime friend of mine. We go all the way back to when I still lived in Paris. His name is Guilliaume Gramont."

Petime's mood snapped from one of terror into trying to hold back laughter. "His name is Guillaume? That's unfortunate."

"I'd take his name more seriously, if I were you." Père Fournier warned. "He's on his way here as we speak. And he'll be the one to light the flame of your pyre."

The surprise must have shown on Petime's face, because Père Fournier smiled. He was back to winning his game. She had expected something bad, but nothing like being burned at the stake. It would be difficult to escape, but now there was a new name and new information being revealed to her. At the very least, she'd need to convey a message.

The priest still had more to say though, and wasted no time in continuing his monologue. "This burning will mark the beginning of the new era. We have everything in place. We've got a new leader, a new face to rise the ranks, and a fresh victory. With that, we can escape from the rubble that the king left us in and rise to a new golden age. Just think about it, witch, your death will cause people from across the country to join our ranks!"

She didn't want to think about it. While it was good to receive the information, the amount that she needed to retain was also quickly spiraling out of her control, and it was hard to balance with maintaining emotional control.

"Poor little witch. I'm sure that you thought you were special, but you're not. You're no one. You're nothing but a girl missing a leg and carrying out The Devil's wishes." He spat.

"You've mistaken me. I am a girl who had nothing else to lose." It was easy to keep arguing. "You've never known a moment of such desperation in your life."

"You're right. I never have, and I never will, because God's light shines down upon me. I'm far from you, tangled up in your mess of curses. I exist for a reason, and God knows it. If I dare say it, destroying you is part of that purpose." Père Fournier raised his hands, as if he were in prayer. His comments were quickly becoming more personal.

"If that is truly what you were meant to do, then I pity you. What an awful fate." Pity. The word was being tossed around so much between her and the church, but what right did either of them have to bestow it? She stared at her crutches which remained just out of reach.

"I'm going to leave you with Juste for the time being. I'm sure that you'd prefer to spend your time with someone that you know more… personally." Père Fournier chuckled, opening the door back up to the room. There was a moment where light flooded in, then she returned to the overwhelming, dark silence.

CHAPTER FORTY-SIX
Juste

Juste wondered what Père Fournier and the witch were speaking about as he waited outside the door. He didn't know what Père Fournier had to say, but if it was anything like his usual rants, he didn't envy the witch for being subjected to it. The other men were lingering in the main room praying. None of them seemed to be bothered by the crucifix, which was strange to him. They had asked if he wanted to pray alongside them, but he declined, not wanting to be under its gaze for the second time tonight. He didn't have a need to gain status with them anyway because he had his own plans in the working. Even if Père Fournier intended for him to be a figurehead, he was going to become so much more than that. Without a doubt, he was going to become the best leader that they had ever seen.

His focus was conflicted though, because as he'd been waiting for Père Fournier to emerge again from the witch's room, he overheard the conversation between the other members of Les Saints Chevaliers. They spoke in hushed voices, but he made out the words "leader" and "Gramont". It was the same thing that he'd heard before, but now it was easier to eavesdrop.

Leaning nonchalantly against the cobbled walls, he was trying his hardest to listen to what they had to say, but it seemed like even though they were talking, nothing important was coming out. No details, no complaints, no anything. No matter what happened though, it sounded like this could be his chance to finally escape the wretched village. If the leader was involved with this, he would be the perfect stepping stone for Juste to make it back to Paris.

Juste's eavesdropping concluded when he heard footsteps approaching the door, so he readjusted his position leaning against the wall. Even if the others couldn't see him, he had no doubt that Père Fournier would be able to tell that Juste was listening to them.

Père Fournier opened the door and pushed past him with a scowl that was worse than usual. "You'd better not mess this up," He grumbled. "There should be supplies in the secret room."

Juste flinched. He didn't dare ask where or what the supplies were, because that would only make him even more sour. The witch had a talent for annoying people, but Juste was surprised that she'd even managed to get to the priest.

He moved the table sitting in front of the painting aside and opened the door to the secret room. It was always a sight to see the large painting pull away from the wall. Thankfully, the instructions Père Fournier gave became clear when it opened. Sitting right at the front of the tunnel down were a length of rope, pitch, and a knife. He was supposed to prepare the witch to be burned. He ignored the voice inside of him telling him that this was wrong. It was only The Devil trying to play his tricks.

Picking everything up in one scoop, he held everything

between his arms and his chest as he made his way back into the witch's room. Upon entry, he was waiting for one of her snappy remarks towards him, but was surprised with silence. He couldn't see initially because of everything in his hands, but once he set it down, he found that she had somehow managed to get a hold of one of her crutches from across the room, and was reaching out with the first to pull the second towards her.

Juste gasped. "What do you think you're doing?!"

There was a clatter of wood and the witch sat quickly back up against the wall of her cage. "Nothing."

Juste kicked the crutch away from her. "Nothing?"

"I am just sitting in my cage. I don't know what else you think I'd be doing." The witch shrugged.

"You are infuriating."

"Likewise." The witch turned her gaze to the pitch and rope. "What are those for?"

"Tying you… to the pyre." He choked on the words as they left his throat, although he couldn't figure out why.

He started the process, figuring that if he could make it as quick as possible, he could escape from being alone in the room with her sooner. The Devil was trying his hardest to convince him that he shouldn't do this, and he didn't want to see whose will, or lack thereof would triumph in this situation.

All that he needed to do before bringing her into the room was tie her up, and cover the rope with a layer of pitch. The rest would be up to Gramont as part of the ceremony.

Juste knew that this was just the tedious part of the process, though. If it were anything the others were interested in, the priests would have done it themselves. Maybe he had decided to join the society because there was no other choice, but that didn't make him gullible. He started wrapping the rope. Soon enough, he would be the one calling them gullible when he outranked them.

The witch remained oddly quiet throughout the process. Even after putting on his gloves and smearing the pitch, she didn't struggle as much as he thought she would. It must have been a blessing from God, which meant that finally, he was starting to see the benefits of his devotion.

He stood, admiring his work for a moment. He had wound the rope around her several times and created an almost perfectly even coat of pitch. "Alright, stand up."

She sighed.

"Stand!"

"Juste." She put emphasis on every word. "*I am missing a leg.*"

"God." This time he wasn't mortified at his incompetence, just annoyed at the witch. "Is it *this* hard for you to live all the time?" He picked her up again.

"Do you ever consider your words before speaking them aloud?" She questioned, looking up at him from the floor.

Juste ignored the question, and picked her up again from the floor. On the way out, he kicked the witch's crutches even further towards the side of the room before he left, which sent her into a defiant wiggle.

"What are you doing with those?!" She wriggled around, trying to see what had happened. "Didn't I say that the priests would want those?! Use them for something! I don't care for what, just don't let them burn!"

"Calm down." Juste grumbled. "If you keep that attitude up, I'll ask them to burn the crutches along with you." He found it strange how protective she was of them.

"Please, I can't let all of me die." She said, voice breaking.

Juste almost wanted to agree with her, but caught

himself. "Why does this matter to you so much anyway? You'll be dead, won't you?"

"It matters because I am proud of them. They can help so many other people. Don't we both want to help people?" She met her gaze with his.

He looked away, refusing to acknowledge the fact that he was losing this battle. "Fine. I'll hide them in a closet somewhere."

The witch smiled surprisingly genuinely. "Thank you."

It was unsettling to see her even somewhat pleased with anything he'd done. They'd been fighting for so long, but this was her bargaining to the last of her ability. It made everything that was happening truly feel real. As soon as he left this room, he would really be greeted by the leader of Les Saints Chevaliers, who would then take the witch from him and really burn her. It was all actually happening.

Juste set down the witch and hid the crutches in the closet like he'd promised, knowing that she wouldn't be satisfied unless she saw it happen herself. Only after that did he take her into the main room of the church.

Juste realized that they had rearranged some of the furniture while he was working with the witch. The pews had all been pushed to the side and were lining the front wall of the church. It gave them more space while also standing as a blockade to the main entrance of the church. There was a large stake in the room's center surrounded by piles of scrap wood and sticks. Juste was still confused on how this would remain discreet, but Père Fournier had done this before and was yet to be caught, so Juste was sure that he had his methods.

When the others took notice of him, they scoffed at the way that he was holding the witch. All except for a new figure whose face and body were masked by a white cloak rather than a red one, whose trims were lined with gold. It had to be Gramont.

When Gramont walked towards Juste, he had an air of confidence that anyone would be intimidated by. All eyes in the room were drawn to his slow move forward. He couldn't see Gramont's face from through the hood, but hundreds of images of powerful-looking men filled his imagination. He took one look at Juste, then the witch, then gestured for Père Fournier to take her.

Père Fournier took the opportunity eagerly, showing no hesitation in taking the witch from Juste's arms. It was a relief to be free of the weight, but it also made him somewhat nervous. No one else in the room knew her as well as he did, so no one else in the room would know the best way to handle her.

While Père Fournier tied the witch to the pyre, Gramont began to speak. "Welcome, brothers. I know that today marks the entrance into a new era." His voice was loud, and projected throughout the entire church. Juste could only take notes.

Even through the veil of the mask, Juste could hear the smile in Gramont's voice. "Are we ready to burn a witch?"

CHAPTER FORTY-SEVEN
Georges

Georges walked alongside Camille and Elise towards the village's church keeping a quick pace. When witch burnings occurred, it wasn't usually long after sunset. It wasn't good in terms of their timing, but the growing darkness helped them to stay hidden as they traveled through the village. Barely anyone was outside this late into the night.

As he passed by all of the houses that he used to know, he realized how much had changed since he was gone. Beyond the new things built, the old things had changed too, like the dirt path that had finally been replaced with stone, or the bush that he'd remembered as a sprout being fully grown. The village that remained in his memory no longer existed in reality.

"Are you alright?" Elise asked, taking his hand. Her other hand held a basket filled to the brim with freshly-oiled torches.

Georges glanced out at his surroundings again. "It's

just… strange coming back here."

"I can only imagine the memories that must be revisiting you now." Elise sighed. "But we won't be here for long, I promise. We have a job to do."

Georges nodded.

He refocused on making it to the church. For a while he'd been basing his directions off of a combination of memory and the faint outline of the church spire in the distance. It was humble, but its outline was still legible against the darkening sky. It had been growing closer until now, when the building came into full view. He realized that this was the one place in the village that had remained exactly how he remembered it.

"I'm surprised you could still find your way here." Camille remarked.

"You'd be surprised at what stays with you." Georges smiled through the pain of his memory. "Right now though, all that matters is getting to that church."

The only thing between them and the building now was the town center. It was the only part of their journey where they would be truly exposed, so they'd need to be careful. After making sure that no one would be there to see them, Georges took off running first, and Elise followed quickly after. Camille followed a few moments behind. When they were around halfway through the circle, they heard a voice. It sounded oddly familiar to Georges, but he couldn't quite pinpoint why. Without thinking, he stopped to listen to it.

"Georges! What are you doing?" Elise half-whispered half-shouted. She had already made it to the other side.

Georges whipped back towards Elise to refocus, but almost as soon as he had, the voice called out again, clearer.

"Camille!" it shouted. "Camille, please come home!"

Camille gasped a little bit too loud, quickly covering

her mouth with her hand afterwards. She'd just revealed their location.

"Who is that?" Georges shot in the same whisper-yell that Elise had used?

"My mother." .

Georges wanted to question it, but he didn't have the time.

"Camille?" The voice said again, much closer. "Georges?"

Georges turned around. He knew the voice now, and sure enough, and a tired, breathless Amelie stood before him.

Her face was much older, worn by time and age, but he still recognized it instantly. Both were too shocked for words. Out of all of the people in the village he'd want to see, it would be anyone other than her.

"You were calling out for…" Georges started, but trailed away connecting the two dots.

"My daughter." she nodded. "Yes."

"Dear Lord, Amelie…"

Amelie didn't address the question. "May I ask why she's with my dead husband in the middle of the night? I thought that The Devil took you."

"Don't call me that." Georges scowled. "And I'd rather not address what happened that night."

"God, are those torches you're holding?" Amelie stepped closer to investigate the basket that was in Elise's hand, but she pulled it out of Amelie's sight instinctively.

"*You're* Amelie?" Elise looked her up and down. "I would have imagined a better-looking woman with how he mourned you."

Georges looked back, clearly embarrassed. "Elise!"

The three of them had all made it into a position to stare

at Amelie with their own versions of confusion and disgust. She took a few disgruntled steps backwards. "I apologize, I just wasn't expecting… all of this, when I was looking for her." She turned towards Camille. "Speaking of which, you are coming with me right now. Do not look back at those agents of Satan."

Camille didn't move. "They're not agents of Satan, Maman, they're doing the right thing!"

"I'm warning you." She cautioned.

Georges looked between the two of them. He realized that Camille was old. Almost too old.

"Camille, how old are you?" Georges muttered.

"Georges." Amelie's tone was daggers.

If Georges had guessed before, but now he was almost certain of it. "No, let her answer the question. Camille, how old are you?"

"Seventeen." She admitted.

"Amelie, don't tell me…" Georges uttered. He didn't have the time to be doing this right now.

Amelie sighed, pressing her fingers into her forehead before speaking. "She is yours, yes. All those years ago I couldn't risk her being ridiculed for being the daughter of a witch, so I did what I had to for the both of us." She turned to Georges. "You have to understand! It was for the good of everyone!"

Georges didn't know how to react. She'd admitted it herself. He was standing in front of his own daughter as they spoke. A girl that he'd thought of as a stranger, the girl that he was supposed to help raise and form into a fully-fledged adult was standing in front of him. Somehow, beyond all odds, they had found each other through the mess.

"Do you see how comfortable a life she has been able to live because of my actions? She takes piano lessons, she's taken etiquette classes, she's got everything that she needs to be married to a wealthy man and live a comfortable life!" Amelie defended herself.

"I never liked any of those things! Couldn't you see that?" Camille cried out. Georges could see the tears forming in her eyes even only under the moonlight.

"They were for your own good!"

"What good could it be if I wasn't happy." Camille lowered her voice, but her tone still cut like daggers. "Maman, I thought that you had sacrificed everything for *me*, but you had really sacrificed everything for yourself."

"I see that even after every attempt I have made to save you from your fate, you still manage to be your father's daughter. If that's what you want, and that's what makes you happy, then so be it, but when you get wrapped up in The Devil's plans, I can't say that I'll still be there to comfort you."

Camille didn't reply, and was left ready to cry in the middle of the clearing, exposed.

Elise rushed over to give Camille a hug.

Amelie turned towards him. "Now you're letting this random woman hug my daughter? *Our* daughter?"

Elise whipped around with a vengeance, still holding Camille as she cried. "I'd urge you to leave if you knew what was good for you."

Georges held up a hand for Elise to hold back. This was his fight. "Amelie, I don't know what you have done over these years, but truthfully, I don't care. You lied to me for your own benefit, saying now that it was for the sake of our child, yet I see her here crying under your care." Georges made sure that he said each word as clearly and as calmly as possible. He wanted the last time he spoke to her to leave an impression. "The "random woman" is my *wife*. What you were supposed

to be, Amelie, but you never became. She has stood by my side
since the time that I spent months on end going from church
to church, only to be met with flames and hostility. She is not
random, and I agree with her. You would do best if you were
on your way now. If Camille chooses to go with you, I will not
fight, but I think she has made her decision."

Amelie started walking towards Camille and Elise
silently.

"Maman, no!" Camille stepped in front of Elise to
protect her. "Leave them alone!"

Georges grabbed a torch from Elise's basket, and struck
a stone to light it. Amelie flinched at the sight of the fire. It was
a tempting thought to make her pay for everything she'd done
to him, to make her feel the same way that he had every time a
church rejected him, to make her feel the same fear that he did,
but he was smarter than to do anything yet.

He turned in the other direction, and walked in the
direction of the church.

Amelie realized what he was going to do, and started
running forwards. "Lord, Satan truly has possessed you!"

He kept walking closer.

Camille pulled away from Elise's hug and turned
towards her mother. "Maman, if you were to choose between
me and the church right now, who would you pick?"

Amelie stared at her for a moment, then shook her head.
"I'm going to get help."

Georges sighed, then tossed the torch against the wall
of the church. It was clear that Amelie had made her decision,
so it was crucial that they work fast.

After Amelie had run, Elise and Camille lit more
torches and set them against the edge of the wall. The progress
started out slow, but once the flames began eating at the

wooden annex of the building, they crept faster and faster along the walls. Georges looked at Camille and Elise, his true family.

Camille, turned around as well, and gave an affirming nod. This was what she wanted to do. This was where she wanted to be. Georges had gained yet another family member, and now they were working together to save each other.

CHAPTER FORTY-EIGHT
Petime

Petime looked out over the church from her spot on the pyre. She had now been tied up properly, and the group of priests had formed a semicircle around who she assumed was their leader. He had been speaking so long that Petime had been able to move past her anxiety and into pure boredom.

"We're going to witness the burning of this witch, whose capture was greatly aided by this new member." A man who she could only guess was Gramont gestured towards Juste.

Juste didn't notice the comment. In fact, he didn't seem like he'd been processing the speech at all for a while now. He kept looking back and forth between the conversation and the top of the room. Petime had thought he was crazy at first, but slowly, there was a cloud of smoke creeping through the door of the annex and into the nave. From Juste's reaction, she realized she wouldn't be the only one burning tonight. Since the pews were along the wall and blocking the only exit to the church, a fire in the annex would trap everyone inside.

"In honor of that, I would like to give Juste the opportunity to light the fire tonight." Gramont smiled, but when he looked for a reaction, Juste was still distracted and staring at the ceiling. Petime wanted to laugh, but she wanted to see how the scene played out more, so she continued to watch silently.

Père Fournier waited for a moment, then had an outburst. "You're going to let him do such a thing with that sort of reaction?! Decision aside, I assure you that he is not experienced enough to-"

"Nonsense, Fournier. I think that he is ready enough." Gramont chuckled.

Petime had never heard anyone refer to the priest so casually. If he weren't about to light her on fire, Petime would have respected him for it. When she looked for Juste's reaction to the comment, she found him staring up at her instead. She knew that he was wondering whether or not she saw the smoke too, but she didn't give him any clue as to whether she did or didn't. It was more interesting that way.

"I think there is something that we should look at…" Juste began, but was ushered by Gramont to come up to the stake.

"Are you coming, son?" Gramont asked, still struggling to push him along. "If you're nervous I–"

"I think this place is on fire." He said abruptly.

Petime was intrigued. She rarely saw such confidence from him.

"Juste!" Père Fournier took a moment to glare before turning to Gramont. "I apologize. He doesn't know what he's talking about."

The other five men looked like they were going to get involved in the argument as well which sent Juste looking up at her again.

If she were able to shrug, she would. "I don't know what you expect me to do. I'm just here, tied to a stake." .

"Brothers, brothers! Calm down, please." Gramont raised his hands to get their attention. "Don't you want to hear the boy out?"

Père Fournier was the first to step forward, looking annoyed at the fact that they hadn't just burned her already. Strangely, he was right in a way. They didn't have time to waste, especially if the building was going to be on fire in the coming minutes. "He is simply causing a disruption for attention." Père Fournier complained. "He's always had a bit of a temper to him."

"He's not wrong!" Petime contributed, winning her the displeased stares of everyone around. "Sorry, I'll stop."

Juste was fuming, and all the other men started arguing at once, filling the room with countless conflicting voices. It continued on like that for a little while until their leader got fed up with things.

"Silence!" Gramont shouted. Only once he had everyone else's attention did he continue speaking. "Follow me, Juste, and I will give you proper repercussions myself." He glanced around at the others to make sure that there were no protests. "Brothers, you may proceed with the burning if you wish. They've lost their novelty to me."

Petime guessed that Gramont had other intentions behind separating Juste. Based on what she'd seen that night alone, he had more perception than the others. He'd caught on to Juste's small conversations with her as well as Juste's staring, so there was no doubt that he'd be able to see the smoke as well. Still, it seemed like no one else had the same thought. Juste looked genuinely surprised, and the priests seemed satisfied being told that they could still do the burning.

"I'd like to apologize for my outburst–" Juste started before being cut off by Gramont.

"Shh." Gramont chuckled. "Now, follow me."

Petime watched Juste and the cloaked figure disappear down the hallway, and along with them went her last hope of any more stalling. All she was left with now was Père Fournier and his lackeys, and none of them would show any hesitation.

From her vantage point, she was able to see Gramont and Juste sharing a quick, quiet exchange of words before disappearing behind the door into the annex. She could understand why they were escaping, but not why they would be walking *towards* the fire. Sure enough, when the door opened, there was a billow of dark smoke. What exactly was back there that was so important to them?

The next thing that her mind flickered to were her crutches. There was a brief moment of panic before she realized that the closet they'd been hidden in was part of the cobblestone portion of the building. They would likely be protected enough from the fire to at least be recognized by her family.

Père Fournier and the other five members of Les Saints Chevaliers happily took the torch that Gramont had handed off to them, and were stalking around her in a semicircle, like predators stalking their prey. Petime only smiled. If she was going to die, she could at least have the solace of knowing that she wasn't the only one.

"You know what you forgot to do?" She laughed.

Père Fournier held his hand out, signaling for the men to pause. "What?"

"You didn't sprinkle your little holy water and salt circle around me this time." She grinned. "I'd almost think that you're asking for Satan to sabotage your plans. In fact, I'm talking to him right now!"

In response to her comment, Père Fournier tossed the torch into the flames. The kindling and logs beneath her lit almost instantly ablaze. She'd been lying, but he'd certainly wasted no time in stopping her. The heat of the fire was uncomfortable, but she wanted to keep her smile for as long as possible. She knew that it would distract the men enough to be trapped by the flames.

The smoke from the annex billowed into the room in large clouds now, and licks of flames were threatening to escape through the door. It wouldn't be long before they started making their way through the pews as well, trapping the priests.It was hard to believe that despite everything happening, Père Fournier and the others still hadn't faced away from the stake long enough to notice the flames.

As the flames crept up the stake, the priests erupted into an argument about the hasty toss of the torch.

"Now, what did I tell you about tossing it in early!" one of the men shouted. "You're supposed to go on my cue!"

It was getting uncomfortably warm now. The fire was getting closer.

"She was spouting curses at us!" Père Fournier spat. "I am the highest ranking member here, and thus you should follow my orders."

"You gave us no orders!"

It was nearly at her feet. Petime closed her eyes.

"Well if she hadn't–" His voice cut off into a pained gasp.

There was a sickening thud paired with it. There was no way that the fire could have made a sound like *that*. Upon opening her eyes, Petime was greeted by Camille, Georges, and Elise standing in the distance. Camille waved, and pointed at Père Fournier, who was holding his hand over a knife in his shoulder.

She paused for a moment in disbelief, then started laughing. "Ha! Look at what God's blessing has done to you now!"

The others of Les Saints Chevaliers had been equally stunned, but now sprang into action, unsheathing knives from their cloaks and running towards the Georges and the others.

The pain in her feet becoming nearly unbearable quickly brought Petime back to the fact that she was still on fire. "Can someone put the fire out?" She shouted over the flames and the scuffle that had broken out. Everyone seemed to be caught up in what was one big knife battle, slashing at each other and running around the back of the nave. If someone didn't notice her soon, she'd be missing more than one leg.

"We're trying!" Elise managed to respond over the fray.

The priests were surprisingly formidable opponents in the fight, managing to dodge attacks and shuffling surprisingly quick for their age around the church. In fact, Petime didn't believe she'd ever seen anyone so wrinkly move so fast.

Thankfully, Elise managed to escape through an opening in the battle. One of the priests had stumbled over the edge of a carpet, which allowed her to sprint towards the relatively unguarded pyre. As she approached though, she was clearly at a lack of what to do.

Petime could feel the warmth starting to reach her hands; it was getting hard to breathe now. If the fire were to reach the rope tied around her, it'd be too late. "Might you think a little bit faster?" She didn't know if her voice carried over the flame, but she could only hope.

"This might be really stupid." Elise started.

"What are you going to-" Petime was cut off by Elise kicking the wood with all her strength. "Elise?!"

She let out a relieved laugh. "It worked, didn't it?"

Thankfully, from a combination of the fire burning the larger logs and a lot of the material being smaller, the part of the fire that Elise had kicked splintered into hundreds of smaller flames. After a few more kicks, the ground beneath her felt immensely colder thanks to the flames being smaller and more spread out. Petime let out a sigh and relaxed within the constraints of the rope. It was a feeling of relief unlike any she'd had before.

Unfortunately, though, the pieces of fiery wood scattered across the floor had gathered the attention of the others.

Elise was stuck in a cycle of looking between Petime and the gaggle of priests running towards her. "Petime, do you see anything from up there that I can use to cut your rope?"

"I've got this one!" Camille shouted from a little way away.

Camille threw an unexpected knife at her attacker and made her way to the altar, practically bouncing from the enjoyment of catching him off guard. Camille had her eyes set on a ridiculously ornate, but sharp, candleholder. Petime silently praised Père Fournier's love for everything that shimmered. Once Camille had secured a firm grasp on the holder, she ran back towards Petime. Georges and Elise were covering her, fighting back-to-back.

Camille approached the pyre, then lifted the holder carefully. At first, only a few threads of the rope snagged on the holder, but after a little bit of sawing on her part, one thread snapped, then another, until the whole rope broke.

"Thank you." Petime sighed as Camille cut away the

ropes. She'd never said the words more genuinely in her life.

Camille smiled. "I owed you one."

Petime tumbled to the floor, and Camille ran back to join the fighting. Petime was alone now, but at least she could focus on untangling herself from the rest of the rope. It was mixed with pitch, which made it a nightmare to try and pry away, but with enough work she could manage to pull it off in chunks.

The others looked like they had dealt with at least one of the priests, which she was glad to see. Georges had also managed to bring a sword along with him all the way to the church, so he was swinging freely while the priests tried to fight back with their knives. Camille was going after the others with a dagger that resembled a butcher's knife. Both were clearly winning their respective fights, and both had never looked happier than when they were working side-by-side. The options for places where she'd be of use were very limited, especially since she didn't have her crutches. She noticed that Elise was busy looking for a way out of the church though, and that was something that Petime could help with.

Petime crawled over to Elise and tugged on the bottom of her skirt to get her attention. "There has to be a way out through there." She pointed towards the door. "I saw two people leave and never come back."

Elise nodded. Discussing logistics a little bit further. Their words, though brief and concise, still carried just as much weight as any other conversation. They were working out the problem *together.* Petime looked along with Elise towards the door. She would need her crutches to do anything useful, so it was the logical next step to go get them.

"Go fight." Petime eventually said. "I'll look for the way out along with my crutches."

"Are you sure?" Elise glanced at Georges and Camille.

"I'm sure." Petime nodded.

Elise didn't hesitate, and ran off to take care of the other priests. It would be better like this anyway. If they killed the priests faster, then they could leave faster as well.

Petime began towards the hallway of the annex. The smoke got worse the closer that she got, but it wasn't nearly as bad as it would be if they were standing. Strangely enough, the hallway itself seemed like it was the last to be affected by the flames, but the side rooms all appeared to be beyond help. *Good riddance* she thought.

She crawled towards the closet that Juste had left her crutches in, ignoring the flames as much as possible. Strangely, it wasn't all too hard for her to do. None of the flames in the rooms were as bad as they were when she was on the pyre, so it was easy enough to make her way to the closet and grab the crutches. It felt like she was returning home as she slipped them back onto her arms. Even if she was covered in pitch, singed with the flames, and covered in sweat from the heat, she was standing. Against all odds she was standing.

"You probably think you've won." she heard a voice behind her. When she turned around, she was greeted with Père Fournier standing immediately behind her, the knife still lodged into his shoulder. There was murder in his eyes.

He tore the blade out and held it in his hands, starting his shoulder bleeding. He had to have known it was a death sentence, but he was bound to take her down along with him. As far as she knew, she was backed into a wall, so he was going to be successful at it too.

Petime screamed as he dug the blade into her shoulder. A searing pain almost as bad as the fire shot through the entire area, and she fell back to the floor.

Père Fournier staggered away himself before falling onto the floor next to her. He was quickly losing blood. "If I am to die here, it won't be alone." he mumbled.

"You should have kept the thing in your shoulder." Petime said through gritted teeth. If there was anything that she remembered from Elise's lesson, it was her warning not to remove an object from her body if she ever got stabbed.

"Who is left to come save me?" He asked Petime. "I did it, I killed her! Now, someone come save me!"

She didn't know who he was talking to for the last part, but it wasn't her. "You're seeing things." Petime commented, but he didn't pay attention. He was still too busy waiting on his nonexistent help.

Père Fournier looked like he was about to collapse, but not before a fleeting moment of realization. He looked directly into her eyes. He knew he wouldn't escape.

She didn't break eye contact with him. "God does everything for a reason."

He fell to the floor.

She didn't have time to waste and succumb to the same fate. Ignoring the pain, she stood up again. For a moment her vision blurred around the sides, but she was able to stay standing. For now at least.

She staggered back in the direction of the main room, but upon leaving, she noticed there was a hole in the wall that had never been there before. It looked strangely similar to the opening that she'd seen in the tunnels. She realized that it was how Juste and Gramont were able to escape. It was a secret door.

The smoke in the hallway was entirely unbearable now, so if they were going to leave, it had to be now. Soon enough, even the villagers would have to realize what was happening too. When she entered back into the main room, it was only Camille, Elise, and Georges. She didn't know, and definitely didn't want to ask, what had happened to the other priests. Camille gasped when she saw the knife in Petime's shoulder.

Petime chuckled as much as she could without disturbing the knife's position. "It's still better than being burned alive."

"You're so horrible!" Camille cried. "Absolutely wretched!"

Petime wanted to give Camille a hug, but it would disturb the knife in her shoulder, so she just nodded. "I am, aren't I."

Petime thought about the door behind the painting. That must have been where Juste and Gramont had left from. "I think I know a way out."

"How?" Georges asked.

"I found some sort of secret exit." Petime explained.

Elise looked around. "It might be all that we have left." She and Petime both know that all the other doors were obstructed in some way or another.

Georges shrugged. "So be it."

Camille and Elise got on either side of her to support Petime as she walked, and she took them down the hall, past the room she'd stayed in, and in front of the new exit point. Thankfully, the three of them had been able to make it before the tunnel had started burning. Although the tunnel itself was made of brick, it had wooden supports, so it would collapse soon enough. When they were escaping, Juste and Gramont had probably believed that everyone left in the building was going to die, so there was no point in covering it up. To be fair, they had certainly been close to having it right.

As the group pushed further into the tunnel, the flames

were beginning to make their way in behind them. With each step that she took, she was able to travel less, and this tunnel didn't show any signs of going anywhere, but there was no way back now.

"Look!" Camille pointed out. "There's a room up ahead!"

With a renewed sense of hope, Petime was able to muster enough strength to make it into the room relatively quickly. This one's walls were made purely of cobblestone as well, so it wouldn't collapse from the flame nearly as fast. It also felt significantly easier to breathe, meaning that it had at least a little bit more breathable air than the tunnel. Something was wrong, though. Instead of everyone being happy, there was a curtain of silence over the room.

Petime managed to turn her head to see what the others were looking at, and was greeted with a room full of torture deviced and witch hunting paraphernalia. It must have been a sort of base for Les Saints Chevaliers like the Tunnels were a base to them.

"It figures." Georges muttered.

Elise added on. "All of them… they're horrifying."

"Is this what Juste has been participating in this entire time?" Camille asked. "Now I sincerely hope our wedding isn't happening." The attempt at brightening the mood was appreciated, but no one in the group had the heart to laugh.

"That's the reality of Les Saints Chevaliers, or at least those like Fournier. He took joy in what he did." Georges said absently. "It looks like they already took everything important out of here though, so it'll be no use searching it for information."

"Information." The word reminded Petime. "I have that… but I also have a knife in my back. I would love to get that looked at." she muttered half-coherently.

"We need to get you back as soon as possible." Camille helped her forward again, although she was practically dragging Petime by this point.

There was a bookshelf clearly pushed to the side, with another tunnel leading out of it. At least they had made it easy for them.

"You all go ahead. I need to do one more thing first." Georges said, taking a torch from the wall. "I don't want anyone else finding this place."

Petime didn't hesitate at all for the chance to be out of there as quickly as possible so she began walking down the tunnel with Camille and Elise. There was a slight breeze, and the air felt cooler than it had inside, which meant that it led to the surface. That relief was the last thing that she remembered thinking.

CHAPTER FORTY-NINE
Juste

Juste trudged through the woods along with Gramont. The passage through the secret exit had been relatively quick, but their time in the woods was proving to be much longer. He realized a long time ago that they were leaving, but was too scared to ask for any more details. However the longer that they walked, the more that the fear was quickly dwindling against his need to know when they would be out of the forest.

He wondered what had happened to the witch as well. Realizing now that the fire had likely been started by her friends trying to save her, there was a chance that she was still alive. If she had made it through the incident, could he really count his job as complete?

"So," Juste finally gave in to his need for answers. "Not that I mind, but how much more woods do you think we'll be walking through?" He was proud of himself for finding a non-confrontational way around it.

"I'm surprised it took you this long to speak to me."

Gramont chuckled. He pulled down his hood as well, revealing a surprisingly warm face. Even though Juste knew he was close to the same age as Père Fournier, he looked much younger and healthier, and his smile was contagious.

"Were you waiting for me to?" Juste was surprised.

Gramont shrugged. "I simply thought that you would have more questions for me. Do you want to know who I am, or why I took you here?"

"You're Guilliaume Gramont, right?" Juste asked without thinking.

Instead of being defensive though, Gramont only smiled. "That's right! You're a lot smarter than they thought you were, aren't you?"

Finally, there was someone who was recognizing his talents.

Gramont looked off into the distance. "I have to admit that I was disappointed by Père Fournier. He thought we were such good friends, so I would have figured that he'd be at least a bit more loyal."

The comment caught Juste off guard. "Were you two not friends?"

"To him we were maybe, but to me, I'd say not."

Juste was surprised, but it made sense. It was better for people to believe that you were an ally if you were vying to become a leader.

Gramont sighed wistfully, then returned to Juste. "They didn't believe you, and with such a keen mind at that. It is truly a shame that they were the ones I trusted to mentor you."

The ones that *he* trusted? Juste wondered. "I thought that it was Père Fournier's decision to take me in?"

"I've had my eyes on you for far longer than that. I was going to take you in sooner, but the opportunity presented itself for you to stay in Edris for a while." Gramont explained. "So I went along with it."

Juste didn't know how to reply. "So… none of my circumstances were an accident?"

Gramont held his fingers to his chin, like he was stroking an imaginary beard. "I suppose you could think of it like that. I think of it more as making the best of what you're given."

Juste thought for a moment. "Then what of the fire? Will you do the same thing?"

"I'll admit that the fire wasn't planned, but it was an intriguing incident to occur. Do you think that there may have been a correspondence between that and the witch?" Gramont spent a moment lost in thought, but didn't wait for a response. "As for the others, they'll most likely die. It is unfortunate to me, but I'm sure that you'll find it an enjoyable thought."

"What do you mean?" Juste didn't know what to think of his answer.

"Well, they've wronged you, right?"

If this was what being treated as an equal was like in Les Saints Chevaliers, he almost wanted to go back to the way that Père Fournier would treat him. While he liked having the information, Gramont's brutal honesty was becoming increasingly off putting to him, especially since they were alone in the woods together. If he made one wrong move, he could just as easily be Gramont's next victim.

Gramont must have noticed the silence. "Do you have any other questions?"

"Will I still be able to become a member of Les Saints Chevaliers?" Juste asked. Part of him wanted to take this opportunity to escape. He had been freed from his chains in Edris, but now he was threatening to become tethered to

Gramont as well.

"Do you want to be?"

Juste swallowed his doubts. This was what God had wanted. "Yes."

"You'll be training with me from now on then. In Paris." Gramont pushed past a wall of foliage.

Paris. That was where Juste's family lived. He didn't think he'd see the day when he'd be returning there so soon, but the idea of it comforting. As long as he had Gramont by his side, he would be able to conquer anything that he put his mind to. Maybe it wouldn't be so bad to remain with Les Saints Chevaliers after all.

Juste had noticed the forest thinning out, and as the two of them escaped the last bit of foliage, they were greeted by a carriage and coachman waiting for their return. It must have cost a fortune to hire the man to wait there overnight for them, but it spoke volumes as to what Gramont was capable of. For the first time in a while, Juste was returning to the noble lifestyle that he had been used to.

Gramont jumped into the carriage immediately, giving a small wave to the coachman, and gestured for him to follow. When Juste sat in the seat, he was welcomed with the familiar pillowyness of his life from before the accident. He was going home.

The carriage started off down the path into the woods, and soon enough, they were on their way back to Paris. The village of Edris was shrinking off into the distance, barely visible through the trees. He didn't know what had become of Camille, Adrian, and the people at the church, but Gramont seemed satisfied enough with him that it didn't matter. He had his answer now. As long as they didn't cause any more issue to him, he counted his mission as complete.

Now it was time to be heading into his next.

CHAPTER FIFTY
Camille

Camille and Elise laid Petime onto the floor of the tunnel. Somewhere along the way, she had passed out from the stress of the night she'd had. Camille was worried, but Elise said that as long as they made it to the tunnels soon, she would be alright. Now that they were in, all that was left was to do their best to heal her. As much as she wanted to trust Elise though, she had a certain degree of worry in her voice that made Camille worried.

"Are you back?" Adrian's voice called from the other room.

No one replied. They were all too focused on Petime, who was deathly pale in the light of the tunnels. Georges and Elise worked together to get a blanket laid out onto the floor.

"Can someone get me some cotton and some honey?" Elise said, crouching over Petime. She was beginning to sweat. That couldn't be a good sign.

"I can." Georges quickly made his way over to the medicine shelf and grabbed the supplies Elise had asked for.

Once Elise had them, she worked hard to get the knife

out of Petime's shoulder and stop the bleeding. She was quick and clean with her work, which made Camille wonder just how many times she'd done something similar. If every member of Les Saints Chevaliers carried a knife, there were bound to be a good deal of stab wounds.

Elise sat back on her knees after a while of working, letting out a deep breath that she'd been holding in for far too long. "I've done everything I can. She's still alive for the time being, just exhausted."

"And fighting off a stab wound." Georges added.

"Can we try to be positive with this?" Elise grumbled.

Camille stayed quiet. She'd always thought of Petime as someone who was invincible, but seeing her like this made her worried. She was standing here, her only major complaint being that she felt tired, while Petime laid, fighting for her life after sacrificing herself for their sake. It didn't feel fair.

Georges noticed her, and put his hand on her shoulder. "If she can survive losing a leg, I'm sure she can survive this."

Camille didn't know how to feel about him being her father. She didn't know how to feel about any of it honestly. If she were to go back home, she was sure that her parents would never let her out of the house again, and she wasn't technically supposed to be here to begin with. It seemed like with any option she chose, she was still left with the question of whether or not she truly belonged there.

"I think I know something that might cheer you up." Georges smiled deviously.

Before she could retaliate, Camille watched as he made his way over to a cabinet on the other side of the room, much to Elise's dismay.

"Georges, no. She needs to rest." Elise glared at him as he started looking through various bottles on the cabinet.

"Georges!"

Once he'd rummaged through the shelf enough to find what he was looking for, he reemerged holding a sack of some sort of rancid-looking pebbles.

"What are those?" Camille asked.

Elise was sitting with her face in her hands. "Not for him to be using!"

Georges, however, decided to be useful. "They're smelling salts derived from deer horns. Smelling them tends to have some… strong reactions."

Elise sighed. "Strong is definitely a way to put it."

Georges laughed, then crouched down next to Peitme. As soon as he held them next to Petime's nose, her eyes shot open and she started coughing. Camille knew that it probably wasn't the *best* thing for Georges to have done, but she could feel it lift a weight off of the room.

An exasperated "What the hell!?" was the only thing Petime managed to say at first. It took a moment longer for her to truly process the situation that was unfolding. "Since when were we back here? The last thing I remember is that secret tunnel." She paused. "Also, what did I just inhale?" She cleared her throat one final time.

Elise sighed. "Smelling salts. You can thank Georges."

Petime stared at her. "Smelling salts? I fainted?" She looked around, as if some context clue would answer the question for her. "When?"

"Do you remember anything of the walk home?" Elise raised an eyebrow.

"Fair enough." Petime worked to sit herself up. "Speaking of, what did you do to my shoulder? It hurts like the Devil ."

"Honey and gauze. It's significantly better than the

knife that was in there beforehand though!" Elise was trying to keep positive about it. "We'll need to be changing it out occasionally though, and you'll be conscious when that happens, so be prepared for it to be hurting a lot more."

"It can't hurt more than getting my leg cut off can it?" Petime suggested hopefully.

Elise smiled. "You can tell me when it happens. Speaking of, I think you should turn around."

"There's gauze in my shoulder though–" Petime strained to turn herself around while sitting on the floor. "Camille! You're here! I would give you a proper hug but I'm still covered in… well a lot."

"You'll just owe me double later." Camille laughed. Although the sentiment of a hug was nice, she couldn't agree more with wanting to be touched by anything other than the pitch, blood, honey, and smoke covered Petime.

There was a pause in the room, a collective realization that the battle was over. All of the stress that had been building for so long was finally over. There were no priests hunting them down, there were no parents keeping her inside, there were no secrets. There was only recovery from this point onwards.

The question of *what now* started to fill their mind instead. Recovery also took work, and they'd made quite a few messes tonight. The church was burnt down, and irrevocable words had been exchanged. None of which would be easy things to avoid the repercussions of. Camille still didn't feel like she had a home.

"I don't think I can go back." Camille said finally. "I don't want to go back to my family."

"What?!" Adrian's voice gasped from behind her.

Camille whipped around, startled by his presence. He

wasn't even supposed to be sitting up for another three days.

"Does no one care for their own wellbeing and recovery here?" Elise said, exasperated.

"You're wonderful darling, but they'll still survive. Let them talk." Georges comforted her. "We've had a big night."

Camille appreciated Georges, and took the chance to collect herself and continue what she was saying. "I know that if I return to them now, I'll probably never be allowed to see the light of day again, or I'll be married off to some other man who turns out to be more of a lunatic then Juste." Camille noticed a pointed snicker from Petime.

After she had finished laughing at the Juste comment, Petime chimed in as well. "If you're staying here, I will stay with you. As much as I would like to return home, I don't think that there is a place for me in that village anymore either, especially if they think we're all dead."

Camille hadn't even considered that much. She was sure that her mother would come up with some excuse or another, but it would be a lot of work to maintain such a story.

"You would do that for me Petime?" Camille was overjoyed at the idea of being able to live a life where they didn't have to work around the stigma of an entire village.

"I wouldn't just leave my best friend alone to fend for herself, would I?" Petime started to laugh, then was quickly reminded of her injured shoulder. "I'm going to have to get used to that, aren't I?"

"That makes two of us." Adrian returned with his own weak chuckle. "I'm starting to feel the bruises on my ribs."

Camille almost felt guilty that she hadn't been injured as well. She'd barely done her part in the fight as it was, relying on Petime and Adrian when fighting with Juste, and Georges and Elise when fighting the priests. Maybe here she could learn to change that fact about herself.

"So, can I stay?" Camille looked towards Georges and Elise with her best pleading face. "I promise that I will do everything you say to the best of my ability, and that I won't tell a soul about this place."

Georges and Elise shared a glance at each other, and Camille felt the anxiety to hear their answer well up in her. It seemed like they both agreed, no matter what the answer was.

Georges left space for a very dramatic pause. "You can stay."

Camille bounced on her toes from the excitement. Her mother would say so many things about how unladylike it was, but she wasn't here to do that anymore. Here, the excitement was returned with the rest of the room cheering and smiling.

"But..." Georges continued. "You can't stay *here*."

"What?" Camille stammered. "What do you mean by that?"

"There is too much risk in too many of us staying here for much longer. Petime said that she saw Gramont, right? He must be on the move to Paris, and we need to warn the other tunnels of their plans."

"About that. I have a lot more information for you two at a later time." Petime interjected. "I can assure you that his plans are worse than you'd think, especially if Juste is still around and they've made it back to Paris."

"That is all the more reason to go then." Georges said. "And I think that Adrian should stay with you two."

"I should what?" Adrian's face displayed a combination between anxious and confused. "I can't leave you two here alone to deal with the aftermath. Who would help you rebuild?"

"I think that it will be good for you." Georges smiled.

"And it would leave Elise and I with more alone time. We've had some plans for a while now, haven't we?" They shared a sneaky smile.

"Ew." Adrian frowned.

Georges stared at him for a moment, then turned bright red, which sent Elise into a fit of laughter. "Clear your mind!"

"You're the one who started it!" Adrian shot back.

"I meant plans about the tunnel! Speaking of which, there is one thing left for us to do before you leave."

"What is that?" Camille asked.

"Become real members of Les Tunneliers."

"Please! I'm ready!" Petime perked up a little too quickly.

Camille realized just exactly what they were implying. "Both of us?"

"Both of you." Elise smiled.

"So, what's the assignment?" Adrian interjected before realizing he ruined the moment. "Sorry, the anticipation was getting to me."

Camille thought that it was cute, but didn't dare say it out loud.

Elise stepped in for Georges to describe the plan. "I think we've all realized what a threat that Les Saints Chevaliers is becoming to our society, especially now realizing that they are recruiting from the general populous, so I think that it is time that Les Tunneliers finally start working together. We've been acting as individuals for far too long." She explained. "I have a list of the other existing tunnels, and I need you to convince them to join us and unite as one. Some are larger, some are smaller, but we need all of them as one unified force if we want this to work. We know it's ambitious, but we need to start now if we have any hope of defeating Les Saints

Chevaliers."

Petime nodded. "Père Fournier mentioned something about a new era when he was talking to me, so I couldn't agree more with your ideas." This only caused more concerned looks between Georges and Elise. "It had to do with Gramont and Juste as well, mentioning something about taking down the tunnels." Petime added in.

"I can assure you that if he is involved in this, then the fight is going to be a lot harder than just a village priest and his followers." Georges worried. "That man is more powerful than any other that I've met, and now he has a protege."

"Why would you choose for Adrian, Petime and me to do this?" Camille asked. "Wouldn't it be better for you two to go if he's really that dangerous?"

Elise sighed. "We're getting older, and as much as I hate to admit it, our adventuring days are probably best left behind us."

Georges looked at them with a seriousness that he hadn't had before. "So, knowing everything, are all three of you in?"

Camille had been correct when she'd said that the battle was over, but there was still a much larger war to be fought. They'd need to be on the road as soon as their health could handle it. They shared a look and a nod between each other, and it sent shivers down Camille's spine. They were a real team now.

"There's one thing left on my mind…" Camille said, trailing off for a moment. "How will we explain what happened in the church if none of us are going to return to the village?"

Georges, for once, looked like he had no idea of how to respond to that, and shrugged. "It hasn't been my problem for a while now. If we just leave it alone it'll probably work itself out."

"I don't think that it'll work like that when they find Père Fournier dead with a stab wound." Petime hesitated.

"And I don't trust my mother to leave us alone either." Camille added.

Adrian looked extremely concerned. "What exactly did I miss?"

"I'll fill you in later." Camille whispered.

"It's true." Elise thought out loud. "We might need to do at least a little bit of damage control."

"I think that I have an idea." Petime said, with a strange amount of confidence to her. "I know someone in the village who will be able to help me from a distance. We can trust him, don't worry."

"Well, if you've got that covered, then I think that it is best if we all *got rest*." Elise glared at Petime and Adrian. Both of them immediately turned their heads in directions that were not towards her. "But let's enjoy the fact that we've won for now."

The rest of that night was spent setting up some extra spaces to sleep while recounting the events of the day to each other. Even though this was Camille's first night sleeping somewhere other than her home, she felt strangely at peace in the unfamiliar place. It was something that she could get used to.

CHAPTER FIFTY-ONE
Petime

Petime walked alongside the edge of the woods nervously. It had been a while since she'd been in the village. The stab wound in her shoulder had taken a while to heal, but now had transformed into a nice, neat scar that traced her left shoulder. She thought of it as a trophy, proof that Père Fournier had no control over her fate. She and the others were going to become full members of the society tonight and leave for Paris the following morning, but she still had one thing left to do in the village. This was her last chance to be just Petime, the one-legged shepherd girl from Edris. Tomorrow she would start the life of secret societies and fighting and science, but today she was just herself.

She arrived at her destination, her house in the field. This was around the time that she should've been doing chores, but as she looked out over the field from the treeline now, it was just her brother. He was basking in the sunlight outside of the house like he always did, but he didn't have a relaxed smile plastered across his face. Instead, it was a more somber face. She wondered if her "death" had affected him at all. Early in the morning after the church burned, Georges and Elise went to hide evidence of their deaths in the church. They couldn't risk anyone thinking otherwise, especially because of what Camille's mother might say.

A few nights after that, they had all seen their headstones in the village cemetery. It was an unsettling feeling being perceived as dead, but Georges said that they would get used to it after a while. Petime still couldn't imagine seeing herself dead more than once though.

She got just close enough to the point where none of the other families would see her, but she could still cross the field one last time to see her brother. At least, it would be the last time for a while. When she thought of saying goodbye, it was this. Just her family and her sheep. She already missed how they would follow her around begging for food.

As she started walking through the grass, her brother noticed the movement. "What do you all think you're…" he trailed off when he saw who was walking towards him. "Petime!"

She could see the tears in his eyes as he ran up to her, pushing through the pile of sheep to wrap his arms around her. "I thought you were dead!" He sniffled. "They said that they found your body in the fire, but I told them I didn't believe them. I told them that you promised you'd see me again."

Petime could feel the tears in her eyes as well. She decided it wasn't time to tell him about what had really happened, at least not yet. For now, he could believe that he knew it all along, and that she'd had a plan this entire time. "I would never break a promise to you." She said through her tears. This time, she meant it sincerely.

Leon was the first to let go from the hug, and as he did he noticed the scar on her shoulder. "Where did you get that?"

He asked, concerned.

Petime looked at it herself. "I told you that I would come back, not that I would stay safe."

"I guess that makes sense." He paused. "So, when will you be telling our parents that you're back?" Leon stood smiling.

Petime went quiet. She didn't know how to tell him about the next reason for her visit. "About that…"

"You're coming back, right?" Leon realized what her silence meant. "Right?"

Petime thought about the best way to word her response. "You know how the priest did some unfair things to us?"

Leon nodded, but didn't back down. "He's dead now though! So you're free to come back!"

"I've known that much for a while. I wouldn't have come back otherwise, but he has others…" She didn't know how much more she could say before she gave away too much. "Some of his friends still made it through the fire, and they want to hurt more people."

"So you're going to leave me behind?" Leon asked, with clear hurt in his voice.

"Not forever." Petime reassured him. "How about I make you another promise?"

Leon thought about it for a moment. "Alright, but only because I know you'll keep it."

"You're growing up, Leon." She said, looking at him with pride. It was true. Over the last few months she'd seen so much change in him. She was disappointed that she wouldn't be able to see that growth continue.

"Of course I am! I want to be just like you!" he smiled.

Petime chuckled. "Just like me, huh?"

"Yeah!" He laid back in the grass. "I want to build all those fancy machines and sneak out at night like you do!"

Petime froze. "What?" She smiled, hoping that she'd misheard all of what Leon had just said.

"I kept our parents distracted for you, don't worry!" His smile turned more sinister. "You owe me so many favors."

"Dear Lord. You're not wrong." Petime sighed. Moving onward, she'd need to realize the danger of Leon's perceptiveness. "How about this? If I tell you a secret, do you promise to keep it?"

"I've been doing that this entire time, have I not?"

Petime had to admit, he had a point. He was ready.

"Follow the trail of ferns." Petime grinned. She wasn't going to give him anything more than that, but it would give him something to work on while she was in Paris, and it would give Georges and Elise some company.

"That sounds very cryptic." He gave her a suspicious look. "But I'll figure it out just like you did."

"If you ever find what you're looking for, expect a letter from me as well." Petime added. She knew that Les Tunneliers had some form of mail system, but she'd need to figure out how to use it.

"I get letters!?" Leon said, jumping up excitedly. "I've always wanted to be important enough to get letters!"

Petime waited to see how long it would take him to realize, and Leon was excited for a few more moments before he stopped jumping around.

"Wait… I can't read."

There it was.

"Don't worry, the people there will help you, and if you ask nicely, they might even teach you." Petime was excited at the idea of her brother being able to read his own letters. "If they ask who you are, say that you're my brother."

Leon gave her a confused glance. "Why would I say anything else?"

Petime laughed. "Don't ever lose that attitude." As she said it, the setting sun caught her eye. She needed to return to the tunnel to get ready for the ceremony.

The concern must have shown on her face, because Leon stepped forward and hugged her one last time. "I understand, or maybe I don't, but I understand that you need to leave. Go defeat those bad guys for me, okay?" He said quietly. "And don't break your promise."

"Understood." Petime returned the hug, then parted ways.

On the way out she was sure to say her final goodbyes to everything in the village. She passed by the river and the stream that ran into it, the hill that lined the fields, the outskirts of the village itself, and one final thing.

She turned onto the shortcut between the village and the shepherds' fields, and stood there for a moment. She hadn't done this since she was a child.

She took a deep breath in, then ran.

She ran so fast that she could feel the breeze in her hair. Her crutches slammed against the ground with every step, and she felt the impact travel up through her arms. It was freeing. This time there was no one chasing her, no wolf, and no memories dragging her down. There was only the dirt beneath her feet, and a smile on her face. It was just like it had been in her childhood. She kept running until she'd made it all the way from the beginning of the path to the very end.

As she slowed to a stop, she could just barely see the tip of the statue that stood in the town center. She didn't feel the same pain in her heart leaving this place as she did with her family. Deep down, she had always known that it was never truly home. Home was the people that filled it, and now those people were going to Paris.

The rest of the trip back to the tunnels was relatively uneventful. She enjoyed the scenery of the woods for a final time, following the trail of ferns, enjoying that she wasn't scared anymore. These woods had become second nature to her over the past days, and she felt like they still would be even when she returned to the village.

When she arrived at the clearing, everyone else was already waiting for her, causing Petime to panic. "Did you all start without me?"

"The sun has been set for ages Petime!" Camille retorted.

Adrian shrugged. "I still see some orange, so that means that it's not fully night time."

"It's close enough!" Camille huffed.

It was funny to see Camille be even more eager for the ceremony than Petime was herself. Out of every outcome that she'd imagined, this certainly hadn't been it. Still though, she wouldn't trade it for anything.

Petime turned towards Georges, ready to begin. "So, Georges, how does this work?"

"Well–" Georges began, but was cut off by Elise.

"He has no idea." She said in a flat, but amused tone.

"They didn't need to know that!" He playfully jabbed her arm before continuing. "Anyways, I was going to say that there is no formal way to hold the ceremony, except for one part. Under the light of the full moon, I am to bestow upon you your Tunneliers coins."

"What are those?" Petime asked, curious as to what a branded coin could possibly look like.

"They are small medallions with the group's symbol on it. Each member of Les Tunneliers has one, and they guard them with their life. It acts as a key into other tunnels, and can serve as a proof of your identity." Elise explained. "It's important when your group is as divided as ours." She smiled. "Although, you all will hopefully fix that."

Georges, Elise, and Adrian led them to a separate clearing in the forest that neither Petime nor Camille had seen before. The entire place was decorated with flowers from the forest, and in the center was a small fire pit that sat unlit.

"You two can do the honors." Georges smiled, handing them both a flint and iron.

Camille and Petime looked at each other.

"Are you thinking what I'm thinking?" Petime asked.

Camille smiled, taking the piece of iron. "I am absolutely thinking what you're thinking."

Petime took the piece of flint, and the two struck a spark over the tinder of the fire together. Once it lit, it burst quickly into a bright orange flame. Even with everything that had happened in the church, this light felt comfortable to her. It felt like she was growing up.

"We did it!" Petime smiled.

Camille clinked her rock against Petime's. "We did, didn't we!"

"No one in this group has survival instincts, I swear." Elise had come to accept her torment, but that wasn't going to stop her from endlessly complaining about it.

With the fire started, there was only one thing left for them to do at the ceremony.

"Petime, Camille, step forward." Georges said with a commendable effort to be serious. "I am now giving to you your Tunneliers coins."

Georges held out two silver coins in his hand. They shimmered under the light of the moon and fire. Each coin was intricately carved out by hand, and shined to a fine gloss. Each also had their name delicately inscribed on the bottom. They were made by hand, and they were made with love. Both Petime and Camille took their coins, holding them in their hands like they were the most precious things on Earth.

After they had enough time to stare at them, Georges spoke again. "It's up to you to decide how you wear them, but you must keep them on you at all times."

Petime knew immediately what she would do. "I'm going to hide mine in a secret compartment of my crutches."

"Your crutches have a secret compartment?" Camille asked, immediately looking over them to examine.

"Maybe they do, or maybe they don't." Petime shrugged. "You'll see what it holds when the time is right." The group laughed.

"What are you going to do with yours, Camille?" Adrian asked.

Camille looked like she was embarrassed to answer. "I was thinking of wearing it as a necklace. Do you think it would look nice?"

Adrian was very clearly blushing at her response.

"What? What does that mean!?" Camille started to panic. "You know what, I won't do it. It was a bad idea anyways—"

She was cut off by Adrian revealing a necklace from under his shirt. The pendant on it was his own Tunneliers coin. "My mother gave it to me."

As the two of them stared at each other, Georges approached Elise and Petime. "How long do you give them?" He whispered.

"A week. Maximum." Elise giggled.

"A week? I'd say a day." Petime replied. "I'll be sure to send you updates along with the reports of our mission."

Elise's face lit up. "I will hold you to that. I need to see our boy find love."

The rest of the night was just as fun as its beginning. They spent the time chatting, playing games around the fire, and just generally enjoying each other's presence before their journey the next morning.

The night passed in a flash, and it felt like it had only been a few moments that she was being loaded onto a wagon headed for Paris. She'd never been as far out of the village as she was now, watching the last tops of the houses disappear over the hillside. Camille and Adrian were sitting in the front seat, chattering away with each other, and she was writing in a newly-started journal. She could only hope that it kept her busy enough on the long journey, whatever it held.

Her time in Edris was coming to a close, but this was only the beginning.

Acknowledgements

I would like to start off by thanking those who saw me every morning at my best, my worst, and everything in between. Room 1313 has been my home away from home for the past three years, and I would not be the same person without you guys. From filling the beanbags to building shelves to just having so many fun conversations, I cannot thank you enough.

Out of everyone, Tirayan, your comments brought me LIFE when I was in the depths of my writing despair. Seeing you yelling so passionately at Juste from the margins of the document and ripping into Camille's mom reminded me why I wanted to keep writing. And Moon, the number of people you have wanted to put in a blender throughout your time reading this will always be a favorite. You kept me going (and grammatically on point) even at my worst. No workshop group will ever compare to you guys.

I also couldn't forget my teacher and mentor for these last three years, Ms. Dyche. You taught me that writing can be anything that I wanted it to be. Whether it be sentient moles or murder roaches in space, you were there to support me and encourage me to be even better than I was already becoming. I never would have made it this far without your support, so thank you for taking the time to help me grow into the best version of myself that I have been so far.

Leaving the classroom for my actual, physical home, I want to thank my parents. You kept me alive and going even when I was at school into ridiculous hours of the night, you put up with all of my last-minute scheduling, and you made sure to turn out the light on nights that I fell asleep on the couch. I don't thank you enough for all that you do, but I appreciate all of it so much, so thank you.

There are so many of you that supported me along my journey writing this novel that I can't even begin to thank you in this small amount of space. My table in Civil Engineering that helped me pick out my font, my orchestra class who listened to me ramble about my plotlines, and all of my friends who put up with my late-night texts talking about what I was going to do next, everyone. I remember you, and I remember that people like you are who I am excited this story reaches. Thank you.

And finally, to everyone who has read this. I thank you for coming along the journey with me and surviving to the end. This is my first novel, so I can only (hopefully) go up from here, and I hope to see you again and again and again in this section of the book.

About the Author

Abigail Mauney is an author with a love for science fiction and fast-paced action. Her love of mixing writing and science continues into her education, being a graduate of the Creative Writing program at Charles J. Colgan High School Center for Fine and Performing Arts, and a current student at Virginia Tech's College of Engineering. Being published multiple times in Charles J. Colgan High School's award-winning literary magazines, and with plans to publish more, Abigail's journey in writing is only just beginning.